CYBER ARMAGEDDON

BOOK TWO: FEAST OF THE LOCUSTS

MARK GOODWIN

ACKNOWLEDGMENTS

I would like to thank my Editor in Chief Catherine Goodwin, as well as the rest of my fantastic editing team, Jeff Markland, Frank Shackleford, Stacey Glemboski, Sherrill Hesler, Carole Pickard, and Claudine Allison.

CHAPTER 1

And he cried mightily with a strong voice, saying, Babylon the great is fallen, is fallen, and is become the habitation of devils, and the hold of every foul spirit, and a cage of every unclean and hateful bird. For all nations have drunk of the wine of the wrath of her fornication, and the kings of the earth have committed fornication with her, and the merchants of the earth are waxed rich through the abundance of her delicacies. And I heard another voice from heaven, saying, Come out of her, my people, that ye be not partakers of her sins, and that ye receive not of her plagues. For her sins have reached unto heaven, and God hath remembered her iniquities.

Revelation 18:2-5

Saturday afternoon, Kate tromped up the wooded hillside through dense brush, an AK-47 slung over her shoulder. She breathed in the fresh mid-October air warmed by a bright yellow sun shining in a clear blue sky. The autumn colors were near their peak, painting the forest in radiant hues. The smell of wet, newly-fallen leaves on the forest floor wafted across her face. She reached the overwatch position above the Apple Blossom Acres entrance checkpoint and scowled. "Vicky, Sam! Sound and light discipline! We've talked about this more than once."

Sam turned the walkie-talkie down.

Vicky objected. "This is important! It's a message from the government!"

Kate knelt by the opening of the rudimentary shelter which offered marginal protection from the elements at best. "How are you getting a radio broadcast on the walkie-talkie?"

With his index finger, Sam indicated a button which read, WX. "It's the NOAA weather band. They're transmitting an emergency message."

Kate let out a sigh of near frustration. "Go ahead, turn it back up. Let's see what they've got to say."

The broadcast was grainy and dry. The man reading the transmission was human but deviated very little from the automated computer voice which typically provided forecasts and hazardous weather conditions on the frequency.

"President Long signed the Federal Emergency Management Reform Act into law today. The law provides sweeping new authority to FEMA and gives the agency temporary jurisdiction over Social Security, Treasury, the Department of Energy, and the Department of Agriculture.

"The law received almost unanimous support from Democrats and Republicans in both houses of Congress.

"In a brief press conference late this morning, President Long laid out an abbreviated plan for getting the country and the broader economy back on track. He said the first order of business would be to issue emergency currency denominated in US Dollars. President Long explained that PayPal would be working with the Social Security Administration to issue $200 in electronic credits per week to all US citizens via their Social Security numbers. Non-US citizens will have to apply for credits through DHS. The funds, created by the Federal Reserve, will be added to the current money supply when the crisis fully abates.

"Citizens who already have a PayPal account will need only to fill out a one-time verification form which will link their Social Security number to the online payment system. New users will have to submit an application before receiving their weekly stipend. PayPal will send out plastic cards to all account holders as soon as possible, but citizens will immediately be able to spend their emergency electronic credits online.

"Additionally, the president has called all first responders, government, and hospital workers to

Evil Solution

return to work as soon as possible. Those who do will be paid their regular salaried amount through the FEMA relief payment system.

"All businesses connected to the fuel and grocery supply chain are encouraged to fill out an online application to FEMA for emergency electronic credits sufficient to cover one month of operating expenses.

"In the meantime, FEMA will be setting up makeshift commissaries in the parking lots of local strip malls and shopping malls. The FEMA Reform Act grants special powers to the US military who will provide security for the pop-up commissaries.

"Finally, the president implored citizens to stay safe and be patient, promising that all branches of government are working tirelessly to resolve the present crisis and get back to normal.

"This report has been provided to you by a collaboration of FEMA, The White House Press Secretary's office, and National Public Radio."

The report began to repeat as if the recording was being played in a loop. Kate took the walkie-talkie from Sam and turned it off. She sat silently on the ground, digesting what she'd just heard.

"Aunt Kate, does this mean we can go back to Atlanta?" Vicky asked. "And will you live at our house, with Sam and me?"

Kate was still trying to process but knew the likelihood of ever going back to Atlanta was slim. "I don't think we'll be going to your house anytime soon. But I'm your family, wherever we go, we'll stay together." She put an arm around her niece and nephew. "You can count on me to always be here for you."

"That's what Dad said after Mom died." Sam picked up an acorn from the ground and inspected it solemnly.

Kate slid her hand up to his hair and pulled him toward her. She kissed the side of his head. "And he meant it. All the things your dad ever taught you, all the love he gave you, it's right here." She tapped his chest. "In your heart. Like your father, I intend to do everything I can to keep you guys safe. And as far as it depends on me, I'll never leave you."

Sam offered a troubled smile, then looked back down at the acorn he was twirling between his fingers.

Vicky issued another inquiry. "What about the police? If they start patrolling the streets again, can we quit spending half the day up here in this rickety old tent? I can't imagine how cold it will be in the winter."

"We'll see." Kate also did not relish the idea of standing watch in the freezing cold. "Things may take a while longer to get back to normal than what the reporter said. The government is always going to sugarcoat the story so people will stop panicking."

"What about PayPal? Didn't they get hacked?" asked Sam.

Kate shook her head. "I'm not sure. If they had a customer database stored offline, they could recreate their system, especially with a little help from the US government. It just wouldn't reflect the previous balances of the account holders."

Vicky leaned close to her aunt as if she were seeking comfort. "What's to stop the hackers from attacking PayPal and taking it down?"

Kate pulled her closer. "Theoretically, nothing. The hacks were Windows-based. If the government and PayPal created a new system, hopefully they built it out on an operating system besides Windows. At least that's what I would have done."

"You mean like Apple?" Sam stood up and stretched his arms.

"Or Linux," Kate replied. "The hacks were very sophisticated. Not many corporations run on Linux, which means there's less of an incentive to write such a complex piece of malware on Linux. Additionally, most white-hat hackers, cyber-security personnel, and computer… enthusiasts use Linux, so it's akin to trying to commit a crime at FBI headquarters."

Vicky cracked a grin. "You were going to say computer nerds?"

Kate messed up her niece's hair. "Yes, but being the guardian of two teenagers, I have to watch my semantics. I wouldn't want the two of you to become labeled as social pariahs because your aunt is a nerd."

Sam's face also lightened up. "You're the coolest aunt ever, Aunt Kate; even if you are a computer nerd."

"You two head on back down to the cabin and get some lunch. And don't forget to wipe down your guns with a couple drops of oil. It's damp out here and we need to keep the rust off those things."

Vicky stood up and retrieved her AK-47.

"You're going to stand guard by yourself? I thought you said we should always travel in twos."

"Gavin will be up here in a few minutes. Besides, the guys down at the gate have things under control. I'm sure we won't get attacked in that amount of time anyway."

Sam shot her a mischievous look. "No, I'm sure the Badger Creek Gang will wait until you and Gavin are making out so they can hit us while no one is watching."

"Ha, ha." Kate crossed her arms. "I'll have you know that Gavin and I are very disciplined, especially when it comes to guard duty." She knew her statement wasn't entirely accurate, but it wasn't for lack of good intentions.

CHAPTER 2

Thus saith the Lord; For three transgressions of Judah, and for four, I will not turn away the punishment thereof; because they have despised the law of the Lord, and have not kept his commandments, and their lies caused them to err, after the which their fathers have walked: but I will send a fire upon Judah, and it shall devour the palaces of Jerusalem.

Amos 2:4

Kate gasped at the beauty of God's creation. She watched the wind rustle through the pale yellow leaves of towering poplar trees. The breeze caused some to flicker like flames and dislodged others from lofty branches. Her eyes followed a shower of leaves falling to the ground. The dropping foliage spiraled past fiery hues; vibrant orange maple leaves, vivid red hickory leaves, and dogwoods which had darkened to a deep plum. Beyond the fading embers of autumn, she saw Gavin ascending the steep gradient from the narrow paved road below. Less than a half an hour had passed since she saw him last, yet her heart leaped at his arrival.

Gavin was winded from the climb, but just barely. "You look beautiful, sitting up here in the midst of this spectacular display."

She concealed her blushing cheeks and gleeful smile by pulling off her ball cap and letting her long blonde hair drop over her face. "Thanks."

"Sorry it took me so long to get up here, but Pritchard stopped me. NPR just aired a report from FEMA. You'll never guess what they're doing."

"Oh, I don't know. I might."

Gavin appeared confused. He half grinned and his eyes shifted from side to side, as if not sure whether she were joking. "O…K…"

"They're going to issue some type of emergency credit to everyone so they can jump-start the economy and put Humpty Dumpty back together again. Probably around…" She closed her eyes, faking a state of extreme concentration. She opened her eyes as if the answer had come suddenly. "$200 each!" She watched his expression. "Was I close?"

He smirked. "How did you hear?"

"They ran the report on the NOAA band."

"I thought it was supposed to be radio silence unless there was an incident to report." His brow creased.

She rolled her eyes. "Sam and Vicky were listening when I came to relieve them."

Gavin propped his AK-47 against the tree and sat next to her. "Teenagers—what are you going to do?"

"So what do you think?" She let him take her hand. "About the broadcast?"

"I don't know what to think. I suppose I'll let myself expect nothing more than the shattered-egg analogy that you so eloquently alluded to. Then, if all the king's horses and all the king's men are actually able to construct something from their pecuniary duct tape and monetary bubblegum, I'll be pleasantly surprised."

"That sounds practical. Prepare for the worst and hope for the best. Do you think the rest of the community will adopt our paradigm?"

He lifted his shoulders. "I'm not sure. I think most of them see us as troublemakers. They blame us for inviting harassment, feel that we brought the attack upon ourselves."

"Not all of them. Jack Russo, Don Crisp, and Scott McDowell all stopped by after the shootout to ask what they could do to help. They offered their condolences once they heard of Terry's death. They're the ones who set up the checkpoint at the community entrance gate."

"Those three families are in the minority, and I'm not so sure they'll stand by our side if the rest of the community puts pressure on them. Scott probably won't be pulling checkpoint duty anymore. The Sheriff's Department will be calling him back."

"We'll still have Don. He's a cop."

"Was a cop. He's retired."

"That just means he's got more experience." She adjusted her ball cap. "Anyway, I think you're being paranoid. Those families were the only ones besides Pritchard that had ever met any of us. If one of the other families down the road had a massive gun battle at their house, I'm not so sure I'd be in a hurry to get chummy with them."

"In this environment? I would. I'd assume that's someone ready to take action and get organized like we've done."

"Well, everyone doesn't think like you do." She watched the two men standing at the checkpoint below the observation post. "Did Pritchard say if he was planning to have church tomorrow morning?"

"He didn't. Why? Are you planning to go?"

"Of course, aren't you?"

"I don't know. Someone has to keep watch anyway."

"It's not your shift. We'll have walkie talkies with us if there's trouble."

"I'm not sure how I feel about all of that."

"You mean God? You believe in God, don't you?"

"Yeah, I mean, I believe in something. All that evolutionary nonsense about everything exploding out of nothing simply isn't rational. But I'm not sure I buy the whole judgement-on-America thing."

"Nobody is going to force you to do, think, or believe anything you don't want to. Coming to church only shows you have an open mind."

"*Nobody*? Have you met your next door neighbor?"

"Okay, *besides Pritchard*, no one is going to pressure you into believing anything." She pulled his hand close to her heart. "I'd really appreciate it. It's important to me."

His smile was less than convincing. "If it's important to you then I'll go."

Sunday morning, the turnout at Pritchard's makeshift church was much lower than the previous week. At the beginning of his message, Pritchard accredited the slim attendance to people trying to spend their emergency credits. His sermon was shorter than the meeting prior. Afterward, he offered a prayer, then made an announcement. "'For I turn y'all loose, the youngin here's got somethin' to say. I believe you'd do well to hear it, too." He motioned to Kate. "Come on up here, girl."

Kate's skin had thickened in the past two weeks and she was no longer bothered by Pritchard's objectionable use of language. She walked to the section of tree trunk used for a podium. Public speaking always incited a feeling of anxiety in her stomach. She recognized most everyone in the audience; the Crisps, the McDowells, the Russos, and her own household. The only family present that she hadn't met was the Cobbs; Corey, Marilyn, their early-30s daughter, Annie, and her 10-year-old son Troy. And then there was Mrs. Dean, an 89-year-old widow.

Even so, Kate felt nervous speaking to the intimate crowd. "Most of you have already heard what I've got to say, so I'll keep it short. Since we're all in one place, this is a good time for us to offer up our thoughts on the current state of affairs.

"I'm going to provide some recommendations and if anyone has any questions, please jump right in. I probably won't have all the answers, but hopefully, someone else here will. I'm not trying to give orders or even a speech. I just want to get a conversation started."

She paused for a moment and pulled a list of bullet points out of her pocket. "As many of you may know, Gavin and I both worked for major banks in the Information Security departments."

Mrs. Dean held up a hand. "I'm sorry, hon, I don't know what that means."

"Cyber security," Kate clarified.

Mrs. Dean shook her head to indicate that Kate's explanation meant little to her.

Pritchard spoke up. "Computers, Rita. They worked on them bank computers that got hijacked."

Mrs. Dean seemed to understand. "Oh, okay."

Once Kate felt confident that Mrs. Dean was satisfied, she continued. "As I was saying, Gavin and I had front row seats for the attacks. I can't get into the details, but the banking system's data was encrypted over and over. Every level of encryption is like solving an impossible puzzle. It's on the order of difficulty of predicting where lightning will strike. Even if the government is able to solve one layer of encryption, they'll essentially need lightning to strike the same place, over and over, and over.

"The emergency electronic credits are only a

temporary solution. The credits may serve to quell the chaos temporarily, but the underlying problem is all but unsolvable. Even if the government is able to come up with a long-term solution, there's no guarantee the new credits won't be attacked. The cybercriminals who launched the attack still have not been identified to my knowledge."

Jack Russo sat next to his wife and daughter. "You said you have some suggestions. I'm eager to hear them."

Kate continued, "Yes, Jack. We're all receiving $200 in credits per week. I recommend spending your credits as fast as possible, in case of further attacks. And, I recommend buying bulk items with the most calories; things like rice, beans, flour, stuff that will last a long time rather than things like meat and milk."

Marilyn Cobb put her hand up. "I don't see why we shouldn't believe the government. They said they'd come up with a solution, and they have. They've lived up to their promise. I feel like the worst is behind us."

Don Crisp crossed his arms. "I hope you're right, Marilyn, but we don't know that for sure. Kate's idea is a good one. We've been given a second chance to get prepared—I think we should put all our resources into making the best of this opportunity. Like Kate said, the window might not stay open for long."

Marilyn shook her head. "I don't know, Don. We've all been through so much, I think it would be best if we just try to move on, get past all of this."

"We can be frugal with our resources and still

(Handwritten margin note:) "I'M FROM THE GOVERNMENT AND I'M HERE TO HELP." YEAH, RIGHT

keep a positive outlook for the future," Don said. "It's not either or. But what I will tell you is that our friends from Orlando said they were coming to stay with us. That was five days ago and we've heard nothing from them. The husband was no sissy. He was my partner on the force for the last eight years of my career. Everyone thinks Orlando is all about Mickey Mouse, but when you work for the Orlando PD, you see a different side of things. And Kirk, the guy who was coming up here, he was one of the finest officers I ever worked with.

("Even in the best of times, the criminal element is violent, deceptive, and watching for any opportunity.) But it's in times like these that they thrive. I assume Haywood County is no exception. Does that line up with your assessment, Scott?"

Scott McDowell rocked forward on his stump. "My thoughts exactly, Don. We've already had a small taste of that right here in Apple Blossom Acres last week. I'm supposed to go back to work for the Sheriff's Department tomorrow. I think it's important that I go. But I'd feel a whole lot better if we had more residents participating in the community watch."

Being the only adult male present not participating in the community watch, Corey Cobb looked away. However, his daughter, Annie, put her hand up to volunteer. "I can help. I don't know how to shoot, but I'm willing to learn if someone will teach me."

Marilyn Cobb jabbed her husband in the side with a sharp finger. Her whispered objection was plenty loud for everyone to hear. "Corey, I don't want Annie having any part of this!"

Corey's brows clenched in annoyance. "I can't stop her." He pushed his glasses up on his perturbed nose and stood up. "Me, too. I've never shot a gun, but I'm also open to being trained."

Marilyn stood up in opposition to her husband. "I'll meet you at the house. I've heard enough of all this for one day." She marched off toward the road.

Once his wife was out of earshot, Corey put his arm around his daughter, "It'll be good to get out of the house. It's been a little…cramped lately."

Annie giggled and hugged her father.

"I can help, too." Annie's son, Troy, added.

Scott McDowell said, "That's very brave of you to offer. We might find something for you to do in the communications department."

Troy didn't seem to understand. He pointed to Vicky. "She's not much older than me and she gets a gun."

Annie hugged him. "When you're Vicky's age, we'll talk about it. But for now, you can find other places to make yourself useful."

"What about me, Dad?" Scott's fifteen-year-old son, David, asked.

His eyes were those of a father who did not want to put his son into harm's way. Yet he could not deny him while letting fourteen-year-old Vicky work overwatch. "Maybe we can work you into the observation post schedule next week."

Vicky bit her lip. "You could work with me, David."

"Can I, Dad?"

Scott cleared his throat. "You need to work with

an adult. You and Vicky have plenty of time to see each other outside of work."

Sixteen-year-old Rainey Russo stood up. "I'll volunteer also."

Jack Russo shot Scott a harsh look and put his hand on his daughter. "I don't think Scott meant that everyone was expected to work security, baby."

"I know. But I want to. I want to do my part."

"We'll talk about it when we get home." Jack's expression showed his unpleasant surprise.

"I could work the same shifts as you, Dad."

"I usually work graveyard. That's not the most desirable time slot."

She added, "I don't care. I don't sleep much when you're out there anyway."

Jack swallowed hard. "We'll see, baby." He pulled her close.

Pritchard walked back to the podium. "If ain't nobody got no more to say, we'll adjourn. I'm a fixin' to wring the head off one of these hens that ain't been layin' if any of y'all want to hang around a spell." He turned to Kate. "The girl here makes a good biscuit for a computer whiz. If y'all can find somethin' to bring, we can have us a fine church dinner. Even if you ain't got nothin', y'all come on anyhow. We'll make do with what we've got."

CHAPTER 3

The earth mourneth and fadeth away, the world languisheth and fadeth away, the haughty people of the earth do languish. The earth also is defiled under the inhabitants thereof; because they have transgressed the laws, changed the ordinance, broken the everlasting covenant. Therefore hath the curse devoured the earth, and they that dwell therein are desolate: therefore the inhabitants of the earth are burned, and few men left. The new wine mourneth, the vine languisheth, all the merryhearted do sigh. The mirth of tabrets ceaseth, the noise of them that rejoice endeth, the joy of the harp ceaseth.

Isaiah 24:4-8

Tuesday afternoon, Kate looked toward the observation post above her position at the Apple Blossom Acres entrance gate. The thinning leaves made the small outpost slightly visible to one who knew it was there. Annie Cobb and Rainey Russo were working the overwatch shift.

Jack Russo was working the checkpoint with Kate. He patted her on the shoulder. "I know what you're thinking."

"Oh yeah? What's that?"

"You're wondering how safe you feel with those two in the sniper's nest. You're thinking you might be better off with no overwatch at all—because if we get hit, they're more likely to shoot you than the bad guys."

Kate didn't want to admit that he'd hit the nail on the head, especially considering one of her guardians was Jack's daughter. "Now that you mention it…"

Jack held his chin high and looked toward the overwatch shelter. "That little girl up there has been going hunting with me since she was ten. I'd let her shoot an apple off my head."

Kate adjusted the strap of her AK-47 on her shoulder. "That makes me feel a little better."

"And Scott worked with Annie all day yesterday. He's helped train plenty of deputies for the Sheriff's Department, he wouldn't have put her up there if he didn't think she was ready. Scott said he worked with your group training with handguns Sunday evening. How did that go?"

"We all feel more confident, but obviously we still need more training."

"It'll come." Jack looked toward the road. "A car is coming. Stay alert."

Kate pulled the rifle from her shoulder and held it at a low ready position.

The vehicle rounded the corner. She could see that it was a Sheriff's vehicle. "Is that Scott?"

"I think so." Jack waved at the oncoming car.

Scott McDowell rolled down his window. "I forgot the secret handshake. Think you can let me slide just this once?"

Jack leaned on the top of the car. "No work vehicles are permitted to be kept overnight in Apple Blossom Acres. We're gonna have to ask you to turn around."

"I see you've had that jalopy of a plumbing van parked in your drive all week. I was thinking of reporting you to the Beautification and Continuity Committee."

Jack held his hands up. "Go ahead. They're all at the FEMA camp down in Greenville."

The two men laughed. Scott turned his attention to Kate. "I made an arrest today that I thought you might be interested to hear about."

"Oh yeah? Why is that?"

"I locked up Lloyd Graves."

The name sounded familiar. "And who is he?"

Scott put his patrol car in park. "The surviving leader of the Badger Creek Gang. His brother was the one whose brains you scattered down your staircase. You might have heard that Lloyd's the vindictive sort. Thought you might sleep a little easier knowing he's behind bars."

Indeed, the name Graves did ring a bell, yet she'd never known the name of the brother. "Yeah, thanks. We had been a little concerned that they might be coming around. Since order is being restored, I'd be happy to come in to give a statement about the attack."

Scott looked from side to side. "Officially, my answer is come on in whenever you're ready."

"And unofficially?" she inquired.

"The department is buried in paperwork, most of it crimes that will never be solved. I know you lost your brother and I don't want to sound insensitive, but your incident had one of the better outcomes. All the perpetrators are pushing up daisies. There's really no bad guys to put away, and the department would probably want all the firearms involved in the shootout. Maybe this is one of those times when it's best to let sleeping dogs lie."

"Thanks," Kate said.

"What did you pick up Graves for?" asked Jack.

"Possession of stolen property, possession of firearms by a convicted felon, and two pounds of meth."

Kate's eyes grew wide. "Two pounds? That sounds like a lot."

"Yeah," Scott nodded. "That's a big haul. It will put him away for a long time if the cogs of justice start turning again. Before the attacks, the FBI told us they believed someone was producing a lot of meth in Haywood County. They thought it was a large-scale operation exporting serious weight to

Atlanta and Charlotte."

"Wow! You think the Badger Creek Gang is that big?" Kate asked.

Scott lifted his shoulders. "This bust is mighty convincing."

Jack inquired, "How's it going with the effort to restore order otherwise?"

Scott shook his head. "Half the guys didn't come back. I don't blame them. If I didn't have you folks watching out for my family while I'm at work, I wouldn't have gone back. Motor pool is running on fumes, the jail is overcrowded, it's not exactly business as usual."

"But people feel safe? They're out spending their emergency credits?" Jack waited for his reply.

"People are out and about, but none of the stores are open. FEMA hasn't opened a commissary in Waynesville yet so there's nowhere to spend the credits. The nearest one is in Asheville."

Kate said, "Maybe we should send a group there to stock up on whatever is available."

Scott looked at Jack. "What do you think?"

"Compile everyone's credits, stock up for the community?" Jack turned his attention to Kate.

Scott jested, "It'll be just like Waco."

Jack tittered. "We'll call ourselves the Branch Jackidians,"

"Don't flatter yourself, Jack. You're barely qualified to work a checkpoint, much less be a cult leader." Scott put his vehicle in drive and pulled through the gate. "You two put together a roster of who should go. I'll make sure the fort is safe while you're gone."

Kate waved. "See you soon."

Jack watched Scott drive away. "Do you think Gavin will want to go?"

"Yeah, I'm sure he will."

"I think you, me, Gavin, and Don should be the ones to go. We need to stay lean and fast. Our best bet of surviving if things get hairy will be to retreat and lay down enough cover fire to make us not worth pursuing. Vicky and Sam can stay with Kelly."

"Thanks, but I'll probably just have Mr. Pritchard keep an eye on them at the house."

"What vehicles do you recommend taking?" Jack leaned against the stone covered pillar marking the entrance to the community.

"Your work van, for one. We can haul a lot of stuff in the back."

"I'll have to clean out my plumbing supplies, but sure, we can take it. That reminds me; I've got some drywall and wood filler in the van. I want to come by after the shift and patch up your walls as best I can. I'm sure looking at bullet holes every day can get demoralizing. Your exterior walls are all D logs. Wood filler will patch them right up."

"That's very kind of you, but why would a plumber have drywall and wood filler?"

"A good portion of my jobs involve pipes inside the walls. With the glacial pace of the handymen around here, I just don't have the heart to make my customers get a separate contractor to repair the walls."

"I'd appreciate it. Not just for me—every time Sam and Vicky look at those holes, it's a painful reminder of the violent death their father had to suffer."

Kate and Jack discussed the details of the coming supply run for the remainder of the shift.

Wednesday morning, Kate <u>loaded magazines into the OD green tactical vest</u> which Scott had given her. The Haywood Sheriff's Department insignia had been pulled off, but otherwise, it was the same as his.

With Sam standing in the doorway, Vicky sat on Kate's bed. "Why can't we go with you?"

"We need to keep the team small." She put her compact 9mm pistol in the holster on the front of her vest.

Sam crossed his arms. "You said we're going to stick together. If we can't go, you shouldn't go either. I thought the point of stocking up all those supplies was so we wouldn't have to get in harm's way by fighting over the scraps."

"We can't survive on our own, and we don't have enough food to feed all of our neighbors. So this actually is in our best interest to get supplies for them. If we don't get the essentials and your neighbors come knocking, who will you turn away?" She looked at Vicky. "Would you watch David McDowell starve?" She turned to Sam. "What about Rainey?"

Vicky huffed and got up from the bed. "You're the only family we have left. If you don't come back, we'll be stuck with Pritchard."

"Mr. Pritchard," Kate corrected. "But I will be back. This isn't a dangerous trip."

"Yeah, that's why you're kitted up like you're going to fight ISIS." Sam let his hands drop and walked out of the room. Vicky trailed behind her brother.

Gavin walked into the room. He also wore one of the decommissioned tactical vests. "Ready?"

"I suppose."

"You sound like you're having second thoughts."

Her maternal instincts began to kick in. "Maybe the kids are right. Maybe my higher responsibility is to them."

"Then stay here."

"Who would go in my place?"

"Pritchard, I guess."

She thought about Pritchard's affinity toward the so-called *Asheville hippies* and let that scene play out in her mind; Pritchard saying something rash or off-color to the soldiers guarding the FEMA commissary. "The team is already put together. I don't want to throw a wrench in the works by making changes at the last minute." She grabbed her rifle. "Come on, let's go."

When they arrived at Don's house, he tossed Kate the keys to his Sierra. "You drove that bucket truck up here. I figure you should be able to handle a pickup. Gavin, you'll ride shotgun with her?"

"Yes, sir."

Don wore his old tactical vest from Orlando. He carried an AR-15 to the passenger's side of Jack's work van. "If we hit trouble, the driver drives, and the shooter shoots. You have to trust that your partner is doing his job. Got it?"

25

"Yes, sir." Kate opened the door to the pickup. "Are we using the same radio channel as we use for community watch?"

"Same channel. Keep it simple." Don closed the passenger door of the van. Jack's work vehicle led the way.

Kate waved at Corey and Annie Cobb as she drove through the familiar neighborhood checkpoint.

The roads had few other motorists and the quick thirty-minute drive to Asheville was uneventful. Once they arrived, however, the surrounding pristine scenery of the mountains was quickly replaced by an apocalyptic landscape. Shop windows were broken out, trash littered the road, and several cars were burned out.

"Wow! For such a small city, this place really looks rough." Kate kept the truck close to Jack's van.

"Not nearly as bad as Charlotte when I left." Gavin held his AK-47 by the barrel.

The radio sprang to life. It was Don's voice. "This looks like our spot straight ahead. We'll park in that shopping center across the street from the mall, as close to the exit as possible."

"Got it," Kate replied.

"Got it?" Gavin lowered one brow. "You're supposed to say *roger* or *10-4*. You played too many outer-space and futuristic video games and not enough present-day, earth-based games."

"Whatever." Kate dismissed his silly critique and followed Jack to the near corner of the shopping center's parking lot.

Don and Jack exited the van and walked over to the Sierra. Don approached Kate's window. "Those soldiers will blow a gasket if you walk up to the commissary all geared up like you are. Why don't you two leave your heavy artillery in the truck? Take your pistols and a walkie. If you get into a scrape, Jack and I will bail you out."

Kate began unbuckling her tactical vest. "What if they have a limit on how much one person can purchase?"

Don answered. "Get as much as you can for two people. If need be, Jack and I will make a second run while the two of you cover overwatch. But this is a highly volatile situation. We don't want to all go in with no one to cover us if things get hot."

Gavin gazed across the road. "The line looks long. It could be a while."

"We've got all day. Take your time." Jack pulled a dolly out of the van which had been configured to lay flat as a handcart. Zip ties secured a section of plywood to the platform of the cart to provide a wider cargo area. "Keep the weight in the center. Light stuff on the edges. Otherwise, it will spill over on you." He handed Kate a collection of bungee cords in various sizes. "Use these to wrap around your goods and keep them together on the way back."

Kate hung the bungees on the handle of the cart and pulled her plaid shirt down over her in-the-waistband pistol holster. She looked at the series of military tents in the mall parking lot across the street. Desert tan Humvees at regular intervals formed a battlement behind coils of concertina wire strung out like an instant parapet. The line of despairing people snaked like a hungry serpent through the mall parking lot and behind the razor-sharp spirals of steel. Sad faces were the ornaments of desperate souls who'd been ravaged by the crisis; all here in a last-ditch effort to gain sustenance which might see them through the gray days ahead.

Only the soldiers posted between the military vehicles looked well fed and clean. The masses seemed to be hanging by a singed and rotting cord. Leery, dusty, hungry, tired, agitated, and on the edge, one after another, more of them joined the tail of the great serpent whose head disappeared into the colossal tent offering a meager hope to an otherwise perishing lot.

"The line isn't getting any shorter." Kate turned her attention back to Gavin. "Are you ready?"

Gavin put an extra pistol magazine in one pocket of his hoodie and the radio in the other. "Ready!"

The two of them cautiously pushed the cart across the road.

CHAPTER 4

And thou shalt become an astonishment, a proverb, and a byword, among all nations whither the Lord shall lead thee. Thou shalt carry much seed out into the field, and shalt gather but little in; for the locust shall consume it.

Deuteronomy 28:37-38

Kate sat on the cart while waiting in line. Her phone vibrated and she pulled it from her pocket. "I got a text from Shu."

Gavin asked, "The cyber-security girl in Silicon Valley?"

"Yep." Kate read the text, standing up to show Gavin. "Tell me if this looks familiar." She zoomed in on the attached picture which revealed a long line of code. "Looks like a locust. What do you think?" Kate's stomach sank at the sight.

Gavin studied the image. "Where did she find it?"

Kate quickly messaged back to Shu. "Where's it from?"

Shu's reply was almost instantaneous. "Can't say."

Kate replied with a question mark.

Shu eventually replied back. "What I will say is that PG&E is a company I do contract work for."

Kate quickly searched PG&E. "Pacific Gas and Electric."

Gavin's face lost its color. "The virus is in the electrical grid."

Kate looked up from her phone. "If a locust has infected one of the companies, they're probably in all of them."

"Ask her if the code was in the Systems Control and Data Acquisitions." Gavin's face was tense.

Kate messaged Shu. "SCADA?"

Shu simply replied back with a mouthless emoji.

"She won't say." Kate let the phone fall to her side. It buzzed once more. She lifted it to see another message from Shu.

"What does it say?" Gavin quizzed impatiently.

Kate looked at her screen. "Good guess."

Gavin shook his head. "Not good. Not good at all."

Kate looked around at the throngs of people in line to purchase basic goods. "I feel like we're wasting time just standing here. We need to get ready!"

Gavin took her hand. "We're doing exactly what we should be doing. We're buying provisions to get the community through the winter."

Kate's anxiety flared up. She wanted to run, to hide, to do something, anything that might burn off the nervousness. Instead, she stood still, her fingers interlocked tightly with Gavin's.

The coming torrent of certain doom weighed on Kate, making the minutes seem like hours. "We should at least tell Don and Jack, so they can be coming up with a plan."

Gavin stroked her arm as if to soothe her. "Our radios are on an open channel. Anyone with a scanner can hear us." He pointed to the military Humvees surrounding the large tent where the FEMA commissary had been erected. "I bet you a million dollars that those guys have scanners."

Kate took a deep breath. "Maybe one of us could run back to the van, tell them in person."

"We're not going to split up, Kate. Let's stick to the plan, and we'll tell Don and Jack after we get our provisions."

Kate agreed to follow his recommendations. (She knew it to be the best course of action, yet she needed to hear it from him, to drown out the screaming voice of her anxiety telling her to deviate from the objective.)

Two hours passed and they finally made it to the door of the tent. Inside, tempers were short, people were pushing, looking at one another with tense, worried, and angry eyes. A large sign hung above the door, which read *$500 Limit, Per Person, Per*

Day. Kate surveyed the pallets of food lined up like a warehouse grocery store. "Where do you think they got all of this?"

"I assume they bought it or commandeered it from the large food processing plants. The actual raw products to make everything were probably already moving through the supply chain."

"I bet they bought it with the new emergency credits that the government created with a wave of their magic wand." Kate loaded several bags of flour onto the cart. "The supply chain locked up once they had no money to keep it lubricated. When the government began pumping out the electronic credits, I guess it was like flipping a light switch back on."

"Exactly—until the raw products already in the system run out. Then, the party is over." Gavin stacked ten 20-pound bags of rice onto the cart. "People will get wise to the fact that these credits are printed out of thin air. Everyone will try to spend them as fast as they can, inflation will skyrocket."

Kate positioned 5-pound bags of beans next to the rice. "I'm not so sure about that. The emergency credits aren't that much different than the money the Fed was printing out of thin air before."

Gavin pushed on the cart, which was getting heavier and harder to move. "Yeah, you're probably right. Never underestimate the naivety of the masses."

Kate loaded cases of pasta sauce onto the cart. "I doubt inflation will have a chance to take off anyway. The locusts will probably take down the grid long before we have to worry about that."

"Good point." Gavin inspected the boxes of spaghetti. "Some of these are name brand and the others just have a white box with black ink."

Kate helped him stack the boxes on the cart. "FEMA probably took over the manufacturing plants and had them print the black and white labels. The name brands were likely already in the warehouse."

Gavin exerted a little more effort to get the cart going. "Are you keeping a total of how much we've spent?"

Kate entered some numbers into her phone calculator. "We'll never be able to fit a thousand dollars' worth of food on this cart."

"Then let's pick up some of that canned meat."

Kate walked in front of the cart. "Chicken, tuna, beef stew, beef ravioli…"

"Get it all. We may not get another chance to spend our credits before the locusts turn off the lights." Gavin began wrapping the supplies with bungee cords so they wouldn't fall off the cart during the long walk back to the van.

"Oatmeal and brown sugar. Think we can keep it on the cart?" Kate picked up a bag of each.

Gavin held up two more bungee cords. "We can try. Those credits won't be worth anything after the grid goes dark anyways."

The cart was soon loaded to absolute capacity and Kate helped Gavin shove the heavy cargo toward the exit door. Once there, they found yet another line to check out. The payment line wasn't nearly so long as the one to get into the tent.

Fifteen minutes later, a FEMA worker scanned the items on the cart. She was a robust woman with short hair. "You'll have to take off the bungees so I can scan the items in the middle."

"Sure." Gavin removed the bands and helped the woman unstack the goods on the outside of the cart.

"That's your limit," said a tall slender man holding a tablet computer.

"Okay, you can put the rest on her account?" Gavin took the tablet.

The man put his hands on his hips. "It doesn't work like that."

"The sign says per person, per day. It doesn't say anything about not sharing a cart," Kate protested.

"It doesn't matter what the *sign* says. It matters what *I* say." The thin man stood upright to assert his authority.

Gavin began off-loading the heavy items right in the aisle. "Okay. I guess you'll have to put all this stuff back."

The lanky dictator rolled his eyes and waved his hand. "Fine, fine. Put it back on the cart. Enter your PayPal information on the tablet and pay so I can ring her up."

Gavin winked at Kate and logged into his account.

After the other goods were tallied, Kate entered her email and password on the tablet. She clicked *Pay Now* and the total was deducted from her emergency credits.

Gavin was already leaning on the cart handle to get it moving when Kate handed the tablet back to the skinny authoritarian. She helped Gavin heave it out of the tent and toward the parking lot.

"Oh no!" said a young hipster. He stepped in front of the cart to stop them.

"What's the problem?" Gavin asked.

The hipster was followed by a menagerie of young people with various hair colors and facial piercings. His hair was black, jet black like from a bottle, and his lip sported a shiny metal ring which looped through like a fish which had been caught but managed to break the line and wriggle free. "You are two people. This is way more food than two people need to get by for a week."

Kate explained rather than escalate the conflict. "It's for our community. We have elderly people and kids, they're back in Waynesville and couldn't come."

"We don't know that." A fat girl with pink hair and tattoos on her knuckles stepped forward. "You could just be making that up."

Gavin's voice was polite. "We bought less than the FEMA daily allowance."

Another brutish girl, thick and meaty with blue hair and a silver stud on her cheek put her hands on the cart. "FEMA can't maintain social equity. It's up to the citizens to make sure everyone is treated fairly and no one steps over the boundaries of social justice."

Kate needed to hear no more. "Let us through."

The blue haired girl picked up a can of ravioli and tossed it to one of her companions. "Or what?"

"I'll tell the soldiers that you're harassing us." Kate glanced at Gavin who nodded his approval.

"Go ahead," said the plump girl with pink hair.

Gavin handed Kate the walkie. "You know what to do if they won't help."

Kate took the radio and sprinted to the nearest Humvee.

The lead soldier kept one finger on the trigger guard of his M-4 and put his other hand up. "Slow down. What's going on?"

"This gang is harassing us. They won't let us leave."

The soldier shook his head. "I'm sorry. We're only authorized to provide support for the tent. The parking lot is outside of our jurisdiction. That's a problem for local law enforcement."

"Can you call the local police for me?"

He shook his head again. "Sorry, we've been specifically instructed not to coordinate with local authorities. But from what I understand they're stretched really thin. Less than a quarter of their officers have reported back to work."

Kate bit her lip in frustration. She turned and walked back toward Gavin who was chasing the hooligans around as they picked items off the cart, one at a time, and tossed them to one another like a wake of vultures. She pressed the talk button on the radio and explained what was happening to Don and Jack.

Don came back over the radio. "Try to bluff them. Tell the ruffians that the soldiers will detain them if they don't disperse. Call me back if it works. If I don't hear back from you in one minute, I'll create a diversion. We're heading in your direction, just in case."

"Got it, I mean, 10-4." Kate hustled back to

Gavin where the cart was slowly being picked apart like a road-kill opossum's carcass.

Kate knitted her brows together and spoke gruffly. "The soldiers said you people have to leave or you'll be detained."

"You people?" The girl with the blue hair stepped forward. "What is that supposed to mean? Like *you freaks*? Are you a racist, homophobe, clinging to your white privilege?"

"What?" Kate was more confused than offended by the accusation. "What does that even mean? You're all as white as me." She pointed to a pale anorexic girl in the back of the mob. "She's even whiter."

"Oh, so she's too white for you?" The beefy blue-haired girl snatched two bags of brown sugar from the cart. "You know what I think? I think you're lying. If the soldiers want us to leave they can come tell us themselves."

The rest of the pack closed in on the supplies like ravenous wolves. Kate reached for her pistol and looked at Gavin.

Without speaking he mouthed, "Don't do it."

Kate let her shirt fall back over the pistol and tried to push the cart. Just then, a hail of gunfire broke out from the parking lot across the street. Kate looked at Gavin. "That's our cue. Come on! Push!"

The gaggle of pixie-dusted delinquents quickly dispersed and began running, along with everyone else in the crowd.

A megaphone atop one of the military Humvees announced the obvious. "Shots fired! Shots fired!"

Kate glanced back only for a moment to see that the soldiers were indeed staying near the FEMA tent and not seeking to pursue the threat. She and Gavin pushed with all of their might to get the cart back to the van. Another round of gunfire echoed off the buildings surrounding the mall.

Kate and Gavin both gasped for air to fill their lungs, shoving the gargantuan load. They crossed the street and came around the corner of the building where Don stood holding his AR-15 with one hand and waving them on with the other. "Come on, come on! Hurry, we gotta go!"

Jack stood ready and waiting by the back of the van. "Just toss it all in here. Don't worry about being neat."

Don stood guard while the other three loaded the van as quickly as possible.

"That's all of it, let's get out of here," Jack said. People were still running in confusion, some spotting Don with the rifle and turning around.

"What about the cart?" Kate asked.

"Leave it!" Jack jumped in the driver's seat of the van.

Gavin shook his head and grabbed the handle. "Come on, Kate. Help me get it in the back of the pickup. They don't know what we know."

Kate quickly assisted Gavin in hoisting the cart into the truck. Then, just before getting into the driver's seat, she drew her pistol in case they were followed.

CHAPTER 5

All thy trees and fruit of thy land shall the locust consume. The stranger that is within thee shall get up above thee very high; and thou shalt come down very low. He shall lend to thee, and thou shalt not lend to him: he shall be the head, and thou shalt be the tail. Moreover all these curses shall come upon thee, and shall pursue thee, and overtake thee, till thou be destroyed; because thou hearkenedst not unto the voice of the Lord thy God, to keep his commandments and his statutes which he commanded thee.

Deuteronomy 28:42-45

The two vehicles raced toward the highway. Kate kept her eyes on the side view and rear view mirror for several miles. After she felt relatively sure they weren't being tailed, Kate picked up the radio. "Do you think it's safe to tell Don and Jack about the locusts over the air?"

Gavin sat in the passenger's seat, his hand on the barrel of his AK. "It's not like back at the commissary. If anyone hears us, it won't make any difference. Go ahead."

Kate pressed the talk key. "Don, I think we should try to hit the other commissary. Scott said another one is near the Biltmore Village."

His voice soon came back over the radio. "No way. This place is entirely too volatile. We need to get home. We picked up quite a lot of supplies. What we have will go a long way in helping us through the winter."

Kate pressed the button once more. "I got a text from a friend while we were waiting in line. I didn't want to say anything over the radio then because I didn't know who was listening. She's in cybersecurity and one of her clients is Pacific Gas and Electric. She's identified another one of the locust viruses in PG&E's SCADA system."

Don seemed to need no further explanation to know this was a serious threat. "We'll stop at that grocery store ahead."

The two vehicles pulled into the parking lot of the BI-LO. All the windows had been broken out and the store appeared to have been looted of anything that wasn't bolted down. Kate stepped out of the truck, watching her surroundings closely. The four of them stood between the truck and the van.

Don stuck his thumbs in the front of his tactical vest. "If the virus shuts down the grid, that's obviously bad news. But it's not like having everyone's accounts erased. The power companies can use generators long enough to wipe the computers and reinstall new software, right?"

Jack let his hand rest on the pistol at his hip. "I would think so. They should be able to fix that in a matter of weeks."

Kate shook her head. "Not necessarily. Stuxnet, the virus used to take down Iran's centrifuges, caused physical harm to the machinery. By attacking the PLCs, it caused the centrifuges to spin out of control and burn out the hardware. The centrifuges were useless after the exploit.

"We're talking about high voltage equipment in this case. Transformers, reducing stations, all equipment which is vulnerable to a surge of enormous voltage. Just think about what would happen to your computer if it were struck by lightning. You wouldn't have anything left to install new software on."

Jack looked at Don. "Maybe she's right. I know it's bad out there, but if the grid goes dark, this will look like a day at the county fair compared to what's coming."

Don thought for a while.

Gavin pointed at the grocery store. "Even if the locusts don't harm the hardware, I'm not sure Asheville and other small cities will survive another two weeks. Atlanta, Charlotte, New York, LA, those places may never be habitable again. The only reason DC is still standing is because the military is keeping the city on 16-hour lockdown. Places like this, they're hanging on by a string."

Deep furrows grew across Don's forehead. "We can go check it out. But if it's rough, we leave right away. We have some provisions. If we get into deeper trouble, we could end up going home empty-handed; or worse, not going home at all."

"I think it's the right move." Kate turned to go back to the truck.

Fifteen minutes later, they were in the Biltmore Village. Kate called over the radio. "The commissary is on the left."

Don replied, "We'll keep driving past that church and take a left. We'll park back behind the commissary and walk up with the cart."

Kate heard a woman yelling. She turned to see a young girl with two small children trailing behind running in the middle of the road.

"Help! Stop them!" she cried.

Kate looked to see two young men in dark hoodies running with a loaded shopping cart, trying to cross the street between Jack's van and the truck she was driving. "Not on my watch!"

She mashed the accelerator and closed the gap. The boys with the cart stopped short and tried to cut behind her. She threw the truck in reverse and backed up, lightly bumping one of the suspected thieves and knocking him to the pavement.

He jumped up from the road and slapped the rear of the truck. "What the heck, yo!"

Kate and Gavin both sprung from the truck, with

weapons drawn.

"Hey, yo! We don't want no problems." The man put his hands up and backed away from the truck.

The other delinquent took off running, abandoning the cart and his friend.

"Yo, Joey! Wait up!" The one left behind stood, hands still up, looking at Kate with worried eyes.

"Go on, and don't let me catch you around here again!" She motioned with her gun. The roughneck seized his opportunity and skedaddled, making haste to catch up with his less-than-loyal comrade.

The woman finally reached her lost cart. "Thank you! Thank you so much!" She motioned for her little boy and little girl to come stand by her side. "I don't know what we would have done if you hadn't come by."

"Do you have a gun?" Kate asked.

"What? A gun? No." The woman seemed confused by the question.

Kate pulled the extra 9mm magazines from the front of her vest. She handed the pistol to the woman along with the extra magazines. "It's probably stolen. I took it off some pretty bad guys. So, if things ever get back to normal, you'll want to get rid of it and buy yourself something else."

The woman nodded and held the gun cautiously. She slipped it into her purse. "Thank you again. I wish I could repay you."

"No need. Just take care of your family."

Jack had backed up the van. He and Don stood watching from the side of the van. Jack called out, "Okay, we did our good deed for the day. Let's get back to the mission."

Hurriedly, Kate returned to the truck. Once inside, Gavin said, "I thought you liked that gun."

"I did. But she needed it more than I do. I've got that .357 that Terry was using back at the cabin."

"Less shot capacity, much slower reload time." Gavin watched out the window.

"Yeah, but a lot more stopping power." Kate followed Jack's van to the parking lot of yet another ransacked shopping center. This one, however, had been much more upscale prior to the attacks. Everyone got out of the vehicles and huddled up.

Kate asked Don for his expert opinion. "What's up with these hooligans stealing food from people? Everyone got the same $200 in emergency credits."

Don replied, "If they can steal someone else's food, they can use their money for drugs. With the ease of transfer, the emergency credits can buy heroine just the same as it buys pasta.

"Addicts have to eat the same as the rest of us. But once food is covered, they're free to expend the remainder of their time and resources on getting high.

"The churches in Orlando provided handouts for the homeless. Some even did their laundry for them. Their intentions were good, but they dropped the ball on execution. They enabled the addicts to stay high. Now in the apocalypse, we have a glut of people who are used to living on handouts. Without the food from the churches, street addicts would have been forced into residential recovery programs in order to keep from starving."

"Wouldn't that have been terrible?" Gavin shook

his head.

Jack added, "It's hard to even say their intentions were good. The Bible says if a man will not work he should not eat. But most churches know better than the Bible these days."

"If they wanted to make a difference they should have opened recovery programs." Don removed his tactical vest. "But it's easier to give someone a hot dog and walk away feeling like the Good Samaritan."

"Some churches probably didn't have the resources to open a facility like that," Kate said.

"Then let them donate their time, money, and resources to larger Christian organizations that do," Jack rebutted.

"I suppose you have a point." Kate redirected the conversation to the mission at hand. "This FEMA tent is much smaller than the one at the mall. The commissary may have less of a selection."

"The line is shorter and not as many people milling around. I'll take that tradeoff any day." Don clipped a concealed holster under his shirt.

Gavin helped Jack remove the cart from the back of the truck. "We'll transfer $500 to each of your PayPal accounts."

Kate took out her phone. "What's the email address associated with your account, Don?"

He seemed hesitant to provide it.

"I'm not going to break into your account or anything." Kate couldn't figure out why he didn't trust her.

"Okay." He stepped forward and spoke softly as she entered it onto her phone. "It's Don the cool cop at Gmail."

Jack began cackling. "What? Don the cool cop? Are you kidding? That's hilarious."

"Okay, funny boy. Laugh it up." Don waved his hands. "Don the cop was already taken. It was Mary's idea. I never should have listened to her. But let's just keep this amongst our little group of friends here."

Jack's face was turning red from laughter. "Oh, no, Mr. Cool Cop, this is going to be your new handle around Apple Blossom Acres."

"Act like it doesn't bother you, and he'll let it die," Kate advised, trying not to giggle.

"Nope! No way. I'll never let this one go." Jack placed his tactical vest in the van and closed the door.

Don's face looked like he'd just eaten a bad pickle. "Let's get serious now so we can finish up and go home."

"Yes sir, Officer Cool Cop." Jack pushed the cart in the direction of the commissary.

"We'll call you if we need help." Don clipped the radio to his belt. "And don't hesitate to give us a shout if you have any rough-looking characters lurking around back here."

Kate tried to conceal her grin. "Okay, we'll do."

Time ticked by slowly, but the guys returned in less than an hour.

"You're back already? What did you get?" Kate let her AK hang from the sling.

Jack pushed the cart. "Powdered milk, powdered eggs, powdered cheese, and military MREs."

"You're joking about the powdered cheese."

Gavin approached the cart.

"I wish I was." Jack stopped by the tailgate of the Sierra. "Slim pickin's in this tent."

Don began loading boxes into the truck. "Low risk, low reward, but that's just fine by me."

Kate helped in transferring the cargo from the cart to the Sierra. She paused to read the ingredients in the powdered cheese. "What could you possibly use this for?"

Gavin took the can from her and inspected it. ("Mac and cheese, you could make a quiche with the powdered eggs…")

"Gross!" Kate protested.

Gavin held the can back when she tried to snatch it from him. "Ah, don't knock it until you try it. You could even make your famous cheese biscuits with it."

Kate successfully wrestled the can back from Gavin and slid it in the truck. "Maybe it will be a good barter item for some real food at a later date."

"That's the spirit!" Jack handed her a case of MREs to place in the back.

With the supplies loaded into the bed of the truck, it was a tight fit to get the cart in. Kate dusted off her hands. "I don't suppose anyone has seen a gas station open."

"I asked the FEMA worker. He said the Department of Energy was going to start sending out tankers to the commissary locations, but that it would be capped at two gallons per person, per day."

"Why even bother then?" Kate opened the door of the pickup.

"We'd use almost that much to make another trip out here to get it." Jack headed for the door of the van.

Gavin added, "If six people came in the van, we'd get twelve gallons and use less than four on the round trip. If we netted eight gallons of gas, it could be a lifesaver when things get really bad."

Kate had a hard time considering that things were not already really bad, but she knew Gavin was right. "Don, what do you think?"

"If the lights stay on long enough for us to come get more food, we can try to get gas as well. But I don't think eight gallons is worth the security risk otherwise." Don opened the passenger's door to the van. "See y'all back at the ranch."

"See you there." Kate thought Don's assessment sounded wise.

CHAPTER 6

For I am persuaded, that neither death, nor life, nor angels, nor principalities, nor powers, nor things present, nor things to come, nor height, nor depth, nor any other creature, shall be able to separate us from the love of God, which is in Christ Jesus our Lord.

Romans 8:38-39

"That's not good." Kate hit the brakes before barreling through the Waynesville intersection where the traffic signal had just gone out.

"That light went out this very second?" Gavin asked.

"It was green when Jack went through it."

Gavin took a deep breath. "No, no, no. We needed to do so many things. I wanted to fill the buckets with water. We'll have no pump. We only have about a week's worth of firewood."

"We have propane." Kate looked both ways then pulled through.

"Yeah, but the thermostat is electric. We can't use a gas furnace without electricity. Most everyone in the community has a chainsaw, but gas is in short supply. Cutting wood is no joke. That's some seriously intense labor."

"At least we can use the propane for cooking on the gas stove."

He replied, "Until it runs out."

Gavin was usually the one trying to calm Kate down. With him coming unglued, her anxiety level was rising fast. She couldn't keep playing the calm one. "You're frightening me, Gavin. I need you to tell me everything is going to be okay."

He was quiet for a moment. "Everything is going to be okay."

"That wasn't convincing. You're just saying that."

"You told me to."

Her heart began to race. "You think we won't make it?"

He reached across the seat and put his hand on her leg. "We'll get through this. It's going to be unbelievably tough, but we will survive. And I mean that, from the bottom of my heart."

She practiced her breathing routine. *A slow deep breath in, hold it for four counts, a slow breath out.* The paralyzing fear began to subside. "Hard is okay. I can handle hard, as long as it's possible."

She pulled in through the gate where Corey Cobb and his daughter, Annie, were still standing guard. Corey smiled and waved, oblivious to the new shade of horror about to befall his community and his home.

Kate followed Jack to his house and parked next to his work van. She quickly exited the truck. "Jack, see if your power is on."

"Why?" He stepped out of the van. "What's wrong?"

"The traffic light, after the overpass, it went dark right after you passed through it."

Don was out and walked around the back of the van. "At least we had a successful supply run."

Jack pressed the remote for his garage door. "Yep. It's out. You think this is it?"

Kelly Russo came to the side door. "What's it?"

Before he could answer, Rainey stuck her head out the door. "Dad, the lights are out in the house."

Jack looked at Don. "Call Scott. I'm sure he's figured out the power is out, but he probably doesn't know why. He'll want to come straight home when he hears this."

Rainey held on to her mother's arm. "Dad, what's going on?"

Jack gave them a quick synopsis of the expected attack against the grid.

Kelly shook her head. "But this might not be it, right? We have power outages all the time. This is the mountains. A dead limb can drop on just the right line and take out half the county."

Kate gave a counterfeit smile. "It's possible."

"But not likely." Jack seemed to want to get on with reality. "Kelly, Rainey, I need you both to power off your phones. I'm not sure when we'll be able to charge them again."

"If we don't have power, the cell towers won't last long. What's the point?" Rainey asked.

"Phones have other uses besides texts and calls. GPS for one thing. We may think of other important uses for them later."

Kate said, "We need to let everyone know what's happening."

"We should unload the cargo first. You always want to stow away your life-saving commodities *before* you tell people the sky is falling in." Gavin let down the tailgate.

Kate didn't like the way he made light of the situation, but she took comfort knowing he wasn't falling apart at the seams. "He's right."

Jack turned to go into his house. "I'll open the garage manually from the inside."

Once the door opened, Kelly and Rainey assisted Kate and the others with stacking the supplies in the garage.

"We need to get everyone in one place; tell them all together," Jack said.

Kate passed a box from the van to Rainey. "Mr. Pritchard enjoys beating on that old pan. I'll have him ring the bell. His yard is already set up as a meeting place."

"Good idea," Jack said.

Don returned to the group.

"What did Scott say?" inquired Kate.

"He's on his way home." Don assisted with the

unloading efforts.

Half an hour later, the assembly had gathered in Pritchard's backyard. This time, most everyone was present. Kate and Gavin stood side-by-side at the podium and explained what they believed had happened. The silence of shock and awe soon faded and the assembly began bombarding them with questions.

"How long will it take to get new transformers? What about solar? Couldn't we still get power from a hydroelectric plant? Isn't the government prepared for emergencies like this?"

Kate held up her hands. "Please. One at a time. But quickly, the source of the electricity isn't the issue. The virus has likely disabled the transmission hardware. Getting new equipment could take years, even decades."

Mrs. Dean stood up. "I was raised in Bryson City, down the road a piece. We didn't have no electricity coming up. I was in my twenties before I had an indoor toilet. Folks in these mountains always did get by just fine without electricity. It'll take some gettin' used to, 'specially for you young folk, but we'll be alright. Don't y'all fret none."

Kate was mesmerized by the old widow's words. The person she'd figured to be the most vulnerable out of the group had proven to be the most stalwart in spirit. Her encouragement transformed the mood of the entire gathering. Her example served to suddenly turn the tide in morale. Kate stuttered, not knowing what to add to Mrs. Dean's wisdom. "Um, well, yes, we, we— can get through this."

Pritchard held up his hand. "We can do all things through Christ who strengthens us."

Scott McDowell seemed to recognize that Kate and Gavin were out of things to say. He stepped forward to the podium, still wearing his deputy's uniform. "Kate, Gavin, thank you for the analysis. Mr. Pritchard, Mrs. Dean, thank you for the courageous examples and revitalizing words. We can and we will get through this crisis. But, we'll have to work together to do it. First and foremost, we need to upgrade our security. I'm going to need all able-bodied adult men to take part in keeping Apple Blossom Acres secure.

"The sheriff's department is essentially non-existent from this point forward. We're running on fumes so even if we wanted to work for free and had no families of our own to worry about, we'd have no way to respond to calls. The jail is running on a generator as of right now. It is also nearly tapped out. Once the generator gives out, the sheriff plans to release the inmates."

The audience began to murmur. The protests grew louder. "How can he do that?"

Scott shook his head. "Leaving them in there would be a death sentence, and it would be one of the most inhumane ways you could kill a person."

"Then take them out and shoot them!" cried another.

"These aren't death-row inmates. This is a county jail, with mostly non-violent offenders, or at worst, people who haven't been convicted yet." Scott remained calm but firm.

"This won't end well!" someone else exclaimed.

Scott pressed his lips tight. "You may be right, but I'm not willing to fall back to the dark ages within the first twenty-four hours of the lights going out."

"And what if they find their way to our community?" a woman from the audience asked.

Scott's eyes were stern. "Zero tolerance. If we're attacked, looted, stolen from, or threatened, we shoot on sight. We'll make handmade signs providing fair warning that trespassers will be killed. As of this moment, we're officially operating under a new set of rules, but I can't justify taking people around back and putting a bullet in their head because they got caught with a quarter bag of pot."

Marilyn Cobb spoke up. "I don't think I'm comfortable with shooting people at all, especially for something as simple as trespassing."

Scott leaned on the tree-trunk podium. "Trespassing typically shows intent to commit further crimes, particularly if the perpetrator has done so after being warned he'll be shot. But your comment is valid. Let's take a vote. Those in favor of adopting my recommendations, please raise your hand."

Marilyn Cobb snarled at her husband, Corey, when he and Annie both showed their support of the new measures.

Scott looked around. "Kate, could you count those up for me and make a note of it? It looks like about two-thirds, but I want this to be official."

"It's not official without Edith and the other board members being present, but that doesn't seem to concern you." Marilyn crossed her arms tightly.

"No ma'am, it does not." Scott remained pleasant. "And those opposed, please raise your hands."

Kate tallied up the *nays,* which were significantly less than one third. It was obvious that several people had abstained from voting altogether.

Scott continued speaking. "Everyone needs to go home for now, take a deep breath and relax. As Mrs. Dean said, we'll get through this. Take inventory of what you have. Write down your immediate needs, and we'll have another meeting tomorrow morning at 9:00 AM. I think it goes without saying, Mauney Cove Branch is our only water source until we figure out a way to get water out of our wells. Let's keep it as pristine as possible. No washing clothes or dishes in the creek. It runs along the road for the most part, so I'm sure no one would have a privy nearby, but just to be safe, I'll say it. No human waste within 100 feet of the creek. Make sure your gray water isn't running towards the creek when you dump it. Jack, you're the water guy, am I missing anything here?"

Jack stood up. "Even with our best efforts, animals can get sick and die in or near the creek upstream from us. And obviously, a raccoon or opossum may not be aware of our 100 feet privy rule, so there's that. Boil your water before you drink it or put eight drops of bleach per gallon. Either one of those things will kill any contaminants."

"How long do we boil it?" asked a man.

"By the time it comes to a full boil, anything that

would hurt you is long gone."

Scott adjusted his holster belt. "Able-bodied adult men who aren't already working security, come on up. We'll set up a schedule and assess how much training we need to do. Don, if you could stick around and help me out with this, I'd appreciate it. If there's nothing else, the rest of you are dismissed."

Amanda McDowell, Scott's wife, held up her hand. "What about the ladies? Some of us can shoot as well as a man."

"Yeah," said Kelly Russo. "I'd like to volunteer for guard detail."

Considering that Kate, Vicky, Annie Cobb, and Rainey Russo were already on the security team, Scott couldn't very well say no. "Okay, any ladies interested in helping out, come on up, but it's not required."

CHAPTER 7

Woe to the bloody city! It is all full of lies and robbery; the prey departeth not; the noise of a whip, and the noise of the rattling of the wheels, and of the pransing horses, and of the jumping chariots. The horseman lifteth up both the bright sword and the glittering spear: and there is a multitude of slain, and a great number of carcases; and there is none end of their corpses; they stumble upon their corpses: because of the multitude of the whoredoms of the wellfavoured harlot, the mistress of witchcrafts, that selleth nations through her whoredoms, and families through her witchcrafts.

Nahum 3:1-3

Saturday afternoon, three days after the lights went out, Kate placed a plate of fried squirrel at the center of the table. It was her first attempt at preparing the small forest creatures which were so abundant in the surrounding hickory and oak trees.

"Yuck! I am not eating those things!" Vicky pushed her chair back from the table.

"That's fine. We have plenty of beans and rice." Kate put two large bowls next to the fried squirrel.

"More for me." Sam forked a piece of squirrel onto his plate.

"I think we should pray first." Kate sat down and looked at Gavin.

"Okay." His face looked expectant. "But you're not asking me to do it, right?"

She lifted one shoulder. "You could."

"I'll forgo the honor."

"Fine." Kate crossed her hands and bowed her head. "God, thank you for our community, and for the food that you've supplied for us. Watch over us and protect us in this dark time. Amen."

Sam looked at his aunt. "That was a good prayer."

"Thanks, Sam. I hope everyone enjoys the squirrel," she turned to Vicky. "But I won't be offended if you don't." Kate stuck her fork in a rear quarter and put it on her plate. "I'm not so sure how much I'm going to like it myself."

"Tastes like chicken!" Gavin's eyebrows were high.

Sam finished chewing. "It's good, Aunt Kate!"

With hesitant eyes, Vicky held her fork gingerly between her thumb and her index finger and slowly prodded a small piece of the meat. "Maybe I'll try one bite."

"It's very good!" Gavin took a drink of water.

They were all quiet for a few minutes while they ate.

Gavin turned to Kate and broke the silence. "So you're working overwatch with Scott after lunch?"

"Two to ten." Gazing at the empty plate in the center of the table, Kate felt pleased with her culinary efforts concerning the wild game. "Why? What's up?"

"Nothing. I miss working security with you. That's all."

Vicky paused from eating. "Aww, how sweet."

Kate smiled. "I do too, but I requested that we be mixed up from time to time. It's important that we work with the guys who have law enforcement experience like Don and Scott; even hunters like Jack." She placed her hand on his. "I hope you understand."

"Absolutely. I think it's good for everyone to work with everyone else. We get to know each other's strengths, and we can all learn something from the other group members."

Kate leaned to the side and gave him the lightest kiss. "Thanks."

"Tomorrow is church, right?" Sam picked a few missed morsels from a squirrel bone.

"I would assume so. Mr. Pritchard hasn't said otherwise." Kate continued to eat.

"I'm going to get my shower today. The bathroom is freezing in the morning," Vicky announced.

"Wash your hair while you're at it," Sam said bluntly.

"Excuse me?" Vicky sounded incensed.

"It's looking a little greasy. That's all."

"Ugh! I skipped like two days washing my hair. That shower bag that Jack rigged up for us barely holds enough water to get a proper body wash, much less to shampoo my hair. I have to heat an entire extra bucket of water if I want to wash my hair. Besides, what do you care?"

Sam's eyes were filled with certainty. "We have exactly four teenagers in this compound. You, me, David, and Rainey."

"So?"

"If you start neglecting basic personal hygiene, you'll upset the balance."

"Ahhh! I skipped two days!" Vicky rolled her eyes. "But please, do go on." She waved her hand at the air.

"Rainey is managing to keep up her appearance, even in the midst of the apocalypse. If you start letting your standards slip, she'll become more attractive to David. Living on the same street, those two already have a well-established rapport…"

"A rapport? Since when do you say rapport? And since when do you care about whether Rainey and David hook up?" Vicky snarled her lip. "You *do* like her, don't you?" She smirked.

Sam set his teeth together and sighed. "I didn't say *I like her*. I'm just pointing out our limited options. And if those two get together, *our* options get catastrophically slimmer."

"Catastrophically slimmer. I see." Vicky crossed her arms and stuck her tongue in her cheek. "You're in love with Rainey Russo. Well, brother of mine, for the sake of your tortured soul, I'll wash my hair tonight."

One side of Sam's mouth curled upward. "I'm sure that has nothing to do with your own smitten heart."

"Maybe, maybe not." She lifted her chin and continued eating.

Kate stood up and put her empty plate in the sink. "How about we see if the radio has any news for us?"

"I thought we were supposed to be limiting our battery usage." Vicky brought her plate to the sink.

Gavin replied to Vicky's comment. "We only have two solar chargers for all the walkie-talkies on the security team. So yeah, we're being frugal with power. But a few minutes of news is considered situational awareness. We can afford to burn some energy for that."

Kate switched on the small AM/FM radio and scrolled to the NPR station.

A male reporter was providing details of conditions around the country. "The US military has stepped in to fill the security void left by failed state and local law enforcement departments in major metropolitan centers since the outage. President Long used his emergency powers to sign an executive order which will permit all branches of the armed forces to participate in the security and recovery efforts. Additionally, he has closed all foreign bases and is recalling each and every US troop currently serving overseas. Bases in allied territories are being temporarily turned over to the host countries. In areas where US relations are stressed, critical weapon systems are being destroyed and the bases will be considered permanently closed.

DOD Secretary Sergio Rosales gave a brief interview to NPR early this morning from the Pentagon. Here's a brief clip of what he had to say to NPR reporter Megan Massey."

Rosales' voice could be heard. "Recovery efforts are progressing best in cities where the population is the most calm. In cities like LA and Atlanta, we've had attacks against FEMA commissaries in which coordinated groups have fired on FEMA workers and security personnel. The groups have managed to steal FEMA delivery vehicles full of relief supplies. Not only does this limit the available food in those areas, but it also requires the military to expend resources on finding the violent criminals."

A female interviewer asked, "Under the president's expanded order, will the military abide by constitutional restrictions in searching for these criminals?"

Rosales replied, "We'll be using rules of engagement similar to those used in theatre where we were battling insurgencies. Technically, that's what these attacks against the FEMA facilities amount to."

The reporter questioned, "Are we talking about

door-to-door searches, like Iraq?"

"Only in the most extreme circumstances, and only until the perpetrators are brought to justice."

"Will the military be confiscating firearms during these searches?"

"The DOD is providing security for these areas. Individual citizens don't need to be armed. Particularly in cities declared to be hostile zones for relief workers, guns are proving to be a hindrance."

"You mentioned recovery efforts. Does the Army Corps of Engineers have a timeline for power to be restored?"

"As you know, much of the infrastructure was damaged by the attacks. The virus caused transformers to be hit with overwhelming surges of high voltage. Many of the components that make up the grid will have to be replaced. Our first priority is getting the capital back online. The DOD is requesting any experienced linemen and electrical workers who are able, to come to Washington DC. It should be seen as a civil service, but you will also be well-compensated. Workers can bring their credentials to the nearest FEMA commissary, and we'll do our best to provide transportation. Once you're here, meals and housing will be supplied."

Sam said, "He still never answered her question about when the lights would be back on."

"He probably won't." Kate poured a gallon of water and a couple drops of soap into a plastic dishpan. "If they say it will take decades, the cities will melt down even faster. Anything else would be a blatant lie."

"Why are they even bothering to try to maintain order then?" Vicky came to the sink to help her aunt clean up.

"What else can they do?" Kate washed a plate, rinsed it and handed it to Vicky to towel dry. "They have to put forth their best effort."

"Or at least make a good show of it," Gavin cleared the remaining dishes from the table. "The government has to appear to be working for the good of the country to justify everything they're dumping into DC. I'm sure the Capitol has water, sewage, and generators humming on every street corner. They probably have internet and cable TV."

Kate put on the feigned look of a sacrificial servant. "We must hold the golden city together, to be a shining beacon of hope for the rest of America—tis our duty."

"But without the rest of the country, their supplies will eventually run out." Sam helped his sister by putting away the dry dishes. "DC doesn't produce anything."

"Yes, but the less they share with the rest of the country, the slower they'll run out of food." Kate rinsed the last plate and handed it to Vicky to dry.

The four of them continued to discuss the trajectory of certain ruin for the nation until Kate had to leave for guard duty.

CHAPTER 8

And the word of the Lord came unto him, saying, Get thee hence, and turn thee eastward, and hide thyself by the brook Cherith, that is before Jordan. And it shall be, that thou shalt drink of the brook; and I have commanded the ravens to feed thee there. So he went and did according unto the word of the Lord: for he went and dwelt by the brook Cherith, that is before Jordan. And the ravens brought him bread and flesh in the morning, and bread and flesh in the evening; and he drank of the brook.

1 Kings 17:2-6

Later that evening, Kate lay prone next to Scott beneath the rudimentary shelter overlooking the checkpoint. The sun sank low behind the mountains in the west.

"How are you guys set for ammo?" Scott asked.

"We have some. I wasn't counting on this being the end of the world as we know it, so obviously, I wish I'd bought more."

"Specifically 7.62. How much do you have, ballpark?"

"AK ammo? I think Gavin brought about 1000 rounds when he came. We might have picked up another 300 from the shootout."

"Yeah, not a lot considering your whole group is running AKs." Scott held a pair of binoculars up to his eyes.

"We also inherited two AR-15s from the fight. But I doubt we even have 200 rounds for those."

Scott continued looking through the binoculars. "I stashed several thousand rounds of 5.56. Most ARs are set up to run 5.56. The department gives us ammo to train with. When Don called and told me what was going on with the power grid, I figured we'd be doing a lot of training, so…"

"You loaded up." Kate squinted in the direction that Scott was looking. "Do you see something?"

"Three does are just inside the tree line on the hill across from us. This is their rut. Lots of times, when you see a group of does together at this time of year, a buck is nearby. And he's likely to be a big one who has chased off all the smaller bucks." Scott passed her the binoculars.

"If you see the buck, you're going to shoot it?"

She looked through the lenses.

"Unless you want to take a shot."

"I see the does, but no buck." She handed him the binoculars.

Scott spoke softly into the radio. "Checkpoint, this is overwatch. I've spotted some deer. I'm going to try to take a shot. Don't get spooked. We're not engaging the enemy or anything."

The radio chirped back. "Roger that, overwatch."

Scott took one more look through the field glasses. "He's probably deep back in those woods. I think we should try to take down two of those does."

"I thought you weren't supposed to shoot does." Kate kept her eye on the deer.

"Like I said Wednesday, we're operating on a whole new set of rules. I'll take the one on the right. You take the one on the far left."

Kate lined up her open sight on the animal. "Where do I aim?"

"Right behind the shoulder."

"It's kind of far." She wasn't sure she could hit something at such a distance.

"Don't worry. Take your time. Tell me when you're ready. We have to pull our triggers at the same time. They'll bolt once they hear the rifles."

Kate watched for a moment. "It went behind a tree."

"That's okay. She'll be back. Do you have a shot for the one in the center?"

"No." A small shrub obscured her view. "But if we shoot the does, won't we endanger the population?"

"It's the apocalypse. All game animals will be hunted to within a hair's breadth of extinction. But, it will eventually come back into balance."

Kate waited for one of the does to reappear. "How do you figure?"

"A few of each species will retreat deep into the mountains, where humans have rarely set foot. They'll reproduce and begin to trickle back into the rest of the country after we've been thinned out to where humans aren't such a threat."

"Thinned out?"

"Kate, most of the country isn't going to survive this thing. I'd imagine half the population will be wiped out before winter is over. By this time next year, we could be looking at an eighty-to-ninety percent die-off."

Kate considered the grim reality and held the AK steady. "I see her butt."

"Just wait. As long as nothing spooks them, you'll get a shot." Scott kept his rifle trained on the doe to the right.

"Why do you think so many people will die?"

"Thanks to you, we took quick action to stock up before the lights went out. Most people didn't seize that opportunity. And thanks to Pritchard's stock-pot-and-wooden-spoon church bell, we were able to come together as a community. We have water and we have plenty of space to farm in the spring. We've been given a fighting chance. But the people in the cities, they have little to no resources. No clean water in most instances. Very little farmable land. Some will try to flee the cities, but if they have nowhere to go, the elements will kill them.

"Unfortunately, the monsters will thrive. They'll be a big part of the die off. Without the thin blue line to keep them in check, they'll grow more aggressive, more violent, and more dangerous with each passing day."

"Monsters?"

"Yeah, monsters. We used to call them bad people, but they'll morph into a completely different sub-species. People like the Badger Creek Gang, they'll get so mean that they'll no longer qualify as human beings."

A chill shot up Kate's spine. "The ones you locked up, they all got out?"

"I'm afraid so. But don't worry about them. We're stronger than they are, and if they come, we'll be ready."

Kate took some solace in Scott's words. "Thanks. I see another deer. I think it's the buck!"

"Can you hit it?"

"I think so."

"I'm still going to try to hit this doe. We've got a lot of people to feed. Take up the slack in your trigger and squeeze on three."

"Got it!"

Scott started the count. "One…two…three!"

Bang, Bang!

Kate watched the buck leap then take off. He ran for a few feet, then dropped suddenly. "I think I got him!"

"I dropped mine also. Good job!" Scott picked up the walkie. "Don, are you listening?"

"Yeah, did you get it?"

"Yep. Kate took a big ol' buck. Can you cover

my position until 10:00 tonight?"

"If you save me a tenderloin."

"Sure thing. And maybe we can have one of the hams roasted by the time church is out tomorrow. Stop by Jack's on your way down the hill. Tell him I'm going to need some help cleaning these animals." Scott stood up from the overwatch shelter. "We're blessed to have you as part of the community, Kate. I thank God that He sent you when He did."

"I'm the one who's blessed. If we'd stayed in Atlanta, we'd have all been dead by now."

CHAPTER 9

How are the mighty fallen, and the weapons of war perished!

2 Samuel 1:27

One week after the locusts took down the power grid, Kate awoke to the distant sound of gunfire early Wednesday morning. Kate grabbed her AK-47, and with her sweatpants still on, stepped into her hiking boots, which she kept near the bed. She snatched the radio from her bedside table on the way out the door. She switched it on and pressed the talk key while bounding down the stairs. "What's happening?"

Pritchard was on the graveyard shift at the checkpoint. "They's shootin' over at the McDowell place."

"How did they get past the gate?"

"Devil if I know. Filthy vermin probably sneaked in through the woods. Just get over there as quick as you can!"

Another voice came over the radio. "This is Don, keep one person on the checkpoint and one on overwatch. This could be a diversion to get a larger force through the gate. Everyone else, meet me at the Peterson's place across from Scott's house."

Gavin stepped out of his room, eyes wide as saucers and wearing his tactical vest.

"Did you hear that?" Kate looked down to see that he'd managed to get his boots on but still wore his boxer shorts.

Gavin's hair was going in every direction. "Yeah."

"Are you going to fight like that?"

He looked down, then back up. "Yeah."

"Let's go!" Kate opened the door and clicked on the flashlight attached to the barrel of her AK-47 with two small C-clamps.

"Aunt Kate! Wait for me!" Sam came out of his room, more dressed than Gavin, with his AK in his hand.

"Get your sister and keep an eye on the house."

"But Aunt Kate!"

She looked up to see Vicky standing at the top of the stairs with her rifle. "This is important, Sam. We don't know how many people are here and what they're up to. You and Vicky have to guard the supplies."

"Okay, we'll defend the house," Sam said.

Kate rushed out the door and down the yard,

walking beside the driveway so as not to make noise by tromping through the gravel.

Gavin stayed close to her side, pacing his breath. "I should have put on some pants."

More gunshots rang out from the direction of Scott's house and the two of them continued running toward the danger.

"Too late for that now." She saw Pritchard along with Corey and Annie Cobb standing with guns ready at the end of the Peterson's driveway. She sprinted toward them. "Don's still not here?"

Corey pointed at the house. "Jack and Don went inside the house. They told us to keep watch out here, in case any intruders tried to get away."

"What about the back of the house? Is anyone watching that?" Gavin inquired.

"Not that we know of," Annie replied.

"But don't just shoot anything that moves," Corey added. "Obviously, Scott will be trying to get Amanda and David out of there."

"Got it." Kate followed Gavin to the rear of the house. More shots were fired in the house. They tucked low to avoid stray bullets.

A man clothed in all black jetted out the back door toward the tree line.

"He's not on our side." Kate leveled her rifle and let the front sight of her AK lead the fleeing culprit. POW!

Gavin's rifle barked out two more shots.

Suddenly, rifle fire came out the back door. Bullets whizzed by Kate's head. She knelt behind a tree. "They're spraying cover fire."

Gavin lay prone on the ground and peeked

around the side of the tree. "We can't let them get away, or we'll have to fight them again."

Kate warned, "Don't take a shot until they've cleared the porch. Otherwise, we risk a bullet going into the house and killing Scott, Don, or Jack.

Gavin growled with his teeth set tightly against each other. "That gives us a short window. They've only got about a twenty-foot sprint to the cover of the woods."

"Okay, let them think it's safe to go and open up when they run." Kate readied her rifle for the final assault.

More gunfire echoed from inside the house.

"There they go!" Gavin fired five rounds.

Kate spun around from behind the tree and let her AK-47 rip through rounds as fast as she could pull the trigger. "I dropped one of them!"

A muzzle flashed from the ground near the tree line. POP, POP, POP!

Gavin grabbed Kate and pulled her behind the tree. "He's not dead yet."

"Nothing is as dangerous as a wounded animal. I have to finish him off." Kate changed magazines, took a deep breath, then used her rifle to pound the area where she'd seen the muzzle flash.

"You hit him. A few times." Gavin put his hand on her back.

Kate waited for a while to see if other hostiles would try to retreat. She listened for more gunfire from inside the house. She picked up the radio. "Don, are you guys okay in there? Do you need us to come in?"

Moments later, his voice came back. "Not yet.

Jack and I are clearing the house. Once that's done, I'll need you and Annie to come in here."

"10-4." She looked at Gavin curiously.

Jack's voice sounded solemn when he finally spoke over the radio. "The house is clear. Mr. Pritchard, head on back down to the checkpoint in case of further attacks. Corey, stand guard outside. Send anyone else that shows up down to the checkpoint. Kate, Annie, we could use your help in here."

Gavin put his hand on her shoulder. "Do you want me to come in with you?"

She shook her head. "No. Go tell Sam and Vicky that the threat has passed for now."

"Okay, I'll be back."

She looked at his muscular legs and fought a grin. "Put some pants on while you're up there."

"Yeah, I was going to." He turned to go up the hill. "But thanks for reminding me."

Kate met Annie at the front porch and the two of them walked into the house.

Don met them inside the door. "Scott is dead. Looks like it was some of Lloyd Graves' boys. Most likely some kind of vendetta for ~~Scott locking~~ him up."

Kate knew that name too well. "The Badger Creek Gang?" She looked around at the four dead bodies lying on the living room floor. "Is that who these people were?"

Don picked up a Glock sitting too close to the hand of one of the corpses. "That's what Jack seems to think."

"Are any of them Lloyd?" she asked.

"Jack said Lloyd is not one of the dead. Three or four other hostiles cut out when Jack and I came through the front door. Scott took out a few before he died. Amanda shot one of them. David killed another. One of them got the drop on Amanda, grabbed her from behind and was using her for a shield. Made David drop his gun. Then, one of them held a gun on David while the other two started tearing Amanda's nightgown off of her. David went wild when they tried that and the one with the gun pistol whipped him pretty good. That's about the time when we came in."

Kate shuddered. "You got here before they…"

"Yeah." Don looked at another corpse on the floor. "But she's shaken up. I think she'd feel more comfortable being consoled by females, considering what she's just endured."

Kate leaned her rifle by the door. Annie did the same. Kate took a deep breath and readied herself for the difficult task at hand. She knew death, was well-acquainted with deep personal loss, and understood, perhaps better than anyone, what it was like to see a loved one taken so violently. She walked into the bedroom. Jack held fifteen-year-old David in his arms. David's anguished moans were of sorrow mixed with wrath. Kate turned to see Amanda wrapped in a blanket, sitting in a corner. Kate took a seat by her and slowly put her arm around the sobbing woman.

Amanda stared longingly at the body of Scott lying on the floor. Someone, Jack probably, had pulled a sheet over Scott, covering his face. Nevertheless, Kate knew it to be him, simply from the way his bereaved widow looked at the motionless mass beneath the pure white sheet with the dark crimson stain.

Kate looked up at Annie. "Could you bring us a glass of water?"

Annie left the room to fulfill the request.

Kate pulled Amanda closer. "Scott was a wonderful person. The whole community will miss him. Not like you and David, but we'll miss him. It's hard to imagine now, but you'll get through this. Do you feel like getting cleaned up?"

Amanda's eyes shifted around the room, looking at the corpses strewn about the floor. She shook her head.

Annie came back into the room. She gave the water to Amanda who took a small sip. "I'm a nurse. I'd be happy to take a look at you… or David if either of you has any injuries."

Without speaking, Amanda shook her head again and gave the glass to Kate.

Kate took the water and set it on the nightstand. "After we were attacked, I remember not feeling safe in my own home. That feeling has passed, but it was very difficult for the first few days. Would you and David feel more comfortable coming up to my place for a day or two? We'll make sure Scott is taken care of."

Amanda seemed lost for a moment. Kate wasn't sure if she was processing the offer or if she'd drifted off to a faraway place. Seconds later Amanda looked Kate in the eyes and nodded.

Kate slowly stood up. "Okay. Let's pack a bag for you, get dressed and head on up to my place.

David, do you want to pack some of your things? You and your mom are spending what's left of the night at my house."

He shook his head. He'd stopped bawling, but his eyes were as red as a raging bull's. "I'm not leaving my dad."

Kate hated to speak about such a sensitive matter, but she'd been forced to deal with the same reality for herself, her niece, and her nephew. "David, I don't want to sound cold, but your father is gone. He was a good man who loved God. He's with Jesus now. He doesn't need you. However, your mother is still here and she does."

David looked at Amanda. Tears began to flow again. "I'm sorry, Mama. I wanted to stop them but…"

Amanda resumed crying also. She opened her arms to her son. The two of them embraced for a long while.

Jack tapped Kate gently on the shoulder. "Let's give them some space for a moment."

Kate quietly dismissed herself and followed Jack and Annie into the living room.

Annie walked toward the door. "David has some serious lacerations on his lip and forehead. Probably not life-threatening, but he could use some stitches. I have some Steri-Strips and sutures up at the house."

Kate looked at Don. "Will you go with her? She probably shouldn't be walking around out there by herself. We don't know where the other thugs could be."

"Sure." Don shouldered his AR-15 and followed

Annie.

"Annie, come on up to my cabin after you collect your supplies." Kate locked the door behind them.

Two hours later, a thin vermillion glow began beyond the mountains, breaking the absolute darkness of the sky. Kate poured another cup of hot tea into Amanda's cup and sat down next to her. "I'll sleep on the couch. You can have my bed."

"I couldn't take your bed."

"I insist." Kate put her hand on Amanda's.

"You're very kind, Kate."

David emerged from the downstairs bathroom, wearing his pajamas. His face was badly injured. Two Steri-Strips held together a long gash on his forehead and three stitches mended the deep cut on his lower lip.

Vicky jumped down from the counter. "David can sleep in my bed."

"That's very kind," said Kate. "Where will you sleep?"

"In my sleeping bag, on the floor."

"What floor?"

"My floor," Vicky said innocently.

"How about you sleep on the living room floor, next to me." Kate's smile indicated that it was more of an order than a recommendation.

David stood behind Amanda with his hands on her shoulders. "Thank you for the offer, Vicky. But if I could just borrow your sleeping bag, you can keep your bed. I'd like to sleep in the room with my mom, if that's okay."

"Oh, sure. I'll go get it. I'll put it in the room

with your mom's bed." Vicky scampered up the stairs.

Amanda put her arm across her chest and took her son's hand. "All the emotion has drained me. Kate, if you don't mind. I think we'll turn in."

Kate stood up. "Sure. I'll be down here if you need anything."

"Thanks again. Good night." With eyes full of sadness, Amanda looked pitiful. David walked up the stairs, his arm around his grieving mother.

Vicky came down as they were going up. "Good night, David. I'm really sorry for your loss. I know it sounds cliché, but I really do know how bad you're hurting."

David paused, his battered face in bitter sorrow. "I know you do, Vicky. Thanks for everything."

Vicky pulled up a stool at the counter next to Kate.

A short knock on the door preceded Pritchard's entrance.

"Come in," said Kate, after Pritchard had already let himself in.

Don and Jack trailed in behind him, both looking somber.

"Isn't Gavin with you?" Kate felt concerned.

"Don't you fret. The boy's down yonder with them Cobbs. They's cleanin' the place up a mite. We got them bodies drugged out of the house. Ain't got enough gasoline to set 'em a fire like we did that last bunch. They'll have to sit 'til we can stoke up a good brush fire in the mornin'. I don't reckon they'll fester much bein as cold as it is and all."

Kate wrinkled her nose at Pritchard's uncanny

ability to make the gruesome sound even less palatable. She turned to Don. "Did you see where they came from?"

"Jack and I are going to track their path once the sun is fully up. I'm guessing they came through Laurel Ridge, on the other side of the mountain."

"From the top of the mountain? Scott's house was near the bottom of the hill. They would've had to pick their way through all that timber. Nobody saw anyone with flashlights?" Kate held her teacup in her hand.

"They could've had night vision." Jack put his weight against the counter.

"Like in the movies?" Vicky leaned forward in anticipation of his reply.

Jack said, "Not necessarily the fancy stuff the military uses—like in the movies. But a lot of folks have Generation 1 or Generation 2 scopes for hunting coyotes or predators that get into their chickens. It wouldn't take much of a stretch to imagine these dirt bags stole one or two good units in a recent burglary. The ones with the night vision could have led the others through the woods. The moon provided some light. It was a clear night."

Kate felt the pressure of the renewed threat. The man responsible for Scott's brutal slaying still had a bone to pick with her for killing his brother. "How are we going to secure the neighborhood from the rear?"

Don shook his head. "It can't be done. Too much real estate. We don't have the manpower. If every resident in Apple Blossom Acres worked security round the clock, the line would still be as porous as a sieve."

Kate didn't like that answer. "But we have to do something. We can't just wait for something like this to happen again—and again."

Jack held up his hand. "Don's right, we can't seal off the community. But we can come up with some measures to make it a harder target."

"Like what?" Kate needed a solution right now, or she'd never get any sleep.

Jack rubbed his jaw. "I'd have to give it some thought, but things like trip alarms, trip wires, stuff like that would help."

"What about booby traps?" Vicky straightened up on her stool. "Pot growers used to hang fish hooks at eye level all around their fields."

"Since when do you know what pot growers do?" Kate crossed her arms.

"Kids at school are always talking about random stuff."

Don's face looked grim. "I don't want to shoot down your idea, but we'd have the possibility of a friendly getting caught in the booby trap. Anyway, brainstorming is good. Keep thinking of anything that comes to mind. Write it down and the security council will review the various suggestions. Jack, the sun is up, high enough for us to track that trail. We should get on it while we can."

Jack followed Don to the door. "Kate, we appreciate what you're doing for Amanda and David. We'll have their place cleaned up in a day or two. I'm sure they'll want to get back home once it's habitable."

Kate put her arm around Vicky. "We're happy to

do it. The McDowells were so kind to us when we lost Terry."

Once the door closed, Vicky looked at Kate. "You know I wasn't going to let anything happen if David had slept in my room, right?"

"And that, my dear, is exactly why you're not ready to make those kinds of decisions. You are underestimating the power of temptation; especially in a volatile emotional environment like we're in."

Pritchard piped up. "You best listen to your aunt. Make no provision for the flesh."

Vicky rolled her eyes at Pritchard. "Yeah, listen to her, the woman who lives with her boyfriend."

"Pardon me?" Kate instantly went from being exhausted to energized by anger. "I don't live with my boyfriend."

"Then what do you call it?" Vicky put her hands on her hips.

"I call it survival. In case you haven't noticed, we are in a violent world. The rules have changed." Kate turned to the old man. "Mr. Pritchard, can you help me out here?"

"The youngin is right. You and the boy are livin' in sin."

"We're not living in *sin*. We haven't touched each other." Insulted, Kate sat with her mouth open.

"That's a lie. I saw you two on the couch the other night." Vicky held her head high.

"Vicky! We were just kissing!"

"Kissing and touching."

Kate's face turned red. "Well maybe, but you made it sound like we were…"

"Doing it? I didn't say that. But you said you two

hadn't touched each other. I'm just stating the facts."

Kate scrambled to bring the conversation back under her control. "We'll try to be more— restrained, going forward."

Kate glanced at Pritchard and quickly turned away. But it was too late.

The old man said, "You can make excuses, you can try to be more restrained, but I'll tell you one thing I've learned in my years upon this earth; if you stand a lookin' at that apple pie in the bakery window long enough, sooner or later, you'll get you a slice of it."

Kate defended her position. "What am I supposed to do, Mr. Pritchard? We don't exactly have a lot of options that would permit us to have separate housing. I stay out of his room and he stays out of mine. I think those are adequate boundary lines."

"Don't have to convince me none. I ain't the one you have to answer to on Judgment Day. And you do have options. Just ain't got none that suit your fancy; that's all."

"And what options might we have?"

"You can get hitched, or the boy can stay with me a spell. Lord knows I've got more room in that old house than I need."

"Get hitched? Be reasonable! We barely know each other."

"Sounds to me like you're gettin' to know each other right quick over here." He waved his hand dismissively. "Don't pay me no mind, but don't think the youngins here don't see right through you tellin' them how to behave one way whilst you do as you please."

The statement cut Kate like a knife. She had never considered what an impact she could be having on her impressionable niece and nephew.

CHAPTER 10

Let him kiss me with the kisses of his mouth: for thy love is better than wine.

Song of Solomon 1:2

Five days passed since Scott had been killed and a state of relative calm returned to Apple Blossom Acres. November arrived and with it came the first serious cold snap. Kate and Gavin worked the checkpoint for the 6:00 AM to 2:00 PM shift Monday morning.

Kate bobbed up and down to stay warm. "It's freezing out here. We need a guard house or something to block the wind."

"One of those big metal barrels with a fire in it would help." Gavin rubbed his arms.

"It's only November. Think about what guard duty will be like in February."

"Don't remind me." He groaned. "How are you doing upstairs? It must be freezing up there with no heat."

"I got cold last night, that's for sure. I put my sweats over my pajama bottoms, two pair of socks, my hoodie, and gloves. We'll have to stoke up the fire and heat the house up really good tonight."

"You could come sleep downstairs."

"Gavin, you know how I feel about that."

"I meant you could come sleep downstairs, and I'll take your room. My room is closer to the fireplace. It doesn't get as cold."

"That's really sweet of you." She looked at her hiking boots. "I've been wanting to talk to you about something."

"Uh oh. Here it comes."

"What? No! Just hear me out."

"Sure, but I can tell by the tone in your voice that it's not good."

"It's not bad either. It just is—what it is."

"Okay, let me have it." Gavin stood erect as if he were bracing himself for a punch in the gut.

"I think you should consider staying with Pritchard."

Gavin looked toward the road. "That's okay. I'll just head to my cousin's in Tennessee."

"No, Gavin! Don't be like that!"

"I'm only here because of you. I knew it was only for a while. I guess I just hoped it would be a longer while."

"Gavin, this isn't about me not liking you, I do—

a lot!"

"Then what's it about?"

"It's about us living together and the example I'm setting for Sam and Vicky. And it's about temptation. We've gone further than I intended, and if we keep pushing it, I'm going to do something I'll regret. I know it's not a big deal to you, but I really believe in God. I want to live a life that's pleasing to Him."

"I promise, I won't even kiss you when we're inside the house. But I don't want to leave you there alone. Not with everything that's been going on. This thing with the Badger Creek Gang has me on edge. I couldn't sleep wondering if something is going to happen to you while you're in the house alone. I don't know if you realize this, Kate..." He took her hands. "But I care about you—deeply."

She looked down at his hands, then up into his eyes. "You never told me before."

"I've tried to show you. I wanted to tell you, but I didn't want to seem—too forward. I've wanted to say that I..." He paused.

She waited with bated breath to hear what he'd say next.

Finally, he said, "Care about you."

She felt disappointed, not hearing the words she wanted him to say. "Yeah, you said that. But unfortunately, we don't have a lot of other choices."

"It sounds like we don't have *any* other choices. It sounds like you've made up your mind and this is the way it has to be."

"Well, Pritchard said we had one other choice but..."

"And what was that?"

Kate laughed nervously and rolled her eyes. "He said we should get married."

"Married?"

"Yeah, that's what I said."

"You would marry me?"

"What? No! I mean, I'm not saying no, but you're not really asking me. But I'm not saying I would either, I, I..." She stopped her belligerent babbling and took a deep breath. "Scratch everything I just said. Can I reformulate my response?"

"Go ahead." Gavin looked completely perplexed.

"I realize that like me, you're from the hacker-slash-gamer culture. We don't have a reputation for having the most well-adjusted set of social skills. Although, I will say yours are far more developed than most people of your technological caliber."

"Is that supposed to be some kind of a compliment?" He looked even more bemused.

"Let me finish." She took his hands. "Even so, being a computer nerd doesn't give you a pass on certain social mores. One of the most sacrosanct of those sociological statutes is that a boy cannot hypothetically pose a question about a girl's willingness to marry him."

He shook his head. "What am I supposed to do now?"

"If you have a question to ask me, then ask it."

"You just said that you'd say *no*. Why are you trying to torture me, Kate?" A tear ran down his cheek and he turned away from her. "I've been in love with you since the moment I saw you at

DefCon. You shot me down, over and over, but by some strange twist of fate, I've been able to break through, to get to know you for these few weeks. While it's been the most horrible period in recent human history, they've been the best days of my life; all because I got to spend them with you. I never hoped that you'd like me as much as I like you, but I simply could not handle the rejection if you turned me down."

She grabbed him and pulled him close. "Gavin, I'm in love with you, too. I wouldn't reject you. I wouldn't say no."

His eyes looked like those of a child on Christmas morning. "You wouldn't?"

She smiled from ear to ear.

He took her hands. "Kate McCarthy?"

"Yes?" She looked into his eyes and her heart fluttered.

The radio chirped. "Checkpoint, this is overwatch. You two better look alive. You've got a vehicle coming your way."

CHAPTER 11

Dead flies cause the ointment of the apothecary to send forth a stinking savour: so doth a little folly him that is in reputation for wisdom and honour. A wise man's heart is at his right hand; but a fool's heart at his left. Yea also, when he that is a fool walketh by the way, his wisdom faileth him, and he saith to every one that he is a fool.

Ecclesiastes 10:1-3

Kate spun her AK-47 off of her back and held it at low ready. Gavin pressed the butt of his rifle snuggly under his armpit. He held up one hand to signal for the oncoming Jeep Wrangler to stop when it turned into the Apple Blossom Acres entry road.

Kate stepped forward to watch the passenger and listened close while Gavin interacted with the driver.

"Sorry, the road is closed to anyone who isn't a resident here." Gavin kept enough distance to be able to engage if need be.

The driver was in his mid-fifties, had a wavy blonde pompadour, which transitioned seamlessly into a shoulder-length mullet. He took a long, deep drag from an unfiltered cigarette. "I'm Rita Dean's grandson. She lives here." When he spoke, smoke poured out of his mouth like a rusty furnace with a stopped up flue.

"What's your name?" Gavin asked.

"James." He flicked the short smoldering butt of the cigarette. "James Dean."

Kate had to pinch herself to make sure it wasn't all some bizarre dream. James Dean had just interrupted Gavin who was about to propose; it all felt so surreal. She pressed her mic button. "Overwatch, can you send a runner to ask Mrs. Dean if she has a grandson. If so, can you ask her to describe him?"

"10-4."

Annie Cobb's voice came over the radio. "I'm just up the road from Mrs. Dean. I can get there faster."

"Thanks, Annie," Kate spoke loud enough for James Dean to hear her. "We're checking with Mrs. Dean right now."

"She's okay then?" James lit another cigarette.

"She's fine." Kate wasn't going to add any more details until she'd confirmed the identity of the caricature before her.

Kate noticed the olive-green duffle bag in the back of the Jeep. Beneath it was more luggage, and what looked like rifle cases. It seemed that James intended to stay a while if he was cleared by his grandma.

Annie called back five minutes later. "She said he's about five and a half feet tall, muscular, with flowing golden locks that would have made Absalom himself jealous. Does that sound like your guy?"

Kate grimaced. "More stocky than muscular, but if you allow for Mrs. Dean's grandiose opinion of her grandchild, I suppose we could be talking about the same person."

"She's on her way down to the gate if you want to wait for a positive ID."

"Okay, thanks." Kate stepped forward once more. "Mrs. Dean is coming down."

"Jimmy! Jimmy! Is that you?" The old woman came down the steep road faster than she should have. "Oh, Jimmy, I just knew you'd come."

James Dean cut the ignition and stepped out of the Jeep. "Grandma!"

Mrs. Dean embraced the parody of the icon for a long minute before pulling back. "It's so wonderful to see you again. How is Columbia?"

"It's bad, Grandma, real bad," said the imitation rebel without a cause.

"You just come stay with your granny for a spell."

James Dean motioned to the gaunt man in the passenger's seat. "Grandma, this is Skeeter. He was my roommate in Columbia. Do you mind if he stays with us as well?" James motioned for the lanky individual to get out of the car. "Come on out here. Introduce yourself."

Skeeter complied quickly, as if it weren't the first time he'd been issued an order by James. "Pleasure to meet you, ma'am."

Kate figured they could do with a few more people to help stand watch. Especially with the onset of winter, she wouldn't mind giving up a shift or two.

Mrs. Dean started back up the hill. "I'm goin' to get some vittles on for you boys. Y'all come on up when you're ready."

"Right behind you, Grandma." With both hands, James Dean gently patted his hair, making sure not one strand had been disturbed by his grandmother's extended greeting. His smile revealed two rows of teeth that weren't exactly straight, and weren't exactly white. However, they were all present and accounted for, which was more than Kate could say about Skeeter. James Dean walked confidently toward Kate and extended his hand. "I didn't get your name, pretty lady."

Her smile was a fractured one at best. She hesitantly obliged his offer of a handshake, hoping he wouldn't lean in for a hello kiss and that her own hand wouldn't be pasted with pomade when she drew it back. "I'm Kate. And that's my boyfriend, Gavin."

James Dean turned and offered his hand to Gavin. "It's nice to meet a man that has the same exquisite taste as myself when it comes to the fairer sex."

Gavin's lips curled into a contrived smile. He seemed to grunt or clear his throat as he shook James Dean's hand. Nevertheless, he cordially entered into polite conversation with the newcomer. "You said you're coming from Columbia? How is it there?"

James Dean shook his head. "Worse than I ever could have imagined. We live close to the high school. FEMA has set up shop over there. We're on 16-hour lockdown every day. Only allowed out of the house from 9 to 5. The military ain't taking no chances. I don't blame them. We've had our share of violence. The iron fist is the only way to keep things under control in a situation like this. I was in Special Forces. If I was calling the shots, I wouldn't do anything different."

"Oh, did you see combat?" Kate inquired.

"Nope. Too young for Nam and too old for Iraq. Kind of a waste; all that training. But, the way things are going, I still might get to hang my fair share of toe tags."

Kate felt repulsed by the method in which the answer had been delivered. But she gave the man the benefit of the doubt. Everyone had their own way of dealing with the terrible environment. Besides that, she'd found Pritchard rather offensive when she first met him. Perhaps she'd be able to warm to James Dean in time.

James Dean looked up the hill toward the overwatch shelter as if he knew exactly where it would be positioned. "What about you folks? How's this little check-point-Charlie thing workin' out for you?"

The question sounded demeaning, but Kate considered the source. "It helps, but we've had our fair share of trouble."

James sniggered. "I bet you have. Something like this would just be painting a bigger target on your backs in Columbia. They'd have eaten you alive."

Kate smiled nervously.

Gavin came to stand by Kate. "Welcome to the neighborhood. We'll be seeing you around. I'm sure you don't want to keep your grandmother waiting."

James seemed to have forgotten all about Mrs. Dean. "Oh, yeah. We better get on up to the house." He got back in the Jeep and signaled for Skeeter to do likewise. "If y'all want some advice on how to tighten things up around here, I'd be happy to help."

"It's not up to us. You'd have to speak to Jack or Don about that." Kate took a few steps back off the road.

"Okay, Jack or Don, I'll do that." James Dean flicked his cigarette out the window and onto the road as he drove away.

Gavin crossed the asphalt and stomped out the glowing butt. "Aren't we lucky to have the legendary James Dean here to help us through?"

"He's a little obnoxious, but so is Pritchard. Sometimes you have to look past the slightly-tarnished exterior to see the good stuff on the inside."

"What good stuff do you expect you'll find on the inside of James Dean?"

"Well, we have to get to know him first." She

glanced up at overwatch. "For one thing, he has Special Forces training."

"Uh huh, and a bloodlust that's never been satisfied. Don and Jack know what they're doing. Unlike Jimmy Dean, Don spent most of his life actually battling the bad guys in the streets."

"I'm not suggesting that we replace Don, I'm just saying let's keep an open mind to what he might have to offer. You'll have to admit, besides the trip lines they set up in the woods, we're no safer than we were the night Scott was killed."

"Yeah, but if Jimmy turns out to be a loose cannon, he's just as likely to get us killed as he is to make the community safer. We've had people like that on our team in Titanfall. They think they know everything and they're unpredictable."

"That one guy who you didn't like ended up being on the winning team in last year's Gears of War playoffs."

Gavin shook his head. "Jimmy Dean could be the world champ at Gears of War, I still wouldn't like him."

"Well, I'm not going to shut him down until I've heard what he has to say."

CHAPTER 12

Draw thee waters for the siege, fortify thy strong holds: go into clay, and tread the morter, make strong the brickkiln.

Nahum 3:14

On the following Sunday, Kate closed her Bible and bowed her head. She held Gavin's hand during the closing prayer. Afterward, Pritchard looked up from the podium. "I've tried to keep the preachin' short. I see everybody out there a shiverin'. But, it ain't gonna get no warmer for a while. Pete Davis has volunteered to let us use his garage to meet. It's that big old metal thing that Edith Ramsey tried to have torn down." Pritchard paused to grin as if he were savoring another thorn which could not be plucked from Edith's side.

"Anyhow, it's a four-car garage plus a shop area. Pete's got him a wood stove out there which ought to break the chill a mite. After we wrap up, I'd appreciate any of you men folk who can lend a hand by helpin' carry a stool or two down to Pete's.

"As some of you may know, we've got a couple new residents with us here on the mountain. I'd like y'all to welcome Jimmy Dean and Skeeter, what's your last name?"

The lanky fellow stood. "Just Skeeter'll be alright." He sat back down.

"Very well, just Skeeter. Jimmy is Rita Dean's grandson. He served in the Army and has a couple ideas he thinks might help us out. He's asked if he could talk to you awhile before we dismiss. I didn't see no harm in it. So, Jimmy, come on up here."

James Dean looked slightly put off, as if the introduction hadn't gone as well as he'd hoped. "My name is James Dean and I served twenty years with the United States Army as a Ranger. The skills I acquired during my time in the service have equipped me to be able to assess a situation like yours and find vulnerabilities.

"I've spent the last week walking around the community and looking at maps of the area. I have a few recommendations that I think will help to make your neighborhood safer."

Don stood up. "Mr. Dean, we already have a security council, and we'd be more than happy to hear your ideas. I know you're new, but typically these types of recommendations will go to us so we can hash them out and make considerations for the residents involved. Then, we present them to the community to be accepted or rejected. It just works better that way. Folks on the council have an understanding of the number of people, ages, and any special needs that might be at each home. I'm sure you understand."

"I understand alright," Dean smirked. "I understand that this is the same security council that was in place when Scott McDowell was murdered in his home. Is that correct?"

"Jimmy, I respect your position, but we have a system in place, and we can't accommodate a lone ranger who wants to upend the entire program."

"First of all, it's James. My grandmother calls me Jimmy, and that's okay, but I'm not seven years old, so I'd appreciate it if you called me James. Secondly, the community has a system in place because it was the only game in town. I think it's their right to decide if it's time for a change.

Thirdly, I've done my homework. I know how many people live in each house, what their ages are, and Grandma has advised me about any special needs they might have. I'll remind you, my grandma has lived here longer than most anyone else. She's seen people come and seen them go. I probably know things about people in this community that you never knew, Don."

"Jack, can you give me a hand? We need to escort Mr. Dean back to his grandmother's house." Don headed for the podium and Jack followed. Gavin stood to join in.

"Skeeter, get on up here," James called to his sidekick.

"Now hold on, Don!" Andy Reese stood up. "I'd

like to hear what the man has to say."

Others in the audience chimed in, supporting Reese's sentiments.

Gene Tifton walked up to the podium and stood behind James Dean. "This ain't no autocracy, Don. We're going to let the man speak his mind. Andy, you come on up here and stand beside us."

Corey Cobb had stood up and was looking at Don as if awaiting instructions on how to proceed. Don's jaw was tight. He motioned with his hand for Corey to sit back down. "Okay, let's hear what you've got to say."

Don and the others returned to their seats. Gavin sat back down next to Kate.

Skeeter remained next to James Dean, like an undernourished bodyguard. Dean's face didn't show the least sign of being rattled, almost as if he enjoyed shaking things up. "Your checkpoint is good, but I'd recommend pushing your overwatch shelter further up on the hill."

Don spoke up. "If you push overwatch farther from the gate, you increase the odds of a friendly fire incident. These are civilians, not sharpshooters."

"Don, I thought we agreed that it was my turn to talk?"

Don replied, "You can speak, but if you propose tactics that will endanger my friends and neighbors, I'm going to speak my mind. That's not negotiable."

"Fair enough." Dean continued, "Training is another big problem. It's been six weeks since the first wave of locusts. That used to be how long the

Air Force spent on basic training. With the proper leadership, these *civilians* would be well on their way to being soldiers. But, I can't fault anyone here for that. The training you need for writing traffic tickets doesn't translate well into a societal collapse scenario."

Don's face was blood red. "I'll also point out that we don't have an infinite supply of ammunition to train as soldiers. And if you'll look around, a lot of the people present are well past their prime fighting age."

"True," Dean conceded. "But I see a good smattering of healthy young folks who look like they'd make hardcore warriors if given the opportunity and the right guidance."

Kate looked to see Sam nodding in agreement. David Russo also seemed intrigued by what the man with the wavy mullet had to say.

Dean picked up on the approval and fueled the fire. "I'm sure some of these young people would like to learn the skills to be able to bring the perpetrators of these violent acts to justice."

Jack spoke up. "Are you selling justice, James, or vengeance?"

"Why justice, of course, Mr. Russo. I'm not trying to make enemies. I want the same thing you and Don want. I'd like my grandmother and everyone else in Apple Blossom Acres to be safe."

Warren Wilcox sat next to his wife, Martha. He said, "Don's done the best he knew, Mr. Dean. I think most of us here would like to see the two of you working together rather than being at each other's throats. What other suggestions do you have for us?"

James put on a sugary smile. "I'd like nothing better, sir. But that's up to Don. As for my other recommendations, we need to blaze a perimeter trail that runs just inside the connecting property lines of the community. It will be used by an around-the-clock roving patrol who watches for activity coming in from the adjacent farms and communities. We'll keep the trip wires inside the perimeter trail, upgrade the alarms, and affix booby traps to the trees outside of the perimeter trail."

"What kind of booby traps?" Gavin crossed his arms tightly.

"I'm glad you asked. Skeeter, bring my bag up front."

Skeeter returned to their seat where Mrs. Dean held up the strap to an old pleather gym bag. Skeeter brought it to James.

Dean unzipped the duffle and retrieved a contraption made from a rat trap and a six-inch length of black pipe affixed to the underside. "This device functions essentially like a zip gun." He fed a shotgun shell into a hole drilled out of the front of the trap. The round rested inside the pipe. "A trip wire would be positioned on the same side as the business end of the device." Dean set the trap and held a length of fishing wire. "Don, this is an inert shell. I've removed the shot, so don't have a coronary on me." Dean jerked the line. POW! The shell exploded, startling everyone in the congregation. Dean laughed at the reaction. "Now that I've got your attention, imagine having a live round pointed at a potential intruder. It's basically like one of those robot vacuum cleaners that cleans the house while you sleep. All you gotta do is empty the thing once in a while.

"If you'd had measures like this in place the night Scott McDowell was murdered, the invaders might have been dead before they ever arrived at his home to terrorize his family and kill Scott."

Gavin leaned over to Kate. "This guy is laying it on thick. He reminds me of a snake oil salesman."

Kate replied, "I don't like the delivery one bit. Neither do I appreciate the degrading manner in which he spoke to Don and Jack. But…"

Gavin cut her off. "But there's a way to do things. And this isn't the way."

Jack stood up. "Anyone who's ever set a mouse trap knows how volatile those things are. The person setting it is at great risk of being killed or seriously injured. At a time when medical resources are nearly non-existent, I don't think it's prudent to use live rounds."

"We have a doctor and a nurse in the community." James looked in the direction of the Cobb family. "Non-existent might even be considered insulting to them."

Corey shook his head. "I'm a research doctor. I have very little experience practicing medicine."

"We have very few supplies," Annie said. "*Nearly* non-existent is an accurate characterization."

"Me and Skeeter will handle setting and reloading the booby traps. I'm sure Jack and Don would have no objection to us putting ourselves in harm's way."

Don stood again. "We also run the risk of a group member or a pet accidentally setting off one of the shells."

"This is the easy part," Dean said smugly. "Don't go outside of the perimeter trail and you won't get hurt. As far as pets, I'll say this as delicately as possible. If you love your kitty or your puppy, keep them inside. Once the deer and squirrel population become diminished, those booby traps will become the least of their worries."

Don had not sat down. "Folks, you know how much I care about you. And you know I'm open to suggestions, but I'll not be a part of reckless plans. So make your decision and let me know." Don took his wife's hand. "Come on, Mary. Let's go home."

"You have a good day, Don." Dean waved. "Skeeter and I will take your stools down to Pete's garage. I'm sure it won't be the last time I pick up your slack."

Jack signaled for Rainey and Kelly to bring their stools and follow him.

The rest of the congregation mumbled amongst one another. The whispers grew louder and soon everyone was involved in a spirited debate over what to do about the newcomer's hardline tactics.

Kate, Gavin, Sam, and Vicky each picked up the stumps on which they'd been sitting. Gavin led the procession down the hill toward Pete Davis' garage.

"These are pretty light. I expected them to be heavier." Vicky hoisted her stool up with little effort. "I wonder what kind of wood it is."

"Poplar," Kate said.

"Wow, Aunt Kate! You know about wood?"

Sam followed close behind her.

"Your grandfather taught me about it when I was young. I'd go with him to collect firewood for the cabin from time to time."

"I thought you weren't supposed to burn poplar, too much creosote or something." Gavin turned to look at her.

"Dad never used it as his primary source. It burns fast and hot. It makes a good wood to get the fire going initially. The harder wood like locust and hickory take a long time to ignite. He'd use poplar to help start the harder stuff. He'd also keep a few sticks of it handy in case the fire died down. Throw a piece of poplar on a bed of hot coals and it will light up lickety-split.

"Dad said all wood produces creosote, the important thing is to use well-seasoned timber and to keep your chimney cleaned out."

"What do you think about James Dean?" Sam asked.

"I think he's rude, but I think he may have some ideas we could use." Kate anticipated a quick response from Gavin.

It came almost instantly. "Good ideas or not, he's a jerk. I hope people know better than to fall for his load of garbage."

Sam retaliated. "Why is it garbage? Everything he said is true. I'm sorry if Mr. Crisp and Mr. Russo were offended but James is right. David's dad might still be here if they'd have been more proactive."

"That's not fair," Gavin said. "Don and Jack are doing the best they can."

"And it's not good enough. Maybe they should

step aside and let someone else try." Sam fell back in the line behind Vicky, distancing himself from Gavin.

Kate sighed, hoping the quarrel would not divide the community. If Apple Blossom Acres lost its sense of unity, it would be ceding a central pillar which made it a refuge against the harsh new world.

CHAPTER 13

And the Lord God said, It is not good that the man should be alone; I will make him an help meet for him. And out of the ground the Lord God formed every beast of the field, and every fowl of the air; and brought them unto Adam to see what he would call them: and whatsoever Adam called every living creature, that was the name thereof. And Adam gave names to all cattle, and to the fowl of the air, and to every beast of the field; but for Adam there was not found an help meet for him. And the Lord God caused a deep sleep to fall upon Adam, and he slept: and he took one of his ribs, and closed up the flesh instead thereof; And the rib, which the Lord God had taken from man, made he a woman, and brought her unto the man.

Genesis 1:18-22

Sunday evening, Kate followed Gavin out the door and onto the porch. "What are we doing out here? It's freezing!"

"It's not freezing. Look at the beautiful sunset behind the mountains."

Kate gazed at the orange stripes of cloud which streaked diagonally upward across the blue background. "It is gorgeous. I use to stare out at this as a kid. I wanted to live up here all the time and never go back to Atlanta."

"Now you have your wish." He put his arm around her.

She pressed her body closer to his, feeling his warmth. "Once the sun is gone, the temperature will drop fast. We need to get back inside soon."

"We will, but it's quiet out here. And it's private."

"Yeah." She looked at him curiously. "Why? You don't think I'm going to make out with you in the blistering cold, do you?"

"No," he laughed. "We were talking about something at the checkpoint on Monday."

"Yeah, about you moving into Pritchard's. Did you talk to him?"

"We were talking about that or…"

"Or what, Gavin?" All week, she'd avoided the

subject like the plague. She assumed he'd done the same. He'd obviously reconsidered his nearly-fatal rushed decision after being saved by a satirical version of the legendary icon, James Dean. The ball was in Gavin's court when Dean's appearance disrupted the conversation, so she'd not seen it as her duty to put it back in play. If Gavin was content for it to be left alone, she had little choice in the matter. But the thoughts and anxiety over being so enraptured by love and the subsequent slow-motion letdown had been eating at her for the past six days, irritating her like a canker sore on the tip of her tongue. Yet she'd held it—until now. "This is exactly why I didn't respond to your flirting at DefCon. I don't like being toyed with, like some kind of trophy. It's not nice to wind someone up, feed them a line of manure about love at first sight, and then toss them aside like a fast food wrapper. What's with you, Gavin? I mean I realize that we don't see eye-to-eye on James, but did you really expect that we'd always agree on everything? Was your deep care and devotion really so shallow? Or am I right? This was actually all just some conquest for you, ever since you painted a target on me at DefCon."

Gavin bit his lip. "Are you done with your scathing rebuke?"

She threw both hands into the air but said nothing.

"James Dean showed up in the middle of my proposal. In a way, I was glad he did."

"I knew it." She turned away from him and looked out at the fading sunset.

"I was glad because I didn't want to ask you to marry me with guns slung over our shoulders and while we were working a security detail, especially after just being lectured about proper etiquette for members of a polite society. Besides all of that, I didn't have a ring."

She whipped around. "Nobody expects a ring in the apocalypse, Gavin. You don't have to make excuses. If you're not that into me, just have the guts to say so. You know what, maybe it would be better if you went to Tennessee."

Gavin's face remained calm. He put his hand in the pocket of his jacket and went down on one knee. He took her hand.

She realized what was happening and covered her mouth with her free hand. "Oh my goodness!"

"Kate?"

"Yes?" Her heart pounded. She wondered if it were really going to happen this time. She thought about how horrible she'd treated him if indeed he really was going to propose. She couldn't imagine that he actually had a ring, but he obviously had some object in his pocket. She watched his hand with eager anticipation.

"Will you marry me?" He slipped a giant diamond on her finger.

The floodgates broke. She began to sob. "Yes! Gavin, yes, I'll marry you." She threw her arms around him and cried. "I'm so sorry for all those awful things I said."

He held her tight. "It's okay. I knew you must have been getting anxious, but I didn't know what to say. I wanted to get a ring and I wanted the setting to be right. I'd hoped we could have the fireplace to ourselves tonight, but it's Vicky and Sam's home, too."

Her emotions of guilt soon turned to tears of joy. She looked at the ring. "It's beautiful, where did you get it?"

"Don't worry about where I got it."

"You didn't steal it, did you?" she said, half joking. The longer she considered the option the more it became one of the few possible options for obtaining such a ring under the present circumstances. "Gavin, tell me you didn't steal it."

"I didn't steal it. I told you when we first found the locusts that I was taking all my cash out of the bank. I don't know what Sky National paid there IS people, but Bank of America was fairly generous."

"But how did you get a ring that fit me perfectly?"

"Can you just enjoy it?"

Kate considered everyone else in the neighborhood who might have the same size hands as hers. "Annie Cobb?"

"Kate! Quit torturing yourself."

"It is Annie's, isn't it?"

"Kate!"

"She was married to Troy's dad?"

Gavin said nothing for a few seconds and said, "She was *engaged* to Troy's dad. He was some financial advisor. He gave her the ring after she got pregnant but took off with another girl when she started getting big. So, technically, it's never actually been through a wedding ceremony. Sort of like a new car that has only gone out on test drives.

I would consider it a brand new ring."

Kate held it up to the sky, watching the evanescing light from the sunset shift through the tiny, crystal-clear facets. "It's beautiful."

"I'm glad you like it." Gavin pulled her toward him and gave her a long impassioned kiss.

CHAPTER 14

A wrathful man stirreth up strife: but he that is slow to anger appeaseth strife.

Proverbs 15:18

Tuesday morning, Kate sipped her coffee and admired her ring. Two days had passed since her engagement to Gavin.

Sam came bounding down the stairs with his AK-47 and tactical vest.

"Where are you off to? You're not on watch this morning."

"Training." He stepped into his boots and went to one knee to tie the laces.

"What training?"

"Ranger training."

Kate needed no further information. "I don't

want you getting involved with James Dean until this squabble between him and Mr. Crisp gets sorted out."

"Mr. Dean doesn't need Don's permission to train us to be soldiers. It's something that should have already been done." He changed knees to tie the other boot.

"Regardless, I don't want you to go."

"Aunt Kate, I love you and appreciate everything you do for us, but you're not my mom."

"No, but I'm the adult in charge of you."

"I don't need anyone to be in charge of me. I can make my own decisions."

"You're sixteen, you do need someone to watch out for you."

"My age is just a number. That whole thing about becoming an adult on your eighteenth birthday flew out the door when the lights went out. I've killed, I watched my mother and my father be murdered. I'm more grown-up than any eighteen-year-old ever was prior to the end of the world." Sam opened the door.

"But I set the rules for this house, and you need to respect them." Kate stood up assertively.

"No, you don't. Dad had two shares in the house, which passed to me and Vicky. We all three have equal say about what goes on in the cabin." He stepped outside and closed the door behind him.

Kate stewed in her anger for several minutes. Then, Gavin came into the kitchen and poured himself a cup of coffee. "I'm going to have to cut wood today. If I have any energy left, I was thinking of taking down that sickly oak out back. It should be seasoned and ready to burn by April. I'm afraid we're going to run out of wood, especially if we have a late spring."

Kate stared at her coffee cup. She didn't respond.

"Hey, are you okay?"

"What? Oh, yeah. Cut down the oak. That's great."

He sat in the stool next to her. "Something is on your mind."

She explained the spat she'd just had with Sam. "I feel like I've lost control of the situation."

Gavin took a long swig from his mug. "You don't really have any recourse, and I hate to admit it, but his point is valid. Maybe you need to let go."

"They're teenagers, Gavin. They need direction, nurturing, they're not ready to be on their own."

"I'm not saying to write them off. I'm simply suggesting that you not expend your energy playing tug of war with someone who doesn't want your counsel. Give Sam all the love, direction, and advice he'll take from you, then wash your hands, knowing you did your best. Hopefully, Vicky still understands how much she needs you to mentor and care for her."

Kate sighed. A knock came to the door.

Gavin stood. "I'll get it."

Kate waited with expectancy to see who the visitor could be.

"Amanda, come in." Gavin held the door open for her.

Kate got up from her stool to embrace the grieving widow. "Hey, how are you?"

"Not good, have you seen David?"

"No."

"He was gone this morning when I got up."

Kate had a terrible thought. What if he'd snuck out the night prior and had fallen asleep in Vicky's room. She didn't want to cause undue alarm. "I'll check to see if Vicky has seen him. I'll be right back."

Kate steeled herself for a possible second confrontation. She felt as if the kids were slipping from her grasp and she could not will herself to let go. She walked gingerly up the stairs and did not knock before opening the door.

Vicky stood, half dressed. "Aunt Kate! Don't you knock?"

Kate quickly surveyed the room but saw no trace of David. "Sorry, I should have. Mrs. McDowell is downstairs. She was wondering if you'd seen David."

"No. How long has he been missing?" Vicky looked concerned.

"Just since this morning."

"Ohhhh." Vicky's brows lifted as if she'd had an epiphany. "And you thought he might be in here. So that's why you barged in. Thanks a lot, Aunt Kate. I thought you trusted me more than that."

"Vicky, it's not like that."

"Just go—and close the door behind you, please."

Kate turned and pulled the door shut. She walked down the stairs feeling worse than when she'd come up.

Upon returning to the kitchen, she said, "Sorry, Vicky hasn't spoken with David this morning."

"Did he have a rifle with him?" Gavin asked.

"Yes. He's been carrying his father's service rifle, an AR-15."

"James Dean is starting some kind of boot camp today. Do you think he might have gone there without telling you?" Gavin offered a stool to Amanda.

She sat down. "We had a long talk about that last night. I told him I absolutely did not want him to participate. I guess it's possible he went anyway."

Kate took her hand. "I asked Sam not to go, but that didn't end well."

"David really likes Sam and Vicky. He looks up to Sam. I think he sees another young person who has endured even more heartache than himself and believes Sam has the path to get through the pain."

Kate's eyes fell to the counter. "I'm sorry if he's leading him down the wrong road. I'm trying to keep them under my wing, but I'm not doing a very good job of being a parent."

Amanda patted her arm. "That's okay, Kate. And if I can offer a little advice…"

Kate looked up, hoping she wasn't about to be scolded. "What's that?"

"Don't try to be their parent. Just love them as much as you can and be the best aunt you can be. Anything else is going to feel fake and unnatural. I think kids see through fake better than we do."

"Okay, yeah, thanks." Kate hugged her.

Gavin finished his coffee. "They're not seeing through the fake in Dean."

Amanda let out a deep breath. "No. Because he's selling them a chance at revenge. Kids will see what they want to see if someone offers to fill a deep emotional void inside them. I suppose adults do that also, but kids have not been bitten by experience yet. Young people are more susceptible to the con."

Gavin grabbed his jacket. "Let's go talk to Don. I'm not content to sit back and let Jimmy Dean wreck our community, at least not without a fight."

Kate put on her coat. "Amanda, will you come with us?"

"Sure." She followed Kate and Gavin.

They arrived at Don's in a matter of minutes. Don and Jack were at Don's wellhead making some modifications.

"What's happening, guys?" Kate inspected the T-shaped contraption which Jack was feeding into the open pipe.

"Hey, Kate, Gavin, Amanda." Jack glanced up but quickly turned his attention back to the project at hand. "I fabricated a simple hand pump for my well. I've been working on the homemade foot valve, but it keeps leaching water. I've given up on perfection and began making replicas of my less-than-impeccable model. They'll save a lot of time if people don't have to haul water from the creek and can pump water from their own property."

"Can I buy one?" Kate asked.

Jack smiled. "I've already made one for you. I don't have enough material to make one for everyone, so you'll have to share with Mr. Pritchard, if you don't mind. I have one for you also, Amanda."

"How does it work?" Gavin looked at the base of the T.

Jack pointed to the thick cylinder near the end. "I cut gaskets out of rubber with a utility knife and spaced them out using a coupling for a larger size of PVC pipe. The thinner pipe extending below the gaskets allows the water to be forced through when I push down on the T handle. The water jets up through the handle and out this side. I put a threaded end on it so you can attach a garden hose if you want."

Gavin pointed to the opening in the middle. "This is the check valve? Air goes in here when you pull the handle back up?"

"Exactly. It's simple, but it works. The problem I mentioned is that the water eventually seeps out through the foot valve and the pump has to be re-primed if you don't use it every few hours. You can remove this cap on the top and pour a couple of gallons of water down the pump. You should be good to go after doing that. Just make sure you refill your bucket for priming before you finish pumping."

Don brushed the dirt off his hands. "Is everything alright, Amanda? You look distressed."

Kate and Amanda each gave their accounts of what happened with Sam and David.

Don's forehead puckered. "I wish I could do something about it, but Dean has a lot of supporters. Jack and I plotted out a perimeter trail that circles the neighborhood yesterday. We're going to take loppers and hedge clippers and cut a path wide enough for a patrol to move freely through the woods without getting hung up on any brambles or bushes."

Home Made Well Pump

"What if the patrol were to spot someone who'd breached the perimeter?" Gavin asked. "Would they be able to get through the woods to chase them?"

"In some places, yes," Jack answered. "In others, no. It would take years to thin out all the briars and undergrowth in these woods using hand-powered tools. Besides, making it easier for us to move through also makes it more accessible to the enemy."

"Then what good does the patrol trail do?" Amanda inquired.

Don said, "If a patrol spots invaders and they can't engage them with weapons, either because they don't have a shot or they lose them in the brush, at least they can sound an alarm. Even if it's nothing but Mr. Pritchard's stock pot and wooden spoon clanging, we can do a lot with a thirty-second warning."

Amanda looked at the wellhead and crossed her arms tightly. "If Scott would've had thirty seconds to wake up before they came in, I think he could have killed them all."

Kate put her arm around Amanda. "I'm sure he would've."

Don pressed his lips together. "We're going to try to put together a better training program also. But with cutting firewood, getting water, trying to keep these winter gardens alive, and everything else, time is in short supply. Jack and I both feel very strongly against the booby traps. We'd be happy to replace the live shells in the devices with inert rounds so we could use them as alarms. That would actually be quite helpful. I hope the residents will recognize that we're doing our best here."

"You have our support." Gavin patted Don on the back. "If it were up to me, I'd allocate those remaining hand pumps to your supporters."

Jack shook his head. "I hate to politicize a commodity as important as water."

Kate considered the situation. "Gavin has a point. Since everyone has to share the pumps anyway, it might as well be our side who is being gracious and letting our opponents have access to the wells. If the shoe was on the other foot, Dean could persuade his followers to restrict access. Not that I expect him to be so rude as to blatantly slap you in the face like that."

Don chuckled at her sarcasm. "Yeah, right."

"On second thought, Gavin," Jack tapped his chin with his finger, "I'm going to take your advice."

Amanda issued one final plea. "Can you do anything to stop Dean's ranger school?"

"I'm afraid not," Don said.

"Not unless he's willing to shut it down for a hand pump." Jack hoisted one of his devices in the air.

Kate gave a faint smile and shook her head. "He'll never cave that easy."

CHAPTER 15

Woe to thee, O land, when thy king is a child, and thy princes eat in the morning! Blessed art thou, O land, when thy king is the son of nobles, and thy princes eat in due season, for strength, and not for drunkenness!

Ecclesiastes 10:16-17

Wednesday evening, Kate prepared a simple dinner of rice mixed with broccoli and cheese soup mix. Sam walked into the kitchen, returning from his second day of ranger school. Kate and her nephew had not spoken since the previous morning's quarrel. She forced a smile. "How was training?"

Sam looked at her, then turned away. He started to walk out of the kitchen without a reply but stopped in his tracks. With his back to his aunt, he said, "It was good. We learned about troop movements, hand signals, all good stuff."

"Dean has skills which could help us out." Kate stirred the soup mix into the rice.

Sam turned around. "Then why are you against him?"

"I'm not against him. I've said from the beginning that he might have some ideas we need to implement. My problem with Dean is his delivery. He was very insulting to Don and Jack."

Sam pulled up a stool near where Kate was working. "I get that, I know your loyalty is with Mr. Crisp. I respect your opinion, but I hope your blind allegiance doesn't get more people killed."

Kate was ready with a quick defense about how Dean's rash behavior was more dangerous than even the Badger Creek Gang, however, she held her tongue, refusing to engage in another argument. "You know, Don and Jack have cut a perimeter trail and are scheduling two-person teams to begin patrolling the trail tomorrow."

"That's good. I hope they give credit where credit is due."

"It's not a competition. We're all on the same side. We're all *literally* just trying to survive." Kate covered the pan and turned off the flame. She let the rice finish cooking with the stored heat in the pan to conserve propane.

Vicky came down the stairs. "Hi, Sam. Isn't David with you? I thought he was coming for dinner?"

"He is, but he wanted to stop by and see his mom. They got into it over him going to ranger school."

Gavin entered the room. "Smells delicious." He greeted Kate with a kiss.

A knock came to the door. Gavin walked toward the living room but Vicky rushed past him. "I'll get it!" she said in a giddy voice.

Gavin stopped and turned to Kate with a look that begged to know what was going on.

Kate grinned and shrugged her shoulders.

"Mr. Wilcox, what are you doing here?" Vicky's reaction betrayed her disappointment.

"Vicky! Where are your manners? Invite him in." Kate placed the large cooking spoon in the sink and wiped her hands on a dish towel. She hurried into the living room. "Warren, good to see you."

"Hi, Kate." He held a piece of paper in his hand.

"What do you have there?" she asked.

"James Dean and Don have agreed to a vote by secret ballot." He handed the paper to her. "Pete Davis' garage will act as the polling station. You may bring your ballot by anytime between six and eight o'clock tonight."

She read the selections. "Don Crisp, Security Council President and Jack Russo, Vice President or James Dean, Security Council President and Skeeter, Vice President." She giggled. "This is silly. No one would vote to put Skeeter in charge of burning the trash, much less allow him to be one heartbeat away from the top security position."

"Oh, I beg to differ, Ms. McCarthy. From what

I'm hearing, the residents are quite evenly split."

"Do you have more ballots?" Gavin asked.

"One per household," Warren explained. "HOA rules have always allocated one vote per property."

Kate argued, "But Dean isn't even a property owner. How can he serve as Security Council President?"

Warren sighed. "The title is just something we came up with to put a definitive end to the squabbling. From the HOA's standpoint, it's no different than hiring an outside company to patrol the street. Prior to the crisis, no HOA provided for their own security, unless it was an informal neighborhood watch or something of that nature."

Kate looked at Sam who was already staring at her. She knew this was going to be another fight. But it was too important. She couldn't back down for the sake of keeping the peace. "Thank you, Warren."

"I've got to finish my rounds. I'll see you tonight when you come by." Warren Wilcox let himself out.

No sooner had he left than Sam asked, "How do you want to do this?"

"We'll decide, by popular vote, which candidate our household will vote for." Kate held up her hand. "All those for Don Crisp."

Gavin raised his hand. "Aye."

"No, no. Gavin doesn't get a vote," Sam protested.

"Why not?" Kate asked.

"He's not one of the owners. He's a guest."

"We're engaged. He's a little more than a guest."

"Even if you were married," Sam continued,

"you'd only get one vote. You have one share of the cabin, I have one share, and Vicky has one share."

Kate could not contest his reasoning. She looked at Vicky. "Who are you voting for?"

"Oh no, I'm not getting in the middle of this." Vicky waved her hands. "No matter who I vote for, one of you will hate me."

"You have to vote for someone, it's your responsibility." Sam took a step closer to his sister. "And it's not just me, David is rooting for James Dean also."

Vicky backed away. "I don't know, Sam! Quit pressuring me!"

"It's a secret ballot. Give Vicky the paper and let her vote for who she wants, privately at the polling station." Gavin walked out of the room.

Kate handed her the paper. "I guess it's up to you."

Vicky took the paper and folded it. "If you'll excuse me, I have some thinking to do." She tucked the ballot in the back pocket of her jeans.

Kate glared at Sam. She felt agitated by the situation. Not knowing who Vicky was voting for didn't help.

Two hours later, Kate sat on top of an old picnic table inside Pete Davis' garage. Vicky sat on the seat below, watching the procession of residents bringing their ballots, one by one, and dropping them in the small cardboard box at the other end of the picnic table. Sam leaned against an iron support beam near the table. David McDowell paced the floor between Sam and Vicky.

Warren Wilcox and Pete Davis monitored the polling activities from the other side of the table. James Dean and his supporters milled about near the rear of the garage while Don Crisp and Jack Russo kept company with their camp by the entrance.

Kate felt the tension in the building, ridged animosity, thick as three-day-old oatmeal. Vicky still had not cast her vote, had yet to retrieve the ballot from her pocket.

"As soon as you decide, we can go home," her brother reminded.

"I know, Sam. This is important. I have to do what I think is best and both sides have a valid argument. I can't base my decision on one of you not liking me or something silly like that. Look at all these people, this is critical."

David's face was serious, much more serious than a fifteen-year-old's face should ever have to be. "Vicky, you know how I feel, and you know why I feel the way I do. But regardless of what you decide, it won't affect our friendship." He took her hand.

A gentle glow seemed to come across her cheeks. "Thanks, David. I really appreciate that. I wish my brother and aunt could be so considerate."

Kate fought the urge to roll her eyes. "Vicky, I'll always love you, no matter what."

"Me, too," Sam added. "But if you vote the wrong way, none of us may live long enough for that to matter."

Vicky stood up from the table. "I'm going to go talk to Mr. Dean and Mr. Crisp."

"Do you want me to come with you?" Kate offered.

"No. I have to do this alone." She pointed at Sam before he had a chance to speak. "And I certainly don't need you to come!" Vicky offered a warm smile to David. "I'll be back in a while."

Apprehension haunted Kate for the remainder of the evening. She watched the crawling procession of events, unable to affect the final outcome.

Warren Wilcox made an announcement. Looking at his watch, he said, "The polls will be closing in five minutes. Afterward, Pete and I will count the ballots and announce the new Security Council President and Vice President. Once we've recorded the votes, we'll make the ballots available for public inspection."

Vicky returned from speaking with the candidates.

"Did you make up your mind?" Kate asked.

Vicky took the ballot from her back pocket. "I think so."

Kate felt proud of her niece. Right or wrong, she'd given more consideration to her vote than perhaps anyone else in the community. She watched Vicky walk with determination to the cardboard box. She took the marker, made her selection, folded the paper, and stuffed it in the box.

"Thank you, Vicky," Warren said.

Pete Davis said in a thundering voice. "Last call. Anyone who hasn't cast their vote should do so now."

Moments later, Warren said to Kate, "Will your group please go stand by the other wall while we tally up the votes?"

"Oh, sure. Come on, guys." Kate made her way over to the Crisp camp. Sam and David did not follow. Rather they headed toward the rear of the garage, with Gene Tifton, Andy Reese, and the rest of the staunch Dean supporters.

"Hey Kate," Don put his hand on her shoulder. "Thanks for coming out."

"Sure." She watched to see what Vicky would do.

After about a minute of milling about in the middle of the room alone, Vicky looked at her aunt and began strolling toward her direction.

Kate felt her innermost being welling up with pride. Once Vicky arrived, Kate put her arm around her niece.

Jack tussled Vicky's hair. "So much for your secret ballot."

Vicky turned to look at him. "I see the improvements you've made to keep us safe. Besides that, you and Don are kind. James Dean isn't a leader, he's just appealing to the mean streak in some people."

"You have wisdom beyond your years, Vicky." Don patted her on the back.

Whether Don and Jack won the election or not, Kate was happy that Vicky had made the right choice.

Minutes later, Pete Davis said, "Our count is fifteen votes for James Dean and Skeeter; sixteen votes for Don Crisp and Jack Russo. Don Crisp is officially the new security council president of Apple Blossom Acres."

Kate and those around her clapped vigorously.

Warren Wilcox held up his hand. "Folks, if you'll hold your applause, I have a few words to say."

The room returned to silence.

Warren looked to James Dean. "Mr. Dean, we welcome your recommendations and advice, but you'd do well to recognize the authority the community has placed in Mr. Crisp and Mr. Russo."

He turned to Don. "Mr. Crisp, while you are the security council president, your authority over Mr. Dean's activities end at neighborhood boundaries and common areas. Mr. Dean is free to protect his property as he sees fit, offer any type of training he desires, and meet freely with other residents at his discretion, so long as it doesn't interfere with the work of the security council. Furthermore, Mr. Dean and Skeeter, being able-bodied adult men, are required to serve security shifts. They are expected to do so without sowing seeds of dissension amongst the other guards. If it comes to light that this is happening, they may be asked to leave Apple Blossom Acres altogether.

"Are these terms agreeable and hereby accepted by both parties?"

"We accept the terms," Don said.

"I'll abide by them as well." James Dean was obviously sore over the defeat but seemed to force himself to swallow the sour bit of crow which, judging by the peculiar movements of his mouth, appeared to be tucked between his teeth and his jaw.

"Very well," Warren said. "Will the candidates please approach the table and shake hands?"

Don and Jack approached the picnic table more quickly than Dean and Skeeter.

"I look forward to working with you, Mr. Dean. We've already implemented several of your suggestions." Don shook Dean's hand.

Jimmy Dean presented a hallow grin. "Same here, Don. Congratulations."

Pete Davis announced, "We'll have a town-hall-style meeting here tomorrow afternoon at 2:00. We'll open it up as a platform for Don to give an acceptance speech and for a brief Q and A afterward. Everyone, please help us spread the word.

"Congratulations, Don and Jack." Kate put her arm around Vicky and they headed for the door. "Good night." She looked around for her nephew, but he and David were nowhere to be found.

CHAPTER 16

Ye are of your father the devil, and the lusts of your father ye will do. He was a murderer from the beginning, and abode not in the truth, because there is no truth in him. When he speaketh a lie, he speaketh of his own: for he is a liar, and the father of it.

John 8:44

Three days passed since the election. Late Saturday night, Kate stood inside the small metal guard shack at the entrance-gate checkpoint. She took off her gloves and warmed her hands over the small wood-burning camping stove. Gavin propped his AK-47 in the corner and did likewise.

Kate took a steaming cup from Jack Russo

who'd poured the hot beverage out of a graniteware coffee pot. "So this was Mr. Cooper's tool shed?"

Corey Cobb passed an empty mug to Jack who poured a cup for Gavin. Jack placed the pot back on the stove. "Yep. I think it's right cozy."

"What if Mr. Cooper comes back?" Gavin blew on the top of his cup before taking a sip.

"I'll put the shed back just as I found it." Jack glanced up at the stove pipe running out the side of the shed. "Except for a small hole, that is. It was kind of musty in here before anyways. The added ventilation should be considered an improvement."

Corey Cobb laughed. "Of course, I wouldn't want to be Cooper if he asked for his shed back. That would be a good way to get all night shifts on the security detail throughout the winter. Jack is in charge of making the schedule."

Jack gave a sly grin. "I'd never do anything so vindictive, Corey."

"Yeah, right." Cobb guffawed.

Kate sipped her cup. "This isn't bad. What is it?"

"Dandelion tea. My grandmother used to make it." Jack refilled the coffee pot from a plastic water jug sitting near the camp stove. "Just boil the roots. I'm glad you like it. Dandelion is one thing we have plenty of around here."

Corey said, "We had Thanksgiving one year with some friends who had a place in Asheville. The lady made hickory nut ambrosia. She crushed hickory nuts, shells and all, boiled them for an hour, then added milk and maple syrup. It was delectable."

Kate considered the concoction. "Huh, I wonder if you roasted the nuts before you boiled them if it might be a good substitute for coffee. That's a commodity which is quickly running out."

"It would be worth trying. The squirrels have about cleaned up all the hickory nuts for this year. But maybe we can beat them to the draw next year." Jack opened the stove and stuck in a small stick of wood.

Gavin sipped his tea. "If we make it until next year, we'll have a lot fewer squirrels to compete with. I've already noticed a significant decrease in their population."

Gavin's comment hung like a dark cloud over the room and seemed to remind everyone that this was not some recreational adventure, but rather a desperate attempt to stay alive.

Kate finished her tea. "On that uplifting, note, I guess we should be getting on with our patrol."

Jack stood from the small stool he'd been sitting on. "Okay. Stop back in to warm up after you make a round."

"Thanks." Gavin picked up his rifle and followed Kate out the door.

Kate and Gavin proceeded toward the perimeter trail, which looped around the community, then back down to the checkpoint. She shined her light up into the trees. Nearly leafless, they looked skeletal and lacked the vibrancy they'd displayed only weeks ago. She and Gavin stepped into the cold damp woods. A shiver went up her back and she reached for Gavin's hand. "The forest is so creepy at night."

Her radio came to life. "Have a good patrol. Let us know when you come back around." It was the voice of James Dean who was in the overwatch shelter with Pete Davis. "We wouldn't want to have any friendly-fire accidents tonight."

Kate pushed the talk key. "No, we certainly wouldn't want that."

Gavin grunted and said to Kate, "Was that some kind of underhanded threat?"

"It's just Dean being Dean." Kate focused her light on the trail and into the forest ahead. "He'd have a real problem on his hands if he ever pulled anything like that."

Gavin focused his beam to the left, then checked behind them. "I worry that Dean is pumping Sam for information."

"What kind of information?" Beginning the steep incline to the top of the mountain, Kate watched her steps carefully.

"Like how much food we have stored, how much ammo, things like that."

"You think Dean is going to rob us?"

"This little all-for-one experiment that we're doing has already proven to be a façade, and a fragile one at that."

"How so?"

"The community nearly devolved into factions because they couldn't decide if they wanted an experienced police officer or a red-neck vigilante to lead us. How do you think we'll look a year from now when our resources are depleted and the memories of a civilized world have all but faded into oblivion?"

Kate wished he could be more positive. "I get what you're saying. I suppose we need to stay focused on the long term. I'll try to talk to Sam, see where he's at."

"Good." Gavin was winded from marching up the hill. "If he sounds like he's open, perhaps you should reiterate the need for secrecy and remind him that the four of us are the real team. You know, what happens at the cabin, stays at the cabin."

"Sure, I'll get him alone after church tomorrow."

"You're going to church? After working all night?"

"Yeah, it's once a week. I'll sleep afterward. Aren't you coming?"

Gavin sighed. "I don't know. That's four hours from the time we get off shift until the time church starts."

"Okay, do what you want." Kate paused to catch her breath. "What about Sam? What if he's been brainwashed?"

"Then we need to start caching some of our supplies—away from the cabin."

Kate resumed her normal speed up the trail. "That might not be a bad idea anyway, considering we almost lost it all when we were attacked. Would we tell Vicky?"

Gavin shined his flashlight from side to side. "You decide, but I'd recommend against it. The easiest secret for a teenage girl to keep is the one she doesn't know about."

"Where would we put our cache?"

"I don't know. I haven't given it that much thought."

Kate pointed her light toward a downed tree. "What about there?"

Gavin's beam followed hers. "Where?"

"Right there, where the roots pulled up the earth when it fell. For one thing, it's a nice big tree, so it's a natural landmark. For another, that ditch behind the roots is a natural hole. We'd have less digging to do if we wanted to bury some supplies."

"A downed tree is also a good candidate for being cut up into firewood."

Kate left the trail and inspected the tree closer with her light. She kicked the soft side and the wood crumbled beneath her boot. "Not this tree. It's basically fertilizer."

Gavin focused his flashlight toward the community. "Whose property is this?"

Kate pulled out her hand-drawn map. "It looks like the Smith's place. They're gone and probably won't be back."

"I'd feel more comfortable if we could find a similar tree on our plot. If not, maybe Pritchard's."

Kate returned to the trail to continue the patrol. "Sounds like a plan. We'd have to haul the supplies for a shorter distance that way."

A woman's voice echoed through the forest.

"What was that?" Gavin asked.

"It sounds like Mrs. Dean." Kate stood still.

"I think she's calling for help." Gavin pointed his light in the direction of the sound.

"We can cut through the Smith's property to the road. Come on." Kate clicked off her flashlight and stowed it in her pocket. She pulled the rifle off her shoulder and used the light affixed to the barrel to pick her way through the brush.

"I smell smoke." Gavin stayed close behind her.

"It's coming from Mrs. Dean's house! I see the glow of the flames!" Kate rushed toward the old woman's home. The muffled cries became clearer. The widow was indeed calling for help.

Kate and Gavin hurried to the site of the fire. Mrs. Dean's attached garage was engulfed in a blazing inferno. Don Crisp was already there with Annie Cobb, Gene Tifton, Rainey Russo, and Harold Pritchard. Don emptied a fire extinguisher and tossed it aside. "The nearest hand pump is at the Cobb's. Get containers and form a bucket line. We have to put this thing out before it reaches the house!"

More neighbors arrived to help. Soon a bucket brigade worked swiftly to convey water from the Cobb's hand pump to the fire.

James Dean arrived on the scene. He snapped at Kate, "Where's Don? Did you catch anyone?"

Kate took a bucket from Pritchard and passed it to Gavin. "Don is inside, putting out the fire in your grandmother's house. What do you mean, did we catch anyone?"

"The arsonist who started the fire!"

"What makes you think it was arson?"

"We're living in a post-apocalyptic world, Kate. Of course it was arson." James Dean stomped off to find Don.

Minutes later, Gene Tifton called, "Hold the line! The fire is out!"

Kate put her bucket down and walked into the garage. Mrs. Dean stood crying and Kate put her arm around the old woman.

Don and James were in a disagreement. "This

never should have happened, Don. It wouldn't have happened on my watch."

"Oh, I thought you were on watch. Which reminds me, who is covering for you at the observation post?"

"Pete is still there, he's got it covered."

"You're sure this wasn't a diversion to lead people off their posts so we could be attacked by a larger force." Don's eyes narrowed. "I understand this is where you live, but you need to have your position covered. Everyone in this community relies on all the others to fulfill their commitments." Don picked up his radio and pushed the talk button. "Can someone send David McDowell up to the overwatch. The post is a man short right now."

"I can run down there," Kate offered.

"If you don't mind." Don looked perturbed by Dean.

"David is up here, at my house, Don." Vicky's voice came over the radio.

Kate pressed the talk key. "What's he doing up there?" She had spoken with Vicky about having David in the house when she wasn't there.

"He stopped by to see Sam."

This subject was a battle for another time. "Can you send David and Sam down to cover the overwatch position?"

"Sure. Talk to you later."

Pritchard came into the open garage and hugged the old woman. "Rita, I'm awful sorry about all this."

"Thank you, Harold." She opened the door to the house and stepped inside. "I think they stopped it before it got in the house. But it smells like a chimney sweep's brush in here." She led the way in and Pritchard followed.

Don surveyed the damage to the garage. "Kate, James believes foul play may be a factor. Would you and Gavin take a walk around the property and see if anything looks out of place?"

"We'll check it out." Kate turned and followed Gavin. She retrieved her flashlight from her pocket and scanned the yard. They walked across the front yard, then down the side of the house.

She let her beam bounce from side to side, then up the wall of the house. "Gavin, look. Someone has spray painted the back of Mrs. Dean's house."

"What did they spray?" He came over to her position and focused his light on the graffiti.

Kate read the words aloud scrawled on the wall in olive-drab spray paint. "Get out while you still can. LR."

"LR? Who is that?"

"Reese, Russo, Ramsey." Kate ticked off the last names in the neighborhood which began with the letter R. "I can't think of anyone in those families whose first name begins with an L."

"It has to be someone from the Badger Creek Gang. Do you think Scott McDowell would have kept any files on the members at his house?"

"I doubt it. But we can ask Kelly to be sure. Let's start by seeing if the initials mean anything to Mrs. Dean."

Kate knocked on the front door.

Pritchard stepped out. "What in the world are you doin', foolin' around out here?"

"We found some spray paint on the back wall of the house. I need to ask Mrs. Dean about it."

"Don't be pesterin' her. She's been through enough for one night."

Gavin stepped past the old man as politely as possible. "We'll be quick."

Kate smiled at Pritchard, despite his soured expression at being overruled. "Two seconds, I promise."

Mrs. Dean sat on the couch. Skeeter stood silently beside her. Rita Dean ran her finger along the coffee table. "Look at this place. Soot's done got everywhere. This place ain't fittin' to live in."

"We'll help you get it cleaned up, Mrs. Dean." Kate sat next to her and explained the graffiti on the wall. Don and James walked into the room as Kate was relaying the information.

"Oh, goodness! Who'd want to hurt me?" Mrs. Dean put her hand on her chest.

"Don't you fret none, Rita." Pritchard stood up. "We'll put an end to these hijinks."

"Those initials don't mean anything to you?" Kate inquired.

She thought for a while. "There was a boy I went with back in school, Larry Rollins, I broke his heart, but I can't imagine he'd want to do anything to me after all these years. I met some sailor who'd just come home from the war and Larry was just a boy, you see."

"I'm sure it's not Larry Rollins." Don interrupted the recounting of Rita Dean's younger years. "Anyone else you can think of? Anyone more recent?"

"What's the name of that community over on the other side of the mountain?" Skeeter asked.

"Laurel Ridge." Gavin ran his finger down the wall, leaving behind a faint line in yet more soot.

"It's Laurel Ridge, LR." Jimmy Dean snapped his fingers. "It's a message to the entire community."

Kate shook her head. "That makes no sense. Why would Laurel Ridge want us to leave? As it stands, they don't have to worry about getting hit by gangs from the back side. At least not until we're all dead."

"I beg to differ," James said. "They probably want to take our territory."

"Why, pray tell, would they want to do such a thing?" Kate waited to hear the man's convoluted reasoning.

"Resources. Forests, firewood, hunting ground, farmable land. If we were smart we would've been doing the same thing." James sat on the other side of his grandmother and put his arm around her.

"Laurel Ridge is mostly high-end vacation homes. They'd never have the manpower to attempt such a move." Don shook his head dismissively. "Besides that, it's mostly democrats. They don't exactly embrace the gun culture. I can't see them starting a war with a working-class neighborhood. It doesn't make sense."

"You met all the people in Laurel Ridge?" James quizzed.

"No, but I've seen what they drive, and I've seen their bumper stickers."

"I would imagine if they're vacation homes it's

because they lived in a city and wanted a quiet place in the mountains. People with any sense would have left when things first started getting bad. Laurel Ridge might have a higher occupancy rate than you think," James said.

"He's probably right about that, Don." Kate hated to side with Jimmy Dean, but it was a solid argument.

"Even so, that doesn't make them aggressive warlords." Don crossed his arms.

Kate hoped Don wasn't being naive. James Dean's analysis of the event made little sense to her, but it was the only explanation offered so far.

James stood up. "Well, whatever happened, it's obvious that our security isn't as tight as it needs to be." He looked at Kate. "I don't suppose you saw anyone on your patrol."

"No. We were on the other side of the mountain from Laurel Ridge when the fire was started."

"Other side of the mountain." Dean nodded condescendingly.

"What are you implying, James?" Gavin sounded angry.

"Oh, nothing about you. One patrol can't be all over the place at one time. But if it were me, I would have scheduled a minimum of two patrols, especially at night."

Don shot back, "We don't have that many people, James."

"You wouldn't need them if you'd have let us put up the booby traps."

"I offered to let you modify the devices, to work as alarms with inert shells."

"Right, you wanted me to waste ammunition by rendering it harmless. In case you haven't noticed, Don. You can't just go to the store and buy more shotgun shells. A live round is worth its weight in gold. I'll have no part in turning them into worthless firecrackers."

"Those booby traps are reckless. I won't allow them."

"You don't have to answer to me," James smirked. "I'm not the one who voted you into office." He turned to his loyal lackey. "Skeeter, run and get our things together. We can't sleep in this mess."

Don offered, "Mrs. Dean, you're welcome to stay at my house. James and Skeeter should find other accommodations. I don't think they'd be very comfortable in my home."

James took his grandmother's hand. "She'll stay with us."

"Where are you going?" Kate inquired.

"We'll stay at the Smith's until we get this place cleaned up."

"The Smith's? You can't just take any house you want," Don protested.

Jimmy looked puzzled. "Why not? The Smith's aren't here—probably never be back. Your second-in-command re-appropriated the Cooper's tool shed for his own personal comfort. You don't have two sets of standards, do you? One set for your buddies, and another for your political opponents?

"I was hoping it was just a coincidence that all of your supporters were getting water pumps while your opponents have to go begging with hat in hand. If Grandma would've had a pump, maybe we could have put the fire out faster. But even if she is a 90-year-old widow, she doesn't get a pump in her yard because she voted for me. It's starting to sound more like Russia than the good ol' US of A."

Kate seethed at the implications. "Maybe it's because the person putting in the pumps doesn't trust that you won't weaponize access to water–use it against your adversaries. And about the tool shed, it's the new guard shack for the entire security team. It's to protect us from the elements so we don't die from exposure. It's quite different from commandeering an entire house."

James winked at Kate. "I hear you've done your share of scavenging, little missy. Do you want to talk about that?"

Kate froze in silence. She wondered if Sam had found out about the things she and Pritchard had taken from the Peterson's. Had he talked to Dean about it? She most certainly did not want to discuss it.

"I thought not." James helped his grandmother up from the couch. "But like you said, we're protecting ourselves from the elements, so we don't *die*." He nodded to Don. "We'll have a town hall meeting tomorrow after church, to talk about how we should respond."

"You don't get to make those calls." Don seemed to be at the end of his rope with Jimmy Dean.

"Oh, of course not. You're the big cheese. You can do whatever you want. But you can't keep me from having a private meeting with my friends to discuss today's events. I'm sure Pete won't mind if we hang around for a half hour after church tomorrow. I just thought since many of my friends are your constituency, you'd want to be there—to defend your decisions. But please, don't feel obligated. I was just trying to be friendly. Now, if you've done all the damage you can do, I'd appreciate it if you all leave. We have a lot to do."

Red-faced, Don walked out the front door. Kate and Gavin followed him.

"You're not going to stay for the meeting are you?" Kate asked.

"I don't know. I'll figure it out tomorrow." Don sounded livid.

"Sure. I don't mean to bug you about it, but if you go, you legitimize the meeting," she added.

"I understand that, but if I don't go, he'll hammer the residents with his propaganda. And the meeting is legitimized by the voters hanging around, not me."

Kate hated the fact that James had pushed Don into a corner once again. "Let me know if we can do anything."

"Thanks, Kate. But the best thing you and Gavin can do now is to get back to your patrol."

"Sure. We'll talk to you tomorrow." Kate watched the man walk furiously toward his house.

CHAPTER 17

The thing that hath been, it is that which shall be; and that which is done is that which shall be done: and there is no new thing under the sun.

Ecclesiastes 1:9

Kate awoke, startled by her niece shaking her arm.

"Aunt Kate, church starts in fifteen minutes. You told me to wake you up." Vicky held Kate's hand.

Kate looked around the room to get her bearings. "Right, sure." She looked at her niece and patted her hand. "Thank you."

"You look tired."

"I only got about two hours of sleep."

Vicky sat on the edge of the bed. "Why don't you sleep in today? You read your Bible every day. I'm sure God wouldn't mind. In fact, He might want you to. He loves you, I'm sure He'd want you to take care of yourself."

Kate stretched her legs and swung them toward the edge of the bed. "Normally, I'd concede to your very valid argument, but today it's important that I be there. James Dean is going to hold a town hall meeting afterward. He's going to use the fire to poison the minds of the residents against Don."

Vicky's mood deteriorated considerably upon hearing about the upcoming discussion. "I thought all that was over with. Why can't people just move on?"

Kate stood and began getting ready for church. "I suppose it makes things harder for you and David, being on opposite sides of the debate."

"Me and David are fine. He has his view and I have mine. We just avoid the subject altogether. It's my hardheaded brother who won't allow me to have my own opinion."

Kate stepped into her boots and laced them up. "Sam is angry. I think he'll lighten up once he's able to move past his grief."

"I'm still angry, too. I loved Mom and Dad as much as he did. I probably miss them even more." Vicky followed her aunt down the stairs. "But I'm not going to let it cloud my reason."

Kate rapped on Gavin's door. "Time for church."

"Hold on!" he replied.

Seconds later he opened the door. "I need some coffee."

"Yeah, don't we all, but we're already late. Come on, we've got to go." Kate opened the front door and the three of them sprinted down the driveway.

When they arrived at Pete Davis' garage, Gavin opened the door for Kate and Vicky. "Take a look at this."

Kate turned toward the direction Gavin had indicated. James Dean had the rangers dressed in all black. Their pants were bloused and most wore black hats. The rangers had a single red bar sewn on each of their shoulders. Sam sat at the end of the row.

"I guess they couldn't find enough brown shirts and had to go with black." Gavin led the way to the seats where they normally sat.

"What's that supposed to mean?" Vicky asked.

Kate hated the devious implication of the comment, but she couldn't deny the uncanny resemblance. "Hitler's youth and the Nazi party wore brown shirts during World War II."

"Oh." Vicky wrinkled her nose at the comparison.

To everyone's relief and enjoyment, Martha Wilcox had taken the reigns of the music ministry. She led the congregation in song with her beautiful voice. Yet, to Pritchard's chagrin, she occasionally mixed in a modern worship song amongst the classical hymns.

An hour later, Pritchard wrapped up his sermon with prayer, then lifted his head. "I reckon everyone has heard about the fire over at Rita's last evenin'. The house wasn't so much damaged, but all her things smell of smoke. If any of you women folk have any clothes or things that might make her more comfortable, you can drop them by the Smith's place. That's where she's staying with Jimmy and Skeeter.

"Don Crisp has a few remarks about the incident. After that, Jimmy wants to speak his peace. If y'all want to hang about, Pete said it'd be alright. Otherwise, you're dismissed, and I'll see y'all next week."

Pritchard came and sat at an empty stool next to Kate. She looked over at the black-clad militia sitting to her right. James looked incensed at having to speak second after Don as well as being publicly referred to as Jimmy.

Don Crisp came to the podium. "Thank you all for staying around. I do want to mention that last night's fire is still being investigated by the security council and despite the opinions of some parties who may be swayed by their feelings, we have not yet determined who caused the fire. I realize that our present environment is an emotionally charged one, especially if it happens to be you who has lost a loved one or had your property damaged. But, staying calm and cool is always going to be our best course of action. We're all free to have our own thoughts about these matters, but if you allow yourselves to get caught up in the fury, it can lead to poor decisions that will further jeopardize the safety of everyone living in Apple Blossom Acres. I'll turn the platform over to Mr. Dean, but I will ask that you all remember that we are in this thing together, and we're all on the same side."

James walked to the podium. Like his minions, he wore all black. He was flanked on either side by Skeeter and Gene Tifton. "Thank you, Don. And I do hope we will remember that we're all on the same side."

Dean turned his attention toward the congregation. "When I look out at you, I see people who want to survive but are worried that it might not happen. Some of you are afraid, scared, concerned that you've made the wrong decision in who you've picked to keep you safe at night.

"Most of you have known Don for years. And at the same time, you don't know me from Adam's house cat."

Dean paused to allow time for the lighthearted titter to travel around the room. "That's understandable. Don is the known and I'm the unknown. But let me remind you that we live in a different world. Two months ago, the officer-friendly approach to security was a prudent path. That was Don's world, patrolling a civilized society. He's overwhelmed and doesn't know what to do with this present reality. That's not his fault. He's never been trained to operate in this environment. I, on the other hand, have been educated to not only survive in this type of setting, but I've learned to thrive. And not only have I acquired the necessary skills, but I was also an instructor. I taught men and women in the United States Army how to push through the worst the enemy could throw at them and come out the other side victorious.

"I won't sugar coat this. Regardless of what I do,

of what Don does, or what any of you do, some of you will die in the coming year. But, I can offer you a path that greatly mitigates the death toll. Our community is surrounded by wolves. We've had violent gangs attack two homes in our community; the perpetrators of those crimes have never been hunted down. Now, the word is out. Apple Blossom Acres is a soft target. We have resources and are unable or unwilling to do what's necessary to defend ourselves. So what did we see last night? It's open season on us.

"The uppity people on the other side of the mountain are trying to run us out of our homes. These are people who likely have very little military training, but they see us as an easy meal. We have two options. We can sit back and wait for them to feed on us in the middle of the night, picking off our most vulnerable first. Or, we can proactively take the fight to them, hunt down the wolf!

"By adopting this course of action, we do four things." He held up his index finger. "Number one, we eliminate the threat." He ticked off another bullet point with the next finger. "Number two, we gain the scarce and badly-needed resources of our adversaries, which will aid us in long-term survival."

Don stood up. "Okay, James, that's enough. We're not having another election, and we're certainly not forming an attack force to take over Laurel Ridge."

"I'll say when I'm done speaking, Don. You had your chance, now it's my turn."

"Nope, this is over. Jack, Corey, Gavin, can you

men help me escort Mr. Dean out of the building?"

The rest of the rangers stood up and surrounded the podium, blocking Don and the security council guards.

"I'll continue what I was saying before I was so rudely interrupted." His ring finger joined the other two. "Number three, we send a message to everyone else who is sizing us up—if you mess with the bull, you get the horns!"

His pinky finger popped up. "And lastly, number four. We gain combat experience for our rangers. Once tested in battle, they'll be ready to finally bring to justice the violent gang who so viciously murdered the fathers of two of these young men."

Kate could see that David and Sam were sold on this vendetta. Dean had sunk his hooks deep within their souls. The room erupted in debate, the volume grew until it sounded as if a bar-room brawl was about to break out.

Pritchard grabbed a heavy wrench from the pegboard tool organizer on Pete's garage wall. He walked to the podium and banged the wrench against the top of the tree trunk. "Y'all pipe down this instant. Now, we ain't gonna have all this fussin'. Pete's been good enough to let us use this place, and I won't have him disrespected like this. You get on home else I'll come around and start peckin' youns in the head with this here wrench." He hoisted the heavy tool over his head, causing a nearby ranger to shield himself with his arms over his head.

Dean commanded, "Rangers, come on. Let's lead by example." He called out orders and the rangers marched in single file to exit the building.

CHAPTER 18

Let the husband render to his wife the affection due her, and likewise also the wife to her husband. The wife does not have authority over her own body, but the husband does. And likewise the husband does not have authority over his own body, but the wife does. Do not deprive one another except with consent for a time, that you may give yourselves to fasting and prayer; and come together again so that Satan does not tempt you because of your lack of self-control.

1 Corinthians 7:3-5

Kate tried desperately to understand what could have gone so wrong. How had this quaint little community been hijacked by Dean's fearmongering?

"So when you two gettin' hitched?" Pritchard trailed behind Kate in line to exit the building.

Kate watched the crowd dwindling after the rangers had marched out. "What?"

Pritchard prodded her diamond ring with the grimy wrench in his hand. "You and the boy, when y'all goin' to tie the knot?"

Kate turned to Gavin. "We haven't really discussed it. So much has been going on, I can't even start to think about a wedding right now."

"Best hop to it, 'for that old serpent gets youns entangled in sin."

Kate glanced at the garage floor. "You're probably right."

"Ain't no probably to it. I know what I'm talkin' about. You two need to get on with it, else the boy needs to move out."

Gavin's brows sank low, either at being threatened with having to move out, being referred to as if he weren't present, or a combination of the two insults. "I'm leaving it up to Kate. I'm cool with whatever, I know how important wedding details can be to a girl."

Pritchard pointed the greasy wrench at Gavin. "That's your problem. You're the one s'posed to be a wearin' the britches here. You tell her when the hitchin's gonna be. If she fancies some particular accouterments of attire or ceremony, you ought to do all you can to accommodate her requests. The girl is a reasonable one, she'll understand everything ain't gonna be perfect under our present circumstances. But both of youns, quit draggin' your feet and hop to it!"

Kate looked at Gavin with suspense, wondering if he'd take Pritchard's advice.

Gavin took a deep breath. "Would Saturday be okay with you?"

She nodded before clarifying. "This Saturday?"

"Is that enough time?"

She bit her lip and nodded again eagerly. "Sure."

Gavin looked deep into her eyes. "Is… that soon enough? Or do you want to get married sooner?"

"Saturday is fine." She felt as if she were coming unglued with joy inside, but fought hard to maintain her composure.

Gavin seemed to be suppressing a smile, which finally erupted and overtook his face. "Good."

"That's settled then. I'll talk to Pete about using the garage and spread the word amongst the womenfolk." Pritchard turned around.

"Wait, Mr. Pritchard." Kate grabbed his arm.

"Jitters already?"

"No, nothing like that. I think a small ceremony might be best. We can announce it to the congregation next Sunday."

"Why in the world would you want to do that? You ain't ashamed of the boy, are you? I know he ain't much to look at, but…"

She interrupted him. "No, I'm not ashamed of Gavin. He's a very attractive man—very attractive. But with all the turmoil, I don't want to be a distraction."

"Young woman, these folks need a distraction. Maybe a wedding would be just the thing to bring them together."

Kate shook her head. "It's like these people are choosing between blue and gray uniforms. I believe their differences have dug a chasm far too wide to be spanned by a wedding. Besides, a big public ceremony would stress me out. I'd only be trying to make everything right for the guests. It would *not* be enjoyable for me."

Gavin seemed to like her answer. "She's a minimalist when it comes to accouterments of ceremony."

Pritchard watched Gavin out of the corner of his eye for a moment, as if contemplating whether he should take offense at the comment.

"But not of attire," Kate added. "I think it would be nice if we get dressed up."

"I can handle that." Gavin gave the affirmative nod of a man who knew he'd gotten off easy.

"Very well," Pritchard said. "It's settled."

"Can I come? I won't tell anyone." Vicky had obviously been listening to the entire conversation.

Kate instantly realized how important it was to include her niece. She took Vicky's hand and pulled it to her heart. "Why of course! You'll be my maid of honor."

Later that evening, Vicky scurried around the kitchen making snacks out of what they had on hand. "I'm trying out some ideas I've had. I want to make appetizers so we can have a little reception after your ceremony."

Kate took a seat on a stool at the counter. "That's very sweet of you. Thank you, Vicky."

"Should we invite Pritchard? After all, he is the officiant, it wouldn't be proper to not invite him to the reception."

Kate smiled warmly. She appreciated that Vicky was putting forth the effort to make the event memorable. "That will be fine."

"And what about ..." Vicky clammed up mid-sentence.

Sam walked in the door, still wearing his black uniform. "What? Don't let me interrupt your conversation."

"We were just having girl talk," Kate said.

"I'll let you get right back to it then. I've only stopped by to get my things."

"Why? Where are you going?" Kate stood up from the stool.

"I'll be staying at the barracks for now."

"The barracks? Where is that?"

"The old Smith residence."

"Dean is transforming the Smith's house into militia housing?"

"It's much more secure to have everyone sleeping in close proximity. It's not safe for you to all be spread out like you are. You're too susceptible to attack, but I'm not here to argue. Don has you all brainwashed into thinking that everything is hunky-dory. I hope you'll come around, but I can't force you."

"Wait, you think we're the ones who are brainwashed?" Kate followed Sam to his room.

Sam stuffed his clothes into his bag. "I'm going

to need my share of the supplies also."

Kate leaned against the door frame. "Sam, we're not divvying up the food. You're welcome to stay here, but Gavin and I bought those supplies."

"Dad gave you money for our share of the supplies. Besides, I went with you on the run to buy the ammo."

"Sam, this is your home. You're welcome to come eat here, sleep here, or whatever you want to do, but I can't allow you to cart a bunch of food out the door. You'd be advertising what we have."

"Don't make this hard, Aunt Kate. You saw what happened today. If you oppose me on this, it won't end well for you."

She stood up straight. "Excuse me! Are you threatening me?"

"Just telling you like it is." Sam zipped up his bag. "I'll be back tomorrow or the next day for the supplies." He pushed past her and left without saying another word.

Kate locked the front door after he left. She felt heartbroken. She turned around to see Vicky crying. She walked over to her niece and pulled her close for a long hug.

Vicky wiped her eyes with her shirt sleeve. "I feel like I've lost my entire family. Mom, Dad, and now Sam."

"I know sweetheart. But you'll always have me."

CHAPTER 19

Two are better than one; because they have a good reward for their labour. For if they fall, the one will lift up his fellow: but woe to him that is alone when he falleth; for he hath not another to help him up. Again, if two lie together, then they have heat: but how can one be warm alone? And if one prevail against him, two shall withstand him; and a threefold cord is not quickly broken.

Ecclesiastes 4:9-12

Monday morning, Kate sat on the front porch swing. The air was cool but the sun shining in the clear blue sky made her feel warm. She sipped a cup of weak coffee. She pushed out the bad thoughts of losing Sam and the animosity in the community by daydreaming about her quiet little wedding at the end of the week.

Kate's pleasant imaginations were interrupted by the sound of boots on gravel. She looked down the drive to see Don and Jack walking toward her.

Gavin walked out on the porch. "Hey, guys. How are you?"

"To tell you the truth, I've been better." Don walked up the stairs slowly. He seemed to be tired. "This thing with the rangers has me all worked up."

"Can we do anything to help?" Kate inquired.

Jack's face was sullen. "I'm glad you asked. The rangers have officially pulled out of community watch. They're guarding the Smith residence and Mrs. Dean's house. We'll have to rework the security schedule."

Don added, "I fear our biggest security problem is growing right here in the middle of the neighborhood. Anyway, Jack and I are going to drive over to Laurel Ridge, see if there's anyone we can talk to."

"About the fire?" Kate asked.

"I'll ask them about the fire, but not in an accusatory fashion. I don't think they had anything to do with it. After 30 years with the PD, you get a feel for these kinds of things. But, as embarrassing as it is, I feel like I need to warn them about Dean and the rangers. If they're not already organized, it's time they start putting a plan together."

Kate pushed her hands in her pocket. "Do you want us to come along?"

Don thought about the proposition before

answering. "Maybe that wouldn't be such a bad idea. I don't think we'll have any trouble, but it may help me to not look like a paranoid kook if I have some people with me who can substantiate my claims."

"I'll get my rifle." Gavin turned to go inside.

"We'll keep the long guns out of sight in the truck," Don said. "I don't want to make anybody nervous. We'll carry concealed pistols. If we get into an altercation, we can shoot our way to the rifles."

Kate quickly realized that a neighborly visit could go catastrophically wrong in a hurry. "Got it." She pulled her shirt over her pistol. Technically, it was covered, but the bulge made by the large revolver required little imagination to figure out what she was hiding. Kate picked up her AK from beside the door and followed Don and Jack down the stairs.

Gavin followed close behind. The team soon reached Don's truck. Don drove, Jack rode shotgun, with Kate and Gavin in the back seats. Don rolled down the window when they came to the checkpoint. "We'll be right back."

"Okay, we'll be here." Corey Cobb waved them through.

Kate had not been outside of the community since the grid went dark nearly a month earlier. "It looks bleak, especially without any leaves on the trees."

No other vehicles were on the road. The only gas anyone had in their tanks was what was left when the power went out. The drive to Laurel Ridge was longer than Kate expected. While it was on the other side of the mountain from Apple Blossom Acres, the route took them all the way out to US-19 and back around.

The shops and businesses that had once lined the highway were all closed, most were looted.

Don turned off of US-19 and followed the side street to the entrance of the Laurel Ridge community. Two men stood at the gate. Each held shotguns and both looked to be in their early sixties.

"These people are in bad shape," Jack commented. "This guy has an over-under model. It only holds two rounds. If that's what they're guarding the main gate with, they obviously don't have many options."

"Why would somebody even have a gun like that?" Kate asked.

"Shooting skeet, quail hunting maybe." Don rolled down his window as they approached. "It's a fancy gun, probably wasn't cheap."

The guard with the pump-action shotgun stepped up to the cab. "Sorry, this road is closed."

"Yes sir, I can see that. My name is Don Crisp. I'm in charge of security at Apple Blossom Acres, the community right behind you on the mountain."

"How can we help you?" asked the man with the over-under shotgun.

"I'd like to speak to whoever is in charge."

"Sorry, we're not in any position to help you," replied the second guard.

"I'm not asking for help. I just have an issue of mutual concern that I'd like to discuss."

The two guards spoke amongst themselves for a

moment. One came back to the truck and the other began walking up the hill. The guard said to Don, "You'll have to wait. He's going to see if the HOA president is available."

"No problem. We've got time." Don rolled the window back up.

"These people don't even have radios!" Kate exclaimed. "How would they call for help if they're attacked?"

"I guess gunfire would be the official sign that says *we need back up*," Don replied.

"Dean will eat them alive if he comes over here." Gavin looked out his window.

Jack turned to the back. "Not if the Badger Creek Gang gets to them first."

"It's amazing that they've survived this long." Kate looked at the single guard at the gate. She scanned the forest for signs of an overwatch team but saw nothing.

Minutes later, the guard with the over-under shotgun came back down the hill with another man. He was tall, late-fifties, and wore a holster with a large semi-automatic pistol. He approached the truck. "What can I do for you folks?"

Don rolled the window down again. "Is there somewhere we can talk?"

"We can talk right here."

"Okay. Do you mind if we get out of the truck?"

"I think I'd prefer if you stay inside."

"Alright then. My name is Don Crisp…"

"Yes, I've heard. You're supposedly the head of security at Apple Blossom Acres."

"That's right. May I ask your name?"

"State your business, Mr. Crisp."

"Very well. We had an incident Saturday night. A widow's home was torched."

The tall man kept one hand on the butt of his pistol. "That's unfortunate, but I don't know what that has to do with us."

"Let me finish. The perpetrator spray painted a message on the back wall which said get out while you still can, LR. Some of the people in Apple Blossom Acres speculated that LR could stand for Laurel Ridge. I just wanted to stop by and ask if that could have possibly been anyone from your community."

"Absolutely not. The accusation is unfounded and preposterous. Good day, Mr. Crisp."

"Hold on, I'm not the one who thinks Laurel Ridge is responsible."

"I don't care what anyone thinks. Turn your vehicle around and leave."

"I think you should care. The widow's grandson has roughly ten militia members convinced that you're a threat and that your community should be eliminated."

The tall man turned around, his face went white. "Us? We haven't done anything. Tell him to leave us alone."

"I've tried to reason with the man. We've had a town hall meeting about it and everything. The issue has caused a split in our community. But he seems dead set on coming after Laurel Ridge. His militia is well-armed and well-trained."

The two guards looked at the tall man. One asked, "Herman, what are we going to do?"

The tall man, Herman, evidently, thought for a moment. "Why are you telling me this?"

"Trying to be neighborly, provide you with a warning."

Herman was shaken. "How do we even begin to prepare for an attack by some psychopathic madman?"

"I'd be happy to provide you with a few pointers, if you'll let us come in."

Herman seemed hesitant. "How do I know this isn't some trick?"

Don pulled out his driver's license. "Here's proof I live behind you."

Herman examined it. "What about theirs?"

Jack offered his ID as well.

Kate leaned forward to address the man. "I'm from Atlanta and Gavin is from Charlotte. We came up to my dad's old place after the attacks."

"That's a common story in our community as well." Herman returned the wallets to Jack and Don. "Pardon my skepticism, but it seems you took considerable risk just getting out on the road. Are you sure charity is the only motivation for your visit?"

"Times aren't getting any easier, may I call you Herman?" Don asked.

"Yes, please. My name is Herman Sweeny. I'm the HOA president for Laurel Ridge."

Don introduced Kate, Jack, and Gavin, then said, "I did feel it was my duty to give you a heads up, however, it's in our interest to not have a security threat in our backyards."

"Pull forward and follow me up to my house."

Don watched the man speak with the guards privately, then followed him up the steep winding road. Herman's home was a huge house. The foundation of the arts-and-crafts cabin was stacked stone. Chinked logs made up the construction of the main level while shaker siding covered the second floor.

Don pulled into the cobblestone drive and cut the engine. Kate and the others exited the vehicle, then followed Herman to the portico which was covered by a grand timber-framed roof.

"This is a beautiful home," Kate walked into the vast open foyer and gazed at the beautiful architecture.

"Thank you. Retrospectively, I wish I'd allocated my money differently, but who could have imagined such a thing would happen. Please, have a seat." Herman waved his hand at the oversized leather couch and loveseat. "You said you could offer some advice."

Don looked down at the wide dark wooden boards of the floor. "I don't have any justification for detaining the widow's grandson, other than him mentioning a possible vendetta against Laurel Ridge. If I were to try such a move, it could further divide our community, push others who are currently not supporters into his arms, so to speak."

"I understand your position." Herman made the large leather chair look small when he sat in it.

"However, if he were to act on his threats, he would be jeopardizing the safety of our community by creating bad blood between us. I believe I would have the support of enough of the community to take action against him at that point."

The lines in Herman's face deepened. "But it would be too late for us."

"Unless we could warn you that the attack was coming," Kate said. "Could we spare one radio?"

"The signal would never go over the mountain." Jack shook his head. "And we couldn't send a runner because James would be going through the woods. He'd probably shoot anyone who he saw as a threat and try to explain it away later."

Don looked into Herman's eyes. "You should pick one property to defend. Without communications, you can't hold this neighborhood. They'll pick you off one at a time. Your people need to gather all your supplies and dedicate one home as a fortress."

Herman looked up the stairs where his wife was eavesdropping on the conversation. He nodded. "My wife actually suggested that. But we've been hoping this would blow over, and it wouldn't come to such drastic measures."

Don continued, "We'll come to back you up if James attacks, but you'll have to keep them at bay until we arrive."

Kate's heart froze. She'd never considered that she might be asked to take action against Sam. She had to find another way.

Gavin said, "Don, can our team have a moment to talk privately?"

"Herman? Would you mind?" Don asked.

"Go right ahead. I'll leave you the room." Herman stood and walked up the stairs toward his wife.

Gavin leaned forward and spoke softly. "We picked up a few extra guns from the shootout at the McDowell's place. Maybe we could arm them with something better than an over-under shotgun."

"We didn't pick up much ammo from that fight," Kate countered. She was usually the first person to be generous, but she knew these guns could end up killing Sam, the nephew she loved so dearly and had promised her dying brother that she'd look after.

Don looked to Jack. "What do you think?"

"Kate's right. We don't have an endless supply of ammo. We could give them some weapons, but they'd have to pull the triggers sparingly."

"One 30-round magazine in an AK-47 could mean the difference in life and death to a man who has nothing but a pistol or an over-under shotgun." Gavin looked at Kate who turned away.

"I guess we could give them two AKs and 100 rounds. We probably have an extra pump-action shotgun. They should have ammo for that," Jack said. "What do you say, Kate?"

"Sure." She didn't want to give them anything but knew it was the right thing to do.

Herman came back down and Don told him their plan.

"That's very generous. What's the catch?"

Don said, "We want you to form an alliance with us. We'll figure out a way to communicate. If we get hit from our side, you'll back us up. If you get hit, we'll back you up. And both of us will make sure no harm comes through the back door, to either of us."

"I'll talk it over with the board, but I think that sounds agreeable. I take it you are worried about other threats than just this James character?"

Kate nodded. "James Dean wasn't the first problem we've encountered, and he won't be the last."

Don stood and looked out at the long-range view of the mountains. "Ernest Martin has the property on top of the mountain on our side. We'll meet you on the ridgeline this evening at 4:00 PM. We'll bring you the guns and walk you through basic operations."

Herman pulled a binder off the bookshelf containing the Laurel Ridge HOA information. He opened it and took out a map. Herman spread the map out on the coffee table. "That should back up to Perry Hine's place. Good. I'll meet you there."

Kate and the others said farewell to the man and headed back to the truck.

On the way home, Don said, "Kate, I realize you have a substantial emotional attachment to one of the rangers, but I'm going to need you to keep this under your hat. Think you can do that for me?"

She looked at Gavin and bit her lip.

Don continued, "I hope it doesn't come to a firefight, but Sam has made his choice. I need to know I can count on you."

"Okay," she mumbled.

"Okay, what? I need to hear you say it."

"Okay, I won't talk to Sam about it."

"Or anyone else. This could spread like wildfire. If Vicky or Amanda McDowell were to catch wind of it, it would go straight to David. Then he'd tell

Dean. This is top secret. We all need to be on the same page for this one."

"Yes, sir. I understand." Kate slumped back in her seat, hating the situation.

CHAPTER 20

But if ye will not do so, behold, ye have sinned against the Lord: and be sure your sin will find you out.

Numbers 32:23

Monday evening, Kate prepared for her shift at the checkpoint. A knock came to the door. Kate looked out the window to see Sam and David standing on the porch. Both were wearing camouflage clothing and tactical vests. She opened the door. "Where are your jack-boot uniforms?"

"Those are our dress uniforms." Sam came inside. "We're training. We don't train in our dress uniforms. David and I are here to get my share of the supplies."

"Okay, but I only have thirty minutes before I

have to go."

"That should be enough time." Sam led the way down the stairs to the garage.

Kate kept a close eye on what he was taking. She'd allow him only so much. "What are you training for?"

"I can't disclose the nature of our missions. I'm sure you understand." Sam opened the door and began loading buckets into James Dean's Wrangler.

Kate watched the two boys taking the buckets closest to the entrance. She felt confident that Sam couldn't fit too many supplies in the Jeep, but hoped he wouldn't come back for more. She noticed the magazine in Sam's vest had been painted OD green. "You painted your magazines?"

"Yeah, those shiny black magazines reflect light; sunlight, even a flashlight beam at night. The paint dulls them out, makes them less reflective."

"Can I see one?"

Sam paused as if he were trying to figure out what she was up to. "I suppose it won't hurt anything. But I'll need it back when I leave." Sam handed her a magazine and continued hauling buckets.

Kate examined the hue. "Sam, this is the same paint that was used on Mrs. Dean's house."

David stopped in his tracks. He remained frozen for a moment. He seemed to quickly calculate the implication of the remark and turned to Sam for an explanation.

Sam looked at him and shook his head dismissively. "They sell that stuff at Wal-Mart. It doesn't mean Mr. Dean set the fire himself."

"No, but it's an awful curious coincidence. You're walking away from your family to go fight with this man. I think you owe it to yourself to consider the possibility." Kate held to the magazine firmly.

David stood staring at Kate.

She said, "You, too, David. Vicky and I have each other, but your mom is all alone in this hostile new world. Would your father approve of you running off on her to follow Dean?"

Sam angrily snatched the magazine away from her. "That's enough, Aunt Kate."

However, her comments were already resonating with David. He looked contemplatively at one of the spray-painted magazines in his own vest. "Are you sure about this, Sam?"

"David, she's trying to get in your head." He stuffed the mag back in his front pouch.

"Why would these people in Laurel Ridge, who were mostly like doctors and lawyers, have OD green spray paint laying around?" David stood in his position.

Sam snapped at both of them in defense of James Dean. "Mr. Dean was on shift when the fire occurred."

"Where was Skeeter?" Kate asked.

"I don't know. That doesn't make him an arsonist. Besides, why would he set his own grandmother's house on fire?"

Kate corrected, "He set her garage on fire. For one thing, it almost absolved him of suspicion. For another, he incited outrage in the community because one of our most vulnerable members was attacked. And lastly, it gave him an excuse to take over the Smith's residence, which is now conveniently being used as ranger barracks."

Sam shook his head but didn't dispute any of the line items Kate had ticked off. "You're judging him guilty over some circumstantial evidence."

Kate made a conscious effort to stay cool. "And you've exonerated him despite some *very compelling* circumstantial evidence. Sam, you're an intelligent young man. The only reason you would refuse to even consider that James had a hand in the fire is that you are consumed with rage. This crisis has taken your mother and your father, and you want somebody to pay. You don't care who it is. Anybody that James tells you to kill will be a suitable scapegoat. I know you Sam; you won't be able to live with yourself if you make a mistake like that."

Sam and David looked at each other for some time. Finally, Sam asked his brother-in-arms, "What do you want to do?"

"Maybe we shouldn't take *all* of your supplies to the barracks. We could look around, see if anything else pops up that indicates Skeeter started the fire."

"I already took Dean's Jeep to get my stuff." Sam looked to Kate as if asking for a way out.

"Did you tell him how much you were bringing?"

"No, I just said some buckets of rice and other foods."

"So take four buckets and tell him that's what you feel was your fair share. You can take some of the ones that got shot up in the raid." Kate picked up a bucket which had duct tape covering the bullet holes.

Sam seemed to mull over the idea. "Okay. But if we don't find anything else, you won't hold out on me when I come back for the rest?"

"Did I hold out on you this time? It's your share, Sam. I hate to see you go, Vicky hates to see you go, but you've obviously decided to make your own rules. I don't want you to make a mistake that you'll regret because I love you, but I respect your decisions."

"Has Vicky said anything about me?" David asked.

"She misses you. I'm sure your mom does even more."

David looked at his boots and bit his lip. "Tell Mr. Dean that I needed to see my mom. I can't make training tonight."

"What if he gets mad?" Sam asked.

"Tell him to come get me if he thinks he can." David walked out the garage door and retrieved his AR-15 from the back of the Jeep. He walked down the driveway, gravel crunching beneath his boots.

"Now look what you did." Sam watched his friend walk down the hill.

"What I did?" Kate's feathers were instantly ruffled.

Sam cracked a mischievous grin. "Relax, Aunt Kate, I'm just kidding."

She resumed her composure. "Are you going back?"

"I have to drop off the Jeep. Maybe I'll leave it in the drive and come right back."

"Dean will know something is afoot if you and David don't return. I need to call Don right away."

"Don't say anything on the security frequency. Mr. Dean is monitoring the channel."

Kate's thumb was on the talk button of her radio. She let it fall to the side of the device. "I'll go talk to him in person. Can you stall a while with the Jeep?"

Sam lifted his shoulders. "I could say we picked up a nail, and we're changing the tire."

"Unlikely, but possible. Let's take the supplies back into the garage anyway."

"So I'm not leaving Dean with four buckets?"

"That was a ruse to buy us time. Now that David has gone AWOL, the jig is up." Kate walked to the Jeep and grabbed two buckets.

Sam followed her and did likewise. "Maybe you shouldn't be quite so convincing next time."

The two of them quickly put the supplies back in the garage and closed the door. Kate sprinted up the stairs. "Gavin is in his room. Tell him what's up, and the two of you wait here for me to come back with Don."

"Roger, that." Sam followed her upstairs.

"Oh, and I need one of your magazines to show to Don." She took the mag Sam handed her and hurried out the door.

CHAPTER 21

Be sober, be vigilant; because your adversary the devil, as a roaring lion, walketh about, seeking whom he may devour.

1 Peter 5:8

Standing outside of Pete Davis' garage, Kate plugged her ears with her fingers while she waited for Harold Pritchard to quit banging the length of rebar against the metal pot. After breaking his wooden spoon on the activity that he pursued with such rigor, the old man had found the iron rod to be a far more suitable material, and it produced a much more desirable ring. When he finally ceased, Kate shivered and removed her fingers.

Pritchard looked at Kate, Sam, Jack, Don, and Pete Davis, all of whom held expressions of extreme annoyance. "What? You want me to get folks over to the garage, don't you?" He afforded no time for a response. Rather he carried his pot and his piece of rebar into the large meeting space. "Well, that's how it's done. They'll be here directly."

Gavin hurried up the road with Corey and Annie Cobb following close behind him.

Pete looked at Don. "Who's watching the gate?"

"No one right now. We need all hands on deck. As of this moment, James Dean is our biggest threat. I'll do everything I can to handle this without it ending in a standoff, but we should plan for the worse. Pete, if things go south, I'll need you to help escort the women and non-combatants out of the building."

"I can handle that."

Warren and Martha Wilcox arrived next. "What's happening?" Warren asked.

Don quickly explained the evidence against Dean.

More residents hurried to Pete Davis' garage, all wondering what matter could be so pressing that it would validate the calling of such an impromptu meeting. Kate spoke to those she knew, encouraging them to be patient.

"Sam, you hang back so Dean doesn't pick up the scent of trouble. Take your rifle up into the woods and watch from there. You never know, the situation could require a sniper." Kate patted him on the back and sent him on his way.

Next, James Dean led a phalanx of ten men across the road. The rangers wore camouflage fatigues, tactical vests, and were heavily armed with assault rifles. Skeeter, Andy Reese, and Gene Tifton were among them.

Kate, Gavin, Pritchard, and the Cobbs stood along the back wall, rifles held at low ready. Jack stood guard next to the podium with his AR-15. The tension in the room had never been higher.

James Dean surveyed the room. He seemed to know the subject of the meeting revolved around him.

Don walked to the podium. "Thank you to everyone for coming on such short notice."

Dean immediately interrupted. "I hope this is good, Don. You've disrupted the entire community's day."

"It will be worthwhile, I guarantee you." He glared at Dean. "The security council has discovered evidence concerning our arson investigation of the fire at Mrs. Rita Dean's home."

Mrs. Dean called out, "It was them rascals over in Laurel Ridge, weren't it? Are you fixin' to bring them in?"

"No, Mrs. Dean, the evidence doesn't support that theory at all." Don's eyes looked sorry about the information he had to give her. "And the evidence has just been paraded right in front of our noses." He held up the magazine from Sam's vest. "If you'll take a close look at the tactical vests being worn by the rangers, you'll notice many of the magazines have the same paint as the one I'm holding."

"What's your point, Don?" Gene Tifton glanced down at his vest, then back up.

"This paint is an identical match to what was used to inscribe the threat on the back of Mrs. Dean's house."

Rita Dean walked to the podium. "Let me see that!" She snatched the evidence from Don.

The room erupted in murmuring.

"Oh, come on, Don! You'll have to do better than that," James Dean sneered.

"I think the evidence is good enough. The security council is going to take James Dean and Skeeter into custody. We will form a tribunal and hold court to determine if they're guilty. If they're found guilty, the tribunal will determine the sentence. Gavin, Kate, will your team please come forward to arrest Mr. Dean and Skeeter?"

"That's not happening," James Dean said. "Rangers!" The militia drew their weapons as did Kate and the other people from the security council.

Rita Dean watched in horror. She looked one last time at the magazine in her hand, then she turned to her grandson. "Jimmy, I'm ashamed of you. You pert near burnt my house down. I reckon you've made up some addled reason in your head that makes it alright accordin' to your twisted mind, but it ain't okay. I'm an old woman, and you were supposed to protect me."

Her words swept like a wave across the crowd. Rita Dean's willingness to accept the evidence was as good as a conviction in the mind of the populace.

"Grandma! It's lies, don't believe them!"

"I don't want to hear no more of it, Jimmy! That

Skeeter boy had been hangin' about the house all day. He disappeared about a half an hour before the fire. Then he popped right back up about the time Don and them came to put it out. Never did sit right with me."

"Grandma, I can explain."

The old woman walked away with her head hung low.

Dean's army remained true to their leader. James Dean looked at Don. "Looks like we've got a Mexican standoff. Only two ways this can end."

Don signaled for Pete Davis to start ushering out the non-combatants. "I'm listening."

"You can let me and my men walk out of here, or we can carpet Pete's floor in carnage. A bloodbath would mean that the rangers and the security council will be completely wiped out. That would make Apple Blossom Acres easy pickin's for the Badger Creek Gang."

Don seemed to recognize the truth in Dean's statement. "Where will you go if we let you leave?"

"We'll vacate the neighborhood. It's obvious our services aren't appreciated around here and I'm not the kind to stick around where I'm not wanted."

"Let me talk it over with Jack." Don's voice could not be heard for several minutes.

Kate listened to the exchange but could not watch. Her eye looked down the sight of her AK-47. On the other side stood Andy Reese with an AR-15 pointed at her. Her palms grew sweaty and her mouth grew dry.

Finally, Don answered. "You'll leave right away."

"I need to gather my things. We'll be out by morning."

"You'll be out in two hours."

"We'll be gone in three."

Don called out orders, "Security council guards, back away from the doors. Allow the rangers to exit peaceably. Keep your sights trained on them."

Kate, Gavin, Pritchard, and the Cobbs stepped to the side of the rear doors.

James Dean and Skeeter left. Then, one by one, the remaining rangers left the building.

Kate sighed after they were gone. "Now what?"

Don and Jack came to stand by the others. Don said, "Now, we get ready for war."

"For war?" Corey Cobb asked.

Don nodded. "Dean already had his sights on Laurel Ridge. Today's events will only cause him to speed up his timeline. The rangers will try to take Laurel Ridge when they leave here."

"We have to warn them!" Kate exclaimed.

"I'm meeting Herman at the top of the hill in a few minutes," Don replied.

No longer worried that the weapons would be used to kill Sam, Kate felt much more generous. "Perhaps we should offer them more guns. Maybe we can even spare a few shooters."

"Are you volunteering?" Don asked.

Kate looked at Gavin who offered a shallow nod. "Yes, I guess I am."

"We'll go too." Annie put one hand around her father and held the other in the air.

Don put his hand on her shoulder. "I need some people at the gate. If Dean sees the front gate abandoned, he'll know something is up. Jack, Mr. Pritchard, you'll go with Kate and Gavin. The Cobbs and I will stand guard at the gate until we see the rangers move out. Then, we'll follow them into the woods. I'm almost certain Dean will take them through the woods."

"How will we know when they're moving?" Kate asked.

Don's brow furrowed. "He has three hours. I expect that he'll use as much of that as possible, but we can't be sure without visual confirmation."

"I can put Rainey in the woods with binoculars and a radio." Jack never volunteered his daughter for anything, but this fight was for all the marbles. He held up his radio.

Kate grabbed it before he pressed the talk key. "No! Remember what Sam said. Dean is monitoring all our channels."

"Then let's use it to put out some false information," Jack smirked and pressed the talk key. "Rainey, I'm going to need your help. Don wants everyone who can pull a trigger to be near the gate this evening. Go ahead and get ready. I'll be down to get you in a few minutes."

Rainey's voice came back over the radio. "Okay, Dad."

"Now they are sure to go over the mountain to get to Laurel Ridge," said Gavin.

Kate squeezed the grip of her AK-47. "And we'll be waiting for them when they get there."

CHAPTER 22

O my God, I trust in thee: let me not be ashamed, let not mine enemies triumph over me.

Psalm 25:2

"Put in a fresh magazine, then push the slide forward." Kate demonstrated the basic operation of the AK-47 for Herman Sweeny and Wesley Holloway, the Laurel Ridge gate guard with the over-under shotgun.

Wesley gently nudged the bolt shut on his rifle. "Like that?"

"Um, you can be a little more aggressive with it. Somali pirates use these guns. You're not going to break it. It's built to withstand more abuse than you could throw at it. And give the bottom of the magazine a good slap after you put it in. If it's not seated properly in the well, the bolt won't catch the round."

Wes seemed to have no idea what she was talking about but followed her directions anyway. The bolt snapped shut with a loud clack.

Kate patted him on the back. "Much better. Mr. Sweeny, your turn."

"Please, call me Herman." The tall HOA president ran his reload drill with much more confidence.

"Good. Keep practicing. Once the bullets start flying, it will be much harder. The more you've done it, the easier it will be." Kate walked out onto Herman's porch where Jack, Vicky, Sam, David, Gavin, and Mr. Pritchard stood looking out over the mountains.

"What do you think? Are they ready?" Jack leaned against the rail.

"Are you kidding? They've never even held a battle rifle before. Of course they're not ready." Kate leaned next to him. "Did you find a good flanking position?"

Jack pointed down into the trees to the right. "That looks like as good of a place as any. We'll have that small outcropping of rocks for cover. That thicket of holly trees will provide some visual concealment, but as you can see, most of the other trees are bare."

"We have to work with what we have," Gavin said.

Jack looked at Pritchard. "You, Vicky, and David will stay in the house. We'll draw the rangers fire, which will provide your team an opportunity to pick them off from up here, a position of relative cover. Be aware of where our team is. We don't want any friendly-fire incidents. When Don's team arrives, watch out for them. Remember, my little girl is going to be with him. God help the person who injures her, friendly fire or not."

Herman stuck his head out the door. "Our wives have made some refreshments for you. We don't have much, but they wanted to show their appreciation."

"That wasn't necessary, but thank you." Kate felt bad for the residents of Laurel Ridge who were barely getting by.

"It'd be an insult not to partake. Y'all come on." Pritchard waved for the others to follow him.

Kim Sweeny, Herman's wife, said, "Please, get a plate and make yourselves comfortable."

Kate and her team walked in and helped themselves to the simple snacks laid out on the counter.

Herman introduced a fourth couple, also in their mid-sixties. "This is Stanley and Judy Hess, they live in the house next door."

Judy Hess had a big smile on her face, which faded when she saw Kate's team. She turned to her husband. "They're mostly children, and girls, and an old man!"

Sam seemed to take offense. "Every one of us has killed ma'am. Most of us, more than once."

Judy stepped back to stand behind Stanley. Her opinion of the rabble seemed to shift rather expeditiously and she made no further comments.

"What about the rest of the homes between here and the ridge? How will we defend them?" Marshall Yates, the other guard from the Laurel Ridge entrance gate held a small plate with some crackers and peanuts on it.

"We can't hold the entire neighborhood." Jack picked at a few nuts from his own plate. "We have to hope that they'll choose to engage us here."

"And if they don't?" Yates asked.

"Then they'll take one of the other houses as a stronghold and force us to bring the fight to them."

"But you said you don't think they'll do that." Herman stood nearby.

Kate adjusted the strap of her rifle. "Dean isn't expecting you to be organized and he certainly doesn't know we'll be here. He's coming because he thinks you're an easy target. I'm pretty sure he'll try to attack this house when he figures out this is where the people are."

"What are we supposed to do?" Wes Holloway asked.

Jack pointed at the possible entry points. "You and the other men will guard the doors and windows in case of a breach. At all costs, you cannot let the rangers get inside."

Ernest Martin's voice came over the radio. "All is clear at the overwatch station."

Kate pulled her rifle off of her shoulder. "That's our cue."

Herman Sweeny looked bewildered. "But the man said all is clear. And how are you getting a signal from your side anyway?"

"That was Ernest Martin. He lives on top of the

hill. He's using his radio to act as a repeater for the two sides of the mountain." Kate double checked that she had a round in the chamber and made sure her safety was off. "All clear means the rangers are coming. Dean and his men are monitoring our frequency."

Jack led the way to the front door. "My team, rally around me. We're moving out."

Kate, Gavin, and Sam followed Jack out the door and into the woods. They found their position behind the rocks.

"And now we wait." Kate looked at Gavin.

He took her hand. "Whatever happens, remember that I love you forever."

She did not want the fear of losing him to cloud her mind but was glad he'd said it. "Me, too."

Time crept by while Kate and the rest of the team waited for the action to start. Gavin looked at his watch. "It's been twenty minutes since we got the call. Do you think they're still coming?"

"They'll come." Jack had been leaning against the rock for some time. He shifted his weight to his other leg. "I would imagine they're rummaging through the first house on this side of the mountain. Herman's is third from the top. We'll hear them when they get next door."

"Maybe we should hit them at that house." Sam recommended.

Jack replied, "No. It's better if we take our time. They'll be on their toes for the first two houses. If all goes well, they'll start to relax, get complacent. That's what we want. Besides, we have a plan that involves multiple teams, we must stick to it."

"Were you in the military?" Kate asked.

"No, but I've watched my share of bucks eating beneath a deer feeder. They act differently the first time than they do the third or fourth time."

Crash, click! The sound of broken glass could be heard in the distance. Kate tensed up. "Sounds like they're coming our way."

"Yep." Jack peered out from behind the rock. "Sounds like they're next door."

"Do you see them?" Sam asked.

"Not yet, but they're coming." Jack signaled for his team to be quiet.

Minutes later, Gavin looked at his watch.

"How long since they broke in?" Kate asked.

"Five minutes." Gavin squinted, trying to see through the holly trees.

Soon after, the low echo of distant voices could be heard. What they were saying was indiscernible, but it was obvious the rangers had left the house.

"Sounds like they went through that house faster," Sam said.

"Yeah, they're probably in a hurry to clean out the residents and stake their claim. They figure they can go back and tally up the loot later." Jack pulled his AR-15 tightly into his shoulder. "Be ready. Hold your fire until I give the order."

Kate felt anxious about the coming encounter. Waiting made it ten times worse. She wanted to get it over with.

"Get down! Here they come!" Jack whispered.

Kate could see James Dean leading the pack toward Herman Sweeny's house.

"Knock, knock, anybody home?" Dean called

out to the house, but no one responded.

James Dean yelled once more, "Little pig, little pig, let me come in."

"Maybe they've all left, went to a FEMA camp or something," Skeeter said.

"Oh they're around somewhere," Dean replied. "The last house had hot coals in the stove."

Most of the rangers could be seen from Kate's position.

"Everyone, pick a target." Jack slowly took aim. "I've got Skeeter."

Kate raised her rifle. "I've got Gene Tifton."

"I've got Dean." Gavin's voice had an air of satisfaction.

"I'll take Andy Reese," Sam whispered.

"On three. One, two, three!"

Kate pulled the trigger. POW! She watched Tifton turn at the last second. She hit him in the arm, but it was not the kill shot she'd intended. Dean dropped his rifle and hollered in agony. He'd been shot in the hand. Skeeter lay dead on the ground and Andy Reese ducked behind a tree, seemingly unharmed.

"Take cover!" Dean yelped. "And somebody get my gun!"

The rangers scrambled to get out of the line of fire. One man ran to retrieve Dean's rifle. Jack and Kate both took shots at him, but he kept moving and neither of them were able to hit him.

"Where are they?" Dean screamed. "Somebody needs to get eyes on them!"

"In that thicket, sir!"

"Okay, rally around me and get ready to flank.

Remember your training." Dean's voice did not sound rattled from having been shot.

Worried, Kate turned to Gavin. "Now what?"

Jack answered her, "Pritchard's team has us covered. This is all part of the plan. Take a deep breath and get ready to fight."

Kate practiced her breathing exercises she'd used to control her social anxiety. A long breath in, hold for four counts, then let it out slowly. She held her rifle up and prepared to engage.

"Right there! I see 'em!" Tifton yelled.

Gunfire rang out in both directions. Kate dropped to the ground and kept firing.

Gavin spun backward, blood spurting from his shoulder.

"Gavin!" Kate turned to check on him.

More gunfire came from the balcony of the cabin above.

"Stay in the fight, Kate!" Jack said.

Gavin winced in pain. "Keep shooting!"

Knowing he was still alive gave her some relief. She turned back to the battle and finished out her magazine. She checked on Gavin once more while she changed mags. He was bleeding heavily.

Dean's men took cover and slowed their rate of fire.

Jack let his rifle drop to the side and called over the radio. "They're conserving ammo. We need to do the same."

Kate took another break to check on Gavin. She tried not to let her fear show. "Can you lean forward?"

Gavin did so but yelped in anguish. "AHHhh!"

Jack took a quick peek. "It went through. That's better than the bullet still being in there. Can you shoot?"

Gavin breathed hard as if in extreme torment. "No. I could fire…" He paused to take a breath. "…a pistol if …" He paused again. "I had to…"

"That's okay, you take it easy." Jack pulled some gauze out of the side pocket of his cargo pants. "I'm going to stick a little of this in the wound channel. It's going to hurt."

Gavin grunted in pain when Jack did so.

Feeling powerless, Kate looked on in horror.

BANG! A bullet struck the rock right behind Jack's head.

"Where did that come from?" Kate looked around.

Jack kept his head low. "We have to move. They're coming around."

Kate slung her rifle over her shoulder and helped Gavin. "Can you walk?"

He looked as if he were about to pass out from the pain. "Yeah."

Kate helped Gavin while Jack and Sam watched the surrounding shrubs for the sniper.

Jack called on the radio again. "Pritchard, we've got a shooter trying to pin us down. I think he's in those bushes to the south of your location. Whether you see him or not, I need your team to put down some cover fire for me."

Pritchard did not answer, but gunfire rang out from the balcony above.

"We have to move! We have to get into a position where we can see our targets." Jack got ready to sprint.

Gavin's eyes were closing.

"He's not going anywhere," Kate said. "You and Sam do what you need to do. I'll stay with Gavin."

Jack looked remorseful. "Okay. Sam, you ready?"

"Yes, sir."

Jack led the way, falling back deeper into the woods.

Kate felt all alone. Gavin was unconscious. Jack and Sam were nowhere in sight. "God, I need your help right now." Her eyes shifted back and forth from her fallen fiancé and the threat just beyond the shrubs.

Another bullet struck the trunk of the holly, inches from her face. Pritchard's team shot in the direction of the shooter. Still, more bullets came. Ping! The final round struck the dirt, an inch from Gavin's head.

"We have to move." Kate looked around for a safe place to drag him. The only spot she could be sure he wouldn't get hit was between the outcropping of rocks and Sweeny's cabin. But that side of the stones was a thicket of holly saplings and brambles. Another bullet whizzed by.

Kate grabbed Gavin under the armpits and pulled him back into the briar patch. Thorns cut into the back of her legs, snagging on her pants. She gently navigated past them. The sniper kept shooting at her. More return fire came from the balcony. Kate continued pulling Gavin deeper into the thicket. She tripped and fell backward into a holly. She lost her grip of Gavin and he slid down the hill, into a maze of thorn bushes. Her face was scratched and cut from the holly but she had to go on. Kate crawled low into the brambles. She carefully retrieved Gavin and began hoisting him back up to the safety of the rocks. Her arms and hands were scratched. A slow trickle of blood ran down her cheek. Once she felt confident that Gavin was out of harm's way, she crawled back to the edge where she could see what was going on.

She heard gunfire erupt from the direction in which Sam and Jack had run. Still, more gunfire came from Pritchard's team above. She saw movement in the branches of a large rhododendron bush near the area the sniper fire had originated. Kate placed the front sight of her AK on the bush and waited for it to move again. Sporadic gunfire peppered all around. Finally, the branches and leaves of the rhododendron rustled again. Kate estimated where the shooter was and pulled the trigger. POW! The bush had one last tremendous shake, then fell still. Kate hoped that it was the last of the sniper but could not visually confirm her kill.

Don's voice came over the radio, "We're headed your way, please advise."

Jack's voice was next. "They're to the south of our location, spread out all over. Be careful!"

Kate pressed the talk key. Desperately, she said, "If Annie is with you, we need medical attention. Gavin was hit in the shoulder and is unconscious."

"She's here. What's your location?" Don asked.

Jack came back before Kate could answer. "Better get Gavin in the house and let Annie take care of him there. Otherwise, you'll all be in a precarious position."

Kate looked at the distance to the house. "I don't think I can get him there on my own."

Vicky called over the radio. "I'll help you get him in. I see where you are."

Kate looked up on the balcony and saw her niece. "Okay. Thanks."

Jack called once more. "Mr. Pritchard, you and David lay down cover fire when Vicky goes out. Do the same while they're bringing Gavin inside. We can provide some support from our position as well. Annie, you need to make a wide circle around the action so you don't catch a stray bullet."

Kate listened to the bullets flying all around her. Moments later, Vicky arrived. Herman Sweeny was with her.

"I'll carry him on my shoulder. I think that will be faster." Herman knelt by the rocks.

"Okay. Vicky, can you help me get Gavin out of the briars?" Kate crawled back into the thicket and pushed Gavin while Vicky pulled from the edge. Once he was out of the brambles, Herman Sweeny bent Gavin's bloody body over his shoulder and stood up. He walked as quickly as his long legs would take him toward the safety of the cabin.

Kate kept her rifle ready and sprinted behind Vicky and Herman. They soon reached the door and Kate heard more gunfire coming from the south. "I think that's Don's team."

"I hope so." Herman gently placed Gavin on the ground just inside the basement door. "Vicky, come with me. We'll get some pillows and towels."

Kate stayed with Gavin, listening to the action

outside. "Fall back! Everybody fall back to the house!" The voice was far away but sounded like Dean.

Kate called over the radio. "Don, I think Dean's men are going to try to hole up in the house next door. Your team should try to cut them off before that happens. Otherwise, they'll have a defendable position to fight from."

"10-4!" Don said.

CHAPTER 23

For, lo, the wicked bend their bow, they make ready their arrow upon the string, that they may privily shoot at the upright in heart. If the foundations be destroyed, what can the righteous do? The Lord is in his holy temple, the Lord's throne is in heaven: his eyes behold, his eyelids try, the children of men. (The Lord trieth the righteous:) but the wicked and him that loveth violence his soul hateth. Upon the wicked he shall rain snares, fire and brimstone, and an horrible tempest: this shall be the portion of their cup.

Psalm 11:2-6

Kate watched Annie cut away the bloody clothes from Gavin's torso. Stanley Hess came down to the basement. "Can I help?"

Annie paused what she was doing. "Do you have any medical experience?"

"I was a lifeguard in college."

Kate tried to picture the pudgy, nearly-bald man swimming with another person in tow. It was far easier to imagine Hess as the one being rescued.

Annie's hopeful expression faded. "Can you boil some water and see if you can find any alcohol or peroxide in the house? I have to get this wound cleaned out."

"Sure." Stanley Hess walked heavily back up the stairs.

Kate watched apprehensively. "Is Gavin going to be okay?"

"I'm not a doctor, but I worked in the ER for a while. This doesn't look life-threatening. He's lost a lot of blood, but the bleeding has slowed. He'll lose some more when I clean out the wound, but we'll close it up right after." Annie turned Gavin on his side to inspect the exit wound. "I'm not seeing any bone fragments. Maybe he got lucky and the bullet didn't hit bone."

Vicky and Herman returned with the pillows and towels. Stanley Hess arrived soon after with a bottle of alcohol and a bottle of peroxide. "Will this help?"

"Yes, thanks!" Annie took the bottles.

Jack and Sam came in the basement door.

"Who's watching the house?" Kate looked up from her bleeding fiancé.

"Don's team," Jack responded. "We need to come up with a plan." He looked at Herman. "Whose house is that next door?" Jack pointed in the direction of the house James Dean's men had entered.

"It's mine," Stanley answered.

Jack said, "The rangers are hurt. We've killed two of their men and injured at least two others. One of the injured men is their leader. Right now is the best time to attack."

"Okay, I understand that my home may be damaged by the fighting. Do you need me to draw you a diagram of how the rooms are laid out?" Stanley offered.

"We're not a trained SWAT team, and we don't have the equipment they use anyway. We'd suffer high casualties if we tried to storm the house." Jack seemed hesitant to continue. "Our best chance is to smoke them out. We'll be positioned to pick them off when they abandon the house. But we need to do it now before they get reorganized."

"Smoke them out? That would cause a greater deal of damage to my home. How can you be sure that the tactic wouldn't burn my house down altogether?"

Jack looked at Herman, then back at Stanley. "That's what we're talking about here, burning it down."

Stanley shook his head adamantly. "I cannot consent to that. Our home is all we have."

Jack sighed. "Our only other option is a siege. We'll have to keep centuries posted all the way around the house until James runs out of food and water."

Kate continued to monitor Gavin's condition. She looked up at the pudgy man standing near her. "Mr. Hess, I understand how much you value your home. Especially in a world that's falling apart, it's the one thing you can count on. But, please, think about the lives that could be spared by smoking Dean out."

Herman added, "Stan, we have plenty of unoccupied homes in the neighborhood. You can take your pick. What about the Mercer's place?"

"We'd lose our photos, our clothing, and all of our belongings." Stanley looked at Gavin lying motionless on the floor and quickly turned away. "I simply can't do it. A home is far more than four walls and a roof."

"Okay then," Jack said gruffly. "You want to put people at unnecessary risk to save your precious home, you and your wife can take the 10:00 PM to 6:00 AM watch, every night until the siege is resolved." Jack put his hand on the doorknob to walk back outside. "And dress warmly, it's going to be nippy."

"Where are you going?" Kate asked.

"To talk to Don, see how many people we can spare for the siege." Jack closed the door behind him.

"Wait!" Stanley called out to the man who'd already left. Nevertheless, he launched his complaint. "I'm not a soldier. Judy hates guns. We can't be expected to be part of a military siege!"

Kate felt the fury boiling up inside. "As your wife so eloquently illustrated for us, our team is made up of mostly high-school-aged children, girls, and old people. If we can do it, so can you."

Herman nodded. "She's right, Stan. This is our neighborhood and our responsibility. We need to be grateful for whatever help they can give us, but we must be active participants."

"Yeah, okay." Stanley Hess started back up the stairs. "I need to talk this over with Judy."

Half an hour later, Kate, Vicky, Herman, and Annie stood around the guest room bed where Gavin lay resting.

Jack returned from speaking with Don and entered the guest room. "How's our boy?"

"His eyes opened and I gave him a glass of water, but Annie encouraged him to keep resting." Kate held Gavin's hand gently.

"So that's good. Is he stable enough to take him home?" Jack inquired.

Annie tilted her head. "He lost a lot of blood. It would be better if he could rest here until tomorrow, especially if he has to hike over the mountain."

Herman said, "He's more than welcome to sleep here tonight. That goes for you, too, Kate."

"Thank you," she said. "We'll take you up on that offer."

Jack said to Herman, "We need to use your home as an outpost. We'll have to keep at least three teams in the surrounding woods to guard Hess' house. But we'll have to keep a backup force here so when Dean moves, we can respond at a moment's notice."

"Whatever you need. What's mine is yours."

"Good," Jack replied.

Pritchard came into the room. "I've been sayin' my prayers for the boy."

"Thanks," Kate said. She updated the old man on Gavin's condition.

Jack said, "Mr. Pritchard, I need you, Vicky, Rainey, and David to guard the checkpoint at Apple Blossom Acres. Mary Crisp and my wife, Kelly, will help you cover security shifts until the siege is resolved. You can even ask Amanda McDowell if she seems like she's ready. The rest of us will set up camp here."

Pritchard's expression soured. "Relegated to babysittin' the women and children, I see." He shook his finger at Gavin. "Me and the boy there fought off them devils who tried to kill Kate all by our lonesomes. I was about to take 'em on single-handedly when the boy showed up with that big ol' rifle of his'n. I reckon he saw some ol' coot a shootin' at them ornery vermin and figured me to be more friend than foe. Good thing of it, too. By the time I knew he was there, he'd done shot two of 'em. Anyhow, it's just to say that you ought not to judge a country ham by the looks of the crust on the outside. Sometimes them ham's that's got a little green mold growin' on 'em is the best ones."

Jack accepted the odd rebuke with grace. "Yes, sir, and believe me when I tell you that you have not been consigned to a lower post. Quite the contrary, my little girl is going to be with you, and she is my biggest prize. I can think of no one else I could trust to single-handedly secure our homes and our families while we're away."

Pritchard looked at him untrustingly and ran his fingers through his beard. Moments later, he seemed to let go of the notion that perhaps Jack's assurance was more condescending than genuine. "Alrighty then, I'll do my best to keep 'em safe."

Jack handed a slip of paper to Herman. "These are the shifts that need to be covered by your people. I realize that Dean came from our neighborhood, but as you said, he's your responsibility now. We expect all of your people to be involved in the siege. Everyone needs to be scheduled to work one of these eight-hour shifts every day. Additionally, when they're off shift, they need to be ready to respond as backup at a moment's notice. Your off-shift people also need to provide support for those on shift, bathroom breaks, bringing them meals, everything they need. Is that clear?"

The tall man nodded as he looked over the schedule. "It's clear and fair. We'll do our best to accommodate your specifications. I see you've already filled in Stanley and Judy's shifts."

"Yes, night shift is the most brutal and the time that Dean is most likely to try to escape. If they want to save that house, they should be the ones putting the most on the line."

"Okay, I'll go present the plan to my group." Herman left the room.

Jack stood next to Kate. "You just worry about taking care of Gavin. I'll need you to participate when the call for backup comes, but I didn't put you on any guard shifts."

"Thanks, Jack. I'll work into the rotation once

he's up and on his feet." She took a seat on the side of Gavin's bed.

"You said you took some ARs off the Badger Creek boys, right?"

"Yeah. We have two, but not much ammo for them."

"You should transition over to an AR. I can help you out with ammo. Scott left a bunch of 5.56 rounds."

"I'm kinda used to running the AK."

"I understand, but when Dean gets ready to move, it will probably be at night."

"I've got a really good flashlight on my rifle. As long as I have a general idea of where the threat is, I can shoot at night."

"The problem with a flashlight is that it makes a really good target for your opponent."

Kate put one leg on the bed. "How will an AR-15 alleviate that problem?"

"I've got an old Gen 1 night vision scope for you. I upgraded to Gen 2 a couple years ago when we had some coyotes in the neighborhood. Scott also had a couple of Gen 2 scopes. David has one and Amanda agreed to let us give the other one to Corey."

"What about Don? Doesn't he need one?"

Jack smiled. "Don was able to buy a really good Gen 3 unit from OPD when his department upgraded. He got that thing for almost nothing."

"Okay, so why can't I put the scope on my AK?"

Jack pointed to her rifle in the corner. "You don't have any rails to mount it on. The hardware for putting a scope on that style of AK is very specific. It's not something you're likely to find laying around in the apocalypse."

Kate looked back at Gavin and put her hand on his arm. "I'm just now getting comfortable with my rifle. I'd hate to start all over."

"You've learned basic combat skills. It won't be starting all over. I think you'll be surprised how easily you transition. If you practice your magazine changes, you'll really like the AR. It's much faster."

"Sounds like I don't have a choice."

"You have a choice. I can give the scope to someone else, just thought I'd give you first dibs."

Kate considered the option. "Okay, I'll give it a try, but I'll keep carrying my AK until I feel comfortable."

"Sounds like a plan." Jack patted her on the arm and left the room. The others followed Jack, leaving Kate alone with Gavin.

"God, please, heal him. And watch over the rest of us." She spent the next hour in silent meditation and prayer.

CHAPTER 24

Rejoice not against me, O mine enemy: when I fall, I shall arise; when I sit in darkness, the Lord shall be a light unto me.

Micah 7:8

Two days passed since the beginning of the siege. Kate stood alone on Herman Sweeny's deck late Wednesday night. A cold breeze made her shiver and made the feeling of being alone in the dark more haunting.

Gavin walked out onto the porch. "Hey, want some company?"

His presence warmed her. "What are you doing out of bed? You're supposed to be resting."

"I've rested. I'm going to get muscle cramps if I lie around any longer. I need to move around."

She eyed his attire. "That's understandable, but why are you wearing boots and jeans? Vicky brought you a clean set of sweatpants from the cabin. And how did you manage to get your jacket zipped up with one hand?"

"Annie helped me, but I can almost get it by myself." The sling for his other arm was still visible from the neck of the jacket.

Kate's lips pressed together to show her displeasure. "I'd hate to think you're considering participating in a firefight in your condition."

"What gives you that idea?"

"Pull up your jacket."

"Why? It's freezing out here."

Kate caught the tail of his coat and lifted it up. "Just as I suspected." She pulled the bottom of his jacket down over the pistol at his waist.

"We're in a war zone, Kate. I feel naked without a gun."

She patted his chest. "How many magazines do you have in there? About four?"

"War zone, I rest my case."

"You can't be effective in a fight with a pistol. Sit this one out and heal up. This won't be your last chance for glory."

"You know that's not why I fight."

"I know, but seriously, I'd like to keep you around for a while."

"That's nice of you to say so, but how would I feel if you get hurt and I didn't do everything I could to keep you safe? A pistol is as good as any other weapon for putting down cover fire."

She pushed the sling of her new AR-15 further

back and took his hand. "I appreciate your concern, but please, just rest for now. Besides, you don't have any reason to worry about an attack tonight."

"Don't I?"

"What is that supposed to mean?"

"I heard you and Jack talking this morning in the guest room."

"I thought you were asleep."

"Resting my eyes, like I was told to do."

She twisted her mouth to one side. "That was all just speculation."

"No, you guys have a point. Dean and Tifton have had two days to recover from their injuries. If Dean's men were carrying three days' worth of provisions, they have one day of food left, assuming Hess had little to no food in his house. Dean will want to move while he still has a buffer, in case they have to hole up again before they can resupply. And he'll definitely want to move when he has the cover of darkness."

"You were eavesdropping."

"You were in the room with me! How could I be eavesdropping?"

"You were pretending to be asleep."

"Resting my eyes, as instructed."

Kate fought a grin. "Regardless of what happens tonight, you are confined to bed rest."

"Yeah, okay." He kissed her on the back of the neck and returned inside the house.

His kiss sent another shiver through her body but had an otherwise entirely different effect than the cold wind. She hoped the siege would be over soon, that all would return to normal or as close as possible, and that their plans for Saturday would not be further interrupted.

Hours later, Kate looked at the antique clock sitting atop Herman Sweeny's fireplace mantel. It was nearly 3:00 AM. She got up from the couch and tiptoed past Sam, Jack, and Annie who were all sleeping on the floor in sleeping bags. Herman Sweeny sat in his large leather chair with his head tilted back, snoring rhythmically. Kate gently pulled back the screen in front of the fireplace and placed another log on the fading flames. Just then, her radio sprang to life.

"We've got movement by the back door!" It was the voice of Wes Holloway who was on guard at the rear of Hess' house. "I think this is it!"

Kate turned to wake Jack, but he was already out of his sleeping bag and shaking Sam to rouse him from slumber. Herman Sweeny sat forward in his chair looking dazed.

"What's going on?" Annie Cobb sat up.

"This is it, everyone grab your guns. Let's go!" Kate clapped her hands to motivate her weary fellow soldiers.

Herman sprinted up his stairs. "I'll be right back. Dianna Yates, Bev Holloway, and my wife will be guarding our home so Dean's men don't try to take this house while we're gone."

"Good." Jack put on his tactical vest and zipped it up. "Tell them that we may need cover fire if we're forced to retreat."

"You got it."

Kate grabbed her AR-15 and hustled down the

stairs with the others.

Gunshots rang out in the distance. Moments later, the radio chirped again. This time, it was Don's voice. "The party is starting without you, get over here as soon as you can!"

"Roger that, Don!" Jack let go of the talk button. "Annie, Mr. Yates, you're with me. Sam, you and Kate wait for Herman, then go back up the Hesses'. I'm sure they'll need it. Kate, you're in charge of your team."

"Got it!" She watched Jack and his team disappear into the night.

"Mr. Sweeny! Come on! We've gotta go!" Kate yelled as loud as she could.

"Coming!" The towering man shook the walls as he stormed down the stairwell.

Kate opened the door and switched on her night vision scope. "Let's go!" She paused when Gavin appeared, dressed for action. "Oh, no! We decided that you'd sit this one out!"

Gavin pushed past her into the frosty darkness. "Correction, you decided. I agreed to no such thing."

Irritated, she led the rest of her team toward the Hesses' house where the rate of gunfire was increasing rapidly.

A sniper took pot shots at Kate's team while they ran across the open yard to Stanley Hess' position behind a gigantic oak. The roots of a nearby fallen tree created a ditch, which Kate jumped into for cover. Sam, Gavin, and Herman Sweeny followed her. More gunfire peppered the area. Judy Hess sat with her hand over her head, balled up in a near-fetal position behind the oak. Stanley, who could have otherwise been of more help, consoled his wife.

"Mrs. Hess, get into the ditch. You'll be safe here." Kate coaxed the panicked woman. She understood Jack's reasoning behind making the Hesses put their lives on the line to retake the house, but she did not agree with his decision; especially now that Judy was part of the problem.

Judy Hess looked up and shook her head. Frozen by fear, she wasn't going anywhere. Kate called out to Stanley, "She'll be safe as long as she doesn't move, but we need you to put down some cover so we can try to get some shots lined up."

Stanley Hess seemed irresolute in complying with the order. He barely stuck the tip of his rifle around the edge of the enormous tree. "Tell me when."

Gavin rolled his eyes and pulled out his pistol with his good hand. "I'll give him some help."

Kate powered off the illuminator on her scope, putting it into passive mode. This would allow her to see the IR illuminator of the sniper but not make her more visible to him. "Both of you, fire five shots in quick succession. Now!" As soon as Gavin and Stanley began shooting, Kate put her sights on the upstairs window where the sniper had been.

Stanley and Gavin's weapons fell silent. Through the night vision scope, Kate saw the glowing light of the IR illuminator of the sniper's rifle reemerge. It shone like a lighthouse in the upstairs window providing the perfect target. She pulled the trigger three times, starting at the bottom of the window and working her way down. She hoped the smaller 5.56 rounds would still penetrate the walls of the wood-framed house and kill her adversary on the other side.

"Did you get him?" asked Herman Sweeny.

"I hope so." She kept her head low and watched for movement inside the window. Seeing no lights from other scopes in the house, she powered her own IR illuminator back on. Through the scope, the illuminator lit up the immediate area like a floodlight, visible only to her.

Jack's voice came over the radio. "They're falling back inside the house. Kate, I'm coming to you, so don't shoot me."

"Roger." She continued to scan the perimeter of the house for movement.

Moments later Jack approached from behind. His face looked grim.

"What's wrong?" Kate asked.

"Corey is hit."

"Is it bad?"

"His thigh. It wasn't spurting, so hopefully it's not an artery. But regardless, he's finished fighting for today. So is Annie."

"Annie was hit?" Sam inquired.

"No, but she's transitioned to her medical role and being that it's her father, I doubt she'll be doing any more shooting."

"I think I got one of Dean's men," Kate said.

"Good." Jack's grave expression didn't change.

"Are you alright, man?" Gavin asked.

Sporadic gunfire occasionally punctuated the quiet in the background.

Jack looked at Kate's team. "Dean is hunkering down. He'll keep taking pot shots to harass us. If we pull back, he'll bolt. But we can't let him keep up his slow-motion assault."

"What other options do we have?" Kate asked.

"We have to go in."

"Storm the house?" Even Sam, who was typically quite gung-ho, sounded apprehensive about the plan.

Jack looked down at the dirt. "We don't have any other choice."

Gavin squatted in the ditch, resting his pistol hand on his leg. "When cops raid a house, they have a guy with a bulletproof shield who goes in first. We don't."

"I know." Jack's reply was sharp.

"Then who is going in first?" Sam inquired.

"I guess I will," said Jack.

Gavin's voice rose. "Oh no! You're not going in first, you have a wife and a kid."

Kate's heart jumped. "You're not going in first either, Gavin! You shouldn't even be out of bed!"

Gavin shook his head dismissively. "Don't you worry about that." He pointed toward the oak tree. "Stanley is going first."

"What? Me?" Stanley's voice quaked with fear. "I can't go in first. I don't know anything about this kind of stuff."

"Neither do I, but it's your precious house, and you're going in first. If you don't, I'll consider that you're abandoning your post, and I'll put a bullet in your sorry head for desertion."

"Gavin!" Kate was shocked by Gavin's outburst.

Judy Hess began bawling. "Stanley! No!"

Gavin gave no quarter. "And you better tighten up, also, Judy. You're going in second."

"Ohhhh!" she wailed in terror.

"Gavin! That's enough!" Kate demanded. "Judy can't even fire a gun. She'd get herself and everybody else killed."

"She doesn't have to fire a gun. Her job is to drag Stanley's corpse out of the way so we can get in to fight."

"This is madness! You are frightening my wife! Knock it off this instant!" Stanley cowered behind the tree.

"Don't blame me," Gavin continued. "You're the ones who think your house is worth sacrificing lives for. I'm just asking that you put your money where your mouth is. In fact, I'll volunteer to go in third, with only one hand to shoot with." Gavin looked at Jack. "Am I wrong?"

Jack sucked in his lips as if he were in deep contemplation. He remained silent for several seconds.

Stanley's eyes seemed to beg Jack to dispute Gavin's monstrous demands. He pulled Judy's sobbing head into his shoulder.

Finally, Jack broke his silence. "Gavin's right. It's your house, Stanley. You should be first in. I'll go second. Herman, you're behind me, then Sam, Kate is at the back of the line."

"What about me?" Gavin asked.

"You'll stay here. We may need cover when we come out. If you use the dirt mound to support Judy's rifle, do you think you could shoot with one hand?"

Stanley waved his hands and yelled over Judy's blubbering squalls. "Wait! Wait! Wait!"

"Speak." Jack held up his hand for the others to be quiet.

"What if we went back to the original plan?" Stanley's voice cracked with pleading trepidation.

"Which plan is that?" Jack seemed perplexed.

"To smoke them out."

"You mean, burn your house down?" Gavin jumped in. "Let's be clear, Stan."

Stanley nodded ferociously. "Yes, burn it down. Whatever it takes."

"It would have been better if we'd had a few hours to put a plan together, but I suppose we could give it a try." Jack looked to Kate for her consent.

"Okay," she said. "So what do we need? Some firebombs?"

"Yes," Jack replied. "Gasoline, Styrofoam, and glass bottles."

"Or Mason jars," Gavin added. "We'd just need to pierce the lids enough to squeeze in some material for a wick."

Kate squatted low and crawled over to the tree. She gently stroked Judy Hess' arm. "Do you think you could go back to Herman's? Ask Kim, Beverly, and Diana to start putting together some materials for us?"

Judy seemed relieved to have someone besides Stanley treating her with compassion. She dried her eyes with her arm and wiped her runny nose. Judy nodded insistently to affirm that she'd accept Kate's offer, as if she'd do anything to get off the front line.

"I'll escort her to the house," Stanley volunteered.

"Oh, no. We need you here." Jack gave an austere smile. "Gavin can escort Mrs. Hess back."

Stanley's expression betrayed his disappointment in Jack's poor choice of chaperon, but he did not argue.

Neither did Gavin appear to find the arrangement agreeable, yet likewise, he did not gripe about it. "I'll get some gas out of one of the vehicles. Can you offer any guidance on that mission, Herman?"

Sweeny pointed toward the house. "Kim's Mercedes is in the garage. It should have half a tank."

"Mrs. Hess." Gavin motioned in the direction of the woods with his pistol. "After you."

She looked fearfully at Stanley once more before leaving.

He smiled tenderly at his wife. "It'll be okay. I'll be along in a while."

Judy and Gavin disappeared into the dark cover of the forest.

"Kate, you guys hold down the fort here. I'll go update Don on the new plan." Jack tucked low to retreat into the woods. "Don't break radio silence unless it's an emergency. Dean is probably listening."

"Got it." Kate lifted her scope to her eye and continued to monitor the house for activity.

CHAPTER 25

> Bow down thine ear to me; deliver me speedily: be thou my strong rock, for an house of defence to save me. For thou art my rock and my fortress; therefore for thy name's sake lead me, and guide me. Pull me out of the net that they have laid privily for me: for thou art my strength.
>
> Psalm 31:2-4

Kate switched rifles with Herman Sweeny to take a break from constantly watching the house. Sweeny's AK reminded her of the trusted weapon that had served her so well in many scrapes. But, her tactical vest was stuffed with 5.56 rounds, so once the battle began in earnest, she'd have to swap it out.

"Coming to you, don't shoot." Jack crawled silently through the trees.

"Hey, is everyone ready?" Kate asked.

"Yeah, but Marshall Yates is by himself since Annie is taking care of Don. I want to send Sam to back him up."

"Sure, I'll go," said Sam.

"Good. I left Don's rifle over there. You can run that. You have a lot more battlefield experience than Yates. Don's vest, containing his AR mags, is next to the rifle." Jack patted him on the back. "Circle wide through the woods to get to Yates' position."

"I will." Sam entered the forest and quickly fell out of view.

"Sam is on his way to you, Marshall." Jack let go of his mic button.

Seconds later, Kate heard a rustling in the woods. "Herman, give me the AR."

He quickly switched rifles with her. She powered on the illuminator and soon recognized the person approaching. "Kim is coming."

Herman's eyes opened wide. "Honey, what are you doing out here?"

"I brought your Molotov cocktails. Judy is a wreck and Gavin is working with one arm. He couldn't very well pack a case of firebombs out here." She gently put down a cardboard banana box filled with various bottles and jars.

Herman lifted one of the bottles out. "Not my Johnny Walker Blue!"

"Relax, dear." She put her hand on his arm. "I

poured it into a Tupperware bowl."

Herman held the bottle like a bereaved master cradling the corpse of his favorite pet. "It won't be the same, drinking it out of a plastic bowl."

"Know that your sacrifice will be remembered." Jack consoled the man in an almost mocking manner. He gave Herman's arm a squeeze and carefully removed five more of the glass containers, leaning them against the mound of dirt at the bottom of the ditch. "I'll distribute the firebombs to the other stations. When I say *commence*, Kate, you shoot out all the windows on the lower floor. That should take less than thirty seconds. Then, Herman, Stanley, and Kim will all light their Molotov cocktails and launch them into the broken windows."

"We can't throw them into the windows from here!" Stanley protested.

"Good guess, Stanley." Jack lowered his brow, as if irritated by the stupid comment. "You'll have to run up to the house and toss them in the windows. Kate will cover you."

"I'll go, but not Kim." Herman's statement was assertive.

Jack looked at the tall man, as if he were sizing up his conviction on the matter. "Fine, but you'll have to make two runs. All six of the firebombs have to go into the windows. We can't take a chance that they'll be able to put out the fire. We can't even give them time to think. They must be forced out of the house quickly so we can kill them when they vacate."

"What about Kate? Why can't she make a run?"

Herman challenged.

"Because she's your best chance of getting back to cover without being shot. Do you think Kim is ready to take out multiple threats in the pitch dark?"

Herman sighed. "I suppose not."

"Okay, have the bottles lined up and pick your course. When Kate starts shooting, ignite your wicks. I should have all the teams ready in five minutes." Jack gingerly carried the box of the remaining firebombs into the blackness of the trees.

Kate watched the house, formulating a plan of attack in her mind. She waited restlessly for Jack's voice to give the command. The seconds crept by. "Is everyone ready?"

"The lighter is in my hand," Herman replied.

"What's taking so long?" Kate adjusted her arm to relieve the tension from holding the rifle.

"Commence!" Jack's voice rang loud and clear over the radio.

Kate squeezed the trigger. She placed one round at the top left corner and one at the lower right corner of the first window. The glass collapsed and fell out. She moved the reticle of the night vision scope over the next window to the right, repeating the process. She heard rifle fire from the other teams during her transition from one window to the next. "Okay, the windows are clear. Go!"

Herman rushed toward the first window, a flaming Mason jar in one hand and his beloved Johnny Walker bottle in the other. Kate carefully watched the windows. "Stanley, what are you doing?"

"Is it safe to go now?" he asked.

"It's getting less so by the moment. You have the element of surprise if you go now. Go!"

Stanley marched out of the ditch and picked up his pace as he stormed toward the second window. The blaze inside the window where Herman had launched his bombs became too bright and Kate had to switch off the night vision scope.

Herman wore a grin of satisfaction as he slid back into the ditch for his second sortie. "Two down, two to go." His next pair of Molotov cocktails were lit and he was out for the next run before Stanley returned.

"I did it!" Stanley called out while hustling back toward cover. A shot rang out. Stanley tumbled to the ground and yelped out in pain.

Kate saw the muzzle flash in the upstairs window but still could not use the night vision scope due to the brightly-burning flames below. She put several rounds into the upstairs window and called to Herman. "Stay on mission!"

He did not comply, rather he placed the two flaming jars at his feet and rushed toward Stanley who lay on his back grasping his right shin. Herman lifted the tubby man off the ground and began carrying him on his shoulder.

POW! Another shot rang out of the same window. Blood erupted from Herman's forehead and he fell forward like a towering pine, dropping Stanley to the ground.

"Herman!" Kim screeched in horror.

Kate emptied her magazine in the window where the shot had originated.

Stanley lay on his belly like a slug. "Help me!"

"Crawl, Stanley! You have to crawl here!" Kate slapped a second magazine into the well and continued firing to provide cover for the chubby invalid inching his way in her direction.

Stanley did not make it to the ditch, but he did finally reach the giant oak which had provided him cover earlier. He put his back against the trunk and wailed in torture.

"We have to get Herman!" Kim sobbed.

"You can't help him now, Mrs. Sweeny," Kate replied. "And I need you to help me out." She grabbed Herman's AK-47 and shoved it into the sorrowful woman's hands. "Just keep shooting at those upstairs windows while I go get the last two firebombs."

"I don't think I can hit anything." Kim's eyes were filled with tears.

"The enemy doesn't know that. Just keep the bullets high so you don't accidentally hit me." Kate popped in a fresh magazine and slung her AR-15 over her shoulder. "Ready?"

Kim obviously was not but nodded anyway.

"Okay, start shooting now!" Kate sprinted toward the two jars sitting in the middle of the wide open yard. They flickered like candles in a great abyss of darkness and peril. She kept her eyes focused on the torches and ignored the danger. She heard Kim's gunshots. "She's firing too fast! She's going to run out of bullets, and I'm not sure she can even change a magazine!" Kate complained to herself.

Kate reached the jars and lifted them from the place Herman Sweeny had left them. She darted toward the final bottom window and launched her payload inside. They exploded in a dazzling display of bright oranges, fiery reds, and brilliant yellows. However, Kim's rifle fell silent.

"She's out." Kate's stomach sank, knowing she'd never make the long dash back to the ditch without cover. She leaned against the wall of the burning house and looked toward the window above her. Rifle fire popped from inside, salting the tree line with lead.

Kate pulled her AR from her shoulder and prepared to fire. She'd have to provide her own cover fire if she was to make it across the yard before being roasted alive by the inferno in the house.

"They're coming out!" Jack called over the radio. "Looks like they're heading your way, Kate!"

"Fantastic!" Sarcastically, Kate voiced her frustration aloud.

Rapid exchanges of gunfire came from the house and the woods. The heat of the flames radiated from the house, baking Kate's backside like an overdone Christmas goose. She inched away from the exterior wall, which was engulfed in flames on the other side. She saw one of Dean's men sprint from around the corner, shooting back toward Jack as he ran.

Kate lifted her rifle. Using the off-set open sights, she fired. "Missed him, and now he's in the woods."

With her back to the flames, she could now re-engage her night vision. Kate powered on the scope. "I see you." She squeezed the trigger. BANG! The enemy combatant dropped to the ground.

Gunfire continued to echo all around. Kate watched closely for more of Dean's men who might pass her in their evacuation attempts. She watched the left side of the house where the last man had come from.

BOOM! She'd been blindsided. Coming in the opposite direction from which Kate was watching, one of the men tackled her to the ground and knocked the rifle from her grip. Kate lay on the ground. Stunned, she turned to see that it was James Dean who'd taken her from her feet. Likewise, Dean appeared bewildered by the encounter. Perhaps he'd been looking backward and not expecting anyone to be on this side of the house. Quickly realizing his predicament, Dean lunged at her with the elbow of his injured hand, knocking her flat on her back. He raised up on his knees and drew his pistol.

Kate wasted no time. She wrapped her legs around Dean's torso and pulled him toward her with a violent jerk. He pulled the trigger but had lost his balance and missed the shot, even at such a close range. Kate grabbed the wrist of the hand with the pistol and forced it to the ground at her side. She released the guard with her feet, sat up, shifted to the side where the gun was and hooked her opposite arm around his arm which held the gun. She clenched her own wrist with her opposite hand and twisted Dean's arm behind his back. He screamed and dropped the pistol. Kate turned toward Dean, forcing his arm further behind his back. Snap! She felt the bone crack in her grip. She quickly crawled from under Dean and got behind him. She wrapped one arm under his chin, the other behind his neck, gripped the inside of her elbow, and squeezed until he went to sleep.

Kate caught her breath from the exertion and stood up. She quickly retrieved her rifle and prepared to shoot. Another man came from around the corner. She quickly placed the reticle on him but froze before pulling the trigger.

"Kate!" Jack threw his hands in the air, letting his rifle fall to his side and dangle from the sling.

She lowered the barrel of her gun. "Oh, thank God! I almost shot you."

Jack looked down. "Is that Dean?"

"Yeah."

"Is he dead?"

"Just sleeping."

Jack drew his Glock, walked up to the man and pulled the trigger.

"Jack! He was completely disarmed!"

"So what were you going to do with him? Take him back, hold a trial, and execute him for murder, right?"

Kate quickly did the math. "Probably."

"I just saved us some time." Jack holstered his Glock and shouldered his rifle. "I think we've got them all, but we need to make a final round and mop up. Are you okay?"

Kate dusted the leaves off her shoulders from rolling on the ground with Dean. "Yeah, I'm good." She followed Jack as they searched the area for more of Dean's men by the light of Stanley's blazing home.

CHAPTER 26

> Live joyfully with the wife whom thou
> lovest all the days of the life of thy vanity,
> which he hath given thee under the sun, all
> the days of thy vanity: for that is thy portion
> in this life, and in thy labour which thou
> takest under the sun.
>
> Ecclesiastes 9:9

Despite wearing multiple layers and piling on the blankets, Kate shivered in bed Friday morning. A knock came to her door.

"It's me, Aunt Kate. Can I come in?" Vicky's voice reverberated through the door.

"Sure." Kate peeked out from beneath the quilts, blankets, and comforters.

The door opened. "I stoked up the fire and left some oatmeal in a pan on the hearth. I'm heading to the checkpoint for my shift."

"Thanks, Vicky. Make sure you stay warm. Go inside the guard shack as often as you need to."

"I will. I can't ever remember it being this cold in November." Vicky sat on the foot of Kate's bed. "Only one more night of freezing to death for you."

Kate tried to act like the wedding wasn't the only thing she'd been thinking of since the shootout the day before. "Oh, yeah, I guess you're right."

Vicky rolled her eyes. "Give me a break! Aren't you excited?"

Kate bit her lip to suppress the grin threatening to make her erupt in a squeal of exhilaration. "Maybe a little."

Vicky watched her carefully. "Mmmhmm. Maybe a lot."

Kate lost control of the smile and covered her head with the pillow. "Okay, maybe a lot."

"I'm happy for you and Gavin. And I'm proud of you, too."

"Oh yeah? Why is that?"

"Because you waited. I know it couldn't have been easy." Vicky stood up from the bed, slipping on her gloves and adjusting the strap of her rifle. "Unless you screw up tonight, of course."

"We're not going to screw up tonight!" Kate huffed with mixed emotions. "But thanks for noticing and thanks for the compliment."

"No, thank you, Aunt Kate." Vicky headed out the door. "For showing me that it is possible to do things God's way."

Kate swallowed the knot forming in her throat. "You're welcome," she said, but Vicky was already gone.

Gavin knocked on the frame of Kate's bedroom door.

"Come in."

"Nope. I can say what I need to say from right here."

Kate sat up, troubled by the strange comment. "Is everything okay?"

"Fine, but you don't know what goes through a guy's mind the day before he gets married. Trust me, it's not safe to have me anywhere around your bed."

Kate blushed. "Oh! Well, I guess that's good to know."

"Anyway, I wanted to talk to you about something. The people in Laurel Ridge literally have nothing to eat. I was wondering what you thought about giving them a couple buckets of food."

"I think that would be very kind. My only concern is that once the word is out that we've got food, we'll become the neighborhood grocery store."

"I considered that. Perhaps we should leave it on their doorstep; anonymously or something."

"I think that would be better." Kate pulled her hair back from her face.

Gavin's eyes looked at her longingly. He moistened his lips with his tongue. He was silent for several moments.

She wanted so badly to ask him to come snuggle,

just for a minute.

He sighed. "I better get out of here."

"Okay. I'll be down in a minute." Kate was glad that she soon wouldn't have to watch him walk away like that.

Someone beat on the door downstairs. The noise startled her, and she quickly got out from under the covers and got dressed. She zipped up her hoodie and hustled down the stairs to see what the matter was.

Pritchard sat on the couch next to Gavin.

"Mr. Pritchard, what brings you by?"

"This cold snap, that's what."

"Oh, do you need some firewood?"

"No girl, I got wood. But all these young chicks we've been a hatchin'. This weather ain't no good for 'em. Folks mostly try to raise 'em up in the spring so they'll have all their feathers by winter, but we's in a pinch thanks to these computer locusts. Gonna have to figure out a way to keep 'em warm. Them little rabbits, too."

"Do you have any ideas?"

Pritchard shook his head as if deeply remorseful. "I've been a ruminatin' on it, but all I can come up with is Edith Ramsey's."

"Edith Ramsey's what?" Kate sat on the corner of the hearth, letting the fire warm her back.

"Edith Ramsey's house, child. What else?"

Gavin looked exceedingly perplexed. "You want to put the chickens and rabbits in Edith's house?"

Pritchard's look of regret seemed slightly feigned. "I reckon we ain't got no choice about it." He tossed his hands heavenward, as if ceding some great debate. "Edith has a good stove. Won't use that much wood, but it'll keep that place good and warm for the critters."

"Where would the animals go to the bathroom?" Kate furrowed her brow.

"Where ever. The carpet, the couch, the counters, Edith's bed, ever where they happen to be when the notion hits 'em, I suppose." Even though Pritchard's thick white beard covered his mouth, the lines around his aged eyes betrayed the smile creeping across his face.

"Mr. Pritchard, are you sure Edith Ramsey's house is the best match for a chicken coop or is this just a good opportunity for you to get even with her? Remember what she said about having us locked up for trespassing when things get straightened out." Kate turned to locate the oatmeal which Vicky had left for her.

"What a disgraceful thing to accuse me of! If you was a few years younger, I'd tan your hide for sayin' such as that. Not that I believe it'll get straightened out, but if'n it do, I'll take full responsibility for it. Anyhow, Edith has that big ol' flower garden all fenced in. We can let the critters out durin' the daylight and shut 'em up of a night. Hear tell she's got a big ol' rack for all them silly shoes she prances about in. That rack will make a right smart nestin' box for them hens to lay their eggs in."

Kate stirred the oatmeal and placed the pot closer to the fire. She looked at Gavin. "What do you think?"

"Sure, whatever." He turned to Pritchard. "Do

you need us to do anything?"

"Them ornery roosters will kill each other if you let 'em get in the same room. We'll have to keep them separated. Also, we need to keep the hens around the light of the stove. If they don't get enough light, they're liable to quit layin'. We'll have to shoo them out of Edith's shoe racks of a night, too. If'n they take to sleepin' in the shoe rack, they won't lay in it. Otherwise, just the typical feedin' ever evenin'. Durin' the day, they'll forage in the flower garden until it's cleaned out."

Kate tasted the oatmeal. "Won't that be tragic?"

"Yep. Edith's prize winnin' flower garden will look like a hog waller by the time them chickens get done with it. But like I said, we ain't got no choice."

Kate shook her head at the old man's insistence that he was not enjoying the prospect of converting Edith Ramsey's home into a barnyard. "Okay, Mr. Pritchard. Just let us know when you need us to help out."

"Best get it done today." He stood and walked toward the door. "I don't reckon none of us will see hide nor hair of you two after the hichin'. I told Jack not to put neither of you on the security schedule for next week."

"Thanks," Gavin walked Pritchard to the door. "Did he ask why?"

"Yep." The old man opened the door.

"Did you tell him?" Kate inquired.

"Get your tails on over to the house in about an hour. We can have the coop set up before lunch." Pritchard pulled the door closed behind him.

Gavin took a seat on the hearth next to Kate. "I

guess that means the cat is out of the bag."

"Yep. Jack will tell Kelly, and she'll tell everyone else."

Saturday finally came. Wearing the only dress she owned, Kate stood in Pritchard's backyard where the makeshift chapel had once been. Her dress was navy blue with a ruffled sash hanging from the waist. It was far from the quintessential white wedding dress, but at least it was new and it did have long sleeves. She shivered in the cold mountain air, wishing the dress were longer.

She had no flowers but Vicky had managed to bind several branches of pine, cedar, and holly together with a length of taupe twine for a bouquet. Mr. Pritchard had another tree trunk set up which served as his podium. Vicky had scavenged together a smattering of candles in various colors and arranged them on sections of firewood in various lengths stood up on their ends and placed carefully around the podium.

Gavin wore a button-down shirt, his black hoodie, and jeans. Despite the imperfect circumstances, Kate couldn't have been more excited about the day.

Pritchard looked at Kate, Gavin, and Vicky, who stood by Kate's side. "The other boy ain't comin'?"

Vicky smiled. "Sam is helping to get everything ready at Mr. Davis' garage."

Kate looked curiously at her niece but wasn't going to make any inquiries at such a solemn ceremony.

Pritchard opened his Bible and read multiple

verses about marriage. Afterward, he closed the well-worn book and tucked it beneath his arm. "Kate, you figurin' on stickin' by the boy here, in sickness and health, poverty and plenty, forsakin' all others, till death do you part?"

She beamed at Gavin. "I do."

"Boy? You gonna hold up your end of it? Love your woman as Christ loves his church? Cause if you ain't, best say so now. Might break her heart but least you won't be breakin' your vow made before God. Hebrews says it's a fearful thing to fall into the hands of the living God. Ain't nothin' to be taken lightly."

Gavin seemed unmoved by Pritchard's caveat. He stared into Kate's eyes. "I do."

"Very well then, I pronounce you husband and wife. From this day forward you are one flesh. You can't go back to bein' two several persons no more than I can separate the corn from the cheddar in a mess of cheese grits."

Gavin appeared to have been stolen from his enraptured state by the allegorical comparison between mountain cuisine and marriage. He turned to the self-appointed preacher and looked at him curiously.

"What're you eyeballin' me about, boy? Go on! Kiss her!" Pritchard waved his hand in an almost threatening manner.

Gavin complied. Kate melted into his arms as they kissed long and passionately.

"Alright, alright, that's enough. There's youngin's about!" Pritchard clapped his hands to break up the matrimonial expression of affection.

"I'm not a kid, Mr. Pritchard." Vicky crossed her arms tightly to protest the accusation of immaturity.

"Well, don't none of us want to see all that. It's why they made honeymoons." Pritchard adjusted his Bible to be more secure under his arm and headed toward his house. "Best get on over to Pete Davis' before the food gets cold. I'll see y'all down yonder."

"What food?" Kate asked. But Pritchard didn't answer. She turned to her niece who seemed to know something of the matter as well. "What is Mr. Pritchard talking about?"

"I didn't tell anyone!" Vicky put her hands up as if surrendering to the police. "I promise!"

"Vicky!" Kate reiterated. "Tell me what is going on."

"Evidently, the word got out. The community wanted to respect your wishes to elope in secret, but they didn't see the harm in throwing you a surprise reception. They've all scraped together whatever they could find to make some really nice dishes. You have to go, Aunt Kate."

She felt touched by the thoughtfulness of the people she'd come to know as much more than neighbors over the last two months. "What do you think?" Kate turned to her husband.

"I could eat." Gavin smiled and led her down the hill.

Upon entering Peter Davis' garage, Kate and Gavin were congratulated by all of their friends and neighbors.

Dressed in a gray suit, Don offered them each a glass of champagne.

"Where did you get champagne?" Amazed by the lengths at which her community had gone to make a nice reception, Kate took the glass.

"It's just the one bottle. Everyone else has punch, which is really just several different flavors of Kool-Aid mixed together. " Don put his arm around his wife, Mary, and pulled her close to himself. "Kim Sweeny sent over the champagne. She'd been saving it for a special occasion and wanted the two of you to have it."

"That was very kind of her." Kate surveyed the attendees. "I don't suppose she felt like coming, being so soon after Herman's death."

Don's eyes were sympathetic. "No. She's having a pretty rough time. The Hesses are staying with her. The arrangement is somewhat out of necessity since the Hesses' house burnt to the ground, but I think it's good for Kim to not be alone in that big old house."

Kate glanced at the concrete floor. "I'll send Kim a thank you note."

Jack and Kelly Russo stood on the other side of the newlyweds. With one hand around his wife, Jack lifted the clear plastic cup containing a reddish-orange concoction. "I'd like to propose a toast."

Kate smiled and gripped Gavin's hand with her free hand.

Jack spoke loudly for all to hear. "To this magnificent couple, may God bless you with happiness, prosperity, perseverance, and hope. And may He shield you from the dangers and anxieties of this troubled world."

Kate and Gavin knocked their glasses together and took a sip from their respective glasses as did the guests.

"I'm so happy for you guys." Annie Cobb hugged Kate. "I hate to rush you but you should go ahead and cut the cake. We only have two people on duty at the gate and the others working security need to get back to their posts."

"Cake?" Kate looked toward the table at the rear of the room. A beautifully decorated cake sat at the center. "How on earth…"

"Kelly Russo made it." Corey Cobb stood next to his daughter, a crutch under each of his arms.

Kate turned to Kelly. "It's so beautiful that I don't want to cut it!"

"Well cut it you will." Kelly escorted the couple toward the back table. "It's what I used to do before the world ended. I'm happy to be able to do it again."

Kate cut the cake making sure two pieces went to the guards watching over the checkpoint. Then, she and Gavin took a seat next to the cake and ate.

Also on crutches, Stanley Hess hobbled over to the table and took a seat next to them. Judy Hess sat next to Stanley.

"Hey, it's good to see you both. Thanks for coming." Gavin shook Stanley's hand.

"We wouldn't miss it for the world." Stanley seemed sincere.

Kate let her fork rest on her plate. "I'm sorry about your house. I wish there had been another way."

Stanley waved his hand in the air. "It's just a

house. We're staying with Kim for now. But perhaps in the spring, we'll take over one of the other vacated homes in the neighborhood." He looked sad and gazed at the table top. "Maybe if I had come to this conclusion earlier, we could have put together a better plan. Then, maybe Herman would still be alive."

Judy rubbed her husband's back to console him.

Kate shook her head. "You can't blame yourself for that, Stanley. It's not your fault that bad people are taking advantage of the crisis and preying on their fellow human beings like animals."

He forced a smile. "Our two families had become the best of friends over the years. And every time I look at Kim crushed by grief, I can't help but think that things could have turned out differently if I hadn't been so selfish."

Gavin patted the man's arm. "Don't beat yourself up. No one is in a hurry to watch their home go up in flames. Were you able to salvage anything?"

"Only your wedding gift." Judy smiled tenderly at Kate.

"Our wedding gift?" Kate felt perplexed, wondering if she'd heard the woman wrong.

Stanley nodded. "Yes. The house is gone. We haven't been able to identify any of our belongings except a few kitchen items which are heavily damaged. But, the chimney is standing erect, like a monument to the world that was."

Kate still didn't understand but smiled anyway.

Judy took over the explanation. "Below the chimney, inside our fireplace is a very nice wood-burning stove insert. We understand you only have an open fireplace and thought it might be of use to you."

Kate's eyes lit up. Thinking about how they'd get through the freezing winter had been a source of great anxiety for her. "What about you?"

"Kim has a wood burning stove upstairs and one in the basement as well," Stanley replied.

Gavin added, "Next year when you move, you might want it then."

Judy shook her head. "We're not even sure that we'll want to move. Kim and I are very close. I hate the thought of leaving her in the house alone, especially in this environment."

Stanley agreed with a nod. "But if we do, we'll probably pick a house with a wood burning stove, preferably one in the center of the house as opposed to an exterior wall."

"I don't know what to say. Thank you." Gratitude welled up inside Kate.

"It's us who should be thanking you," Stanley said. "We'd have never survived if it hadn't been for the good folks of Apple Blossom Acres. I haven't been able to inspect it, but the flue liner should still be intact. Jack said he'd pull it out and install it inside your chimney. I'd help him get the stove over to your place but..." Stanley glanced down at his bum leg.

"We appreciate it, more than you can imagine," Kate said.

"We're only sorry that we couldn't have had it installed for your wedding night. It would have been so cozy and nice for you." Judy lifted her fork and began eating again.

Mr. Pritchard had sat down behind Kate midway through the conversation. With a mouthful of cake, he said, "Ain't no need to be a worryin' about these two youngins. They ain't about to freeze tonight. Matter of fact, it's liable to be so hot in there that they'll have to open a window."

Kate's face turned red. "Mr. Pritchard!"

"Simmer down girl! Ain't no secret to nobody in here what y'all fixin to do!"

She buried her head in her husband's arm. Even Gavin began to blush.

Kate and Gavin mingled with the other guests for the next hour, then they made their exit.

CHAPTER 27

The thief cometh not, but for to steal, and to kill, and to destroy.

John 10:10a

Monday evening, Kate, Gavin, Sam, and Vicky sat around a foldable card table, which they'd set up in the living room in front of their new stove insert.

Sam tallied up the score from the last hand. "That's it. Guys win again. Looks like Kate and Vicky will be doing the dishes for the next *two* weeks."

"No way!" Vicky banged her fist on the flimsy table. "Double or nothing, come on, Sam. Deal the cards!"

Kate put her hands in the air. "I'm going to cut my losses right here. Besides, I think we're going to turn in for the night."

Sam shuffled the deck. "Gavin, if we keep this up, we could get out of household chores all the way through the spring."

Gavin pushed away from the table. "Hate to disappoint you, but I'm beat."

"Beat? It's eight o'clock. Come on, bro. We're on a run!" Sam pleaded.

"Where's your sense of romance, Sam?" Vicky shot her brother a dirty look. "Let it go. They just got married. This is supposed to be their honeymoon. It's bad enough that they have to share the house with us."

"Oh." Sam seemed to have a revelation.

Embarrassed, Kate bit her lip and quickly dismissed herself from the table.

The security walkie-talkie came to life. It was Rainey Russo. "Main gate checkpoint calling for Kate."

Kate stopped in her tracks and turned to retrieve the radio from the kitchen counter. "This is Kate, go ahead."

"Your brother is headed up to the house."

She pressed the talk key. "My brother? Why is he coming up here? Why didn't you call me before you let him in?"

Rainey replied, "He had ID. I verified that it was your brother. I figured he wasn't able to make it to the wedding and was coming by to congratulate you. Mr. Wilcox is on duty with me. He agreed that it was the right thing to do. Did we do something wrong?"

Kate set her teeth tightly against one another and

squinted in regret. "It's okay, you didn't know, but he's not welcome in the neighborhood. Where's your dad?"

"Having dinner probably. He and Don are coming on shift at ten."

Kate pressed the talk key again. "Let your dad know that Boyd is here and tell everyone to be on the lookout. My brother showing up spells disaster."

A knock came to the door. Kate motioned toward Gavin. "Get your rifle ready and hang out in the bedroom. Stay back and listen for trouble."

Kate waited for Gavin to get to the bedroom before answering the door. "Mr. Pritchard?"

Pritchard came in carrying a bag of salt. "Boy that stove sure do keep it warm in here, don't it? Anyhow, I ain't come to take up your time, 'specially it bein' your weddin' week and all. I just wanted to drop off some salt. Pitch a handful of it in the fire now and again and it'll keep the creosote from buildin' up in your flue. Them rich folk over in Laurel Ridge don't take care of nothin'. Ain't no tellin' when they last had that liner cleaned out."

"Thanks, Mr. Pritchard but we have salt." Kate passed the bag of rock salt back to the man.

"No, you keep it. I stocked up on salt and a few other items. Like I said, I knew the judgment was a comin' based on what the good book said." Pritchard looked into Kate's eyes. "What's a matter with you, child? Buyer's remorse?"

"What?"

"Cold feet, you already wishin' you hadn't hitched up with the boy? Is he treatin' you right? Cause if'n he don't, I'll haul him out behind the woodshed quick as a fly over a frog pond."

"No, Gavin treats me fine."

"Then you best just count your blessin's. Besides, I'm too old for you, so you wasn't gonna find no better lookin' man anyhow."

"No, Mr. Pritchard, I'm in a state of absolute wedded bliss, but my dirt bag of a brother decided to stop by and I know it can't be good."

"Oh, him. Where's that devil at?"

"He's walking up from the checkpoint now."

Another knock came to the door.

Pritchard grabbed the doorknob and jerked it open. "Now you listen here! We told you not to show your sorry hide around these parts no more! What in the world are you a doin' comin' around here? Carry yourself back to the rock you done crawled out from under 'for I jerk a knot in your tail!" Pritchard pointed beyond Boyd without giving him a chance to speak.

Boyd's face was contorted into a look of vast annoyance. "Kate, tell this old man to get out of my way and let me in. I've got something you're gonna want to hear."

Kate bit her thumbnail. "Mr. Pritchard, let him in. Let's see what he has to say."

"Don't you be a eyeballin' me, boy!" Pritchard raised his hand as if to back slap Boyd when he walked in the door.

Boyd winced and quickly moved away from the cantankerous old man.

"Say what you have to say, then get out of here." Kate crossed her arms tightly.

"That's no way to speak to someone who's just

trying to do you a favor." Boyd made himself comfortable on the couch.

Pritchard followed him like a hound dog circling a treed raccoon. "We don't need no favors nor no help from you, boy. If'n you see me in a fight with a bear, don't raise a finger to help me. If you want to help somebody, help the bear. I'll take my chances."

"Stop calling me boy!" He stitched his brows together. "Kate, I come in peace on behalf of Reverend Graves."

"Reverend Graves? Who is that?" She stepped closer to the couch but did not sit down.

"Lloyd Graves, he's found Jesus and he wants to forgive you for killing his brother."

"Which Jesus did that ol' polecat find?" Pritchard quizzed.

Boyd held up his hands as if bewildered. "I don't know, old man, how many Jesuses are there?"

"There's the Only Begotten Son of God that the Good Book teaches us about, then there's that pot smokin' hippy that they worship in most of the churches I've ever set foot in, you've got the Jesus them devils from the Spanish Inquisition was a prayin' to." Pritchard ticked them off one by one with his fingers. "There's more Jesuses than you can shake a stick at. People cobble together attributes from the real Jesus and mix 'em up with their own wicked notions of how God ought to be; like some sacred Mr. Potato Head. Then, they bow down to their little Mr. Potato Head Jesus same as you would any other idol."

Boyd stared at the old man with his mouth open,

as if he were completely befuddled.

Kate brought the conversation back on topic. "You were saying, Boyd?"

"Ahhh, yeah. So, Reverend Graves is willing to let bygones be bygones."

"How magnanimous of him," Kate said. "Considering his brother killed my brother and was intending to add Vicky and me to his stable, I think he should be sending me a thank you note for ridding the earth of that scumbag."

Boyd wrinkled his nose. "Where's your sense of forgiveness?"

"Oh, I forgive him, I just don't want to share a planet with people like Jason Graves. And I hope Lloyd is truly reformed. Thank you for delivering the message. I'm glad to see you've made some new friends. So, if that's all, I guess you should be going."

Boyd crossed his hands and sat forward on the couch. "We still have the matter of reparations."

Kate sighed. "Okay, Boyd. Enlighten me. Does the good reverend want to reimburse me for the damage his brother did to my house? Try to compensate us for our pain and suffering? Nothing he can offer will replace Terry, so I think it would be best if we just stay clear of each other."

Boyd sucked his teeth. "That's not exactly what the reverend has in mind. He feels that you owe him."

"Get out! Get out of my house!" Kate screamed and kicked Boyd's leg violently to hurry him out.

"Hey!" Boyd tried to get out of her way but tripped when he tried to stand up. "Don't shoot the messenger." He scrambled on his hands and knees toward the door. He finally regained his bipedal position and brushed himself off. "You need to think this over. The reverend isn't going to like it if you deny him this request."

"I don't care what he thinks. Tell him that if he sets foot in Apple Blossom Acres, he'll be reunited with his sorry excuse for a brother faster than he might want. And that goes for you, too. If you come back, I'll kill you, Boyd."

Boyd shook his head. "You don't stand a chance against the reverend."

"That's what his brother thought. Now get out!"

"I was only trying to help." Boyd walked toward the door. "You're underestimating the reverend. Prior to the collapse, his dealings put him in tight with some of the worst gangs in Charlotte, Knoxville, and Atlanta. As you can imagine, lots of those folks left the cities because resources are so scarce. Many of them have come to the reverend for food and shelter, joined his flock."

Kate considered the threat. Her face felt pale.

"This won't end well for you." Boyd started down the porch stairs.

Sam yelled, "It won't end well for you either."

Boyd turned to look at his nephew.

BOOM! Boyd's head jerked backward. Blood spurted into the air as his body was flung to the earth behind him.

Kate's heart stopped for an instant. She turned to see smoke trickling from the barrel of Sam's .45. "Sam! What have you done?"

"I did what had to be done, Aunt Kate. If there's

going to be a war, we have one less person to fight. Additionally, Uncle Boyd was probably going back to Graves to tell him all about our security layout."

Kate walked out on the porch. Gavin followed her, his AK slung over his shoulder. He put his arm around her. "I wish it could have been handled another way, but Sam is right."

She wasn't ready to admit that fact. The haunting feeling of being the only one left of the three siblings sent a chill up her spine.

Jack and Don hurried up the gravel drive with rifles ready.

"What happened?" Don called out.

Gavin debriefed them on the events.

"Then we better get ready." Jack's expression was glum.

"We need to bring everyone into one or two houses." Don's brow was heavily furrowed. "We need to bring all of our weapons, ammo, and provisions. We need to do it now. For all we know, Graves and his hoodlums could be a quarter mile up the road waiting to hear our answer."

Kate looked at Don and pushed her hands into her jeans pocket. "We might have some supplies here, in case we needed to ride out a prolonged blockade."

"I've got some vittles about. Reckon my homestead might be a good spot to hunker down." Pritchard brushed his beard.

Jack pointed across the yard. "Kate's cabin has a water pump close to the house. Still, we should fill up every container we can."

"What's to stop them from burning us out, like

we did Dean?" Gavin leaned against the rail of the porch.

Jack dragged his foot through the gravel. "That's a good question."

Don exhaled his disgust at the situation. "We'll just have to keep them far enough back. Snipers in every window."

Vicky stood in the doorway. "What about those booby traps that Dean made? I know you guys don't like to use them, but desperate times call for desperate measures."

Jack nodded. "Yeah, desperate times call for desperate measures. Mr. Pritchard, can you stop by Pete Davis' and the two of you go hold down the gate? Send Rainey and Warren up to the overwatch position. But if you see trouble, just let us know and get out of there. Take the perimeter trail through the woods and get back here as fast as you can."

"What about the road?" Kate looked to her niece for more ideas. "Is there any way we could booby trap the entrance so they couldn't get in?"

Gavin quickly said, "We probably can't stop them, but we could at least slow them down."

"What have you got in mind?" Don listened curiously for his reply.

"We have chainsaws. We can drop some of those massive pines and oaks along the road. It would force them to approach on foot rather than in their vehicles." Gavin turned to his wife.

She added, "That would limit how much supplies and ammo they could bring up at once."

"Okay, spread the word. We need to get moving," Don said.

"What do you want done with this ornery critter?" Pritchard pointed at Boyd's corpse lying at the bottom of the stairs.

"Just drag him over to the woods. We'll probably have plenty more to deal with by morning." Jack turned and followed Don back down the drive.

CHAPTER 28

This is my commandment, that ye love one another, as I have loved you. Greater love hath no man than this, that a man lay down his life for his friends.

John 15:12-13

Kate stood looking out her old bedroom window. Since the wedding, she'd moved downstairs with Gavin, but Don and Jack were manning the first floor and their families were sharing the downstairs bedroom. Kate, Gavin, Sam, and Vicky were all stationed in her old room.

"Do you see anything?" Sam stretched out on Kate's bed.

"Still nothing," she said. "This could be a long

night. You and Vicky should try to get some sleep. You two will have second watch."

"Yeah, right. Our tiny village is getting ready to be attacked by the worst gangs from Charlotte and Atlanta. I could get some pretty restful sleep about now." Vicky's voice overflowed with a degree of sarcasm that could only come from a teenager.

Kate knew her comment had been unrealistic. She felt tired though. The past three hours had been spent scurrying about like a squirrel getting ready for winter. Water had been collected, trees had been felled, and booby traps had been set up around most of Kate and Pritchard's yards, leaving only two access points by which the early warning teams could get to the houses from the perimeter trail.

The next two hours moved by at a snail's pace. Kate glanced at her watch. "It's after 1:00 AM. I feel like my eyes are going to close. Think you could keep watch by yourself?"

Gavin ran his hand across the back of her head. "Sure. Go ahead and get some rest if you can."

Vicky and Sam lay on Kate's bed. Both were breathing heavily as if in deep restful sleep. Kate wriggled down inside the sleeping bag on the floor next to Gavin. She felt warm and safe, despite the impending peril. She closed her eyes and drifted off.

"This is it, they's a-comin'!" Pritchard's voice over the radio startled her awake. "I count headlights from no less than twenty vehicles runnin' headlong towards the gate."

Jack's voice came over the radio next. "Rainey,

get out of there! Make your way to Kate's as fast as you can. The rest of you, get to Mr. Pritchard's!"

Vicky rolled out of the bed and retrieved her weapon. She didn't have a tactical vest but had extra magazines for her AK-47 in an oversized purse that hung on her shoulder. She looked under the bed.

"What are you doing?" Sam inquired.

"Making sure we have plenty of ammo up here. I don't want a repeat of the last attack."

Kate zipped up her tactical vest. "We have as much as I could fit under the bed, plus some in the closet. Obviously, we had to share the AK ammo with the other people who needed 7.62, but we've got more shotgun shells and handgun bullets in the closet."

"Okay." Vicky still didn't look to be at ease but seemed to accept the accounting.

Kate leaned her AK against the trim around the window and chambered a round in the AR-15 which had the night vision scope attached. She opened the window and looked through the scope down the driveway.

"It will take them a while before they get up the road. If anyone needs a drink of water or to go to the restroom, now is the time." Gavin propped the barrel of the .270 deer rifle on the window sill.

Cold air poured into the room, making the chilling situation that much more frigid.

"They've got night vision!" Kate saw the glowing beams of infrared illuminators coming up the drive.

"That gives you a good target." Gavin watched

patiently through his scope.

Kate wasted no time. She zeroed in on the closest beam and took her first shot. POW! The man collapsed to the ground. All the other IR beams ceased moving for a moment and then turned in her direction. She took three more shots, which dropped two more of the attackers. Then, the reverend's men commenced firing.

"Get down!" Kate yelped. Gunfire ripped through the window and struck the interior walls. She watched the exterior walls closely. "The logs seem to be stopping the bullets from coming through. Everyone get your back against the outside wall. It's the safest place to be."

Sam shook his head and began crawling for the door. "I'm not waiting to get trapped up here again. I'm going downstairs to fight with Don and Jack."

"Me, too, Aunt Kate. We can use your room for a fallback position." Without waiting for a reply, Vicky followed her brother.

Kate's brows drew together. She looked to Gavin hoping he could stop Vicky and Sam from running off.

"All the ammo and extra guns are up here." Gavin's plea did not dissuade them.

The gunfire slowed and Kate peeked out the window. "They're already in the yard!"

Gavin looked over just in time to watch three of the booby traps explode. The homemade zip guns ignited, taking out two of the hostiles and injuring three others. "The tripwire shotgun shells are working."

"Until they're all tripped. It's an overwhelming

enemy force." She found a target and took a shot, putting down another of her opponents. "I don't see how we can make it through this."

"Live or die, we're not going to make it easy for them." Gavin took a shot and then returned to cover.

Don's voice came over the radio. "Everyone, put a flashlight in the window facing out. It will limit the effectiveness of their night vision."

Kate took the extra light from her vest and set it in the corner of the window. Immediately, gunshots peppered the corner of the window where the light rested. Kate rolled away from the window and waited for the shooting to die down. She popped up again and tried to find another target. More sporadic gunshots hit the exterior logs of the house around the window, forcing her to retreat to cover. "They're closing in."

"Like they're going to attempt a breach?"

"Yeah." Kate felt anxious.

"Maybe we should go downstairs, in case they storm the house." Gavin inched away from the wall.

"Okay. Let's stash these weapons up here. We'll leave them under the mattress and carry only our handguns and AKs."

Gavin crawled to the edge of the bed and lifted the top mattress. He shoved the .270 between it and the box spring. Kate placed the AR-15 next to the .270.

Gavin pointed to the shotgun in the closet. "Get that one also. I don't want them finding our guns and using them against us."

Kate quickly stowed the shotgun between the

mattresses and followed Gavin to the door. The two of them hustled down the stairs.

Don peeked out the front window. "Feels like the Alamo. We're completely surrounded."

"I think they're getting ready to breach the door." Kate walked to Don's position.

"Then we should take covered positions and light them up when they come in," said Jack.

Kate rushed back to the refrigerator. "Gavin, give me a hand."

He helped her pull the massive box away from the wall and position it as a barricade from behind which to shoot.

"Rainey, come on. We'll do the same thing with the stove." Jack motioned for his daughter to assist him.

"Here they come!" Don spun around from the window, pushing Sam and Vicky toward the kitchen.

Kate took aim at the front door. Seconds later, the sound of a shotgun preceded the lock shattering and the front door being kicked open. Kate and her team opened fire at the intruders. Then, more gunshots came from the back door. Kate turned to see three men had already gained entry.

Don cried out to his wife in the downstairs bedroom. "Mary, get upstairs! All of you!"

Mary emerged from Gavin's room followed by Kelly Russo and Amanda McDowell. The three women all carried guns and fired toward the front door while making their dash for safety.

Kate ducked between the stove and the counter. She continued firing at the three men who'd come in the back door. Soon, her team cut them down. A temporary lull in the shooting gave them a moment to breathe. "I think we should all get upstairs."

Don watched the front door. "No. Then we're trapped with nowhere to move."

Jack looked upstairs where his wife had just gone. "The house is going to be overrun. I think Kate is right. We need to get up there and hold them back so the girls can get out the window and over to Pritchard's."

"If his house hasn't been taken over as well," Gavin said.

"What's your situation, Mr. Pritchard?" Kate called on the radio.

"Wonderin' if we ought to come help y'all. Looks like you've got more than you can handle."

"Yeah, almost. But stay put. We're coming to you." Kate clipped her radio back on her vest.

"Let's go!" Jack motioned for everyone to head upstairs.

Kate led Vicky and Rainey toward the stairwell first. Gavin and Jack came next. Kate looked down over the banister. "Don, Sam, let's go!"

"I'll hold them off until the girls are out. You get going." Don's voice came from the kitchen.

Next, Sam's voice echoed from below. "I'm going to stay with Mr. Crisp."

Kate's stomach sank. She knew what they were doing. Kate opened her bedroom window and looked down below. She saw several of the Badger Creek ruffians positioning themselves behind trees for the next attack. "Vicky, take everyone to your room and go out your window. You can tie off bed sheets to the toilet and climb down. Gavin and I will provide cover fire from my window. Jack, you can put down cover fire from Vicky's window while the girls are escaping."

"Got it!" Jack left the room. "I'll tell you when they're ready."

Enemy shooters took pot shots from behind trees toward the upstairs windows to harass Kate and her team. She looked at Gavin. "I don't know if we're going to get out of this."

His face was grim. "No matter what, I love you."

She leaned against the exterior wall waiting for her cue. She took his hand. "I love you, too."

"Okay, Aunt Kate, we're tied off," Vicky yelled from the other room.

"Cover me," Jack said. "I'm going first, to draw their fire."

"What?" Kate spun the barrel of her rifle out the window and began shooting at trees which looked like they might be harboring her adversaries. She watched Jack shimmy down the bed sheets from the next window over. He sprinted to a tree between her house and Pritchard's, then began firing. Likewise, the people in Pritchard's house also provided cover fire.

Next, Vicky climbed down and hurried across the yard. Mary Crisp went after Vicky, then Kelly and Amanda.

Suddenly, the raid began. What seemed like dozens of invaders streamed across the yard toward Kate's house. She heard shooting downstairs. "We should go backup Don and Sam."

"Graves' men are shooting at the girls." Gavin

grabbed her arm and pulled her toward Vicky's room. "We need to focus on saving the people who can be saved."

Kate slung her rifle over her shoulder and climbed out the window while Gavin covered her with rifle fire. "Okay, I'm down." She went to one knee and emptied a magazine in the direction of the hostiles while Gavin climbed down the sheet.

"Change your mag!" Gavin let out a volley of bullets while Kate reloaded.

Still, the enemy persisted in shooting at them.

"Kelly!" Jack screamed from halfway between the two houses.

Rainey's voice cried in distress. "Mom!"

Kate looked to see that Kelly Russo had been shot crossing the yard.

"Come on, we have to cover them." Gavin fired toward the enemy line as he ran.

Kate followed him, pulling the trigger on the way. Jack and Rainey sprinted toward Kelly, slinging their weapons over their backs and picking up the wounded woman.

With her legs pumping as fast as they could carry her, Kate continued shooting all the way across the two lots. She turned and walked backward so she could keep the bullets flying. She heard the voice of Corey Cobb. "Kate, Gavin, hurry up!"

Kate turned to see the man holding Pritchard's side door open for them. She took one last look at her house before going inside. Through the windows, she saw flashes of light from so many muzzles illuminating the inside of her cabin in short bursts. The momentary flares ceased and the sound of gunfire grew silent. Kate understood what had happened to Don and Sam. She stepped inside the house and closed the door behind her.

Unconscious on the foyer floor lay Kelly Russo. Corey Cobb helped Annie strip away the bloody clothing from the wound in her torso.

Jack looked on in unbelief while Rainey gripped her father's arm and wailed in sorrow.

CHAPTER 29

The pangs of death surrounded me, and the floods of ungodliness made me afraid. The sorrows of Sheol surrounded me; the snares of death confronted me. In my distress I called upon the Lord, and cried out to my God; He heard my voice from His temple, and my cry came before Him, even to His ears.

Psalm 18:4-6

Kate's radio came to life. It was an unknown voice. "Your obstinance before the Lord has cost the lives of your friends. Repent now of your unholy defiance and save the souls of those who remain."

Pritchard picked up a nearby radio. "I figure this is the man who calls himself the reverend. Let me tell you somethin', boy. I remember when you and your no-account brother wasn't nothin' but a couple little punks runnin' around town causin' mischief. You ain't foolin' nobody but yourself with this reverend business, Lloyd Graves. You ain't no preacher and you ain't no man of God. You just a heapin' up more punishment for yourself come judgment day."

Graves called back over the radio in response to Pritchard's rebuke. "Thy fate is sealed! Prepare yourself for the wrath of the righteous!"

With his rifle over his shoulder, David McDowell embraced his mother. "I guess he's coming here next."

Kate looked to Jack for orders but saw that he was in no position to lead. "Annie, Corey, we need to get Kelly upstairs so you can work on her there. We'll hold them off downstairs as long as we can."

Gavin took Jack by the shoulders. "We need you to stay with us. Annie is going to do all she can for Kelly, but for now, Rainey needs you to keep her safe."

Jack watched Annie and Corey lift his wife's listless body from the floor. His eyes moved to his daughter, then to Gavin. He gave a shallow nod. "Okay."

Vicky was obviously holding back the tears. She shouldered her rifle and glanced at her aunt. "Sam is …..?"

Kate gave her a quick hug. "I'm afraid so, honey. But he did what he did so we could get away. Let's make him proud.

"Jack, you, and Rainey go upstairs with your wife and hold them off. The rest of us will fight from down here."

Pritchard led Kate, Vicky, and Gavin to a downstairs bedroom which had a view of the front and back of the house from the doorway. "Y'all shoot from here. David McDowell, Warren, Pete, Ernest, and me will guard the rear. I'll put the menfolk from Laurel Ridge across the hall from you. All the women have guns, too. They'll be upstairs with the Russos."

Kate nodded. "How many do you think there are?"

Pritchard held his rifle and stroked his beard. "Hard to say. If there was five in each vehicle I reckon that'd make about a hundred. Might a done killed twenty or thirty of 'em."

Kate hated the odds. Her group was slowly getting picked apart.

Stanley Hess nodded at Kate when he limped down the hall with his rifle. He was followed by Wes Holloway and Marshall Yates.

"Kate, Gavin, Vicky, good to see you. Sorry the circumstances are so dire." Wes waved as he went into the room across the hall.

Kate forced a smile, knowing that soon she'd likely be reunited with Sam and Terry. She stood in the doorway, positioning her rifle to shoot toward the front. Gavin aimed toward the back of the house. Vicky knelt on one knee below Kate, also ready to fire forward.

A hail of bullets pounded the front door like

metal rain, some of the rounds piercing the door. Kate ducked behind the cover of the bedroom door frame until the shooting subsided. Next, the door flew open and Graves' men came pouring in like a flood. Kate and the others opened fire cutting down the first wave of intruders, but more kept coming, crawling like a plague of locusts over their fallen comrades.

"I'm out! Cover me!" Vicky struggled to change magazines.

Kate slowed her rate of fire so she wouldn't run out until Vicky had reloaded. "They're closing in on us, hurry, Vicky!"

Vicky resumed firing and Kate swapped her mag. Gavin grabbed them both by the shoulder and pulled them inside the bedroom. He slammed the door behind them. "Come on, we have to go."

"What are you doing, Gavin?" Kate began to open the door and re-engage.

"This battle was over before it started. It's going to be an absolute slaughter. We need to escape out the window." Gavin shoved a large desk in front of the door and opened the window.

"And abandon our friends?" Vicky's face was contorted with fear and grief.

"They're already dead. We can't save them. But I might be able to get my wife and my niece to safety." Gavin tugged Kate's arm toward the window. "I don't see anyone on this side of the house. Run straight for the woods. I'll cover you and Vicky until you get across."

Kate knew he was right but still couldn't stand the thought of running out on the others. "Okay.

Vicky, you go first."

Vicky crawled out the window and Kate followed.

"Go now! Run!" Gavin screamed as he began taking shots at men who noticed the girls running across the yard.

Kate led the way and slid behind a thick tree trunk. "Come on, Gavin!"

Vicky looked back in horror at the window through which they'd just escaped. "They're coming in the room!"

"Hurry!" Kate coaxed.

Gavin sprinted toward the trees with gunfire biting at his feet. Kate shot back toward the window where two of Graves' men were shooting at Gavin.

Gavin tumbled to the ground as soon as he reached the tree line.

"Vicky, keep shooting!" Kate lunged toward her husband to help him up and into the cover of the forest. "Are you hit?"

He winced in pain. "Left arm."

Kate couldn't stand the thought of Gavin going unconscious again; not in this situation. She stuck her fingers in the bloody bullet hole of his shirt and tore away the material. She positioned her flashlight on the wound. "You're bleeding pretty heavily, but it looks like it just nicked you."

Rifle fire peppered their area. "Aunt Kate, you have to turn off that light. It's giving away our location!"

She nodded and complied with Vicky's command. "Gavin, can you walk?"

"No, but I can run. Let's go!" He directed the

girls deeper into the woods.

Kate took cautious steps so not to trip over any branches. "Where are we going?"

"We'll take the perimeter trail to the top of the hill. We'll head over to Laurel Ridge and hide inside one of those houses for a day or two." Gavin looked back over his shoulder to make sure they weren't being followed.

"What if they search Laurel Ridge?" Kate asked.

"One of us will stay on watch at all times. We'll hear them coming. If they do, we'll be ready to bug out with a moment's notice. We'll disappear into the woods. But I doubt they'll go there. Laurel Ridge doesn't have enough supplies to make it worth their time. In fact, I don't think they have anything except the few buckets of food we gave them. We can live off those for a week or so. That will give us time to come up with a plan."

They finally reached the perimeter trail. Kate turned around to have one last look at the neighborhood that had been her home. In her heart, she felt that she was saying goodbye to everyone she knew. "Look, through the trees!" She pointed down the hill.

"Are those reinforcements?" Gavin watched in amazement at the stream of flashlights coming up the winding narrow road toward Pritchard's house. The beams scanned through the barren trees.

"Quick! Get down or they'll spot us." Kate pushed Vicky to the forest floor.

Gavin lay prone next to the girls. "Don't move a muscle." The ultra-bright lights scanned through the woods bouncing left and right directly over their heads.

Kate heard one of them speak into his radio.

"Second Lieutenant, bring your platoon up through the woods and flank the house from the right. Make sure you're taking precise shots. I think we've got civilians being attacked by a local gang. We don't want to accidentally hurt the people we're trying to help."

"That's not the Badger Creek Gang!" Vicky whispered.

"It's the military." Kate remained still.

Gunfire was exchanged for several minutes between the military and the Badger Creek Gang. The soldiers moved closer and closer to Pritchard's house. Many of Graves' men escaped the house, fleeing into the woods.

"This guy is coming right at us!" Vicky took aim.

Gavin shoved the barrel of her rifle to the ground. "No! You'll give away our position."

"We can't just let him get away!" Vicky protested.

Kate watched the man. He was headed straight in her direction with no clue that they were in his path. He stopped just short of Kate and looked down in absolute surprise. She grabbed his ankle and jerked his foot out from beneath him. He fell to the ground on his back. Kate jumped on his chest, put one arm around the back of his neck and slid her other arm beneath his. Using her bicep, she pushed his arm over his throat and held it there with her head. Moving like a crab, she crawled over the man's torso in the opposite direction of where she was holding his head and rotated away from him. With each inch that she moved, the pressure on the man's neck grew tighter and tighter. She felt him go limp and she sat up.

Gavin drew his knife and slit the man's throat. He wiped the blood from the knife on the man's jacket and put the knife back in his pocket.

Vicky turned away from the gruesome sight.

The gunfire gradually died off. Kate, Gavin, and Vicky continued to watch from concealment.

Pritchard and Jack emerged from the house with their hands up and their weapons hanging by their slings.

"Gentlemen, keep your hands up. Step forward and the sergeant will remove your weapons." A man in an Army uniform motioned for them to approach.

"We're residents of the neighborhood. My ID, which lists my address as being on this street, is in my pocket. We were attacked." Jack walked slowly toward the man giving the orders.

"Okay, I'll check that out, and you'll be free to go." The man went into Jack's pocket.

"What about our weapons? Will we get those back?" Jack kept his hands up while the man inspected his ID.

"You can put your hands down." The man handed Jack's wallet back to him. "We'll be providing security from now on. DC has chosen Asheville as one of the major reconstruction projects. The Army will be taking control of a fifty-mile perimeter around Asheville. The Army Corp of Engineers will be re-establishing electrical service in Asheville, then the surrounding areas."

Pritchard objected to losing his rifle. "I appreciate you boys comin' along when you did, but you can't be everwhere at once. We need to be able to fend for ourselves. These Badger Creek fellas is meaner than a nest of pit vipers. A heap of 'em took off through the woods when you boys showed up."

"We'll handle them, sir." The man inspected Pritchard's ID and gave it back to him.

Kate whispered, "We need to stash these guns before we come out."

"Agreed." Gavin gradually got up from the ground and backed toward the perimeter trail.

"How about that downed tree by the Smiths'?" Kate asked.

He nodded and signaled for Vicky and Kate to slowly lead the way. "I think that's the place."

Vicky motioned toward the dead man. "He has weapons."

"Get them, too," Kate said.

Quietly, Kate, Gavin, and Vicky slipped through the woods and stowed the rifles, handguns, and magazines in the shallow ditch made by the fallen tree. They raked a thin layer of leaves over the guns to hide them from view. Then, they walked back toward Pritchard's house.

One of the soldiers spotted them. "Hands up! Come on out of there."

They did as they'd been instructed. "We live here. We were attacked," Kate said.

"Okay, let's see some ID."

She replied, "We just moved here after the crisis.

But the other residents can verify that we live here."

"Vicky! You made it!" David McDowell came running toward her. He embraced her and held her tight.

The soldier nodded at Kate. "Okay, I guess you guys are alright. You didn't have any weapons?"

"Ran out of ammo and had to run." Gavin held his palms up.

"Okay." The soldier looked at Gavin's wound. "We have a medical tent set up down by the entrance gate. You should have that cleaned up."

"Thanks, I'll take you up on that."

"Do you want me to go with you?" Kate inquired.

"No. Go check on everyone else." Gavin put his good arm around her neck and pulled her in for a tender kiss. "I'm sorry about Sam and everyone else who didn't make it, but I'm glad you're still around."

The adrenaline which had been keeping Kate going was fading fast, making room for a wave of sorrow to come gushing in. "Me, too."

"See you soon." Gavin started down the drive.

Kate looked at David comforting Vicky. Her niece seemed to be in good hands, so she walked into Pritchard's house. Inside was a display of carnage unlike Kate had ever seen. She'd witnessed her brother's death, been in multiple shootouts, taken the lives of many, and endured her own home being turned into a bloody mortuary. Yet, she was unprepared for what her eyes beheld. Bodies were stacked up in piles, Pritchard's floors were crimson red and sopping wet. Some of the corpses she recognized but most she did not. She found Pritchard standing in his kitchen surveying the remains left behind by the butchery. "Where's Jack?"

"Upstairs, with his youngin." Pritchard didn't look up.

"Rainey is okay?"

"Okay ain't the word for it, but naw, I don't reckon she got shot."

"What about Kelly? Did she make it?"

"Nope; 'bout all of 'em's dead." He looked up. "What about Gavin and the girl?"

"They're okay."

Pritchard's eyes were filling up with tears. "The hand of the Lord saved you, Gavin, and the girl. Me, too, I reckon. Them what was in the back of the house with me is all dead, the men from Laurel Ridge, too."

"What about the people on the second floor?"

"Them devils went up there. Killed Corey and a bunch more of 'em." Pritchard looked up and counted off names on his fingers. "Jack, Rainey, Kim Sweeny, Judy Hess, Annie Cobb, and her little boy, David and Amanda McDowell. They stuffed Rita Dean back in the closet to hide her before the fightin' commenced. Them's the only one who survived, I reckon."

Kate couldn't even remember how many of her friends and neighbors who were no longer among the living, according to Pritchard's list. She watched as soldiers marched past, carrying the bodies of the dead. The commanding officer came up to her and Pritchard. "I know this is a hard thing to ask, but it's necessary. We can make an educated guess about which side each of the dead were on, but it would be better if one of you could make positive identifications of the residents."

"I'll do it." The lines around Pritchard's eyes showed his grief. He followed the officer out the door.

Kate traversed the open grave, careful not to step on any of the dead, but eager to get out of the house. The first light of dawn was glowing over the mountains. The sun would soon be warming the frigid night air.

Kate walked back to her own cabin where other soldiers were carrying out more of the dead. She readied herself for what she knew awaited her. She ascended the porch stairs and stepped across the bodies of two intruders. She looked down the hallway.

There on the floor, slumped up against the wall was Sam. Don lay face down in a pool of blood only three feet away. Kate covered her mouth in dread. The soldiers had already taken their rifles and stripped off their tactical vests. Her nephew looked so peaceful.

Two soldiers came in and started to pick up Sam. Tears streamed down Kate's face. "That's my nephew. Could you bring him upstairs and put him on the bed instead of taking him outside with the others?"

One soldier looked at the other. The second soldier nodded. "Sure. Just show us where."

Kate led the way upstairs to her room. The soldiers put Sam on her bed and left her alone to mourn. She pulled up a chair next to the bed and took his hand. "We're going to miss you, buddy— especially Vicky. But we all made it out alive, thanks to your valiant sacrifice. And I'll make sure it was not in vain. We'll give ourselves some time to grieve, we'll say goodbye to you and all the others, then we'll pick ourselves up and move on. But we'll never forget you, and we'll always remember what you did for us."

She turned to see Vicky and David standing behind her. Vicky dried her eyes with the sleeve of her shirt. She knelt by the bedside and stroked Sam's lifeless arm. "Ditto."

Kate pulled Vicky's head gently to her chest. She kissed the top of her soft hair. "We'll get through this. We have to, for Sam."

DON'T PANIC!

Inevitably, books like this will wake folks up to the need to be prepared, or cause those of us who are already prepared to take inventory of our preparations. New preppers can find the task of getting prepared for an economic collapse, EMP, or societal breakdown to be a source of great anxiety. It shouldn't be. By following an organized plan and setting a goal of getting a little more prepared each day, you can do it.

I always try to include a few prepper tips in my novels, but they're fiction and not a comprehensive plan to get prepared. Now that you're motivated to start prepping, the last thing I want to do is leave you frustrated, not knowing what to do next. So I'd like to offer you a free PDF copy of *The Seven Step Survival Plan.*

For the new prepper, *The Seven Step Survival Plan* provides a blueprint that prioritizes the different aspects of preparedness and breaks them down into achievable goals. For seasoned preppers who often get overweight in one particular area of preparedness, *The Seven Step Survival Plan* provides basic guidelines to help keep their plan in balance, and ensures they're not missing any critical segments of a well-adjusted survival strategy.

To get your **FREE** copy of *The Seven Step Survival Plan*, go to **PrepperRecon.com** and click the FREE PDF banner, just below the menu bar, at the top of the home page.

Thank you for reading *Cyber Armageddon, Book One: Rise of the Locusts*

Reviews are the best way to help get the book noticed. If you liked the book, please take a moment to leave a five-star review on Amazon and Goodreads.

I love hearing from readers! So whether it's to say you enjoyed the book, to point out a typo that we missed, or asked to be notified when new books are released, drop me a line.
prepperrecon@gmail.com

Stay tuned to **PrepperRecon.com** for the latest news about my upcoming books.

If you've enjoyed *Rise of the Locusts*, you'll love my end-times thriller series, *The Days of Noah*

In an off-site CIA facility outside of Langley, rookie analyst Everett Carroll discovers he's not being told the whole truth. He's instructed to disregard troubling information uncovered by his research. Everett ignores his directive and keeps digging. What he finds goes against everything he's been taught to believe. Unfortunately, his curiosity doesn't escape the attention of his superiors, and it may cost him his life.

Meanwhile, Tennessee public school teacher, Noah Parker, like many in the United States, has been asleep at the wheel. During his complacency, the founding precepts of America have been systematically destroyed by a conspiracy that dates back hundreds of years.

Cassandra Parker, Noah's wife, has diligently followed end-times prophecy and the shifting tide against freedom in America. Noah has tried to avoid the subject, but when charges are filed against him for deviating from the approved curriculum in his school, he quickly understands the seriousness of the situation. The signs can no longer be ignored, and Noah is forced to prepare for the cataclysmic period of financial and political upheaval ahead.

Watch through the eyes of Noah Parker and Everett Carroll as the world descends into chaos, a global empire takes shape, ancient writings are fulfilled, and the last days fall upon the once-great United States of America.

If you have an affinity for the prophetic don't miss my EMP survival series, *Seven Cows, Ugly and Gaunt*

In *Book One: Behold Darkness and Sorrow*, Daniel Walker begins having prophetic dreams about the judgment coming upon America for rejecting God. Through one of his dreams, Daniel learns of an imminent threat of an EMP attack which will wipe out America's electric grid and most all computerized devices, sending the country into a technological dark age.

Living in a nation where all life-sustaining systems of support are completely dependent on electricity and computers, the odds of survival are dismal. Municipal water services, retail food distribution, police, fire, EMS and all emergency services will come to a screeching halt.

If they want to live, Daniel and his friends must focus on faith, wits, and preparation to be ready . . . before the lights go out.

You'll also enjoy my series about the coming civil war in America, *Ava's Crucible*

The deck is stacked against twenty-nine-year-old Ava. She's a fighter, but she's got trust issues and doesn't always make the best decisions. Her personal complications aren't without merit, but America is on the verge of a second civil war, and Ava must pull it together if she wants to survive.

The tentacles of the deep state have infiltrated every facet of American culture. The public education system, entertainment industry, and mainstream media have all been hijacked by a shadow government intent on fomenting a communist revolution in the United States. The antagonistic message of this agenda has poisoned the minds of America's youth who are convinced that capitalism and conservatism are responsible for all the ills of the world. Violent protest, widespread destruction, and politicians who insist on letting the disassociated vent their rage will bring America to her knees, threatening to decapitate the laws, principles, and values on which the country was founded. The revolution has been well-planned, but the socialists may have underestimated America's true patriots who refuse to give up without a fight.

ABOUT THE AUTHOR

Mark Goodwin holds a degree in accounting and monitors macroeconomic conditions to stay up-to-date with the ongoing global meltdown. He is an avid student of the Holy Bible and spends several hours every week devoted to the study of Scripture and the prophecies contained therein. The troubling trends in the moral, social, political, and financial landscapes have prompted Mark to conduct extensive research within the arena of preparedness. He weaves his knowledge of biblical prophecy, economics, politics, prepping, and survival into an action-packed tapestry of post-apocalyptic fiction. Having been a sinner saved by grace himself, the story of redemption is a prominent theme in all of Mark's writings.

"He brought me up also out of an horrible pit, out of the miry clay, and set my feet upon a rock, and established my goings." Psalm 40:2

Made in the USA
Columbia, SC
14 December 2020

Medical School:
The Unwritten Curriculum

2017 Edition

organizations, companies, and URL links out of our own interest and potential educational benefit to the readers.

LEGAL

Table of Contents

Welcome,

Thank you for choosing this book. The author and contributors are graduates of US undergraduate universities and competitive US medical schools, having firsthand experience navigating through the admissions system for medical school and residency.

Medical school admissions have significantly changed over time, and the approach taken to evaluate and choose applicants involves a broad scope of an applicant's life experiences far beyond their GPA, MCAT score, and college education. Having extensive extra-curricular experiences shadowing physicians, performing research, tutoring, volunteering, and even having other graduate degrees are quickly becoming essential for a successful medical school application.

Succeeding in medical school and securing a residency position is just as a competitive and complicated process. To be successful, residency applicants need to have solid grades in the fundamental science classes, have aced their clinical rotations and boards, and secured strong letters of recommendation.

This book was written with the purpose of helping pre-medical and medical students attempting to navigate and succeed in the overwhelming and complicated process of preparing and applying to medical school and then residency. This book provides a timeline outlining how a student should approach the medical school admissions process and covers commonly asked questions and essential topics, including the importance of undergraduate majors, GPAs, MCAT scores, extra-curricular activities, personal statements, obtaining letters of recommendation, interviewing, and beyond.

In this book, I've attempted to shed light on many aspects of the admissions process while giving the reader essential tips learned through my own journey in college, medical school and residency. A large part of this book is also serves as an introduction to medical school with tips on how to succeed. There is also a mini-medical school section where I review interesting cases/pathology, the basics of medical imaging, laboratory values and note writing and presentation highlights.

Visit the website www.premedadvisor.net for even more information.

Wishing you the best in your journey ahead.

AJ, M.D.

Why Medicine?

Before embarking on a career in medicine, the single most important question you need to ask yourself prior to applying to medical school is *"Why Medicine?"* This question may seem simple at first, but needs to be examined on multiple deeper levels. The answer to this question should constantly evolve and become more defined with time and experience. This question will also almost definitely come up on nearly every medical school interview, and your answer may be a deciding factor in whether you are admitted to medical school or not.

The decision to pursue a career in medicine will be one of the biggest decisions in your life, involving years of studying and preparation, as well as major financial sacrifices for you and your family. Being confident and passionate in your decision to pursue medicine is essential. Deciding to switch careers as a practicing physician is often costly and difficult, so your answer this question will define your commitment to the field.

Stepping back, this question is really asking what experiences in your life have led you to make this choice. If you ask yourself this question when you're first starting college, you probably won't have a well-defined or thought-out answer yet, and in all honesty, you shouldn't. The way you structure your undergraduate years and the activities you choose to involve yourself in will hopefully help you develop a well constructed answer to this question by the time you apply to medical school.

In some cases, students discover that medicine is not their real passion, and many pursue other careers like nursing, dentistry, business, law, computer science, or engineering. Other students are passionate about medicine, but struggle through the admissions process due to academic issues or minimal experiences in medicine; some never get an admissions offer and have to look into other careers.

A common answer I hear to the question of *"Why Medicine?"* from students with little experience in the medical world is "I want to help people." While this is an admirable answer and goal for any individual, this is considered a weak and poorly thought out answer from the perspective of those on admissions committees. Many different careers both in and outside of medicine offer individuals the opportunity to help people in need or make significant positive changes to the world.

Why a career as a physician over that of becoming a nurse, dentist, teacher, police officer, engineer, etc.? Some of the most significant changes to our daily lives have recently come from the tech and start-up industry, so you must ask yourself why being a physician over these other potential career paths. This is a question everyone should have a unique answer for and it should encompass and summarize the influences of multiple life experiences.

For many, medicine provides a unique opportunity to combine multiple interests into one career. Many physicians are passionate about science including anatomy, physiology, pathology and pharmacology and also enjoy applying their scientific interests in a way that positively affects the health of individuals in their community.

Medicine is unique in the responsibility that comes with the position of a physician, and the countless interactions one will have with patients and their families. For some, personal experiences with illness fostered a passion for medicine, and for others providing care to impoverished communities abroad is a major influence. Each individual has unique experiences driving their passion for medicine.

11

There are also many benefits to pursuing a career as physician. Doctors often have very reliable job security, and there is a need for physicians throughout the world. Physicians are often well-regarded members of their communities with a unique skill set that is essential regardless of economic stability or turmoil. Such a career also provides many with great job satisfaction, knowing their work contributes to the good of their patients and community.

As you begin your pursuit of medicine, keep these things in mind, and continue to question and develop the foundation driving your passion for becoming a physician. Here are some reasons why I chose medicine:

- I was always interested in pursuing a career that was science based and could be applied practically into a fulfilling career.
- I wanted to pursue a career that would be intellectually stimulating and worthwhile.
- I enjoy medicine, as it is a constantly evolving, dynamic field.
- I wanted a career where enhancing others live and caring for patients would be a priority.
- The ability to give back to the people of the community is gratifying.
- I find the study of anatomy, physiology, pathology and pharmacology worthy of lifelong study.
- My personal experiences with illness motivated me to succeed.
- Medicine has provided me with a career that I can be proud of.

If you spend enough time on the Internet you'll eventually come across several popular forums that premeds and med students use. While many of these forums are useful, I've noticed that they are also extensively filled with misinformation. I've also found a significant pessimistic attitude towards medicine that up and coming students need to be wary of. On the other extreme, several popular book authors exaggerate their positive experiences in medicine and their experiences are obviously sensationalized. These authors do a disservice to students and really don't offer a realistic perspective into the medical world.

While you read other resources, here are some things to keep in mind. No career is perfect, and any profession you choose will have its ups and downs and you will have to make significant sacrifices to be successful in any field. Medicine is not immune to this, and it's no secret that to be a successful physician, you'll need to make significant sacrifices to survive the process of college, medical school, residency and fellowship, and finally, the stresses of being a practicing doctor.

I have found medicine to be worthy of the sacrifice and I could not be happier with my choice. That being said, getting to this point was filled with stress, long sleepless nights, scary decisions and serious dedication, but it was definitely worth it. Don't allow yourself to get overly influenced by the extensive pessimistic attitudes about medicine. If you plan things out right, medicine has the potential to be one of the best decisions you'll ever make.

Remember that the spectrum of medicine is wide, and there are dozens of specialties, all with different expectations and overall happiness levels. The life of a surgeon is very different from that of a pathologist or pediatrician.

Choosing a specialty that fits your personality and expectations will likely affect your future happiness level more than anything else.

General Approach: Undergraduate Years

Whether you are just starting out at your undergraduate university, or you've been at school for a few years, the general principles of applying to medical school outlined below will apply to you. If you started undergrad relatively recently, then you have a good amount of time to implement the tips I'll describe, regarding everything from choosing a major to being mindful of your GPA/science GPA and how to schedule extra-curricular activities.

College is an incredibly exciting time that will help you grow and mature in fundamental ways. You'll learn a huge amount of new information academically, and you'll grow significantly as a person. You'll also have to make many more important decisions on your own, such as deciding what major to pursue, deciding on a career, and learning to live relatively independently. Juggling these new responsibilities with the new academic expectations of college can be overwhelming for some. Here are my suggestions for getting started and planning ahead.

Freshman Year

As you start college, you'll likely be taking introductory courses into the basic sciences including biology, chemistry and physics. You will also likely take other required degree introductory courses, including some type of math class such as Calculus. Although the course load this first year may seem boring and cumbersome, the above also serve as pre-requisite courses for medical school and are extremely important to your application. You need to have one primary academic objective in the first semester, and that should be to settle in to an effective study/lecture routine and *ace these classes*. Learn where the best place on campus is to study, whether it's in your dorm, a coffee shop, or in the library and train yourself to go there regularly.

It's important to quickly figure out the most effective way for you to study and do well. See my personal recommendation further on in the book regarding high volume studying. Also be very wary of doing so called "study groups" with your friends. 99% of the time these become completely useless, especially if you just sit around and chat or gossip the whole time. The best way to utilize group study sessions is after you gain a good understanding of the material yourself, and then use the sessions to quiz each other on the material for extra-reinforcement.

The first semester will also be a good time to start getting involved in different extracurricular organizations and groups throughout campus. Most colleges/universities will have student organizations and fairs around the time of orientation. This is a great opportunity to get out there and see what's available as well as meet like-minded people. Make sure to swing by the premed office and join any premed society too. This can be a good resource to stay on track and also meet other fellow comrades embarking on the medicine journey. Its not too early to start, so go get involved. I tended to avoid any societies that required a paid membership, as I saw no benefit to these programs. Usually, the local premed club is good enough.

To Greek, or not to Greek? If it's a house that's all about not studying and doing well academically, I say that it's probably best not to. However, there are fraternities/sororities with academic focuses and GPA requirements. Many students are able to find a great social circle this way and feel having that sense of community decreases overall stress of venturing out into adulthood. This can also be a good way to be involved in philanthropic activities in the community.

If you are planning on volunteering at the nearby hospital, you'll need to look into applying for a volunteer spot early. Every year hospitals get tons applications from starry-eyed students armed with an eager smile and a hop in their step that all want to be candy stripers. This process can take several months (up to 8 months for me), so it's best to get your application in by the fall.

One last great habit you should continue/acquire is regular exercise. Not only is it good for your physical health, exercise will overall improve your mental well-being, release endorphins and all that. Take advantage of the student rec center. Once you're out of school and responsible to pay for a gym/health club, you'll miss the free access to a gym. Intramural sports are a fun way to get exercise and meet people if you don't fancy going to the gym, and there's a variety of available sports including soccer, dodge ball, and basketball. Come on, who wouldn't want to join the Quidditch team?

On a related health note, learn to eat a healthy, balanced diet. This can seem difficult on a student income, but it is important. Having a well balanced diet will make your body and brain function better and you will feel better overall on those long study days. Additionally, follow good sleep hygiene, so you don't become over-dependent on caffeine. Life will seem hectic if you are doing all the above, but there really is time for it all. It's just about time management. Okay, you have a game plan for the first year, now go do it.

Freshman Checklist

- Register for classes and go to them. Do well in all classes, but particularly in any medical school pre-requisites.
- Figure out your best study method, consider my study tips and see if they work for you.

- Go to TA sessions and professor office hours. This is essential for getting good letters of recommendation.
- Join the local Premed society and stop by the premed office.
- Join student organizations.
- Apply to volunteer at the local hospital or clinics.
- Get into a good workout routine and eat well.

Freshman Summer

Once you get through freshmen year, you have your first college summer ahead of you. Now although you may be tempted to spend your summer sleeping in until noon and watching TV (which I did quite a bit of), realize that summer is a perfect time to get key components of your application taken care of such as research and volunteering/shadowing. Throughout the preceding year, keep your ears open for professors looking for students to help on research projects and approach them in the spring to get a spot in their lab/group. If you can get a project going by late spring (this can take a while), you'll be able to dedicate quality time throughout the summer. Additionally, if you start early on a project you may be able to develop it enough to publish it (BIG plus) before you graduate.

Summer should also be used to retake any courses you need to. If they are pre-requisite courses, this should definitely be a priority. If you are feeling motivated, look into taking the next level of pre-requisites. Keep in mind, though, summer classes consist of the same amount of material as a regular course, but crammed into either a 1 or 2-month period. Be prepared to dedicate some serious time, particularly for science courses that require lab hours. Time you put in now is time that will be saved later, freeing up time in your junior and senior years for fun electives, project completions, study abroad programs and travel.

17

Choosing a Major

Good news - you can pick any college major you want and still go to medical school. The only requirement is that you complete a set of pre-requisite courses in the sciences and social sciences. For most people completing a science degree, these courses will likely be a part of your degree plan. For others, this may mean extra classes and perhaps even extra semester(s). Whatever your major is, you are going to want A's in all your pre-requisite courses, period.

It's your choice, but choose a major and a course load that you know you can do well in. Don't think you have to get a biochemistry or biomedical engineering degree to get accepted into medical school (unless you really want to). These "impressive" degree plans will not help you while you are applying if your grades suffer due to an extremely difficult workload. Also, since practicing medicine requires the natural ability to express and feel human compassion and empathy, many people feel a degree in the social sciences can be very advantageous. A non-traditional major can also help you stand out in a sea of biology majors with a perfect 4.0 GPA (you'll be surprised how many of those are out there).

Here's another piece of advice as you make your way through the curriculum needed to apply to medical school. Be active in your classes. That means attend class, ask questions if you don't understand something, visit your professor's office hours, and go to the TA sessions. Your professors will appreciate it. They are human too and like it when students show interest in the subject matter. Also, you will find that doing these things will make it easier to do well in the courses and this is also a good way to get to know your professors (and for them to get to know you), which will come in very handy when its time to ask for letters of recommendation. This is particularly important at larger universities where your class sizes are >200.

Professors of big science classes often get flooded with requests for letters of recommendation when it comes time to apply for graduate school, so unless you've made the effort to get to know them personally, you really can't expect much more than a generic letter of recommendation. As an example, I often went to office hours during my physics course during the year and got to know my professor pretty well, as these groups were usually pretty small. The following year I decided to tutor student athletes in the same physics course, and had the opportunity to engage with the professor on a regular basis. By the time I asked for a letter of recommendation, he had known me for several years, as a student and tutor for his classes.

So my advice is to pursue a major that you're genuinely interested in. This can be anything from psychology, English to aeronautical engineering (people in my med school classes had these majors). As long as you complete the pre-requisite courses for medical school, which you can work into your schedule, then this can even be advantageous to you as an applicant, as you bring a non-traditional skill set to the medical field.

You should also pursue a major that you're interested in because if you're in a situation where you don't get into medical school, you'll still be secure with a major that you are passionate about and can pursue a career in. It's always wise to have a back-up plan, as nothing is guaranteed in medical school (or any graduate school) admissions process.

Obviously, if you are passionate about science then definitely pursue a science degree and consider anything from Biology, Chemistry, Biochemistry, to Bioengineering or other interesting majors. I personally was very interested in the science programs at my college, and ended up majoring in Microbiology. I enjoyed the smaller class sizes, the interesting laboratory projects I was involved with and the relevance of the topic to my medical school pursuit.

Importance of the Pre-requisites and the *"Science GPA"*

The importance of your undergraduate GPA cannot be overstated and may be the single most important component of your application to medical school. Do your best to maintain a strong GPA, and strive for a GPA of 3.5 or better. Definitely strive to maintain as close to a 4.0 GPA in the pre-requisite science classes as you can. If your GPA does fall below this, it doesn't spell the end for your career ambitions, as admissions committees also look at aspects other than your GPA, and look favorably at a strong trend in an improving GPA. Don't forget that schools also look at your *"Science GPA"* which is an average of the science courses you'll take to be considered for admissions, and serves as a way to compare your academic performance alongside students from other universities aside from the MCAT.

Let's say you've messed up in one of your pre-requisite classes and got a D (too much partying, huh)? What should you do? It's generally recommended that you retake the course if you can. This only works if you are being realistic about doing better the second go around. That means some more self-reflection and dedication to studying. It usually boils down to too many external distractions (parties, sports, clubs, etc.). If you are really serious about applying and being admitted to medical school, then you're going to need to cut the distractions and get on with it. Maybe that means you aren't going to Burning Man this year, but hey, you'll eventually get an MD for it.

Another option you may consider is retaking the courses at a local community college. Many will offer night classes and tend to be substantially cheaper than a university. Some will also point out that they may even be easier (not sure about this one, maybe it's smaller class sizes and more individual attention from the professor). You will definitely want to discuss with your school pre-medical advisor regarding your best options.

If you can do well the first go around, you will save yourself a great deal of hassle and stress later on. However, don't get too discouraged if you have to retake some courses to improve your GPA. The important thing is to continue to show a strong improving trend in your GPA. This is essential. The rigors of the medical curriculum are far beyond that of undergraduate courses, and admissions committees want to be sure that you'll be able to handle the workload once you're admitted. This is your chance to prove it to them.

Also, its important to familiarize yourself with the website run by the AAMC® (Association of American Medical College) which you will need to use for your application process.

Most medical schools require a set of pre-requisite courses, which generally include the following courses:

- A full undergraduate year of biology
- A full undergraduate year of chemistry
- A full undergraduate year of organic chemistry
- A full undergraduate year of English
- Often required (biochemistry, mathematics, statistics, several years of humanities studies) – depending on the individual school

"High Volume Learning"

An essential element to being successful in college is adapting and being able to mentally absorb and retain large amounts of information. I like to call this method of learning "*HVL*" or "*High Volume Learning.*" Like the transition from high school to college, the transition from college to medical school will be significant as far as expectations go for the amount of material tested on exams. This will also dramatically increase in residency, when you are studying for your board examinations.

It took me a while to develop study methods that were both effective and efficient, which was one of the single best skills I learned in college. Through trial and error I explored all types of memorization techniques, but found several key factors that were essential to doing well and retaining information successfully. The first was the importance of repetition. I found that the more I was able to review material, the better I did. This seems pretty obvious, but being able to do this effectively is important. Another important component in studying and repitition is separating study blocks with time and sleep.

My approach for most classes was as follows. The first thing I did was to quickly skim whatever chapter or set of notes I was planning on studying. I didn't try and memorize anything initially. Instead, by quickly skimming the entirety of the material, this would allow my brain to develop an overview and begin to compartmentalize the topics. You can imagine that by skimming and seeing the main topics you're planning on studying, your brain begins to form new pathways and compartments under which you'll add details to later. This part of studying is essential. One of the biggest mistakes I initially made was to try to start memorizing details right away, without initially forming this framework. This is a huge mistake that makes life and studying harder than it has to be. Once I started doing this essential pre-study step, the efficiency and productivity of my studying improved.

After reviewing all my material quickly, I then take some time away from the material. On the next round through, I get a highlighter and read through all my notes/chapters again, but now reading intently for details, not necessarily trying to memorize everything. I just allow whatever material sticks naturally to stick. I highlight things I think will be tested or important concepts, but not memorize them yet. Once I finish this process, I usually take a break from the material for a day and sleep on what I've read. I've noticed that sleeping after studying is essential and really helps the brain organize and remember material.

My next time through the material is where I do a large part of my preparation for my high volume learning. Once again, I go through all the study material/notes intently, focusing on the details and things I outlined the day before. This time around though, I make a notecard for each fact or concept that I don't know cold from the day before and/or jot down notes or drawings on a paper that I want to review again. This takes significant time, but will really pay off for you soon. You have to invest this time now to make studying less painful as the test nears.

This is usually the longest part of my studying process. I've actually found making notecards on my phone notecard app or computer to be the fastest way of preparing my study materials and making them easily accessible wherever I might be. Once you finish going through and making your notecards, you should again take a break from studying, take a nap/sleep a night before studying your notecards.

A couple days before an upcoming big test is when I start going through my notecards and notes I jotted down (for the big classes there can be 100's of notecards). At this point, I'm trying to memorize each detail, and I found the best way to do this is to go through them in small batches. I aim to go through all my notecards a few dozen times for continued reinforcement of the material.

Anytime I start feeling tired during this process I don't fight the urge to sleep. I go and take a nap, as this is usually a sign from my brain that it needs time to process all the information I've been memorizing. I've found that fighting the urge to sleep or nap is very counterproductive and leads to wasted study time. Going along with what your body is telling you will greatly enhance your learning. There's a reason you're tired, so don't ignore it and give your brain what it wants.

Right before any big test I attempt to go through all my notecards/notes quickly one more time, and study things that are very difficult to remember, like specific numbers, right before the test so that they are fresh in my head when I take the exam. This approach to test taking, especially in classes with very large amounts of material, seems to work well for me and may work for you. I suggest trying it out and see how you do.

Top 20 Tips For Pre-Medical Students

Looking back at college life now with the perspective of a resident, here are the top 20 tips every pre-medical student needs to know:

1. *College is great.* Period. Take advantage of all the opportunities you have as a student. This is a great time to explore your academic interests and take classes you are genuinely interested in and those you want to take for fun. You're unlikely to ever have another opportunity to explore all your interests like you do in college, so make the best of it. Try to learn as much as you can, you'll be surprised by how much of what you learn in college will be applicable later in life when you least expect it.

2. Don't forget the *importance of your GPA,* especially in your science classes. It can be very difficult to repair your GPA once its low, so remember, every grade counts. This should be your number one priority academically if you are serious on applying to medical school. Your GPA gets harder and harder to fix the longer you are in school, so it's essential to start out strong.

3. *The college/university you go to isn't as important as how well you do there.* Most of us went to state universities and ended up getting accepted to excellent medical schools. So don't think that by going to a state school you are somehow at a disadvantage to other students who went to Ivy League schools. Your performance and how you made the best of your academic opportunities will be the most important factor in the end.

4. Things you learn in college *will be relevant* even in medical school and residency.
   1. Biochemistry, psychology, microbiology etc., will all be studied again in the first two years of medical school.

2. Even classes like calculus and physics are relevant in your future. For instance, in diagnostic radiology residency, we are required to know physics and its applications to medical imaging. This involves re-learning the basics of atoms, protons, electrons, radiation, and even some aspects of quantum mechanics in order to understand MRI physics. These concepts are even tested on the medical boards for radiology. Never saw that coming!

5. *Never ever get into any legal trouble.* This may seem obvious, but it's surprising how many people don't realize the importance of this until its too late. These sorts of issues are often permanent and will put you at a severe disadvantage, as there are just too many applicants without any legal issues. Also, having legal issues shows schools you engage in risky or illegal behavior, and many schools will not want to risk limited class space on that kind of candidate. These issues will also cause you issues applying to other graduate programs and jobs in the future. Always think of the long-term consequences.

6. Use your time in college as an *opportunity to explore other career choices,* not just medicine (engineering, dentistry, business, etc.). I was asked on multiple interviews what other careers I considered and had experiences to back it up. Medicine is a great career, but there are many other gratifying careers out there that give you the opportunity to make a huge impact on the world (think about all the recent tech start-ups, etc.).

7. *The friends you make in college* will likely be your life-long friends.

8. *Enjoy your summers off* while you have them, make the most of this free time and consider traveling as much as possible. Don't forget that it is also a great time to start research projects, do volunteering or possible work a summer job.

9. *Pursue your other hobbies*. Don't sacrifice doing things you enjoy (like painting, the outdoors, fishing, etc.) as they are what make you a well-rounded person. Admissions committees will ask you about your hobbies and your non-academic interests so be sure to keep those going. It's what makes you, you.

10. *Set healthy, consistent habits and workout routines*. These will be essential to getting through medical school and staying well during times of high stress. The importance of this can't be overstated.

11. Try to accumulate as *little debt as possible* while in undergrad. The debt you'll accumulate during medical school may easily be well over $200-300,000, so do your best to get as many scholarships and pay off your debt while in school as best you can.

12. If the major you are pursuing doesn't include these classes, then think about taking some *classes on finance and business*. Many medical students and residents have significantly limited knowledge when it comes to these topics. Medical students have some of the largest amounts of debt, along with dental and other health professional students. Being educated in personal finance and business is a must now days, and starting to educate yourself in college will help you from making costly mistakes in the future.

13. If you can maintain good grades, try to *work some part-time jobs* while in college and during the summers. Medical schools want to know that you have practical job experience in the "real" world. I had a variety of part-time jobs, several non-science related, which I was asked about during both medical school and residency interviews. This also helps show that you are well-rounded individual and appreciate the work those do around you.

14. *Consider going overseas* for a semester or year during your undergraduate years. Many of my classmates took advantage of this opportunity, and where extremely happy

with their experiences. College is a time where you have a chance to take this unique opportunity, which will otherwise be very difficult to accomplish at any other point in your life. This will also exhibit your cultural diversity and will be a great once in a lifetime learning experience. It will also make a great topic of discussion for interviews.

15. Get involved in your school's *pre-med club.* Learn from the students ahead of you in the application process and be actively involved. If your school doesn't have a pre-med club, then start one.

16. *Be active at your university.* Pursue extra-curricular activities starting freshmen year, don't wait until junior/senior year when you realize you have few extra-curricular activities compared to other applicants. I describe this and give you ideas in more detail below. You want to show a long trend of volunteering and being active, you don't want to look like you rushed at the last minute to do some extra-curricular activities just for the sake of doing them.

17. *Network, network, network.* You'd be amazed at how successful (and how unsuccessful) the people you are friends with from college may end up becoming in non-medical careers. College is a great opportunity to network with people and be sure to stay in touch after graduating. You never know what opportunities, business or otherwise, may present themselves for you in the future.

18. *Consider pursuing a double major or getting a minor* in another field that interests you. For instance, I pursued a science degree for my major (microbiology), but was also genuinely very interested in learning more about psychology, which I decided to get a minor in. This also keeps more open for you in the future and shows a well-rounded education.

19. *Try to set aside savings.* If you are able to pay off your undergraduate debts, try to set aside savings for medical

school and residency. You'll want to minimize the amount of loans you take out, as interest rates on loans recently have been exceptionally high, over 6-7% for many student loans. To put that into perspective, if you have $200,000 in medical school debt at a 6.5% interest rate, that debt is accumulating at approximately $13,000 per year. OMG. You'll thank yourself later on for having set aside savings which can help pay off debt later on, especially during residency when you have to start making payments on a limited resident salary.

20. *Have a back-up plan.* There is no guarantee that you'll be admitted to medical school. I knew of people with MCAT scores and GPAs higher than mine who ended up getting rejected multiple years in a row, some of which ended up pursuing other careers. The admissions process to medical school is extremely complicated, and at many times subjective and confusing. Sometimes, it's flat out unfair. Even stellar students get rejected. You don't want to be caught at the end of the application cycle rejected without a plan for what to do the following year or two if your plan to re-apply. I was extremely fortunate, and got admitted my first go around. My plan was to continue on at my college, possibly pursuing a graduate level degree while continuing to do research. I was very fortunate to get accepted during my first application attempt, but many others weren't as fortunate. Having a back-up plan will be essential especially if you have plans to re-apply. Admissions committees will be very interested to know how you spent your year or two off, and they will expect major improvement in your application in any areas where you were weak. You may have to take more science courses to strengthen your science GPA, or you may pursue further graduate degrees, you might even start working in bio-tech or some other industry. In the event you don't get accepted the second or

third time around, planning ahead will keep you on track to re-apply or have a new career path.

Extracurricular Activities

Having a wide variety of extra-curricular activities that you have been involved with for long periods of time (years) is essential to a successful medical school admission. When planning out which extra-curricular activities to get involved with, you'll want to start early on in your undergraduate years, preferably freshman year.

Things to remember are that admissions committees will be looking at the extent of the time commitment you've put rather than just the pure number of hours. It's much better to volunteer at a hospital for 200 hours over the course of two years than to do so in the course of 2-3 weeks. This shows commitment and dedication over time. Also, it's important to start planning for these experiences early on, as there are often long waitlists to join the volunteer group at hospitals and you may expect to wait six months to a year before you can actually start logging volunteer hours.

One thing that was difficult for me was figuring out what activities/volunteer experiences to pursue. I wanted my experiences to be unique but also relevant to my application to medical school. So I compiled a list for you of different activities I, and others I know pursued. This should give you a good idea on how to get started. Some of my activities were not directly medically related but I felt that admissions committee members were happy to see applicants like myself pursuing non-medical extra-curricular activities, and mine went a long way with committee members.

When deciding on which volunteer/extracurricular activities to pursue, plan to dedicate at least 2-5 hours per week for each activity. Try to consistently go each week, and obviously its okay to skip during test weeks or finals weeks. Try to do several different activities at once, like volunteering one day a week and tutoring another day of the week. Here is a list of some of the extra-curricular activities I took part in.

Volunteering at the Local Hospital

Essentially every hospital I know of has a volunteer division. Doing hospital or clinic volunteer work is an absolute must for a successful medical school application. You will want to contact the volunteer department early in your undergrad career, preferably freshman year, as getting volunteering setup can take months if not a year at some hospitals. You will also want to do this long-term, over the course of years. I did approximately 4 hours of volunteering per week for approximately 3 years. My duties were relatively simple and included stocking supplies in the ER, assisting patients, assisting medical staff and running errands. I also volunteered at a clinic for two summers performing similar duties.

Tutoring On/Off Campus

During college, once I felt I had mastered basic biology, chemistry and physics, I started tutoring college athletes in these subjects at my undergraduate university. I thought this was a worthwhile activity for several reasons, first, it provided me with a small supplemental income. It also provided me experience teaching in subjects that I enjoyed learning about.

Activities like this show that you have a great understanding of the topics you're teaching, and you have the social skills necessary to teach other students successfully, which is extremely important in medicine. During my medical school interviews, I was actually asked about my tutoring experience quite a bit, and I felt it actually went a long way in getting an admissions offer. I felt that some of the committee members I interviewed with looked on this more favorably than much of my clinical and hospital volunteer work.

Teaching English

I participated in the international student group on campus, and served as an English teacher for students that were doing an exchange at my undergrad. This was great, as I got to meet students from different countries, work on my own time, and do this over the course of several years. This turned out to be a great topic of discussion during my interviews, especially about how I dealt with some of the language barriers and how this would be relevant to practicing medicine.

Scientific Research

I pursued a science major, so it was fairly easy for me to go to my advisor in college and ask for a list of professors that were interested in having students work in their lab. I ended up in a microbiology lab and worked there for several years, and even ended up getting an honors thesis out of it. This was also a great topic of conversation during my interviews. If possible, try to get involved in research, as it teaches you a completely different skill set that you don't learn from you classes including how to formulate a hypothesis and then using scientific methods and tools to reason and evaluate your hypothesis. You also learn a lot about scientific writing and gives you chance to publish your work and maybe even go to a scientific conference.

Try to get started on a project during your freshman or sophomore year, as some projects can take a year or more to complete. Your project does not have to be directly related to medicine. For instance, my research project spanned about two years and focused on marine microbes. All my interviewers found this very interesting and discussed it with me extensively.

Your goal should be to either get your research project published in a scientific journal, or to attend a scientific conference and present your research as a poster or as a presentations at a relevant scientific conference. Accomplishing this will go a long way in helping out your application.

The reality is that most medical school applicants will have quite a bit of research under their belt, so make this a priority as you set up your schedules and plan out your coursework. I allotted about 10-20 hours a week to my project depending on my class and testing schedule.

Work as a Scribe, Medical Assistant, CNA or EMT

A fairly popular undergraduate activity is to work as a scribe, usually with ER physicians at the local hospital. Working as a scribe usually entails working alongside physicians and helping them with documentation and note taking. This is a great opportunity, as you get to know physicians directly and actually get to be involved in patient care.

Usually these programs require students to attend and pass a training program. The benefits are huge, and include learning much of the medical terminology associated with medicine early on, and getting to know physicians personally, which is important down the road when you are looking for a physician to write you a letter of recommendation for medical school.

Other things you can strongly consider include getting certified as a medical assistant, CNA (certified nursing assistant) or EMT (emergency medical technician). Getting certified in these fields will allow you to go beyond just volunteering and actually be involved in patient care.

Many of these certifications can be completed in your extra time during college, or even during a summer break. You can then get a part time job during college and gain invaluable work/clinical experience that you just can't get as a volunteer. In my opinion, this would be the way to go if you have the time to complete a certification course and extra hours during the week to do some part time work.

Overseas Volunteering

Personally, I did not do any volunteering overseas, though I had many classmates that did. I don't think it's essential to do this, but having either study-abroad or volunteering experience overseas will definitely be beneficial. There are many different types of programs out there, and I would ask your local pre-medical advisor, which programs students at your university found to be the best.

I chose against doing any overseas volunteering because I found it difficult to find a reputable program through which to go with. I also found that there were ample interesting volunteer opportunities here at home, so I really didn't feel the need to pursue anything overseas. I would highly suggest looking into at least studying (as opposed to volunteering) overseas for a semester or so. Its important to show that you have a diverse cultural experience in your application, as the patients you'll be taking care of in the future will come from all sorts of backgrounds. By at least studying overseas for a semester, you'll gain insight into other cultures and ways of life that you might not have gotten otherwise, and admissions committees like to see that in applicants.

Club Involvement

You'll definitely want to show that you are active on campus. I joined the pre-med club and found it much more useful than I initially thought it would be. Pre-med clubs are helpful in that they help keep you on track with what other students are doing, and making sure you stick to the timelines and various deadlines when it comes to application time. Many pre-med clubs that have a medical school nearby will host alumni students to come back and visit and share their medical school experiences, which can be very insightful.

Learning from the experiences of older students helped me greatly, and I learned quite a bit about the state medical school there before even starting. These clubs also often have students who recently successfully got admitted to medical school, and they can be a great resource for the whole application process. Overall, this experience was extremely beneficial and I highly recommend getting involved, the earlier the better.

Sports/Hobbies

Being involved in collegiate and intramural sports is a major plus, not only for your health, but also for your application. Being active and engaged in multiple activities at school again shows that you are a well-rounded individual and that you can balance multiple different activities. Some very successful medical school applicants from my college were also student athletes and they attended top-level medical schools. Medical school admissions committees look very favorably upon students who can juggle the multiple responsibilities of being a student athlete and succeeding academically.

Be sure to keep up your hobbies throughout college as best you can. Medical school admissions committees want to see that you are a normal person too and that you have interests outside of academics and school. Whether it is sports, the outdoors, biking, painting, or whatever...be sure to keep it up. It might end up being a big topic of discussion you can relate to with an interviewer. From personal experience, I secured a fellowship position in a competitive sub-specialty through a common interest I shared with one of my interviewers.

Shadowing

Shadowing physicians during your undergraduate years is also considered an absolute must. It's very difficult to understand what a physician's job entails until you actually get the opportunity to shadow. You'll learn how incredibly varied the different specialties are, and how dramatically different the day-to-day work of each type of doctor is. You'll want to get involved shadowing as soon as you can, usually around your sophomore or junior year. Summer is also a great time to do some shadowing as well, since most students have a fairly flexible summer schedule.

To get started, your undergraduate pre-med advisor should have a list of local physicians that have a history of taking on local high school and college students for shadowing experiences. If you don't have a pre-med advisor, then ask local friends who may have parents that are physicians or nurses and can put you in contact with physicians who would be willing to take you along. You can also ask other students in your pre-med club to put you in touch with physicians they have shadowed.

Once you find someone who's willing to let you shadow, you'll likely have to take a HIPPA course for that particular hospital or clinic. I would aim to shadow for about half a day per week over the course of several months, or a summer break. This way, you don't overwhelm the doctor, and you are there long enough to learn quite a bit. You'll also need a letter of recommendation from a doctor, so remember to represent yourself well during your shadowing experience. I'll go over how to ask for a letter below.

What to Expect

As the name implies, shadowing involves quite a bit of observation. As a student, there is only so much you can do while shadowing. You should expect to meet the physician at the time you both decided on, and literally expect to be his or her "shadow." You'll go along with the doctor and see patients alongside him/her, go to surgeries, and follow them throughout the hospital. The experience is supposed to give you a glimpse into the daily life of a doctor. Many physicians will take the time to teach you the basics of a physical exam, show you interesting findings, and work to involve you as much as they can.

How to Dress

You should expect to dress in professional type clothing – by this I mean nice slacks, shoes and shirt and tie for the guys, and slacks or professional skirt or pants for the ladies. Remember, you are joining the physicians in their place of work, so you want to represent them well. Unless you are told otherwise, I would dress like this. Sometimes, you may accompany a surgeon or anesthesiologist to the operating room, and they may have you dress in scrubs at that time. There's generally no need to bring much else, no need for a stethoscope or notes when you are first starting out. Just observe and try to learn as much as possible.

What Questions Do I Ask?

You should generally reserve asking any questions until the patient encounter is over. Good questions include inquiring about the different types of conditions and diseases you are seeing, how the doctor comes up with a differential diagnosis, and then a final diagnosis. It's also fun to ask the doctor you're shadowing how they first got interested in medicine and how they came to practice where they do today. This will also give the doctor the opportunity to ask you how you became interested in medicine, and they'll have a chance to get to know you much better and hopefully lead to a great letter of recommendation.

Getting a Letter

Getting a letter from a physician will be essential to completing a strong medical school application. Your best chance to get a letter is usually from the doctors you shadowed during undergrad. You should put quite a bit of effort into demonstrating interest and impressing whomever you're shadowing.

When you ask for a letter you'll want to have several things prepared including your personal statement, CV and any other relevant things. Give your letter writer 3-6 months to finish their letter for you, as this can be a very time consuming process. See my suggestions for getting a good letter of recommendation as those general tips apply here.

The MCAT®

The Medical College Admissions Test® (MCAT® is a registered trademark of the AAMC®) is a standardized computer examination required of most US medical school applicants. It will primarily test the knowledge from your required medical school prerequisite courses including biology, general chemistry, organic chemistry, physics, sociology and social sciences.

The test is divided into 4 sections: Biological Science, Physical Science, Verbal reasoning, and the newer section, which includes Sociology/Psychology/Behavioral Sciences. Sounds scary? It is, and it can become the gigantic monster that haunts your nightmares, but just like anything else in this application process, proper preparation and a good game plan will go a long way to doing well on the MCAT.

Score Goals

Like everyone, you are probably asking yourself how high of a score you need to get to get into medical school. There's no definite cutoff, but averages for each school can give you a good idea of what to shoot for. Many medical schools offer up this information on their admissions websites, so it's wise to visit those and get a feel for what's competitive. Contrary to what a lot of students think, your MCAT score is not the single most important thing in your application, and plays a small but important component in the big picture. Don't get me wrong, its definitely important and the better you do, the easier it'll be to get interviews at schools you're interested in. Many schools are rumored to use MCAT scores as a filter, and there's probably some truth to that. Also, doing well on the MCAT will allow you to use the rest of your application to highlight what makes you special and sets you apart, as opposed to admissions committees being focused on why you got a subpar score.

The exact score you need to get an interview invitation and acceptance into medical school depends on multiple factors. The AAMC® (Association of American Medical Colleges®) has reported the 2013 MCAT scores for applicants/accepted for multiple demographic groups. This is a good guideline to start with as you create your plan of attack for the exam. I encourage you to take some time to get a feel for what is a good score and how your GPA affects your MCAT goal. You will soon realize that MCAT scores and GPA have an important relationship: The lower your GPA is, the higher your MCAT aim should be.

When to Schedule the Test

You must register for your selected test date within an allotted time several months in advance. Earlier registrants get a discount. When you take the MCAT is entirely up to you. Most people take it in the late spring/early summer of the year they are applying. This timeframe is favorable as it allows for the remaining summer to be used concentrating on the rest of the AMCAS® (a registered trademark of the AAMC) application as well as ensuring the MCAT score report is available at the time of application submission.

Also, in the event your score is undesirable, you will have time to retake the test without sacrificing application submission time. Be aware, test dates can fill up fast so plan ahead so that you don't miss out on the application cycle and so that you give yourself enough prep time.

How to Choose Prep Materials

Let me insert a bit of a disclaimer before I discuss prep material. The most ideal way to prepare for the MCAT is to actually learn the material in your pre-requisite courses and retain as much of the information possible. If you concentrate on doing this, you will make your life much easier when it comes time to study for the MCAT.

You will need some self-reflection when choosing prep material for the MCAT. Are you an independent learner who can motivate him/herself to study multiple hours alone. Do you need a structured class with set times? Have you done well in your pre-requisite courses (and actually remember anything), or do you need a more comprehensive review? Do you prefer having a bunch of different books or like things concise and prefer to only have one resource?

As you know, there is a huge amount of test prep material out there including books, audio files, classes, practice exams, flash cards, etc. Which you choose should depend on your level of knowledge, time commitment/constraints, learning style, and overall desire to prepare. There are classed offered by private companies such as Kaplan and Princeton Review which are very comprehensive, but can also be very time consuming and costly. These are particularly useful if you need an in-depth review of the material, or have been away from school for a while.

There are multiple prep books available are well suited for the independent-learning student. A personal favorite is the *ExamKrackers* book set. This set is reasonably priced, printed in color, and the material is presented in a funny and simplified way. I recommend also getting the companion Audio-Osmosis to listen to in the car, while running, etc. It's pretty funny and you'd be surprised how far a humor goes to help keeping you focused on those long study days.

One thing I highly recommend is taking/studying the AAMC practice MCATs. These can be purchased from AAMC directly and will be the best indicator of your preparation. Take one before you begin your MCAT studying to get a sense of what your strengths and weaknesses are (you might find you need more/less time/resources to reach your score goals), then schedule the remaining ones throughout your prep time. These practice tests can take over four hours. Also, don't forget to go back and study each question/answer. Remember to understand why you missed what you missed.

Letters of Recommendation

As you begin to seriously consider preparing to apply to medical school, in the back of your mind you'll want to keep track of potential people you can ask for a letter of recommendation. I suggest planning on obtaining approximately 4-6 letters of recommendation from professors, researchers/bosses that you've worked with and also from physicians that you've shadowed.

You will want to obtain letters from individuals that you have taken the time to get to know well and from those that can attest to your abilities and vouch for you with a strong letter of recommendation. Avoid getting letters from family friends or people that know you on a casual basis.

You'll want letter writers who can attest to your academic abilities, your work ethic and can advocate for you as a strong applicant for medical school. For example, I had letters from two physicians that I shadowed, 3 professors from undergrad (biochemistry, history, and physics professors), and one from my research mentor. My pre-med advisor then went through my letters and selected the strongest ones to include in my application.

When thinking about which professors to approach, the topic the professor teaches likely won't be quite as important as how well they know you and how strongly they will advocate for you. For instance, I obtained letters from my history, biochemistry and physics professors as mentioned above. These were all professors that I had multiple classes with and I spent time going to office hours for help and assistance with the classes. This showed my engagement and interest in the material during class, and also let them get to know me over the course of the academic year. During these office visits, the professors have a unique opportunity to get to know you personally and what your goals are. This is an excellent opportunity to lay the groundwork to obtain a letter for your medical school application.

I also obtained a letter from a family physician and cardiologist that I had shadowed over the course of years. They were able to write me a strong letter of recommendation and attest to my future potential in medical school and beyond.

In retrospect, I feel that having strong letter writers is extremely important to having a successful application to medical school. During my interviews, the strength of my letters was brought up on multiple occasions and played a critical role in my overall application.

Tips for Getting Great Letters of Recommendation

- Plan in advance. If you are seriously considering applying to medical school, start planning which professors or researchers you'll be asking for letters. You'll want to approach professors in classes that you did well in, and those that had an opportunity to get to know you well. Make sure to get to know your professors by putting in the extra effort to go to office hours on a consistent basis; express you interest in medical school early on and set the foundation for a strong future letter.
- Give your letter writers plenty of time to write you a great letter. Definitely don't wait until the last minute to ask for letters of recommendation. Writing a good letter for a student is a time intensive process and many professors/researchers/physicians are extremely busy. I usually gave my letter writers a several month notice so they would have plenty of time and not feel rushed.
- When you ask for a letter of recommendation, be sure to provide your letter writer with your CV and a draft of your personal statement for medical school. This will allow them

to write about your background and accomplishments and help them build a strong case for you as an applicant.

- Shadowing physicians is essential; make sure to get to know one or two that can get to know you and be sure to ask for a letter.

Asking for a Letter

This is easier than it sounds. When you decide to ask for a letter, you can go about it several ways. Once you've felt that you clicked well with a certain faculty member/physician, you should make the attempt to approach them during their office hours or during a time when he/she is not busy, and ask them if they would be comfortable writing you a letter of recommendation. Gauge their answer, and if they offer to do so, you can meet with them later on and come prepared with your CV and personal statement.

The process is similar when you're shadowing a physician. Set the foundation early on during your shadowing experience. Let them know what your timeframe is for getting your application in, and then see how the experience goes. If you feel that you clicked well with the doctor, then towards the end of your shadowing experience, ask them if they would feel comfortable writing you a letter of recommendation for med school. Most physicians will be happy to write you a strong letter. Provide them with a CV and personal statement after they agree, and give them several months to work on it.

Occasionally, your letter writers will get so busy that they may forget to work on your letter. It's definitely okay to occasionally send them an update on when you're sending in your application, and by this way you politely remind about your letter. Only do this if your application date is fast approaching and you still haven't heard from your letter writer.

Be sure that your letters are also submitted confidentially to your application. Your pre-med advisor at your school will be able to review your letters and help you choose the best ones, but you should not be able to see them. Sometimes letter writers will let your read them, and that's okay, but give them the option to keep it confidential.

Once you do get a letter from a faculty member or physician, its definitely good form to let them know how appreciative you are for them taking the time to do this for you. Stop by their office hours and thank them, and consider giving them a thank you card. Remember that writing a letter is time-consuming, and showing that you're grateful for their time is good practice.

That essentially summarizes getting a strong letter of recommendation. It's much simpler than it sounds as long as you stick to the tips above.

Committee Letter

While you are preparing your application and meeting with your pre-medical advisor at your school, you will also need a committee letter from your pre-medical advisor. This will essentially be a synopsis of your performance in undergrad and may or may not contain comments from the other letter writers. Your pre-med advisor at your school will help you with this part.

Personal Statement

When you start getting closer to finalizing your application, you'll be asked to write a personal statement describing why you chose to pursue a career in medicine. This question is purposefully meant to be quite broad and somewhat vague. A personal statement, though, is a very important component of the application, and gives you the opportunity to describe your unique life experiences which comes back to the question..."*Why medicine?*" As the name implies, a personal statement should be a concise and unique to you. This is an opportunity for you, the applicant, to tell the reader how you arrived at the decision to apply to medical school and pursue a career in medicine. Use this essay as an opportunity to discuss your unique life experiences and characteristics, so that the reader can remember you.

When writing the personal statement, approach this as an opportunity to tell your story. Reflect on what experiences led you to discover your passion for medicine. Topics to consider when writing your personal statement include:

- Personal experiences with illness.
- Mentors in a medical research lab and how they influenced you.
- Physician mentors that you shadowed.
- Volunteer experiences.
- Your non-medical experiences, and how those validated your dream to pursue medicine.
- You academic pursuits.
- A significant research project and how it motivated you.
- Why you think you're a good fit for medicine.
- Why medicine is a good fit for you.
- What you'll bring to the profession.

- What qualities have you developed through your experiences that will help you succeed in medical school and beyond?
- This is your chance to make your case for why you want to be physician.

When planning out how to write your personal statement, remember that writing an effective essay will take multiple revisions and a substantial amount of time. This process can actually take months before you are finally ready to submit your essay. Make sure you get an early start (usually in the winter to early spring of your junior year) and have as many people (family, friends, professors, advisors) as possible read your essay and give you their feedback.

Keep in mind that the topics you write about in your personal statement will almost surely be used as discussion points during your interview. So, make sure you know your personal statement very well. Be ready to anticipate a question about anything you may have mentioned in your essay and be able to elaborate on it during the interview.

Breaking Down the Personal Statement into Sections

Here is how I like to think about breaking down the parts of the personal statement. The personal statement should be well-organized, like any essay, and should demonstrate a logical progression of the major experiences that led you to apply to medical school. You also have a character limit of 5,300 characters (including spaces), which you'll need to keep your essay within.

Introduction/Opening

One way to approach writing the first paragraph is to think about a major life experience that served as a catalyst for inspiring you to pursue medicine. What major life experience or moment made you want to become a physician? This could be just about any experience that you've had and was significant to you. You'll want to make your introduction interesting, and capture the reader's attention. Keep in mind that many committee members read dozens, if not hundreds, of essays, so you'll want to write a memorable introduction to your personal statement. Whatever it is, your opening sentence should be a reflection of that moment or experience. Then go into more detail about this through the rest of this paragraph.

Body

So now you've set the stage with your introductory paragraph capturing an important moment about your path to medicine. You will want to transition from this point into the body of your paragraph. You can go in several different directions at this stage of writing. Now can be a good time to reflect on what inspired you to pursue your chosen undergraduate degree. You can also transition into talking about your childhood or important events you experienced growing up that shaped your character and eventually led you to pursue your interests in medicine.

You can also begin writing about other plans you may have had, that were not related to medicine, and how these influenced you. For me, I discussed personal experiences with illness in my family and then transitioned to discussing my experiences growing up (family, school, outside interests) and how this shaped my decision for why I chose to pursue biology and then microbiology in college. I gave a brief overview of my outside life interests and tied them together to show why I decided to do a science major.

Body Continued

In this paragraph, you may consider starting to tie in how your experiences in college (and/or after college if you are a non-traditional student) really inspired you to further consider medicine as a career. This is a great time to talk about the shadowing, volunteer work, or research that you've done. Transition smoothly between each section, and show how this would be a natural, logical progression for you. At this point I would start talking about your major, and how the research you did in that also pointed you in the direction of medicine, alongside the other experiences. If you have any weaknesses in your application (low GPA for example) you can tie in an explanation for why this may have happened, and what process you went through to remedy this issue. Discuss how these experiences developed characteristics in you that will help you be successful in medical school and in practice as a physician.

Conclusion

The final paragraph is where you now bring it all together. Explain how the summation of the experiences you described above really make choosing medicine a natural choice. The conclusion can be tricky to write well, as you need to succinctly tie the entire essay together and elaborate on how your experiences led you to apply to medicine, and at the same time helped you develop the necessary characteristics and skill set to be successful in medicine. You'll want to express why medicine is a good fit for you, and how you'll be the same for medicine.

M.D. vs. D.O.

There are actually two pathways to becoming a physician in the United States, which isn't known to all pre-medical students and much of the public. There is the more traditional and well-recognized M.D. pathway to becoming physician, aka obtaining a Medical Doctorate. Another recognized pathway to becoming a physician is to get a D.O. degree, or Doctor of Osteopathic Medicine. Medical credential committees recognize both as fully capable of practicing medicine in the United States and many countries, though there are differences between the two.

Many pre-meds often hear about the D.O. pathway while in college but many get confused about the differences between D.O. and M.D. The differences between the two degrees are becoming more of a historical point with time. There are currently approximately 34 medical schools (more being added) offering the osteopathic degree. The primary historical difference between M.D. and D.O. is that the osteopathic schools have focused on incorporating training into what is essentially musculoskeletal manipulation, a form of hands on physical manipulation and therapy. Otherwise, the curriculum for the both M.D. and D.O. schools is very similar, including book work in the first two years and then clinical rotations in the last two years.

When it comes to deciding whether or not to apply to a D.O. medical school, the choice is personal, and likely won't have too much of an impact on your overall career in medicine. In the past, admissions to osteopathic schools have been viewed as somewhat less competitive, as many osteopathic schools were felt to use a more holistic approach to choosing applicants and are more forgiving of poor grades, etc. Though, as the number of pre-meds continues to increase year-by-year, admissions to D.O. schools is also significantly increasing in competitiveness.

When it comes to taking boards and applying for residency, D.O. students take a D.O. examination similar to USMLE Step 1, and many students also take the M.D. boards. By taking the M.D. boards (USMLEs) many D.O. students apply to allopathic residencies. There also exist osteopathic residency programs in multiple specialties, but these are much smaller in number than the traditional allopathic residency programs.

Going through residency, I've worked with medical students, residents, and attendings from all different backgrounds, including many with D.O. degrees. From experience, I can say that there is little to no difference between M.D. and D.O. holders aside from mostly historical stigma and potentially some challenges obtaining residency positions in very competitive locations and programs. In almost every case, if I hadn't know the persons degree, there would be no way I could know if they were M.D. or D.O. That being said I've also personally known D.O. medical students who have gone on to match into ultra competitive residencies like allopathic dermatology programs. I also know many specialists, including orthopedic surgeons, who are excellent physicians.

For those interested, I've included a list of osteopathic schools you can look into and apply to in the US. I highly suggest you look into these schools and see which ones have the best match rates into competitive specialties, and seriously consider applying to these schools, especially for some of the more non-traditional students or those who had some academic struggles but overall had a very strong application.

Overseas Medical Schools

Another option that many pre-meds end up considering is attending medical school overseas, usually either in the Caribbean or in Europe. Students have lots of reason to consider these options and I'll bring up some points to consider. If given the option, I personally would first try getting into a U.S. allopathic M.D. school or osteopathic D.O. school. If unsuccessful the first time around, I would work on improving my application and then trying again, with the caveat of applying to these schools as a backup on the next go around. I personally know quite a few residents and practicing physicians who completed their medical school overseas and have very successful practices.

Generally, overseas schools can be a bit more forgiving of lower academic standings or MCAT scores, so some students find that it's a bit easier to gain admission into these programs. That being said, you need to seriously consider some of the downsides. For many of these programs, you'll have to move to a country where English may not be the native language, so on top of tackling a medical school curriculum, you'll have to adapt to new unfamiliar surroundings, people, culture, and way of life. The cost of these schools is generally very high as well, so you need to be financially prepared.

Another reality of doing medical school overseas is that there is no guarantee of obtaining a residency position in the United States. Competition for US residency slots is intense and securing one as a US graduate can be hard enough. Securing a residency spot coming from an overseas medical school will be a challenge, especially when it comes to more competitive specialties. If your focus is on pursuing a career in the primary care specialties such as Internal Medicine, Family Medicine, or Pediatrics you generally shouldn't have much of a problem securing a residency slot. My opinion is that as long as you do well in your classes and clinical rotations, you should be fine. Getting into more competitive specialties such as anesthesiology, radiology, orthopedic surgery, ER, etc., will be much more of a challenge and will require excellent board scores and outstanding performance in your clinical rotations.

When looking at overseas medical schools, you should also bear in mind that some of these programs allow you to do some or even a majority of your clinical rotations in the mainland of the U.S., which is crucial. By doing rotations in the U.S. you form connections with various faculty members at the programs you'll rotate through and if you do well this might be a foot in the door for you when it comes to securing a residency spot. Be sure to research each program intensely, look at things such as their boards pass rates, their residency Match results and the percent of students who actually matriculate from the program once they enroll.

AMCAS®

(American Medical College Application Service®)
A program of the Association of American Medical Colleges

When you start getting ready to apply to medical school, you'll definitely want to visit their website which is where you can find the official online medical school application that is run by the American Association of Medical Colleges®. You will use this site multiple times in your future: for medical school, residency, and fellowship applications. You'll definitely want to get familiar with the website, the different parts of the application, and various application timelines and due dates. We won't discuss the application in too much detail here, as the official AAMC® website has great modules and explanations for navigating the application process, and we highly recommend you visit and become very familiar with it.

The overview of the application is as follows:
- A section where you will input your **background information** (Demographics, Education, etc.).
- A section where you will put in all of the **coursework** from undergrad (and graduate school if your pursued other degrees). This section will require you to put in the different classes you took and grades you received in each. Your overall and Science GPA will be calculated out.
- Information on **work experiences and activities**: here you will essentially put in the dates and hours of all your work, volunteer, research, and shadowing activities that you have participated in. You'll be expected to put in the number of hours per week, and add a short description of the activity.
- **Letters of recommendation**: this is the section where your committee letter and your letters of recommendation will be uploaded and sent to the schools that you designate.

- You will select the **medical schools** to which you want to apply to in a separate section.
- There will be another section for you to type in your **personal statement**.
- The final section includes uploading your **official standardized test scores**.

Interviewing

Overview

If you finally get to this stage of the application process, then congratulations. Getting to the interview stage of medical school admissions is extremely competitive, and you've gone through quite a bit of the competition to get to this stage of the process. Doing well at the interview stage cannot be overstated. A great interview will often make it easier for admissions committees to overlook other application weaknesses, but it can also work in reverse. A poor or weak interview performance can quickly hurt even a great applicant's chances. So how did we, and others we know, prepare ourselves for interviews? Several ways, as I'll describe below.

First of all, you will want to prepare and try to anticipate the huge variety of questions you might be asked. The range of questions you may be asked is quite extensive, and sometimes difficult to predict. Questions can range from interviewers asking about how you became interested in medicine, to difficult topics regarding complicated geo-political views you may read about in the news.

Some interviewers may also ask detailed questions about your personal statement, your research, and other activities. At times, applicants are given a difficult ethical question to see how they work their way through it. Be ready to discuss everything mentioned in your application in detail. Some physicians may even have done research on topics similar to yours, so be prepared. To start off, we've included **50 questions** that I had received on my interview trail to give you a better idea of what to expect.

1. Why medicine?
2. Why medicine over other health professions?
3. Tell me about yourself.
4. Tell me about your family.
5. What makes you a better candidate than the many other applicants we are evaluating?
6. What is your greatest strength/weakness?
7. What motivates you?
8. What was your biggest failure?
9. What is the greatest challenge you've ever faced? How did you overcome it?
10. Why was your (GPA or MCAT) low, compared to the other applicants?
11. How do you deal with stressful situations?
12. Tell me about a memorable patient encounter you had during your shadowing experiences.
13. Why did you choose to do research in _____ at your undergraduate university?
14. What is the last book you read?
15. Who influenced you the most in your life?
16. Who do you look up to?
17. What do you read for fun?
18. What hobbies do you have?
19. How do you feel about (current news event)?
20. What work experience do you have?
21. Did your parents or family push you to pursue a career in medicine?
22. How would your best friend describe you?
23. What's your favorite movie?
24. If you were stranded on an island, what 3 items would you bring?
25. Tell me more about your hometown.
26. What do you think will be greatest challenge for you in medical school?

27. How will you be able to handle the demands of medical school?
28. If you could meet any historical figure, who would it be, and why?
29. What are your plans after medical school?
30. Do you know what specialty you want to pursue?
31. What are the major issues in healthcare in the United States at this time?
32. How do you feel about the Affordable Care Act?
33. Is healthcare a right or a privilege?
34. I see that you spent time in (other country), what is their healthcare system like? How is it different from ours?
35. What would you change about healthcare in the United States?
36. Do you think the US should have a single-payer system?
37. Do you have any experience with the underserved population?
38. What will you do if you don't get into medical school this year?
39. Why do you think you weren't accepted to medical school last year (if 2nd attempt)?
40. I see that you have a graduate degree in _____, why are you leaving that career path?
41. What made you decide to change careers (if non-traditional student)?
42. How did you spend your gap year(s) (if you took time off after college)?
43. How do you think you compare to the other applicants we have?
44. What should I tell the admissions committee about you?
45. Why do you want to come to medical school here?
46. Why did you choose to go to undergrad where you did?

47. **Various ethical scenarios**:
48. A patient comes to you seeking help and guidance in having an abortion. Your personal views are against abortion. What do you do?
49. You notice that one of your medical school/physician colleagues is behaving differently than normal. You find out they may have a substance abuse problem. How would you deal with this?
50. How do you feel about physician-assisted suicide?

General Approach to Answering Questions

So how did I prepare for interviews? Generally, I practiced interviewing for weeks and months leading up to my interviews. After studying the types of questions and answers, I also made sure to read up on daily news and current events, as interviewers like to see that applicants are well-informed about world events. I also rehearsed these and many other questions with friends and professors and staged "mock interviews" to work on my interviewing techniques. One valuable lesson I learned was to videotape myself while being interviewed so that I could see what my interviewing weaknesses were.

There is also an art to answering the different types of questions, especially the ethical questions. Admissions committees want to know that you are able to see both sides to a certain scenario, and expect you to work through it without letting personal bias interfere. They want to know you will be fair and put the care of the patient before your own biases, but they also want to know that you'll respect your own personal/moral boundaries when making decisions.

My advice is to find the middle ground in these questions. For instance, when faced with the question about abortion that I posed above, an acceptable response could include helping the patient find a provider that would be able to assist her with an abortion, rather than completely not aiding the patient at all. These are tricky questions, and admissions committee members will want to see how you work through them.

The Night Before

The day and night before your interview do your best to relax and do some preparation for the big day. Take some time to review commonly asked questions, like the ones I mentioned above. Stand in front of the mirror for a while, and go over answering the questions you know you'll get asked. Your answers should sound well thought out, but not overly rehearsed. You want to sound like you're speaking naturally, and didn't just memorize various answers you think the interviewer wants to hear.

Be sure to get as much sleep as possible so you appear well rested and composed the next day. Also, make sure you know exactly how to get to the interview spot -- I would make sure I knew exactly where I was going the next day, I'd take a little trip and made sure the directions I had to the medical school or building on campus where accurate so I wouldn't run late the next day. Consider taking a taxi to the medical school in the morning, so you don't have to worry about parking on campus.

The Day of the Interview

Most importantly, arrive early, and definitely do not be late unless you have some extenuating circumstance. You should be dressed formally, and looking clean and well put together. Be on your best behavior, this includes being respectful of everyone you meet, from the taxi-driver in the morning, to the receptionist, your interviewers, and the other applicants. Admissions committee members may ask different people who may have interacted with the applicants whether they were polite and appropriate; trust me on this one. Be genuine and respectful of everyone. Under no circumstance should you have your phone out texting, especially if you are being interviewed or people are talking with you. I've seen med students do this who are interviewing for residency, and it's essentially an immediate rejection.

How to Dress

Guys should be dressed in a suit and tie, preferably dark gray/black/navy. No pin-stripe suits. As an applicant, you will want to avoid being the candidate that sticks out in the clothing department; instead, in my opinion you want to be aim to be conservative. Make sure your suit is appropriately fitted. Be clean cut for the day. Ladies, professional slacks or skirts are advised.

Thank you Letters

It is considered good form to send your interviewers a thank you note in the week or two after your interview. Usually, people write about whatever they discussed during their individual interviews. Try to make note of an interesting topic you and the interviewer talked about to jog their memory about you, and thank them for their time. It's best to write a unique thank you note to each interviewer.

Here is a sample thank you letter that I have used in the past, which you can modify for yourself:

Dear Dr. Smith,

Thank you for the opportunity to interview at University of _____ on February 5th. Meeting with the faculty and other staff was a great experience and I sensed a true commitment to the advancement of medicine at the program.

I really appreciated the opportunity to meet with you and enjoyed having the chance to discuss my background growing up in _____, my interests in and outside of medicine, and for the opportunity to learn more about _____ medical school and the surrounding area.

Based on my interview it is clear that the University of _____ provides superb, well-rounded educational opportunities with faculty committed to providing excellent care and teaching. It would be a privilege to be a part of the University of _____. I am thankful for the opportunity to have met you and the other members of the medical school.

Sincerely,
John Doe

Extra-Tips

Be sure to have several questions to ask the interviewer when they ask if you have any questions. You don't want to say no to this. Some example questions are as follows:

- Do you expect any changes to your medical school curriculum?

- What is the greatest strength of the medical school?

- What is your favorite thing about the medical school?

- What advice would you give a pre-medical student, such as myself?

- What are some of the opportunities students have for research?

Remember, you are the one being interviewed. Don't try and take over the interview, let the person interviewing have the lead role and guide the questions. I've seen medical students try and lead the interview when interviewing for residency, and it just does not go over well with the faculty doing the interviewing. Stay composed and calm. It's normal to be a little nervous, don't worry.

After the Interview

The time after the interview can sometimes last a while with little to no feedback from the schools you interviewed at. At some point you will receive updates on the status of your application, and often times you will either be accepted, rejected, or placed on the waitlist. Dealing with an acceptance is easy, but having a strategy for dealing with rejections and waitlists is trickier. If put on a school's waitlist, sometimes it's advisable to send an update letter to the school, explaining your continued interest in their program, and include any major updates to your application. This can sometimes bump a candidate higher on the waitlist, but you'll want to do this sparingly.

I Messed Up: What To Do

Lets say that you just went through the application season and you were unsuccessful for one reason or another, whether it was low grades or MCAT scores, or not enough volunteer and extra-curricular activities. At this point in the game, it's very important to get to the bottom of what went wrong. Things to consider as you go forward. You need to show significant improvement and progression in your application before re-applying to med school.

If you got low grades or a low MCAT score, you will have to show significant change for the better on your next go around. If you feel you didn't have enough volunteer activities or whatever, you'll need to put in significant time to show your commitment to the field. Keep in mind though, that I knew many excellent students that had great applications that just didn't get in, and sometimes it's just bad luck.

In the event that you got rejected and are now graduating college without a definite backup plan and had a lower GPA or MCAT score, you should strong consider pursuing a science based graduate program, such as Master's, to show that you can handle graduate level course-load and show excellence in academics by getting the highest GPA you can. This might be your last chance to prove your abilities to admissions committees, so before you re-apply, make sure this stuff is taken care of. If you were a science major, consider applying to post-bacc programs or Master's programs in your related fields or programs like Anatomy/Physiology.

These are generally not too crazy competitive so you could potentially secure a spot at your alma mater or close by. You'll need to continue to do significant volunteer work during this year or two. The hardest part of this process is taking your time and making sure to get your application perfect before applying the next go around. The tendency is to immediately re-apply the following after getting rejected, and unless you've done something to significantly improve your application, you might just end up hurting your chances more by doing so.

So even if it means waiting another year or more to apply, do that before re-applying. I had several friends you were science majors, ending up doing a Master's in Anatomy or a similar science field, did research and continued volunteer work and successfully got into great medical schools. You have to be patient, persistent, and dedicated. You really start getting your application in trouble if you get rejected two or more times in a row. Each time you re-apply it decreases your chances of getting admitted unless you show drastic improvement in your application.

Another thing to consider is that if you only applied to MD schools the first time, branch out and consider applying to DO schools and maybe some of the overseas schools such as the Caribbean programs which I talk more about below. This can save you years of life and is a really good other option to consider.

Final Thoughts

Now that you've made it to the end of this section I recommend you keep reading through the medical school half of the book. You'll get a taste for some of the topics and things you'll encounter in medical school and you can learn some interesting information that you can apply during your shadowing experiences.

Remember some of the most important tips when applying to medical school:

- Grades and MCAT scores are some of the most important parts of your medical application. The longer you are in school, the harder it is to make significant changes to your GPA (because each class has less value in the GPA calculation the more classes you have), so do your best to ace your courses from the first semester.

- When you do your extra-curricular activities, remember that showing commitment and interest over an extended period of time is more important than just the sheer number of volunteer hours.

- Apply broadly to lots of medical schools, as many as you can afford so that you have a better chance of securing interviews and an admission.

- Expose yourself to other career options in college, such as dentistry or engineering. Admissions committees like to see that you considered other options and these could serve as good career options in case you don't get into medical school.

Part 2:
Medical School

Now That You're Accepted

I still remember the feeling of driving home from college one weekend in the spring, filled with anticipation, as if it was just yesterday. My parents had called to tell me that an envelope had arrived from a medical school, one I had been waiting to hear back from since my interview, which also happened to my first choice in my home state.

The feeling of opening an acceptance letter is life changing, and comes with a feeling of both comfort and anxiety. On one hand, all of your hard work and effort finally pays off with the acceptance letter in your hand. In a way, your future arrives planned out for you, and no longer having the uneasy feeling of possible rejection gives you great peace of mind. The surreal thought of actually becoming a physician now seems plausible and totally within reach. On the other hand comes anxiety, as you wonder if you'll have what it takes to survive the extreme academic demands of medical school.

You may be asking yourself, what exactly is the point of this book? Well, it started with me taking a look back to my med student days, now as I'm finishing up with my residency program, realizing how much I wish I had known when I had first started medical school. I finally learned the meaning behind the "unwritten" medical school curriculum. If you haven't heard this term yet, you might within the first few weeks of starting classes. Essentially, the "unwritten" curriculum describes the underlying set of principles and lessons medical students learn through their journey through medical school. These lessons and principles are never actually taught or described in a book, but are learned, and includes the things when you tell yourself "*If only I had known that before starting this class or rotation, I would've done so much better.*" Some of the factors that play into this curriculum are extremely important, and may play a larger role in securing a residency position than actual grades.

This umbrella term encompasses principles such as clinical and operating room etiquette, understanding and successfully operating as a student in a hospital and preparing excellent written and oral patient presentations. I discuss developing advanced study and memorization techniques, understanding what interviewers are looking for in a future resident, learning how to interact with patients in an efficient and empathetic manner, and developing the appropriate technical, knowledge, and social skills necessary to be an excellent resident physician.

Medical school is a completely different animal than the classes you had in college, and the experience will significantly change and mature you as a person. For the remainder of this book I will attempt to address many of the important lessons I learned in medical school and describe how you can utilize these lessons and go through medical school successfully. I'll talk about how to go about preparing your application and how to successfully interview for residency.

I'll also go over many clinically relevant topics to give you a flavor for what you will learn in medical school, including common pathological processes, basics of laboratory tests, EKG basics, and radiologic interpretations, as well as resources I highly recommend as you start planning your approach to medical school. The mini-med school chapter has 40 disease processes that I think are fundamental to knowing along with interesting radiology. Some of the topics I discuss may sound obvious at first; while the importance of others will only become more evident once you start medical school. I hope you find the advice useful and practical, and if successfully implemented, will help you secure a residency position in the specialty of your choice.

Top 16 Things I Didn't Expect in Medical School:

1. There's literally a thing called "*Medical Student Syndrome*," that happens to lots of students, myself included back in the day. What happens is that in school you start learning about all these countless diseases and symptoms, and eventually you start imagining that you or someone you know has developed every single disease process. You literally start to worry about everything, every cough, bump, sneeze or other symptom you discover. Keep things in perspective and don't get carried away.

2. No longer feeling like you are at the top of the class. In college, most pre-meds generally do a pretty solid job in their classes, and the transition from being a top performer in college to just average or below in medical school is humbling. You are now classmates with all the other high-performing students from around the country and you'll be graded against them. So get used to potentially feeling like this.

3. Feeling like you are studying for college finals every other week. The volume of material and detail you are expected to know can be overwhelming at first and you'll have to use your study skills from college and adapt them to keep up with the huge volume of information.

4. The personalities of the people in your medical school may be very different from the friends you had in college. Pre-meds and med students are an interesting group of people, so just know what to expect.

5. You will be ranked in medical school. Keep this important fact in mind as you start out. Most medical schools will rank you into quartiles based on your performance on tests and on clinical rotations, which will be extremely important for your application to residency. Your ranking in each individual class against your classmates will be documented and will be sent to the residency programs you apply to, and

often times, will again be sent to fellowship programs you apply to thereafter.

6. Astronomical amount of student debt. It may be easily over $200,000, plan accordingly. Do your best to pay off as much of your loans as fast as possible and apply for scholarships.

7. Your first two years will be primarily non-clinical. You will be mostly in lecture and memorizing a large amount of material in classes such as anatomy, physiology, pathology, biochemistry, microbiology, etc.

8. The most important test in medical school is called USMLE Step 1® (United States Medical Licensing Exam®). This will be taken after your first two years of medical school and will play a major role in your competitiveness for residency. You will take parts 2 and 3 later on.

9. Understand that different medical specialties are more or less competitive. The most competitive at this time include dermatology, plastic surgery and orthopedic surgery, as well as several others. Many medical students go unmatched into these specialties, unless you're the top of your class. Don't go to medical school with the expectation that you're going to end up in one of these specialties, I knew several incredibly smart people that didn't match into super-competitive specialties.

10. Your grades in your clinical rotations (third and fourth year) are based largely on subjective evaluations from supervising physicians and residents. This is hard to get used to and can be extremely frustrating since these evaluations can determine much of your future.

11. You almost definitely change your mind on what specialty you want to pursue multiple times. Don't worry, this is completely normal.

12. Keep an open mind to the different medical specialties as you rotate through them. You might find that a certain specialty you didn't even previously consider might be the

74

right fit for you and this might be your only chance to find that out.

13. Learn as much as you can from the residents on your rotations. They were med students not too long ago and remember what it's like to be in your shoes. They'll also vouch for you to the attending when it comes to your evaluations, and will help you enormously during your rotations.

14. Be respectful to everyone you meet. The medical world is small, and everybody knows everybody.

15. Your study habits will likely have to evolve to keep up with the new, more intense expectations of the medical school curriculum.

16. Choose a specialty that you find to be a natural fit for you, regardless of what compensation may be at that time. With budget cuts, and constant changes to the reimbursement system, you'll want to choose a specialty you can practice happily for years to come.

Moving through the ranks of the medical system, now as a resident, I finally feel like I'm beginning to gain an understanding into the somewhat chaotic medical education system. The feeling of what it's like to be a pre-med and med student is still fresh in my head, but now I've had the opportunity to work with, teach, and evaluate medical students. Over time, I feel like I have developed a pretty good understanding of what it takes to be "good" or even an "*outstanding*" medical student. This is only my opinion, but here we go...

Being a medical student is incredibly hard; I can say that I definitely didn't do a perfect job, and it's very different from being a college student. The way you are evaluated is completely different, especially during your third and fourth years. Your evaluations become more subjective and based on people interacting with you and assessing your clinical and social skills. I have noticed some trends in the most successful medical students I've worked with, and they all usually share the following 15 characteristics, in no particular order:

Top 15 Tips to be a Successful Medical Student

1. **Keeping it Real:** This is usually a natural trait in a person. The med students we enjoy having on our service, we can tell are genuinely good people, and don't put on a fake smile and to try and impress us. They take their medical education seriously, show empathy to their patients, and show a level of interest and concern that doesn't seem forced.

2. **Don't Backstab:** I learned about this important rule from an anesthesiology attending in medical school. He told me that an important characteristic he looked for in medical students is that a med student never made a fellow student look bad for their own benefit. This is a great piece of advice. I actually experienced this multiple times during my 3rd and 4th years with people in my class. Obviously, people see right through this behavior. Admirable behavior we watch for is how med students help each other on the rotation, and how they work together to help their classmates look good. Essentially, in my mind, I'm thinking "would I want to be co-residents with this person?"

3. **Street Smarts:** Many, many medical students are very intellectually smart, but having social smarts is a totally separate skill set. The ability to pick up on social cues from the residents, attendings and patients is essential to success. These are things we observe, which are important in making a good physician.

4. **Well-Dressed:** This is fairly obvious, but successful medical students are always well-dressed and well put together. Remember, you are working with patients, families, other healthcare workers, and doctors. You should make every attempt to represent the workplace and the people you work with well. Showing up looking like you just spent a night out drinking is definitely not a good idea.

5. **Professional:** This encompasses multiple aspects of the way you present yourself. Successful medical students are always conscientious of how they are presenting themselves to people. This involves dressing appropriately, being well spoken, refraining from inappropriate language (especially in patient care areas), the way you interact with other students and health care workers all play into this.

6. **Smart:** I still remember several medical students I've worked with, and how truly impressed I was with their fund of medical and non-medical knowledge. These medical students generally go above and beyond the others. The way to get to this level includes the basics: hard work, studying, and knowing your patients well.

7. **Don't Fake It:** No one in medicine is capable of knowing everything. Attendings and residents are always looking things up and learning new things. Medicine is something that you continue to learn throughout your life. In no way do we expect medical students to know everything. The best medical students I've worked with always admit when they don't know the answer to a question. Having a dependable medical student that you can trust is incredibly important for residents. We would rather know that the student doesn't know the answer to a question, such as the patient's lab values, than to give us the wrong values, which could lead to patient safety issues.

8. **Don't Try Too Hard:** There is a fine line between being a hard worker and going too far in trying to impress those around you. The best medical students are always on time, done with their work and ready to help the residents/attendings at the end of the day, and then head home when the work is done. Each team you are on works differently, so you need to be able to adapt to various expectations.

9. **Help Out:** Great medical students generally check in with the residents throughout the day and before heading home

offer to help out with any unfinished work. They generally understand that everyone wants to get home after a long day of work, and while we don't want medical students to do extra-work, the offer is always nice and well received.

10. **Don't Complain:** The days during medical school and residency can be long and arduous. Generally, the best medical students don't focus on the negatives and do a great job of making the work environment fun and enjoyable. Complaining, while easy to do, doesn't change anything for the better for anyone.

11. **Care for Patients:** Great medical students are well liked by their patients. Generally, these students show compassion and empathy towards their patients and are genuinely interested in the care their patient is receiving.

12. **Respectful:** Essentially self-explanatory.

13. **Empathetic:** An important characteristic every doctor needs to have.

14. **Able to Adapt:** To do well in medical school, you have to be able to adapt to changing environments on a constant basis. You will be changing teams and rotations, as well as meeting new attendings and residents constantly. Having the ability to quickly adapt to new environments is essential. In a span of two months you may go from working in a rural family medicine clinic to working on a high-stress surgical sub-specialty team with completely different expectations, hours, and personalities.

15. **Easy to Get Along With:** Our favorite medical students are usually the ones we enjoy hanging out with throughout the day. They have the ability to make the day more enjoyable, while still keeping things efficient with the goal of doing well and getting home at the end of the day. This takes a special social skill that some people just seem to possess.

Years 1 & 2 of Medical School

Medical school ended up being quite different from what I initially expected. One thing that I didn't expect was that the first two years would be primarily classroom-based with only some clinical exposure (it's quite compared to what you'd expect). The first two years are generally based around a set curriculum established for medical schools in the United States. While the order of these classes may vary by school, the common coursework includes the following:

- Anatomy
- Embryology
- Cell Biology
- Biochemistry
- Microbiology
- Pharmacology
- Histology
- Physiology/Pathology of the Major Organ Systems
  - Cardiopulmonary
  - Gastrointestinal
  - Reproductive
  - Immunology/Allergy
  - Neurology
  - Hematology/Oncology
  - Endocrinology
  - Nephrology
  - Neurology

Each medical school organizes these classes slightly differently, and follows a required curriculum provided by the governing body. In most schools, the first class students start with is anatomy, followed by the rest of the curriculum. Some of the classes will be repeats from college, but with a more clinical approach and often studied in much greater detail than during undergrad.

During these classes, you will be given a syllabus with notes and presentations, and you will also have these supplemented with book readings. Many schools will also record their daily lectures and post the videos on the school website. This way, you can come back and watch the lectures at a later time and take more detailed notes. During each block you will be tested with multiple choice tests and the class blocks will often end with a cumulative final. This process will be repeated ad-nauseum for two years; it's a pretty painful process depending on where you go to school.

Students are expected to memorize the provided syllabus and required readings in especially high detail. Exams are generally given every couple weeks, with the tests often graded on a curve. The grading scale in medical school is different than in college, and most schools use either an Honors/Near Honors/Satisfactory/Fail or High Pass/Pass/Fail grading system. Usually Honors or High Pass would correlate with an A in college. Near Honors or Pass would be equivalent to grade ranges from C to B and anything below would be considered failing. Several schools use only a Pass/Fail grading system.

The interesting thing I learned about grading during the preclinical years is that some schools begin to divide you into quartiles, based on your exam results. Top performing students would fall into the top quartile, and lower scoring students would fall into the other groups. Your quartile will then also be adjusted based on your performance on your clinical rotations. By the time it comes to applying for residency, your grades will have landed you in one of the four quartiles, which will be reported on your **Deans Letter** for residency programs to know. A Deans Letter is a document that is included in your residency application that summarizes your performance in medical school and gives your class rank. As I quickly learned, doing well on each test was incredibly important, as these results had a major impact on your overall class ranking and chances of locking down a great residency position.

So, how can a student be successful during the first two years? First, you need to know what to expect. The volume of information you are expected to learn over a short period of time is much higher than it was in college, and often feels as if you are studying during finals week in college, except now that feeling is repeated with every test in medical school. In college I often procrastinated and put off studying until right before my exams. In medical school, this definitely wouldn't work, and I had to adjust my study methods accordingly.

My studying in medical school significantly changed. After a few courses, I also realized that my classmates fell into two broad categories. There was one group of students, a small subset, who seemed like they rarely studied and somehow managed to memorize everything in perfect detail on their first pass through the material and always got the highest scores on the exams. This was the natural genius group. On the other, you had the larger group of students (myself included), who had to read the material over and over, only learning the material through extensive repetition and note taking/flash-card making. By this time, you probably know which group you fall into and you should plan out study time accordingly.

One of the most important things I learned to do was to try and pre-read the lectures for the next day the night before, and also review older lectures the same day. This is obvious, but like many of us were guilty of in college, the temptation to procrastinate is powerful, but will make it difficult to pass medical school classes.

Many of our lectures were also presented in slide format, which I find difficult or nearly impossible to study. So, the night before I would retype the slide presentations into well-organized text documents on my laptop, for easy memorization. I also learned that it really helps to retype or re-organize the notes yourself, as you end up remembering where you wrote certain topics or graphs on your notes, which makes recall easier. I allotted approximately 5-6 hours per day to studying on non-test weeks. During the days leading up to tests, I studied as much as possible, sometimes well over 12-15 hours a day.

By the time you start third year, in theory, you should now have a solid grasp for the physiology and pathology of each of the organ systems as you head into clinical rotations. Many schools have also started introducing introductory classes to clinical medicine during the first two years, intermingled among your science classes to give you a head start for when you begin your clinical rotations. These classes review the basics of a clinical exam, basic note taking and presentation formats and other duties of a medical student while on different rotations.

The point of taking all these classes and studying the material in such detail is to prepare you for what may the single most important test of your academic career, commonly known as the USMLE Step 1. This exam tests your knowledge on the fundamental basic science classes you took during the first two years and is one of the important criteria residency programs use to compare you against other applicants, much like the MCAT was for medical school. This test is usually taken in the late spring or early summer of your second year of medical school, just before starting you clinical rotations.

If you're reading this book sometime before medical school, then it's entirely possible to get a little bit of a head start during the summer before. I wouldn't suggest going all out studying, but would recommend getting the *Netters Anatomy Book* and

Flashcard set, as well as two books called *BRS Physiology* and *BRS Pathology*. If during your summer off, you get a chance to skim through these books, it'll give you a nice head start on what you'll learn when you first get to class, and you'll feel more comfortable with all the new terminology.

How to Study

As I described earlier, my study habits had to undergo a fairly significant change once starting med school and I employed a method for high volume learning, which is essential to be being successful in medical school. For one, the amount of material and the detail tested on each exam seemed to be far beyond that of the tests I had during undergrad.

During most of my undergraduate years, I found that I usually crammed for several days prior to each exam and utilized dead week to study for finals. While there was quite a bit of procrastination, it seemed to work out well and I had quite a bit of free time between tests. I wouldn't say this was the best approach, but it happened to work out for me.

I found this study approach to be a bad idea pretty quickly in medical school. Now instead of having multiple small tests scattered throughout a quarter or semester, I was anticipating one large test every 1-2 weeks with a "*cumulative final*" at the end of each block. You are also generally only taking 1 or 2 different classes at the same time instead of having 4-6 different classes during a quarter.

Lectures generally spanned each day starting at 8 or 9 am and went into the late afternoon. This was different from undergrad, where I usually had about 4-5 hours of lecture per day. Thus, I had to change my study tactics to adapt to the new expectations.

- I developed a pattern where I would pre-read the provided syllabus/book material at least 1-2 days ahead of the lectures. At this time, I didn't try to memorize the small details at this time; instead I focused on building a foundation of concepts upon which to memorize details at a later point.

- Many of our lectures were put together as slide presentations. Like many of my classmates, I found (and still find) studying and memorizing large amounts of material from slides nearly impossible and useless. I spent my late afternoons re-writing the material and making it into normal handwritten notes or typed documents, which would be much easier to organize, memorize and study.
- I allotted approximately 2-3 hours each day to re-writing my notes, and then approximately 3 hours to studying old material and pre-reading for the upcoming lectures.
- During weekends I spent approximately 6-8 hours studying and took the remainder of the time off, unless it was the weekend prior to an exam, where I studied most of the time.
- I made sure to save my notes, as many of our classes had a cumulative final.
- Several friends and I would get together once or twice a week and quiz each other on all the material for the upcoming test. This was a good way to gauge how we compared to our classmates as far as knowledge base, and also exposed us to material we thought we knew but didn't.
- I also utilized notecards extensively to really memorize the fine details of the lectures.

These study tips may seem obvious, but the importance of adhering to a rigorous schedule wasn't apparent to me until I experienced my first few medical school exams. You will need discipline and you will need to stick to a system that works. I had classmates who didn't take these things seriously when we first started med school, some students even did so poorly they had to repeat classes and a couple dropped out. Refer back to the pre-med section, where I describe my approach to high volume learning if you're interested to hear more.

OSCE's and Clinical Medicine

The OSCEs (Objective Structured Clinical Examinations) are a type of examination that you will take prior to starting your clinical rotations, and also during your clinical years. This is also how you become familiar and comfortable performing various types of physical examinations and patient workups.

The OSCE is essentially an examination that tests your abilities with various patient interactions and physical exams. During your first two years in medical school, you will have classes separate from your pre-clinical classes that will develop and teach you clinical skills. As you approach your clinical years (years 3 & 4) you will likely undergo a more standardized OSCE examination where you will be put into a clinical environment, and you'll be asked to see various standardized patients. Students are graded on their interactions with the patients, their medical knowledge, their physical exam thoroughness, and their ability to form a differential diagnosis and treatment plan.

Another point to doing these OSCE examinations is to prepare you for the USMLE Step 2 CS, which is the clinical skills component to the licensing exams. For this test, which you'll take in your 3rd or 4th year of medical school, you'll fly to one of several locations in the country that offer the exam. This part evaluates your clinical skills. You and many other medical students will meet at a large building where you will be put into multiple clinical scenarios and graded on both your clinical performance and note writing abilities. Essentially you'll take part in multiple clinical scenarios with "actor patients."

Each component of the test will put you in a simulated clinical scenario, as if you were seeing a new patient in clinic. The test focuses on whether or not you can correctly do a history and physical exam that is relevant to the problem the patient presents with. The whole experience is videotaped, and examiners then review your performance to see if you acted appropriately. While this experience sounds scary, it has been historically thought of as the easiest part of the USMLE exams, and generally has the highest pass rate.

USMLE™ Step 1

(The United States Medical Licensing Examination (USMLE™) is a joint program of the Federation of State Medical Boards (FSMB®) and National Board of Medical Examiners (NBME®))

While you study for each of your classes, keep in mind that the USMLE Step 1 will essentially be a cumulative final of nearly all the material you'll learn during the first two years. While studying for classes, I would also read the associated *First Aid for the USMLE Step 1®* (essential book for this exam) chapter and make additional notes into this book from my class material.

I also ended up buying a year's subscription to *UWorld Q-Bank* (an online question bank that is also essential to doing well on this exam), and would do the associated questions with my coursework. This way, over the course of the first two years of medical school, I could familiarize myself with how the material would be tested on Step 1. This is important, because just as the MCAT was very important for getting into medical school, doing well on Step 1 is essential to securing a good residency program in the specialty you want to pursue. Many students view this as one of the most important exams they ever take.

Testing though, doesn't end after Step 1. The USMLE is a three-part examination, and you should expect to take the Step 2 (2-part examination) during or after your third year of medical school, and Step 3 during your internship year. You need to pass all three to become licensed as a physician in the US, so it's essential that you do well.

Should I Study the Summer Prior to Starting School?

The short answer is yes, but it's generally recommended you take the time off and enjoy your summer. In hindsight, I wish I had studied some prior to starting classes. Much of the difficulty of medical school is getting used to the new terminology associated with the material. If I could do it again, I would have pre-studied casually during the summer and would have pre-read the following books:

- I would familiarize myself with the *BRS Physiology* and *Pathology books* (commonly known as the Blue and Red book). These books contain all the fundamentals of physiology and pathology that you will learn during your first two years, and being familiar with the general material will put you ahead. Try to read each book once through as they are relatively short. While a lot of the material will go over your head, it'll pay off later.
- Buy a copy of *First Aid for the USMLE ® Step 1* (*2017* or whatever is newest). During the summer, just aim to become generally familiar with this book. This is the essential book for the USMLE Step 1, which all students take late spring/early summer after the first two years of medical school. Skim through this book; start understanding how it is laid out and what kind of material it contains.
- Consider buying *Netter's Anatomy*, as most medical schools use this book to teach anatomy alongside the anatomy lab. You'll almost definitely be buying this book for Anatomy, and I highly suggest buying the *Netter Anatomy Flashcards* and getting familiar with these prior to starting school.

Overview of Years 3 and 4

The third and fourth years of medical school are better known as the clinical years of medical school. You will rotate through the following specialties:

- Internal Medicine
- Surgery
- Pediatrics
- Family Medicine
- Psychiatry
- Obstetrics/Gynecology
- Neurology
- Surgical sub-specialties

During your rotations you will usually be put into a team comprised of attending physicians, residents, and other medical students. Your goal during 3rd year will be to learn how to function like a resident, and learn how to perform the clinical duties of a physician. You'll learn how to obtain a clinical history from a patient, perform an appropriate physical exam, structure a differential diagnosis, and come up with a plan regarding tests and treatment.

As a 3rd year med student, you want to be good at three things: You want a good differential, you want to know how to treat both common and rare diseases, and you want to ace the shelf (a test at the end of each rotation).

You'll also learn how to present your findings to attending physicians. Attendings and residents will then evaluate you on all your abilities. During your rotations, you will also take standardized tests on the material for each rotation (book recommendations for these tests is discussed on the website).

During your fourth year, you'll be able to pick more specific rotations that are more interesting to you. You'll be able to rotate through specialties such as cardiology, nephrology, orthopedics, plastic surgery, etc. You'll also spend fourth year applying to residency and getting ready for internship year.

During the end of your third year, you will have to take the USMLE Step 2 (divided into two parts, CK and CS) and during the beginning of your fourth year you will have allotted time to rotate through other non-core rotations that you may be interested in, including: Dermatology, Radiology, Plastic Surgery, Anesthesiology, Radiation Oncology, Ophthalmology, etc.

During the end of your third year, you'll also finally decide on a medical specialty to pursue and you'll begin your application for residency. This will occupy most of your fourth year as you send out your application and beginning interview around the country for residency spots. During the spring of your fourth year, you'll go through what is famously known as The Match, which I'll discuss later on, but will essentially decide where you go for residency. During your third year rotations, you will be usually be assigned to a medical team comprised of attending physicians (the bosses), residents, other medical students, and allied health practitioners (pharmacists, PA students, etc.),

Your goal during the third and fourth years is to take the knowledge base that you built during the first two years and learn the practical clinical implications of these concepts. You also get to learn about how to treat all the varying pathology and be able to provide a prognosis. On top of this, you really begin to learn how to perform the clinical duties of a resident and attending physician.

During this time you'll learn how to function like an effective medical resident, learning how to obtain a clinical history from a patient, perform an appropriate clinical exam, structure and form a differential diagnosis, and come up with a treatment plan for your patients. Your ability to perform these functions accurately and efficiently will be how the residents and attendings grade you during these rotations. At the end of each rotation, you will also generally take a standardized test on the material for each rotation. Here is a brief overview of how you can prepare for and expect from the major rotations you'll go through:

The Clinical Rotations

Medical Hierarchy:

One thing to quickly realize is that there is a well-established hierarchy in the medical world and it pretty much goes as follows: *med student, intern, resident, fellow and attending* at the top. You'll quickly find that the level of respect and acknowledgement you get will be directly correlated with your standing on that hierarchy scale, and it'll get old fast. In my experience, med students are essentially treated like dirt (I definitely felt this way), and being an intern is only slightly better in that you get paid something rather than paying tens of thousands of dollars to be at work. As you go up the residency ladder (higher PGY level) things will get better and better. My advice is to respect the hierarchy, be patient, and with time you'll earn your spot towards the top. It's a lot like the military and there's really no getting around it.

Below, I go over the major rotations you'll go through and my tips for surviving them, doing well, and hopefully acing the rotation.

Surgery:

Known to be the hardest rotation, the hours and expectations on this service can be grueling. This is one of the core rotations all medical students must somehow get through. One of the best ways to prepare for this rotation is to read *Dr. Pestana's Surgery Notes*, which is widely regarded as the most important book for the surgical rotation in medical school. It's short, to the point, and has 180 questions in the back, which test your knowledge of the material. What I like best about this book is the brevity. The truth of the matter is that on your surgery rotation you simply will not have time to read a full-scale book like *NMS Surgery* or *First Aid for Surgery*.

I read selected chapters out of those texts, but don't feel that I gained an incredible amount beyond this book. Instead, I chose to read this book 3 or 4 times. This book will teach you and test you the main things covered on the surgery shelf, fundamental things to know like what's the next step when a patient presents with certain signs and symptoms. A loose example of the kind material tested on the shelf that this book will etch into your head is: A patient presents with right lower quadrant pain of one hour to the ED (Emergency Department), what's the next step? US, CT, or straight to the OR for appendectomy?

Internal Medicine:

Better known as the essential or core medical specialty, this really serves as the foundation and building block for the rest of the medical specialties. Internal medicine deals with medical problems including but not limited to cardiac, pulmonary, and renal issues. Internal medicine docs are often primary care doctors and somehow find a way to manage extremely complicated patients with extensive medical problems. Internal medicine doctors nowadays either function primarily as an outpatient doctor (clinic doctor), or a hospitalist (doctor that rounds on patients in the hospital), with some doing a hybrid practice of both. This rotation can be exhausting, as you'll be expected to see a variety of patients every day, most with very complicated medical histories. You'll be expected to know how to manage their multiple issues and a huge amount of trivia related to their disease processes.

When you do your internal medicine rotation, most likely you'll have a mixed experience where you'll rotate with a team of residents and a hospitalist, and you'll also be assigned to a doctor who primarily functions in the clinic seeing outpatients. The best way to prepare for internal medicine is to have solid grasp on patient workups and presentations.

You should review the book *Step Up to Internal Medicine,* which was the number one resource I used on my internal medicine clerkship. I also used it for preparing for the Internal Medicine shelf. Every single attending you work with on internal medicine will tell you to read *Harrison's Principles of Internal Medicine*, but this just can't be done. Harrison's is thousands of pages of thick text, and is suitable for residents and attendings alike who are devoting their lives to internal medicine.

To review, as a med student, you want three things: You want a good differential, you want to know how to treat both common and rare diseases, and you want to ace the shelf. The next section of this book will prepare you for all of these without breaking your back. There are plenty of good images, good mnemonics (though you still might rely on some from *First Aid for Step 1*, I did), and covers all the bases. This is a bullet point stylebook, so keep that in mind if you learn better from a different writing style. Use this in conjunction with the USMLE World Q-Bank for Step 2.

Pediatrics:

Many med students find the pediatrics rotation surprising in that the most difficult part is dealing with the patients' parents. Pediatrics is a whole different world from adult medicine, and deals with conditions and syndromes you'll rarely if ever see on other rotations. Many of the kids' parents have spent a huge amount of time in the hospital with their kids, so they can be very knowledgeable but also demanding on the medical staff (rightfully so). You'll want to read a lot on this rotation, as the there are multiple syndromes and associations that you'll be quizzed on daily.

The best book I found for this rotation is the *BRS Pediatrics* book, though it is somewhat old (2004) and a lot of the information is a bit dated. With that said, I still think this is the best text available for the pediatrics clerkship. The organization in this book is better than found in any other. Reflecting back on the pediatrics shelf, I think the most important thing to recognize for the shelf is the epidemiology and risk factors of pediatric disease and conditions. The book highlights the most important aspects of the pediatrics shelf and questions that really fill out your knowledge after each chapter. I recommend doing the questions immediately following reading the text, and then reviewing the questions again several days later. The questions really focus on the aspects that will be tested on the shelf. In short, its a dated text, but pediatrics hasn't changed that much.

Psychiatry:

This may be one of the most interesting and strange rotations you'll go through during med school. You'll just have to experience it for yourself to see.

First Aid for Psychiatry is probably the most used book for the psychiatry shelf. As with above, the book is short. There's no fluff to be found here. DSM-V has many changes made to diagnosis, including diseases that have been added, removed (Asperger's is no longer recognized as an independent entity from Autism), and changes to diagnostic criteria. I like this book because it lists exactly what the shelf will be testing, the diagnostic criteria of the major psychiatric disorders. If you know the diagnostic criteria, you will pass this shelf. If you know the appropriate drugs for conditions and what alternatives to use, you will ace it. And I'll be honest, though this book is for a previous version of the DSM, if your knowledge is good enough that you are recognizing these discrepancies, than you are just fine for the test. This is a test for medical students with a basic knowledge, not a test for psychiatry senior residents. One note from my own experiences was that Lithium came up a lot on the shelf for treatment in instances other than bipolar disorder.

Family Medicine:

Family Medicine: Essentials of Family Medicine. There are a lot of different sources for family medicine, and this is the one that I decided to read all the way through based on reading through various medical school family clerkship web pages. I believe this is simply the best text available. The problem with the family medicine shelf is that it tests the things you don't think are worth studying for internal medicine, and it includes pediatrics and basic OB/GYN. This book has a huge emphasis on giving the grades of evidence for management strategies of various diseases. I think it really helps to have the evidence grade found along with the guidelines and suggestions to know if what your learning is RCT proven (Grade A) or just something a couple experts decided over a couple cold ones at the bar (Grade C).

Is black cohosh an RCT-proven treatment for post-menopausal syndrome? The family medicine shelf will test stuff like this, and this book will teach you, the answers.

Anesthesiology:

This was one of my personal favorite rotations. I found the attendings and residents to be extremely med student friendly, the hours reasonable and the rotation fun. I learned how to do procedures like intubate patients, start arterial and venous lines and a ton about pharmacology. If you're thinking about pursuing anesthesia as a career I highly recommend it.

Affectionately known, as "*Baby Miller*" among anesthesiologists and residents, this book is the abbreviated version of Miller's Anesthesia. Speaking with residents and attending physicians, I know that not one of them has ever read the entirety of Miller's Anesthesia, but I do know that almost all of them have read *Baby Miller*.

In fact, I recently spoke with the director of anesthesiology at a program and he noted this as the most important book any med student could read to impress on their anesthesiology clerkship. It has all the information that is essential for residents and attendings, but is written in a manner that feels almost casual to read. You will get questioned on the material in this book, and if you bring up some of the information found in this text on service, they will know you read (what comes to mind is the image in this text of the proper alignment of axes for easy intubation via direct laryngoscopy).

Radiology:

Another one of my all-time favorite rotations, the residents and attendings at most hospitals are very laid back and treat med students great. You have the opportunity to learn more than you thought and hang out with radiologists who are sometimes referred to as the "*doctor's doctor.*" A branch of radiology, interventional radiology is procedure heavy and deals with cutting-edge procedures involving all aspects of the body and all organ systems. Interventional radiology recently became its own independent specialty and until recently was a subspecialty of diagnostic radiology. If you get a chance, make sure to rotate through both departments and it might convince you that radiology is for you. Highly recommended.

As far as reading material, almost everyone recommends that med students read *Felson's Chest Imaging* book, which goes over the basics on how to read a chest X-ray. That's probably not quite enough, so I recommend the book "*Learning Radiology*" by Dr. William Herring, which is perfect for medical students (the website is really good too).

OB/GYN:

One of the more difficult rotations I went through in medical school, and not exactly my favorite. I found the people and lifestyle to be exhausting, but you may have a very different experience so keep an open mind.

As far as book recommendations, of all the texts "*Blueprints: Obstetrics and Gynecology* " is probably the one I offer with the lowest of all the recommendations. I believe it's the best book available for OB/GYN, though it's not perfect. Everything you need to know for the shelf will be in this book, the question is whether you have the patience to read the chapters and memorize the content. There are questions at the end of each chapter, but I didn't find them as critical to ingraining knowledge as *BRS Pediatrics*. In short, the information is here, but it's a tough read.

Write-up and Presentation Basics

Presentation Basics

A big component of how you're evaluated during 3rd and 4th year is your ability to effectively and eloquently communicate. A tradition in medical school and residency is the patient presentation, usually given by the med student or resident to the attending. Even though it'll seem a bit useless when you first start doing them, the aim of this process is to teach you how to filter and organize information on many different patients and communicate these findings to other physicians. Presentations will be broken up into oral presentations, of which there will be new full patient presentations, or small update style presentations for patients that the team knows. You'll also have the written portion, which will include the first big work up called the history and physical, and then your daily progress note. These are written in a SOAP format (subjective info, objective info, assessment, plan).

Written Component

H and P
Stands for history and physical, this document is a fully comprehensive work up of the patient performed during the initial evaluation by the physician. This is written documentation of a discussion of the patient's current presenting medical problem, medical and surgical history, medication list, social and family history, review of systems, physical exam findings and your assessment and management plan for the patient. This has a very specific format and is conventionally followed between specialists and parts of the country. The breakdown of an H and P in the conventional order is:

Chief Complaint: One sentence that summarizes why the patient came to the hospital or clinic.

HPI (History of Present Illness): When writing this section you present the age and sex of the patient, you'll put the patients medical status into perspective by mentioning relevant current medical issues, and then you'll go into an in depth discussion on the current issue that brought the patient to the hospital. You'll want to fully characterize the current presenting symptom or symptoms making sure to discuss time of onset, severity, alleviating and worsening factors, change in symptoms, history of similar event, other symptoms. Remember to address the PQRST factors (provocative/palliative, quality/quantity, region, severity and timing).

Surgical History: Get a detailed history of all the patient's surgeries. This will also help in the work up; if patient has a history of an appendectomy then you won't be looking for that, and its important to document for yourself and other specialists that may be reading the document. Duh.

PMHx (Past medical history): You'll want to get a detailed medical history on the patient's current and past medical problems. These may change how you manage the current issue or may clue you in to the source or etiology of the current problems.

Social History: Does the patient drink or smoke? If so, how many drinks per day and how many packs of cigarettes per day. Learn about their marital status, living situation, occupational exposures (like type of work environment), any recent travel or exposure to sick people, any pets (like birds).

Family History: Ask about any medical issues that run in the family, affecting parents or siblings. Remember that some people are adopted so be clear about biological family.

Allergies: Ask about allergies, with a special emphasis on medications.

Current Medications: You want to ask the patient and document all their current medications, the doses, how often they take them.

Review of Systems (ROS): This is usually a checklist to run through from head to toe regarding any other symptoms.

Physical Exam: The patient should get a comprehensive physical exam, especially on the initial work; you'll document your findings in this section.

Vital Signs: Heart rate, blood pressure, respiratory rate, temperature, O2 saturation.

GENERAL: How does the patient look overall (well-appearing, distressed, disheveled).
EYES: Extra-ocular muscles, pupils.
ENT: Ears, nose and throat.
CARDIAC: Listen to the hear sounds; describe whether there is a regular rate and rhythm, whether you hear any murmurs, gallops or rubs.
LUNGS: Are the lungs clear when you listen? Describe whether you hear rales, crackles, rhonchi, wheezing or anything else.
ABDOMEN: Palpate the entire abdomen and document whether the abdomen feel soft, distended, tender to palpation, any masses that you might feel.
GENITOURINARY – Genital exam if appropriate.
EXTREMITIES: Look and examine the arms and legs. Document any amputation sites. Is there any leg or arm swelling, redness, ulcers, etc. are the pulses all intact.

MUSCULOSKELETAL: Strength, range of motion, swelling.

NEUROLOGICAL: A basic neurological exam involves testing cranial nerves 2-12, and evaluating for symmetric sense of touch, strength and proprioception. Is the patient alert and oriented to person, place and time?

Cranial Nerves:
CN I (Olfactory) – Check smell (not usually done).
CN II (Optic) - Visual acuity and funduscopic exam.
CN III (Oculomotor) - EOMs (Extraocular muscles).
CN IV (Trochlear) – EOMs.
CN V (Trigeminal) – Sensory nerves to face. Motor nerves to muscles of mastication. Have the patient clench their teeth, open jaw, and make sure they feel light touch to the jawline, cheek and forehead. Corneal reflex also.
CN VI (Abducens) – EOMs.
CN VII (Facial) – Motor innervation to the muscles of facial expression. Have the patient raise their eyebrows, frown and show their teeth, smile and then puff cheeks.
CN VIII (Vestibulocochlear) – Innervates hearing structure of the ear. Whisper in each ear, evaluate hearing; Weber/Rinne tests.
CN IX (Glossopharyngeal) – Sensation to the palate. Check gag reflex.
CN X (Vagus) – Make the patient say "ahhhh." Watch to see the palate and uvula move upward.
CN XI (Accessory) – Motor nerves to sternocleidomastoid and trapezius. Have the patient shrug their shoulders. Turn their head against the resistance of your hand.
CN XII (Hypoglossal) – Evaluate the tongue for atrophy and fasciculations. Look for atrophy or deviation of the tongue to one side.

Laboratory Results: Current labs that have returned. Mention any important trends if there are old labs.

Radiology Results: Include radiology exam findings.

Assessment and Plan: In this section of the write up you bring all the information together into a nice summary, and you discuss what you think the patients most important issues are in order of importance, what you think is causing them, and your plan for each issue as how you'll work it up further, how you'll treat it, and whether you'll consult a specialist.

Oral Component:
Once you finish the write-up, as a med student or resident you're going to be expected to present your work up to the attending, and if you are getting a bunch of new patients you might be presenting multiple patients which can make this pretty challenging to do well. As always, practice and repetition will make you good, and understanding your audience will make you even better. The kind of presentation that your surgery attending wants to hear is very different from your internal medicine attending. Some of the major things to keep in mind while doing these is that people have short attention spans, which is made worse by listening to confusing or poorly done presentations.

You'll want to practice your presentation quickly before giving it, follow the format, try to speak confidently, and refer to your notes as little as possible. Maintain eye contact with your attendings and adjust your discussion to your audience. I found that on internal medicine for instance many attendings would make you go through the whole work up initially, but as you get better they would let you summarize it down shorter to just the relevant points. On surgery, our presentations were 1-2 minutes max, and on internal medicine they were up to 10 minutes or more, but this is attending and specialty dependent.

Progress Notes:
Once the patient has been on your service then you'll see them every day and write progress notes. These notes are much more brief than the H and P and usually include a brief summary of the patient and progress in the hospital stay, major developments or interval changes, updates on physical exam and labs, and update on the problem list, assessment and plan. You'll also present this orally to the attending daily, which will also be quite succinct.

Basics of Anatomy

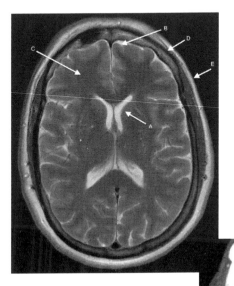

A – Lateral Ventricles
B – Gray Matter
C – White Matter
D – Skull
E – Scalp

CTA examination shows the
blood supply to the brain, which
is the Circle of Willis with its
branches taken on one cross-sectional image.

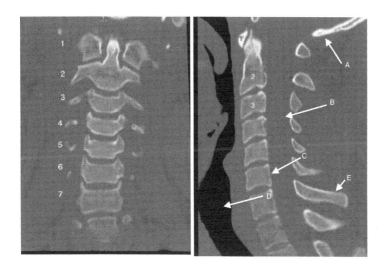

CT images taken reformatted in coronal (left) and sagittal (right) views show the 7 vertebral bodies of the cervical spine labeled on the left.

A – Skull base
B – Spinal canal with spinal cord
C – Vertebral body
D – Trachea
E – Spinous Process

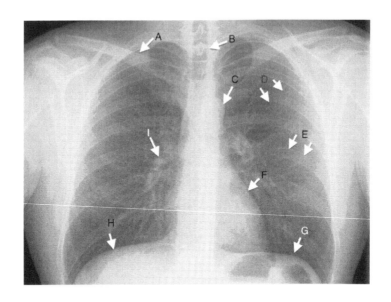

A – Right clavicle

B – Trachea

C – Aortic knob (top of the aortic arch)

D – Anterior rib

E – Posterior rib

F – Left heart border

G – Left hemi-diaphragm

H – Right hemi-diaphragm

I – Pulmonary vessels (arteries and veins)

Have system that you use each time to look at a chest x-ray. I get a general overview, and then I look at the bones (fractures, tumors), spine, heart (big, normal), lung apices (for pneumothorax), costophrenic angles (for pleural effusion), heart and mediastinum and the lungs (pneumonia, CHF, other).

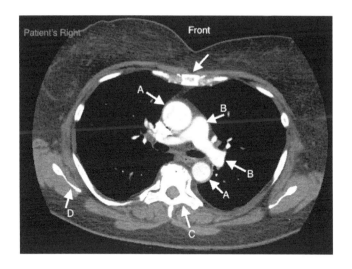

Cross sectional, contrast-enhanced CT image through the mid chest shown in the axial (cut like a sausage) view, in a "*soft tissue window*."

A – Aorta, ascending (top) and descending (bottom) portions
B – Main pulmonary artery and left pulmonary arterial branch
C – Vertebral body
D – Scapula
Single Arrow - Sternum

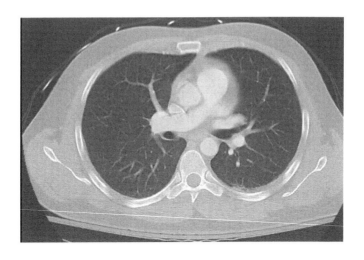

Contrast-enhanced CT through the mid-chest now shown in a special *"lung window"* that allows one to see the lung better than on the prior image. The window is set by changing the way the raw data from the CT scanner is interpreted and shown on the computers. We change windows to look for different things. For instance, on the lung window we can look for things like pneumonia or the processes that affect the lungs. On the prior page, the "soft tissue window" is better for evaluating the muscles, vessels and other things more dense than lung. Understand this stuff, even advanced residents in some specialties don't understand these very basic concepts.

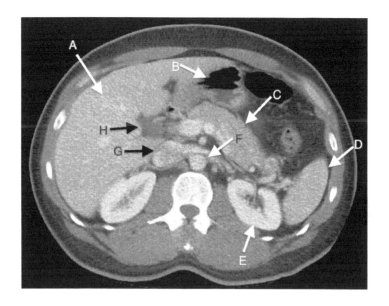

Contrast enhanced CT through the upper abdomen, shown in the axial slice and "soft tissue window."

A – Liver
B – Part of the distal stomach
C – Pancreas
D – Spleen
E – Left Kidney (patient's left on the image right)
F – Aorta
G – Inferior Vena Cava
H – Small part of the Gallbladder

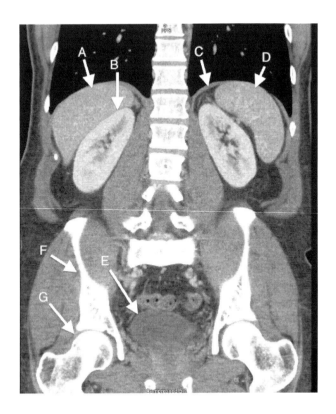

A – Liver

B – Right kidney (remember the patient's right is actually the left side of the image).

C – Left hemi-diaphragm

D – Spleen

E – Urinary bladder

F – Pelvis

G – Right hip, femoral head in the acetabulum

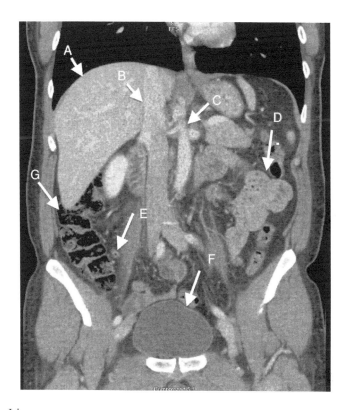

A – Liver
B – Inferior Vena Cava
C – Aorta
D – Portion of small bowel
E – Normal appendix, partially visualized
F – Urinary bladder
G – Cecum (ascending colon)

1. CASE: You're working in the ER and an 85-year-old female is brought to the ED by her family. They state that the patient suddenly developed problems seeing and had trouble forming words. Your emergency room training prompted you to order imaging of the brain. You call radiology for the results, but discover that the radiologist has wandered off in search of elusive Pokémon© in the hospital, leaving you to look at the images by yourself for the time being. What do you think the diagnosis is based on the images? (Pokémon is a registered trademark of Nintendo).

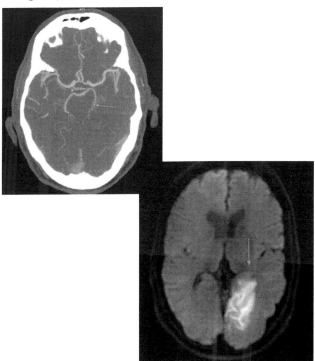

Stroke – The images above show an abrupt cutoff of a branch of the Circle of Willis (the left PCA). The second image shows a corresponding bright area on MRI diffusion based image. These findings are consistent with infarct, which leads to the symptoms of stroke. Stroke is a condition that's discussed all the time in the media and amongst the public. If you ask a random person to describe what a stroke actually is, few can actually describe the details about the pathophysiology. In order to understand what a stroke is we first have to review the basic anatomy and physiology of the brain. The brain is composed of gray and white matter. Each type of cell serves a particular function. The brain is also divided up into how it controls and responds to the human body.

If you have some time, you should Google "*homunculus.*" Essentially the homunculus is an artistic description of how each part of the brain controls different parts of the human body. Like every organ in the body, the brain has a complex blood supply. The main blood supply to the brain arises from the aortic arch in your chest, where the common carotid arteries originate. These then course up your neck and split into the external carotid arteries (supplying the muscles in your face) and the internal carotid arteries (supplying your brain). The internal carotid arteries course up through you neck and eventually form what is known as the Circle of Willis in your brain.

The arteries that make up the Circle of Willis allow for the distribution of blood to different parts of your brain. Patients classically develop symptoms including arm or leg weakness, loss of sensation and/or control to parts of their body, facial droop, blurry vision, and inability to speak or understand speech normally. Other symptoms exist, but these are some of the most common. Patients are usually rushed to the emergency room after a family member notices some of these symptoms, and in the emergency room the physician will assess the patient for a stroke (through a specific set of guidelines).

The next line of evaluation usually involves obtaining a CT examination of the brain. This checks if there are any other things in the brain causing the patient's symptoms such as brain tumor or active bleeding. The second portion of the exam is performed with contrast, which makes it possible to visualize the vessels in the brain. This allows the radiologist to evaluate whether any of the vessels to the brain are occluded or causing the symptoms. If an occlusion is suspected or found, patients are treated with clot-busting drugs such as tPA, or they undergo minimally invasive surgery with a neuro-interventionalist, who is able to go after the clot and get it out of the artery in the brain using advanced vascular techniques with catheters and wires under image guidance (with an x-ray machine).

Below is a non-contrast and contrast-enhanced CT examination of the brain. The non-contrast portion of the exam helps to evaluate for abnormalities in brain structure, look for any bleeding, or other changes in the brain. Contrast is then injected into the patient's veins and is timed so that we can see the vessels in the brain. If a patient is having stroke symptoms, we worry that one of the vessels might be occluded or clogged up with clot or narrowed from bad atherosclerosis. Above, contrast is seen in the vessels of the brain, known as the Circle of Willis. Each branch has a name and brings blood to different parts of your brain, controlling different functions. When looking at these images, one can actively scroll through different layers of the brain and also look for things like aneurysms (abnormal out-pouching in the vessels) in the brain on top of many other things like occluded vessels or vasculitis.

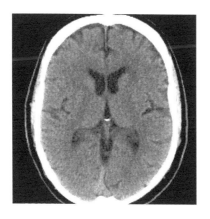

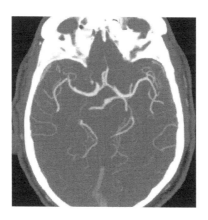

2. **Myocardial Infarction (Heart Attack)** – This common term is also discussed every day among the public, but again few people actually understand what it means. Heart attack in the medical world is known as myocardial infarction (an MI). Again, like with the brain or any other organ or muscle group, the heart needs its own arterial blood supply. This is provided by the coronary arteries, which arise from the very proximal parts of the aorta and dive back onto the heart and into the heart muscles. The coronary arteries course over different aspect of the heart, and provide oxygenated blood to the beating heart muscles (whom have a high demand due to the high activity of the muscle). The big coronary arteries to know about are the left and right main coronary arteries, as well as the left anterior descending (LAD), posterior descending, and circumflex arteries.

When one of these arteries becomes occluded, either with a buildup of plaque (from a lifetime of bad diet, smoking, diabetes, etc.) or thrombus (clot), the blood supply to certain portions of the heart is cut off. As you can imagine, when this happens, the heart stops receiving its optimal amount of rich, oxygenated blood. Patients begin developing chest pain as blood flow is decreased, and the heart muscle starts to strain and become ischemic from lack of blood flow, this is especially worsened when the heart increases its oxygen demand with exercise or strenuous movement.

Patients classically present with symptoms that include chest pain (feels like an elephant is sitting on my chest), left shoulder pain, diaphoresis (sweatiness), headache and nausea. Evaluation for MI is performed with an EKG (which can shows signs of an acute heart attack), and also labs including troponins, which is a chemical marker for cardiac injury. Patients can be further evaluated through nuclear medicine examinations, like a myocardial perfusion

118

scan, or the heart vasculature can be evaluated with angiography. Patients are usually treated with medications or angioplasty by an interventional cardiologist.

3. **Congestive Heart Failure (CHF)** –This is a very common heart problem experienced by millions of people in the United States. Essentially, due to different issues (prior heart attack, alcohol abuse, infections, heart valve and pulmonary problems) the heart eventually beats non-optimally, and flow through the heart starts to go, essentially, back up into the lungs. This often manifests as pulmonary edema, which means excess fluids in the tissues of the lungs, as the heart doesn't move the blood forwards well enough. Patients often feel short of breath, present coughing, and feel unwell. You can evaluate for CHF by getting an EKG, a chest radiograph (which will show an enlarged heart and increasing fluid in the lungs), and a lab called Brain Natriuretic Peptide, or BNP (a marker for heart failure). Patients are treated by a cardiologist, who tries optimizing heart function with certain medications and getting rid of excess fluid with diuretics such as Lasix, a diuretic, to get rid of excess fluid.

4. **Pneumonia** – One of the most common ailments in the chest, pneumonia is an infection of the airspaces in the lungs. The most common cause of pneumonia is generally from bacteria, such as streptoccocus pneumoniae, and others such as klebsiella or legionella. Other common causes of pneumonia include viral infection. It's also possible to get a fungal pneumonia, especially in patients who are immunocompromised such as those with HIV. One of the most common fungi to cause pneumonia includes aspergillosis, pneumocystis pneumoniae and coccidiomycosis. You'll learn about these in detail in med school. These kinds of infections generally present themselves in patients as chest pain, shortness of breath, fever, and overall ill-feeling. Most of these bacterial infections can be treated with antibiotics. Here is an example of a diffuse pneumonia (bottom) versus a normal chest x-ray (top).

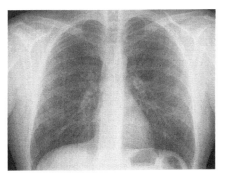

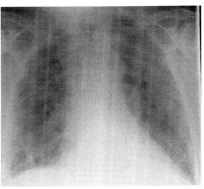

5. **Diabetes** – Occasionally you'll hear people call this "*the sugars*" (no joke, I have heard someone seriously say this to me, in actual life). Basically, this is a problem that exists in the balance between insulin and glucose in the bloodstream. Insulin is a hormone normally produced by particular cells in the pancreas known as beta-cells. When you eat food, glucose is released into your bloodstream. The body senses this increase in blood glucose and then releases insulin as a response, which attaches to receptors on various cells in your body and then stimulates them to take up glucose. In diabetes, people don't create or respond to insulin appropriately. Thus, you get diabetes, of which there are two types, I and II.

Type I Diabetes is generally seen in younger patients and happens when there is an autoimmune reaction in which the beta-cells of the pancreas are destroyed. This leaves little to no cells to make insulin, so the patient becomes dependent on insulin medication for replacement. The onset happens somewhat quickly, and the exact cause for why the body reacts to beta-cells isn't completely known, but genetics and possibly a reaction to a virus are some theories. Patients usually present with excessive urination, thirst and fatigue, and are usually on insulin replacement medicine for life. There are also some studies out there showing promise in a novel technique of implanting working beta-cells into patients' pancreatic tissues.

Type 2 Diabetes generally occurs in the older population and affects children less frequently. This type of diabetes has to do with decreased production and increased resistance to the insulin hormone, generally in people with poor lifestyle choices, including obesity and poor diet. This type of diabetes also results in excessive urination, thirst, fatigue and hunger. Type 2 diabetes is managed with diet and exercise, as well as insulin medication and medications like Metformin, which increase cellular sensitivity to insulin and increase insulin production. Type 2 diabetes has the potential to be reversed and cured if patients watch their diets well enough, and some studies have shown bariatric surgery to cure it as well.

6. **Deep Venous Thrombosis (DVT)** - A relatively common problem. This disease involves the development of thrombus, aka a blood clot, in one of your deep veins, usually in the leg at the level of the thigh or calf. This is one of the reasons that people are encouraged to get up and walk around when they are sitting for a long time, like on long flights or at work. These bloods clots develop in your veins because when you are sitting or not moving around enough, the blood becomes stagnant and is prone to clot off (this makes intuitive sense). Now, if this does happen, then the blood drainage from this area isn't optimal so this could lead to swelling of the extremity where you've developed the clot. The more feared complication of a DVT is the development of Pulmonary Embolism, which I describe in detail below. DVT is usually treated with anti-coagulants, medicines that break down or keep clots from forming.

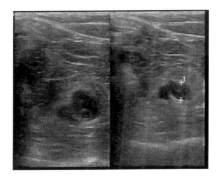

7. CASE: A 30 year-old man presents to the ED late one night during your shift. He states that he developed sudden chest pain and shortness of breath after being on a long 10-hour flight. He tells you he's never experienced anything like this before. You order imaging of the chest to check for something you suspect, but you find out the radiologist heard Sasquatch may be outside and ran out to look for him. You're on your own for right now. What are your thoughts?

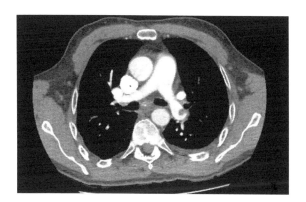

Pulmonary Embolism (PE) - A feared, potentially deadly process is usually secondary to a DVT. This is when a DVT (described above) that has developed, most likely in your leg, dislodges and travels up your leg, in the central veins in your body, and back to the heart. Once in the heart, the clot then gets pumped into the pulmonary arteries (carry deoxygenated blood which was returned from the body to the heart, and now being sent to the lungs to get oxygen). You can image that if a clot were to get lodged in a pulmonary artery, this will lead to significant increase in back pressures into the heart, causing straining of the heart, and you'll also have a lack of new oxygenated blood.

People generally present with sudden onset of chest pain and shortness of breath, sometimes after a long flight where they developed a DVT that then dislodged. This process can be fatal, and needs to be quickly diagnosed. You can get a blood marker called a D-dimer, which can indicate the presence of pulmonary embolism, and further evaluation is usually performed with a CT Chest PE with contrast. Treatment options for PE include anticoagulation medications, or interventional radiology using catheters to essentially break down and suck the clot out of the pulmonary artery. The image below shows a filling defect in the left pulmonary artery, which is compatible with a PE.

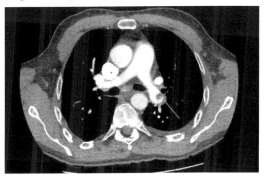

8. **COPD/Emphysema** – One of the big reasons you should never smoke, aside from increasing your risk of lung cancer, is developing chronic obstructive pulmonary disease (COPD) and emphysema of the lungs. Simply put, smoking causes severe damage of the substance of the lung, or the lung parenchyma, including the alveoli (which function in gaseous exchange). Smoking causes destruction of the structures, which leads to abnormal lung function. Your lungs have a tough time working correctly, when the fibers have been broken down, the normal lung can't expand and contract normally. As you can imagine, this leads to significant issues with breathing, exercise tolerance, predisposition to infections, and subsequent heart issues as well.

9. CASE: A 25 year-old male presents to the ER complaining of right lower quadrant abdominal pain. You find that he looks ill, has a fever and abnormal labs. You order an imaging test and find out that the radiologist is gone as he heard there is a UFO outside (he wants to believe). You are forced to look at this single CT image alone. What are your thoughts?

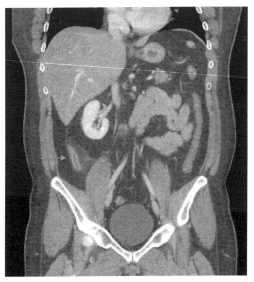

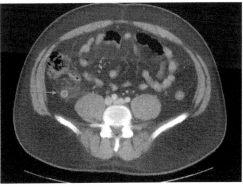

Appendicitis – The most common reason for an emergent surgery in the US, appendicitis is probably the best-known abdominal issue to just about everyone. The appendix is a small tube like structure arising from your ascending colon (also known as the cecum) in the right lower quadrant of your abdomen. Its thought to be a remnant from prehistoric times and doesn't serve too much of a function nowadays. Occasionally, the appendix can get inflamed and infected where food or a little stone (appendicolith) can get lodged at it's opening to the cecum, and you get this stagnant buildup of bacteria and colonic material. This leads to inflammation of the appendix. Sometimes, the appendix can get so inflamed it bursts, and you get spillage of the infected contents into the abdomen. If this happens, doctors worry that these contents will form into an abscess in the abdomen, which makes treatment more complicated. This is the reasoning behind going to surgery a lot of the time.

Most patients present with dull abdominal pain that starts around the mid-abdomen near the umbilicus and eventually migrate to the right lower quadrant. Patients present looking pretty sick, with fevers and worsening abdominal pain. The workup usually involves taking a good history and physical exam, checking laboratory values, such as a white blood cell count, which is a marker for inflammation and infection, and then evaluating the abdomen with imaging, including looking at the appendix with ultrasound, and more commonly CT.

10. **Cholelithiasisis (Gallstones)** – The gallbladder is a little sac-like organ that lies in the gallbladder fossa in your right upper quadrant, right alongside the liver. Its function is to make bile, which gets secreted through a series of ducts that connect the liver and gallbladder, and empty into your small bowel. The bile contents aid in digestion. A common issue

is the development of gallstones in the gallbladder. The contents of the gallbladder form into little stones and usually sit in the gallbladder without causing any issues. Occasionally, the stones may get lodged in the gallbladder neck or in the cystic duct that allows the gallbladder to excrete bile. When this happens, there is backup of bile in the gallbladder, increasing tension, and you develop acute cholecystitis, as described below.

11. **Acute Cholecystitis** – This is a common problem for many people each year, and when you hear about people having to have their gallbladder taken out, this is generally the reason. Occasionally, people with gallstones will get one lodged near the gallbladder outlet, which is the cystic duct. When a stone obstructs the gallbladder outlet, and it can't excrete bile like it normally does, then you get a buildup of pressure and stasis of bile, which can lead to infection and inflammation. When this happens, we call it acute cholecystitis and it generally requires the attention of a surgeon and may lead to surgery for a cholecystectomy.

12. **Hepatitis** – Generally, when a disease process name ends in "*itis*" it usually signifies an inflammatory process. Hepatitis essentially means liver inflammation, which can have lots of different causes. The most well known is hepatitis from viruses, including hepatitis A, B, and C. Other things that can cause liver inflammation include various medications, autoimmune response, alcohol, etc.

13. **Fatty Liver Disease (Hepatic Steatosis)** – One of the most common issues that affects peoples' livers in the United States and attributed to poor diet and obesity. This also goes by the more formal name of hepatic steatosis. Essentially, due to non-optimal lifestyle choices including poor diet and exercise, you get a buildup of fatty deposits in your liver.

This leads to a chronically irritated liver which can progress changes of fibrosis. This is generally reversible with improvement in diet and lifestyle. The most worrisome complication is progression to cirrhosis as described below.

14. **Cirrhosis** – Repeated bouts of inflammation and healing eventually can lead to an irreversible state for the liver where it fibrosis down and scars. This is called cirrhosis, and the most common cause in the United States is alcohol abuse followed by causes such as Hepatitis C. Cirrhosis is a very serious medical condition, and leads to further issues such as portal venous hypertension, ascites (abdominal fluid) and puts the patient at significantly increased risk for hepatocellular carcinoma. Treatment for this condition is essentially a liver transplant.

15. **Abscess** – You'll commonly hear this term and it's pretty important to understand, as it can happen almost anywhere in the body. An abscess usually develops when there's some sort of infected fluid collection that gets walled off. This can make you very sick. This can happen anywhere in the body, including the brain, spine, chest or abdomen. Pretty much, if bacteria can get there, an abscess can form. These things need to get antibiotics and then drained, either by surgery or by an interventional radiologist using a surgical drain or catheter.

16. **Bowel Obstruction** - Until starting residency, I didn't realize this was as big a problem in medicine as it is. This process happens most common secondary to adhesions, which are small little fibrous bands of tissue that develop in your body oftentimes years after surgery. These adhesions can get bowel loops caught up in them, and the bowel can get obstructed. Bowel obstructions can also be caused from masses like cancer, and infections and inflammation.

Sometimes you have to have surgery to fix this problem, as bowel obstruction can be very serious. Below, you can see a CT of the abdomen with dilated, fluid filled loops of bowel in the upper left hand corner of the image, which can be seen with a bowel obstruction.

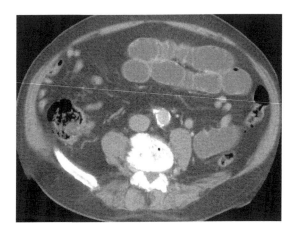

17. CASE: A 56 year-old man presents to you in the ED after developing a sudden, sharp excruciating chest pain while at the store. He states he's never felt a pain like this and it causes him to feel short of breath. You order imaging, STAT! You call radiology as soon as the scans are done, but you find that the disgruntled radiologist has yet again disappeared, this time to a Justin Bieber concert (a once in a lifetime opportunity). You need to start figuring out what's going on based on the images. What do you think?

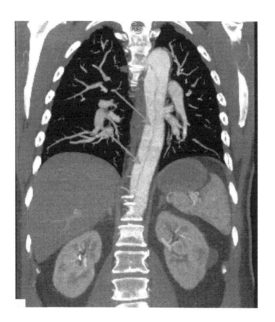

Aortic Dissection – A very serious medical emergency, aortic dissections usually happen in adults and older patients who are often hypertensive and involves the aorta, the great vessel of the body. The aorta is the large vessel that carries blood away from the heart and helps distribute it through branches throughout your whole body. The aorta runs from the heart, loops in the chest and comes down into your abdomen where it branches and then goes down to the legs as the iliac and femoral arteries. As you can imagine, this artery is really big, up to 3-4 cm in diameter, and the wall of this artery is pretty thick and made up of several layers.

When the inner layer of the aorta rips, blood can squeeze in and track between the inner and middle layer creating a new channel filled with blood. Thus, you get a true lumen and false lumen in your aorta. In the CT images, you can see what is called the "*dissection flap*" separating the true and false lumen. Dissections are divided into type A (involving the ascending aorta and aortic arch) and type B (involving the descending aorta). Type A's are generally treated with surgery, and type B is often treated with anti-hypertensive medicines.

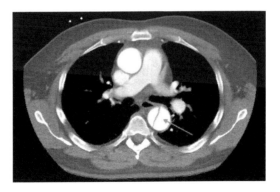

18. **Aneurysm** – An aneurysm is an abnormality of a vessel wall, usually an artery, which usually leads to an out-pouching and dilatation of a focal part of the vessel wall. When the vessels do this, you can kind of imagine how this part of the vessel becomes weak and prone to rupture. Now if this happens to an artery in the brain, or a major artery like the aorta, these generally need to be treated especially to try and prevent future rupture. Once an aneurysm ruptures, treatment can be complicated depending on where in the body the vessel has ruptured. If an aneurysm in the aorta in the chest or abdomen ruptures, this can be life threatening, as very large amounts of blood pass through the aorta. There are various size cutoffs for treatment depending on where the aneurysms are and what vessels they involve, and you'll study this all in more detail in med school.

19. **Brain Tumor** – There are a host of different types of brain tumors, all with different levels of severity and have different treatments and prognoses. One of the main way tumors are broken down is by age, with pediatric tumors usually having a somewhat different differential than adult tumors, but there is some cross-over. Some of the more common pediatric tumors include medulloblastomas, pilocytic astrocystomas, gliomas, astrocytomas on top of several others.

   More common adult tumors include glioblastoma multiforme, meningiomas, subtypes of gliomas and astrocytomas. These can occasionally be seen on CT examination but are better evaluated by MRI, which looks at soft tissues in the brain much better.

20. **Brain Hemorrhage** – This is most commonly caused during trauma, like car accidents or falls, and is the most likely reason you'll get a brain CT scan if you are taken to

the hospital. Things like hypertension can also cause bleeding. There are different types of brain bleeds, and they are managed differently depending on where they are seen. The three types of brain hemorrhage classifications include subarachnoid hemorrhage and then subdural and epidural hematomas. The most emergent of the three are epidural hematomas, which can grow and cause brain herniation as they compress the brain and shift it in the skull causing major issues. Subdural hematomas are still serious but can be managed without urgent surgery as can subarachnoid hemorrhage. I've included a picture of a large brain hemorrhage as seen below.

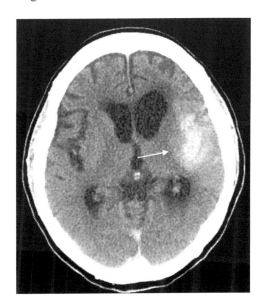

21. **Meningitis** – You hear about this disease quite a bit in the news, usually having to do with outbreaks on college campuses or wherever people are in close quarters. Meningitis means inflammation of the meninges. The meninges are a special layer of connective tissue around the brain. When this tissue around the brain gets infected, it's named meningitis and can be very serious and needs treatment. This can be diagnosed by doing a lumbar puncture, which is when physicians use a needle to access the fluid surrounding the spine, which can be tested to see if there is meningitis on top of many other things. You can also sometimes see meningitis on MRI examination of the brain.

22. **Sepsis Spectrum** – SIRS (Systemic Inflammatory Response Syndrome) and Sepsis is a spectrum of systemic response patients get following progression of an infection, such as pneumonia. The spectrum of severity progresses from *SIRS > sepsis > severe sepsis > septic shock*. When patients get progressively sick following infection, a body response is mounted which include a release of inflammatory markers, which then set off a cascade of reactions in the body.

Sepsis usually first starts with an infection such as a pneumonia or urinary tract infection, which goes untreated. The patient then starts to develop symptoms of fatigue, tachycardia, low blood pressure, fever, and decreased urination as the body continues to mount a reaction to the infection with a stronger response. Eventually, a progression of organ dysfunction and breakdown start occurring. There are specific diagnostic criteria for diagnosing the differing levels of SIRS and sepsis, using some of the criteria below:

- *Heart Rate*: > 90 beat per minute
- *Temperature*: <36 °C (96.8 °F) or >38 °C (100.4 °F)

- *Respiratory Rate*: >20 per min or PaCO2<32 mmHg
- *WBC Count*: 4×10^9 per L (<4000/mm³), >12×10^9 per L (>12,000/mm³), or 10% bands

This condition is treated in the hospital, and can become extremely serious. Patients are usually treated with IV fluids and antibiotics to combat the infection. Sometimes, people end up in the ICU because the infection and inflammatory response become disabling that they need life support and intense high-level observation and treatment.

23. **Pancreatitis** – Meaning inflammation of the pancreas, pancreatitis is also seen along a spectrum ranging from a mild inflammation of the organ to severe inflammation and necrosis of the pancreatic tissue, which can be life threatening. The most common cause for pancreatitis is alcohol abuse, but there are a ton of other causes including medications, trauma, infection, cancer, hypertriglyceridemia or most interesting, from the sting of a scorpion from Trinidad/Tobago (everyone's favorite med school factoid). If pancreatitis gets really bad, parts of the tissue become necrotic (dead tissue) and you can get fluid collections (pseudocysts) and infection. Treatment can be quite complicated, and you'll learn how to treat and manage it during your clinical rotations.

24. **Pyelonephritis** – This is commonly known as a "kidney infection" and is quite common. Most people start out having a urinary tract infection that progress up to the kidney. Generally, this can be treated with fluids and antibiotics, but as with everything, it can get more complicated.

136

25. **Renal/Ureteral Stone** – Super common reason for people complaining of abdominal pain, and I'd say the most important thing to know is the different types of stones seen. Most stones are made up of calcium oxalate and pyrophosphate. You can usually see these things sitting in the kidney, ureter, or bladder on a CT scan without contrast. If the stone is big, it can obstruct the ureter and cause a back-up of fluid/urine and keep the associated kidney from excreting normally. This dilates the kidney and can lead to hydronephrosis (dilation of the renal collecting system). If the stones get big enough, a urologist has to go in and extract the stones using various methods.

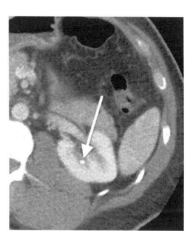

26. **ACL Tear** – People talk about having their ACLs torn all the time, but I find that a lot of laypeople have a hard time describing what it means or where exactly it's located. To break it down, first you need to know there are a bunch of ligaments in the knee, but two of the really important ones are the ACL (anterior cruciate ligament) and the PCL (posterior cruciate ligament). There are also the medial and lateral collateral ligaments. These 4 main ligaments stabilize the knee and help you do your normal movements. The most commonly torn ligament in the knee is the ACL and it connects from the back end of your femur to the front of your tibia. I've included a normal MRI of the knee so that you can better visualize what I'm talking about. In sports like soccer or basketball that require a lot of changes in positioning and pivoting, this ligament is prone to injury and tear. When the

ACL gets torn, there's often a triad of findings with the medial meniscus and medial collateral ligament also getting injured in the process. Below are MRI images of the knee, taken in a sagittal position (you are seeing the knee from the side with the patella in front, or on the left of the image). Top image shows a normal PCL ligament. The lowest image shows a missing ACL consistent with ACL tear.

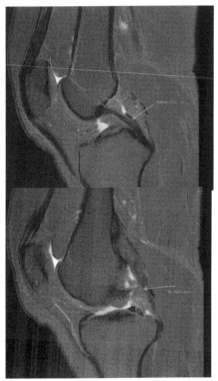

27. **Intussusception** – Most commonly seen in the young pediatric population, this can be an urgent finding that may need immediate treatment. This occurs when a loop of bowel *"telescopes"* into another loop of bowel, effectively causing an obstruction in the bowel that needs a quick fix. The most common location for this to happen is at the level of the ileum and cecum, but this happens in other locations as well. This is important to know for your pediatrics rotation. The best way to evaluate for this is with an abdominal ultrasound.

28. **Pleural Effusion** – There is a lining that surrounds the lung that is called the pleura, and it is made up of two layers called the parietal and visceral pleura. In different medical conditions, fluid builds up in this space and it is called a pleural effusion. These can develop from infections, cancer, heart disease, liver disease and multiple other causes. It's relatively common and can be treated with a thoracentesis, which involves inserting a needle into the space and draining the fluid. The contrast-enhanced CT below demonstrates a large pleural effusion along the right posterior chest. Something this large can usually be drained with a needle and the fluid can be sent to the laboratory to evaluate it and hopefully provide information on the origin of the pleural fluid.

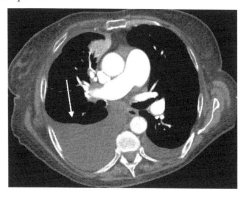

29. Pneumothorax – In certain situations such as trauma, instead of fluid building up in the pleural space, you can get air that builds up. Depending on the mechanism by which this happens, it could be life threatening. A tension pneumothorax is a subtype of this process that is most worrisome and can cause death if not treated with a needle to get the air out of the pleural space. Here is what a pneumothorax looks like on CT. The arrow is pointing to a pneumothorax along the patient's left lung. This patient was involved in a trauma and had multiple fractures and a pneumothorax.

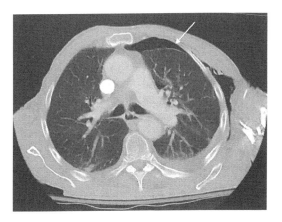

30. **Locked in Syndrome** - This is a very rare and terrifying diagnosis that results from a stroke involving a very specific area of the brainstem. A patient is characteristically only left with the ability to communicate with eye movements, with complete loss and paralysis of almost all other functions (there is a spectrum of affected loss of function).

31. **Hypertension** - There are two components to measuring blood pressure. Normal blood pressure ranges include the systolic pressure which ranges from 90-119 mmHg. The bottom number is the diastolic pressure and normally ranges from 60-79 mm Hg. The hypertension cutoff is usually 139 systolic and 89 diastolic. There are several levels of hypertension. High blood pressure as you can imagine is like having an abnormally high water pressure in pipes. There are many causes for hypertension. Hypertension can lead to problems such as aneurysm development and brain hemorrhage.

32. **Diverticulitis** - Commonly occurring in older patients, small colonic out-pouchings called diverticula start coming off parts of the colon, most commonly at the level of the sigmoid colon. These can number in the dozens or hundreds. These outpourings can get inflamed for various reasons and can lead to diverticulitis. This can be a recurring issue for lots of people. Sometimes if the inflammation is bad enough you can form abscesses and even get a bowel perforation. Treatment is usually with antibiotics and/or surgery, like partial colectomy.

33. **Atrial Fibrillation** - You can think of this as a quivering of the atria, which leads to an irregular heart rhythm. Because the atria don't normally contract there is some stasis of blood in the atria, which can occasionally form a clot or

thrombus, with the fear that it could get dislodged and travel to the brain and cause a stroke, or could go to a limb and cut off normal blood supply leading to ischemia.

34. **Celiac Disease** – An immune reaction to gluten (proteins in grains) with the patient's bowel reacting in inflammation and classically causing diarrhea. Patients are at risk for developing complications from repeated bouts of inflammation such as scarring and fistulas as well as anemia. Patients are also at increased risk for lymphoma.

35. **Crohn's Disease** - One of two main inflammatory bowel diseases. This disease results in outbreaks of severe bowel inflammation that skips around in the GI tract directed by the bodies immune system. It classically involves the terminal ileum and causes diarrhea, weight loss, fevers and rashes. Patients are treated with long-term medications such as steroids or drugs targeting the immune system with potential complications of developing bowel obstructions and fistulas.

36. **Ulcerative Colitis** - The other main inflammatory bowel disease, also causes severe inflammation and ulcers in the bowel, usually the colon. Classically involves the rectum and usually is continuous in its involvement of the GI tract. Complications also include development of strictures and fistulas. Also treated with steroids and drugs targeting the immune system.

37. **Volvulus** – A potentially emergent finding when parts of the colon, usually either the cecum or sigmoid colon twists and flips about itself causing a high grade bowel obstruction that may need the immediate attention of a surgeon. A sigmoid volvolus usually involves older people (S for

seniors) and Cecil volvulus is seen more in kids (c for children).

38. **Colitis** - Inflammation of the bowel, which can be from a multitude of reasons. Ischemic colitis is caused by a blocked off blood supply to the bowel, usually from bad atherosclerosis or a clot/thrombus blocking an artery. Infectious colitis is usually from bacteria or viruses, and is classically caused by *Clostridium difficile* in hospitalized patients on antibiotics.

39. **Necrotizing Fasciitis** - A scary rapidly progressive severe soft tissue infection that requires the immediate attention of a surgeon and often leads to surgical debridement.

40. Ascites – This is the build-up of fluid in the abdominal cavity. This can also be from many causes, but the most common include liver failure from cirrhosis, infections, or cancer. Below is an ultrasound image of the abdomen that shows a lot of darkness in the abdomen. On ultrasound, clear fluid is dark and the frond like parts you see in the image are likely parts of small bowel and attachments.

Ascites can cause patients quite a bit of discomfort and the problem can usually be taken care of, at least temporarily with a paracentesis, which involves putting a needle into the abdomen and draining the fluid off. Ascites often re-accumulates so many patients need to get this drained routinely.

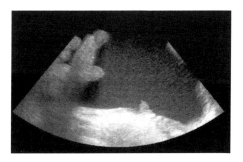

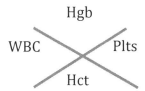

Above is the traditional way of documenting the basic lab values and approximate normal ranges are below (these vary slightly by institution and laboratory).

Na (Sodium) – 133-143 (abnormalities can indicate hypo/hypernatremia)
K (Potassium) – 3.5 – 5.1 (high or low levels can be dangerous)
Cloride – 98 – 106
CO2 – 22-30
BUN – 7 -20 (marker of renal function)
Creatine – 0.6 – 1.2 (marker of renal function)
Glucose – 70 – 100 (watch especially in diabetics and with insulin)

WBC (White Blood Cells) – 4.5 – 11.0 (marker of infection)
Hgb (Hemoglobin) – 12.o – 16.0
Hct (Hematocrit) – 41 -53

Plts (Platelets) – 150-350

Other Important Labs to Know

D-Dimer – This is a marker in the blood that can be seen with a pulmonary embolism, though it is not specific for it and can be seen with lots of other medical conditions. You usually use it to rule out a PE (if its negative, its unlikely there's a PE).

BNP – Brain natriuretic peptide is a blood marker that people use to evaluate for CHF. This is a peptide that secreted by the heart, specifically the ventricles in response to stretching from increased pressure, like that seen in CHF. Remember, congestive heart failure leads to increased vascular pressure because the heart isn't functioning well.

Troponin – This is a blood marker for a myocardial infarction, and its frequently ordered in patients presenting with chest pain and suspicious for heart attack.

ESR – Erythrocyte sedimentation rate. An inflammatory marker in the body.

CRP – An inflammatory marker in the body. This is known as an acute phase reactant.

Lipase and Amylase – Pancreatic enzymes, elevated levels can signify pancreatitis.

AST/ALT - Liver markers.

.

Medical Imaging Basics

I'll be the first to admit that in med school I thought imaging was a pretty dry topic and I wasn't too interested. That being said, I quickly realized how wrong I was, especially during my clinical rotations. Being able to understand the basics of medical imaging is crucial to being a good physician. Most of the diagnoses and management decisions made in medicine are based on diagnostic imaging, and even if you're not a radiologist, you need to know what exams to order, what to do with the results, and how to explain imaging to patients. In my experience, even specialists like anesthesiologists need to know what to order (you do an epidural injection and the patient develops back pain later on, how are you going to work this up?).

To make this process a little more interesting and easier, I've included the basics of the major imaging modalities. I briefly explain how the images are made and under what general circumstances you'd use each different type of modality. Keep in mind that many specialists outside of radiology need to understand imaging. Cardiologists read nuclear medicine exams and echocardiograms, and surgeons need at least a basic understanding of how to read x-rays, CTs and MRIs, etc.

Understanding medical imaging planes, or what direction images are taken in is one of the basic fundamental skills. I know advanced residents in specialties and even attendings that can't tell what the name of certain slices is, so it's time to make sure you know how to distinguish the different imaging planes. There are three basic ways to visualize cross-sectional images and that is in the axial, coronal and sagittal planes. The axial plane is if you placed someone down on the ground and imaginarily sliced them like a loaf of bread. A coronal image is if you sliced the images of the person across, so that you would look at them like you do normally, but at different levels. Sagittal means you look at them from the side. Look at the examples below and be sure to understand the terminology, its important.

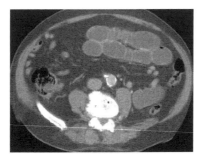

Figure: Axial slice.

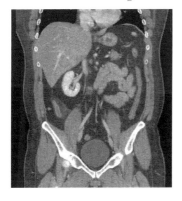

Figure: Coronal slice.

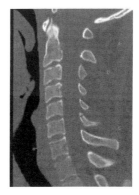

Figure: Sagittal slice.

X-Ray

So we've all heard about x-rays, but if you're headed to medical school it's time to increase your depth of knowledge regarding all imaging modalities.

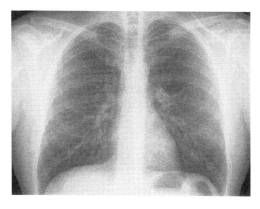

Imaging nowadays is a core diagnostic element. Many diagnoses and management issues are decided by imaging and many procedures are even image guided so understanding this stuff is crucial.

The x-ray or radiograph is most basic form of imaging. It was first developed in the late 1800s. X-rays are not too complicated to make, all you need are several things including electricity, an element such as tungsten and way to direct and collect the x-rays. To simplify the process, you run electrical current through a filament and element like tungsten, this is your cathode. This heated element then shoots out electrons towards another thing called your anode, which may also be tungsten.

A series of reactions undergo with the electrons coming in, and the elements own electrons, resulting in release of energy and out of this come x-ray photons, which are directed at a person. As they pass through the person, thick, dense material like bone absorbs some of these. The others pass through other body tissue easily, like lung. That's why lung looks dark on x-ray, and bone looks white. X-rays that pass through will darken the digital film

149

and thus you get an image of the body. The actual process is much more complicated, but that can give you a good basic understanding for how an x-ray is made and used.

CT

CT, commonly referred to as a CAT scan, actually stands for computed tomography. A CT scanner is based on the same principles as an x-ray machine. It uses ionizing radiation based imaging, aka x-rays. CT scanners have now been around for a few decades, and current generation scanners are very advanced and give amazing images of the body accurate to the millimeter.

A CT scanner works like a rotating x-ray machine with multiple detectors (often refereed to as 128 or 256 slice scanner etc.). The actual machine looks like a gigantic white donut standing on its side. A person lies on a table and goes through the hole in the donut, while inside the donut, the components that make and shoot x-rays spin around the person. A computer reconstructs the very complicated information from the detectors into an image of a person, with the ability to scroll through whatever was imaged.

CT scans are done either with or without IV or oral contrast and many clinicians have a hard time understanding when contrast should and should not be used. To understand it better, first we need to understand what CT can look at, and what contrast is. CT is great for looking at things like organs and bones, including the brain. MRI on the other hand, is much better at examining soft tissues in great detail, and giving information on tissue composition. Contrast is a dense iodine based material that absorbs x-rays. It is a fluid and is injected into the patient's venous system, usually through an IV during a CT exam. The contrast then mixes with the blood and goes to wherever blood goes. So contrast goes where blood goes, and blood goes to vessels and organs throughout the body.

Some reasons to use contrast include:
-   Desire to visualize solid organs better.

- Looking for infection (infected areas have inflammation and more blood and thus contrast goes there).
- Looking for tumors/cancer.
- Evaluate the vessels in the body, looking for things like aneurysms, vessel injury.
- Evaluate trauma patients and look for active bleeding from organs (if an organ is bleeding you can see blood with contrast hemorrhaging).

You might then ask yourself: Why would I ever order a study without IV contrast? There are several reasons:
- The patient is allergic to contrast.
- You are looking for something that doesn't require contrast to be seen, such as a stone in the kidney or ureter.
- Following lung nodules.
- Looking for fractures.
- Looking at the brain for trauma.

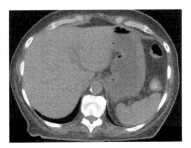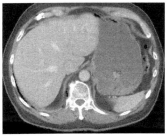

Non-contrast exam on the left and contrast-enhanced exam on the right so that you can compare and see how it affects imaging of organs like the liver and spleen.

MRI

MRI is a completely different animal than x-rays or CTs. The huge advantage of MRI over the others is that no radiation (x-rays) is used to get images of the body. The way an MRI works is based on very complicated physics and chemistry, which I will briefly go over. MRI wasn't developed until after CT, and it was coming into development in the 1970s. The importance of MRI imaging is so great that the inventors who created the ingenious equipment received the Nobel Prize.

An MRI works by utilizing 3 main things: a big magnet, a radiofrequency pulse (like a radio wave), and the spin of the body's hydrogen atoms. It was discovered that utilizing some crazy physics the body's hydrogen atoms can be coerced to spin in unison. This is some quantum mechanics business, but when this happens you can utilize radiofrequency pulses and detectors to image a body. Each type of tissue has different spin characteristics in their hydrogen atoms, so you can see different chemical properties in the tissues. That's probably all you really need to know about how it works for now.

MRI is great for looking at some tissues, abnormalities in the brain and spine like tumors and infections, as well as imaging of the joints, muscles and extremities. MRI is also used to examine the breasts for cancer in certain cases. MRI is also classically now used to diagnose acute stroke in a patient, as it's the best way to see if there is a brain infarct with a special imaging sequence called diffusion based imaging.

Ultrasound

Another completely different way of evaluating the human body is ultrasound. Ultrasound is performed using a small probe that contains piezoelectric crystals within the end of the probe. Using electricity, these crystals vibrate and transmit a sound pulse into the body, which then bounces off different tissues and back to the probe. All this stuff again involves some physics and math, but these pulse characteristics can be used to generate an image of what the ultrasound pulses are traveling through.

Ultrasound is really good at looking at vessels and blood flow, scanning through solid organs to look for masses or other abnormalities, gallbladder evaluation, looking at the appendix for first line appendicitis workup, looking for fluid in the abdomen and evaluating pregnancies on top of other things. You can also look for DVT, aneurysm, or other vessel abnormalities, which I talked about previously...just to name a few.

You also use ultrasound quite a bit during procedures, so even if you're not reading ultrasounds as a radiologist, you need to understand the basics of how these work. Placing lines, such as central lines nowadays requires ultrasound guidance and being able to guide your needle tip into a vein, so even interns working on the medical wards will be expected to know how to work an ultrasound machine and understand what is shown.

Nuclear Medicine

Nuclear medicine has an entire medical specialty dedicated to it and encompasses an entirely different method of imaging. Nuclear medicine is based on using radionuclides that are given to the patient and are emit particles like gamma particles from different organs. One of the more common exams most people have heard of is a PET scan (Positron Emission Tomography).

This exam utilizes FDG (fludeoxyglucose), which is similar to glucose and the body treats it in a similar way. When given to the patient, it localizes to areas that have high glucose uptake and activity. The organs and muscles use glucose for energy, so you can see uptake in them. More importantly, cancers and infection also take up glucose and this test can highlight metabolically active cancers. This exam is very important for diagnosing and following cancer in patients.

Nuclear medicine is also utilized for many other medical issues including thyroid, cardiac, bone and gastrointestinal imaging. Instead of using x-rays like in CT, imaging modalities such as gamma cameras are used to detect the ejected photons from the radionuclides the patient has ingested. Common nuclear medicine exams include but are not limited to:

- HIDA scan
- V/Q scan
- PET scan
- Tagged RBC scan
- Bone Scan
- Thyroid and Parathyroid Imaging

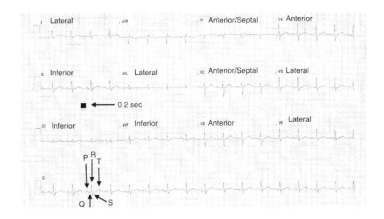

P Wave –Atrial depolarization.

QRS Complex– A complex, representing ventricular depolarization and contraction.

T Wave - Ventricular repolarization.

Black Box – A measurement of time, the black box above represents 0.2 sec and is made up of 5 tiny boxes representing 0.04 sec.

Rate – The easiest way I use to determine the rate is to find the first QRS complex that falls on or near a dark time line marker (making up the outline of the black box above), then count backwards (300, 150, 100, 75, 60, 50), with each QRS complex until you hit another that is in a similar spot to the initial one you chose. This estimates the rate, which is in beats per minute, by convention.

Rhythm – The next thing that is generally assessed on an EKG. Basically, you want to make sure the heart has a regular rhythm, and you do this by making sure that the P and QRS relationship is normal, if P is up then QRS should be up, and that it appears the same throughout the course of the beats.

Axis – This gets more complicated and you'll learn the specifics later on.

Pathology – There is a ton of pathology you can discern from an EKG including many rhythm disorders, things like atrial fibrillation, ventricular tachycardia, ventricular hypertrophy, STEMI (ST segment elevation MI), and lots of others. If you're interested you can read up one these more with an EKG textbook, but the above are the bare bones basics.

Common Surgeries/Procedures

CABG - Pronounced "cabbage," this stands for coronary artery bypass graft. Performed by a cardio thoracic surgeon and done for the purpose of providing a more normalized blood supply to the heart. When the heart's own blood supply via the coronary arteries gets so bad from atherosclerotic disease that patients develop myocardial infractions or angina not amenable to angioplasty or stenting, this is the next line of treatment. Parts of veins are generally taken from the legs and are sutured around the areas of bad vessel disease to help the blood bypass areas with severe narrowing in the vessels. Depending on how bad the disease is, these can involve 1-2 vessels or more.

Angioplasty/Stenting - These are two common interventional procedures performed by interventional radiologists, cardiologists and vascular surgeons. Utilizing a minimally invasive surgical technique where the patients arterial or venous systems are accessed via specialized wires and catheters and are used to open blocked or narrowed vessels with angioplasty (balloon on a catheter that's expanded in a vessel to open it) and stenting, which involves placing a small metallic stent shaped like a vessel to keep it propped open or to repair a diseased vessel. For instance you can place an aortic stent graft across an aortic aneurysm.

Embolization - Performed by interventional radiology and vascular surgery, embolization involves the placement of special materials or chemicals to stop bleeding also done by accessing the patients vascular system. You can use special embolization coils or chemicals to promote clotting and/or restrict blood flow.

Colectomy - Can be either a partial or total surgical resection of the colon. Performed for various reasons including colon cancer and recurring colitis.

Anastomosis - Basically means the suturing and connection of two things. For instance if resect a part of the bowel and then reconnect the ends of the remains bowel this is an anastomosis. This can also apply to vessels and other things

Central Line - One of the most common procedures performed in the hospital, you can think of this as the placement a really big IV in a big central vein, usually the internal jugular vein, subclavian vein or femoral vein. These lines or catheters have multiple uses, including being able to draw blood, administer drugs, etc.

Intubation - Usually performed by anesthesiologist and ER docs, this means placement of an endotracheal tube for patients that will require mechanical ventilation, like those going for surgery with general anesthesia, or patients who can't breathe on their own.

NG Tube - Stands for nasogastric tube, places through the nose with the tip in the stomach. You can use this tube to give medications through it, or relieve pressure in the stomach if the patient has a bowel obstruction.

Feeding Tube - This is a tube put in from the mouth and put down until the tip of the tube goes down the esophagus, through the stomach, out the pylorus into the duodenum and usually parked by the ligament of Treitz area near the proximal jejunum.

Lumbar Puncture - Very common procedure performed for the evaluation of patients with suspected meningitis or other infectious or inflammatory issues in the nervous system. Also helps to evaluate for any cancer cells. Generally performed by ER docs, internists and radiologists. Commonly known as a spinal tap, this is performed by accessing the spine using a spinal needle, for the purpose of obtaining cerebrospinal fluid, which is then evaluated for infection, cancer, etc. most commonly done at the levels between L2-L4.

Arthrocentesis - Using a small needle to get into the joint space, usually of the shoulder, hip or knee to drain fluid in the joint that may be there for various causes.

Paracentesis - Using a small needle and tubing to drain ascites from a patient's abdomen. Usually done by ER docs, internists, or radiologists.

Thoracentesis - Also done with a small needle advanced into the pleural space to drain a pleural effusion.

PICC - Stands for peripherally inserted central venous catheter, this is like an upgrade from an IV that can stay in place for a while and is used to give medications and other functions. Usually placed in the upper arm in the basilic or brachial vein.

Nephrostomy - A tube placed into the collecting system of the kidney from the side or back through the soft tissues in cases where the kidney can't drain normally on its own.

ORIF - Short for Open Reduction Internal Fixation, which is a common surgery to fix fractures performed by orthopedic surgeons.

Epidural - Often performed by an anesthesiologist for pain relief during childbirth. A spinal needle is advanced into the spine in the lower back. The tip of the needle is parked in the epidural space and numbing medication is injected. This causes numbness from that level of the spine down.

I and D - Simple term meaning incision and drainage, often done by surgeons or ER doctors for abscesses in the soft tissues. Usually just requires some local anesthetic for pain.

Laparotomy – When surgeons make an incision in the abdomen for surgery.

Laparoscopic – When surgeons use fiber-optic instruments to evaluate or operate in the abdominal cavity through small incisions in the abdominal wall. Notice the similarity in wording between this and laparotomy.

TEE - Trans esophageal echocardiogram performed by inserting the imaging probe into the esophagus. Provides better images of the heart than a TTE.

TTE - Trans thoracic echocardiogram, performed by imaging the heart through the chest wall.

ERAS and The Match

Once it finally comes time to applying to residency in the fall, you'll want to get pretty familiar with the ERAS and Match system. I've gone through the process of using both systems twice, once for my residency match and also for my fellowship match. The process is fairly well streamlined but it's a good idea to get familiar with everything early, and I'll go over some of the tricks I learned from my latest experience.

The first thing to realize is that ERAS (Electronic Residency Application Service) is separate from the entity that runs the infamous Match. The first thing you'll need to do is register an account with ERAS and start filling in all the necessary information to complete your application. There's a spot to do everything, including your CV, which you'll manually put in all your work experiences, volunteering, publications, etc. You won't be uploading a CV that you have, instead you'll generate one through ERAS that is standardized for all applications. There will be a section for you to put in your demographic information, upload your transcripts and USMLE scores as well. You'll also upload the personal statement that you've prepared.

You'll also include your ***Deans Letter*** in the application, which is a summary of your performance in medical school. Your grades as well as the comments you received during your clinical rotations will be included in this document.

The hardest part of the process I found was arranging for the letters of recommendation to get uploaded into the ERAS system. The process is a bit complex and requires either emailing the authors of your letters, or the medical school deans department a special link through which they can upload their letters into the system. Once you finish this whole gauntlet, you'll get to select which residency programs you want to have

162

your standardized application digitally sent to. You'll get a list to select from and you'll get charged a certain amount depending on how many programs you've chosen to apply to. I applied to a ton of programs and thus paid a ton of money for my applications.

Once programs receive your electronic application, it will take some time for them to review all your materials. Eventually they will start emailing you with either invitations to interview, or rejections. This is definitely a super exciting time in the process, as you'll be really surprised by which programs will and won't interview you. Once you start accepting interview invitations, you'll have to start planning which rotations and days you'll be able to miss to go on as many interviews as you can. Most places recommend making your fourth year schedule a bit easier during the months of December and January when it seems a lot of the interviews take place.

This can be an exhausting time, as you'll have to juggle interviewing all over the country and your remaining rotations. You'll need to be prepared much in the same way that you were for medical school interviews. You'll get many of the same questions as before, but you'll also get more clinical questions on some interviews. I've even heard of students applying to orthopedic surgery having to exhibit their hand-eye coordination skills by doing various puzzles or putting different things together during their interviews…seriously.

Once you get through interviews and sending thank you letters to the programs you interviewed at, you'll want to sit down and think about how you're going to rank the programs for the match. The general, consistent advice is that the Match algorithm works in the favor of the applicant (you) and that you should rank the programs in the order that you want to go to them. Many students think that the match algorithm is more complicated than this but the general rule will be to rank the programs by which ever was your favorite. It worked out well my friends and myself.

The match traditionally takes place sometime in mid-March and this is when you find out where you'll end up for residency. There's usually a formal envelope opening ceremony that takes place at each medical school and peoples' families fly in for this event. On that morning you'll receive an envelope that will reveal where you'll spend the next good portion of your life.

Rarely, some students go unmatched into their specialty, especially some of the applicants to very competitive specialties like dermatology and orthopedic surgery. In that case, applicants will go into the "scramble" now known as the "SOAP" or Supplemental Offer and Acceptance Program. Applicants will be notified before match day that they didn't match. In the scramble un-matched applicants will be able to apply for open positions in pretty much any specialty.

By the end of the whole process, almost everyone finds or gets a spot in the match. This is one of the most exciting times in medical school.

Be sure to check out the document released by the NRMP called the *Charting Outcomes* summary of the Main Residency Match (a quick Google search will bring this up). This gives you important information on the applicants to each specialty regarding average board scores, number of programs ranked, etc.

Extra-Things (Research, Away Rotations)

If you're planning on applying to some of the more competitive specialties, including dermatology, plastic surgery, orthopedic surgery, ophthalmology or another specialty in a competitive location then you're going to need to prepare a very competitive application. On top of acing all your classes, clinical rotations and rocking Step 1, you'll need to do a few other things to set you apart.

Your residency application will be open for submission via ERAS in early September of your fourth year. With all the other things you have going on like studying for classes and Step 1, this leaves you barely any time for anything else. If you're applying to competitive specialties you'll really need to try and do some research in the field that you're interested in, but not at the expense of your grades or board scores. Those should always be your first priority. When you finally get your study method down, then ask your medical school advisors to help you get into contact with specialists in your field of interest that are performing research.

Once you get in touch with someone, you'll need to choose a project or join something already in progress with the goal of publishing it in a journal and/or presenting it at a conference. Submitting research abstracts have strict criteria for each journal or conference, and preparing these on top of doing the actual research is extremely time consuming. I found that the end of 1st year during your summer off to be an ideal time to start a project and get the ball rolling on this. During this summer you can also begin gradually studying for Step 1.

The next thing you'll need to do is make sure that you work in clinical rotations into the field you're interested in during third year or early fourth year. This is a must and you'll need to perform well and ace the rotation and also get to know some attendings well enough so that you can ask for a letter of recommendation by the time the application is due.

If there is a particular program that you're interested in going to for residency you can consider doing an away rotation at that program usually during fourth year. In this case, you won't have to hurry to try and do this by the time applications are due. A lot of med students schedule these for mid fourth year after they've sent out their applications. The programs you rotate at often give out a courtesy interview if you rotate there, so this might give you a shot at matching into a program you otherwise might not have gotten an interview invitation from. You need to be careful though, as this can work both ways. You need to think of an away rotation as a month-long interview at whatever program you rotate at. If the residents and attendings like you then this helps you a lot. On the other hand, if people don't really like you when you rotate their then you may have done better by not rotating there. It's a difficult choice and you have to decide on your own.

If you do decide to do it, then plan for this many months in advance. Many places will have an application you'll need to fill out long in advance, and it may be very competitive, especially for some of the top-notch programs. It'll also have to work with your availability for electives in your schedule. Some places you rotate at will help you with housing while at other places you're on your own, so you might have to rent out a place for a month or so. It's pretty complicated, so plan ahead.

As an aside, I decided to do an away rotation and ended up at my residency program because of the connections I made during that month. I really don't think I would've even gotten an interview there if I hadn't done an away rotation, so for me it was a success story. During my away rotation one of my requirements was to put together a presentation on a topic of my choice relevant to the specialty. I also submitted a write up on an interesting case and had it accepted for publication. I put in a lot of effort into both and I feel it went a long way.

Residency Personal Statement

I've included a copy of a personal statement used to successfully gain admission to residency, which may help you get some idea of how to approach writing this essay. The following material is copyrighted, and no part of it may be reproduced. Notice the transitions between sections and how to tie it all together at the end.

"I was four years old when my brother and I were diagnosed with _____ a condition requiring close medical attention during childhood and adolescence. While growing up with _____ was a challenging experience, it also introduced me to the medical world at an early age. From my pediatric physician, I learned that my condition could potentially affect my growth, which had to be closely monitored with radiographic bone-age studies of my hand. I later learned that the first X-ray image of the human body was that of a hand taken a century before I was born.

During my preclinical years in medical school, I initially became interested in medical imaging during classroom anatomy lectures given by several radiologists. The visual aspect of human anatomy and pathophysiology fascinated me. This compelled me to investigate radiology as a career choice by becoming involved in and leading, the radiology interest group.

During my clinical years in medical school, I came to appreciate the broad variety of medical specialties, and learned during my core clerkships about the clinical value of radiology, my attraction to medical imaging, and how it affects clinical decision-making. While on my pediatrics rotation, I was fortunate to have the opportunity to learn from my own, former pediatric physician. In the clinic, I learned about the importance of assessing bone-age hand radiographs, and how such images are invaluable in determining the correct course of treatment in these patients.

My rotations in diagnostic and interventional radiology, allowed me to understand the central, multi-faceted role that radiologists play in patient care. During my diagnostic radiology rotation, I began to recognize the great breadth of clinical knowledge, and attention to detail that a radiologist must possess in order to make a correct diagnosis. While working with several physicians, I learned about various imaging techniques and encountered a variety of interesting cases.

One was of a young woman who was diagnosed with superior mesenteric artery syndrome, a rare condition that often presents a clinical diagnostic dilemma. This case helped me to appreciate the critical role a radiologist plays in patient care. The discovery of these radiographic findings, along with close collaboration with the medical team, led to a curative diagnosis.

During my elective in interventional radiology, I realized that radiologists stand at the forefront of diagnostic and therapeutic procedures. Interventional radiology revolutionized medicine by allowing patients to undergo minimally invasive procedures, expanding once-limited treatment options, and replacing more invasive surgical procedures. I had the opportunity to work with, and learn from, nationally renowned physicians who were role models. They possessed clinical knowledge spanning many medical specialties to make various diagnoses, and also had intricate procedural skills to treat a host of medical conditions.

While on the clerkship, I observed a variety of procedures, and was given the opportunity to assist with inflation of balloon catheters and deployment of embolization coils. These electives taught me about the central role that radiologists play in patient care, solving diagnostic dilemmas, acting as advisors to other physicians, and employing procedural skills to treat complex medical conditions.

Many factors contributed to my choice of pursuing radiology. My initial interest in biology and science was kindled by my own medical condition and fascination with radiographic studies. In college, and medical school, I found learning about human anatomy, physiology, and pathology intriguing. Yet, it was not until medical school, where I was drawn to medical imaging and radiology.

My personal attributes will be suited in radiology, as I have enjoyed interacting with patients, physicians, and staff during medical school. I am a visual learner, and enjoy the challenge of complex problems while approaching them with a methodical and detail-oriented approach. Radiology is at the forefront of medicine, and the future will hold many exciting changes and technological advances. Being a radiologist will allow me to play a central role in patient care, while presenting me with a continuously evolving, challenging, and intellectually stimulating career."

Residency Interview

Before I even discuss interviewing and the interview process, I want you to Google pictures or videos of guilty dogs smiling. Become familiar with these expressions, as your face will be almost permanently contorted into a similar position during your entire interview period. Your facial muscles will hurt after all the forced smiles that come with this season.

With that aside, lets discuss the daunting interview process for a residency position. With any luck, you've positioned yourself such that you will have a number of interviews at some of the top programs that interest you, and you will also visit some programs that might be lower in your plan of places to go, but are essential nonetheless for guaranteeing yourself a residency position in the coming year. In general, if you can afford it, you should go on just about as many interviews as possible. During the process I found that programs you think will be your dream programs on paper end up being subpar in real life. On the other hand, some programs that may seem to be mediocre before visiting will impress you at the interview and simply sweep you off your feet with the interest they show in you and how well you get along with the residents. There really isn't any way to predict where this will happen, and that is the benefit of going on more interviews.

Most interviews will have an interview dinner the preceding night. This is an opportunity to sit down in a low-key environment with current residents and discuss some details of the program that might not be available from the website, how residents and faculty interact, and any other questions you might have. In general, attendance at the dinners is strongly encouraged by programs, and I believe it is in your best interest to attend. One of the most important aspects of deciding if a residency program is for you is simply your interaction with

171

other residents. There is no better opportunity to sit with current residents and have a normal conversation to see if you could get along with these people for several years, or if there's just no way that you could tolerate them. Remember that the sample of residents who attend dinners may be skewed toward those who are more outgoing or who are happier with the program they matched to, and in general any strong negativity expressed toward the program should alarm you.

Another thing that must be set straight upfront about the dinner: You will be told that you will not be evaluated based on the interactions at the dinner. This is probably false or not completely true. I have had co-residents who attended these events tell me that faculty asked them about certain applicants after the interview. Also, consider that the residents who attend the dinner have a vested interest in matching applicants to their program who they want to interact with for several years. If they see alarming or annoying behavior after just several hours with you, what can they expect with several years?

In one situation that comes to mind, I remember an applicant at a dinner who clearly became intoxicated during the interview dinner. This individual became loud, obnoxious, and quite frankly annoying, and was informing all the applicants and residents that this was her first choice for a residency program. If you think such behavior will not make its way back to the residency program decision makers, than you are gravely mistaken. Additionally, you will find that residents who attend the dinners will remember your name the following day if you see them at the interview day, and I strongly believe this is so they can contribute to discussion of your rank for the program. So, with the dinner, the goal is to be laid back and friendly. Contribute to the dialogue between the residents and other applicants. Ask pertinent questions regarding the residency, but I encourage you to avoid asking excessively detailed questions.

"Will I take 3 calls per month or 4 calls per month?" is probably not that important of a question in choosing a residency program, probably varies based on the rotation you are on, and is something that probably varies greatly from year to year.

Sometimes applicants will ask such detailed questions, and you can just feel it when the resident answering the question goes into auto-pilot regurgitating information about the program that is of little value and isn't interesting. Remember the residents will likely go on at least several dinners, and they want to have fun and interesting conversations with the people that they meet. I encourage open-ended questions regarding favorite parts of the program, favorite activities in the city, and other such discussions. Avoid discussions regarding other programs. Focus on topics that let the residents' and your own passions come through.

Most actual interview days are quite varied. Many involve meeting with several attendings, discussing how you got interested in whatever specialty you chose, and answering any questions you may have about the programs. Some specialties, like orthopedic surgery have been rumored to have difficult interviews that even involve having to put together puzzles and do tasks requiring hand-eye coordination. Also, always remember to have several questions for each interviewer. Some good questions include: What is your favorite thing about the program? Where do graduates usually end up practicing/what fellowships do they usually get?

40 Residency Interview Questions I Was Asked

1. Why medicine?
2. Why did you choose _____ specialty?
3. Tell me about yourself.
4. Tell me about your family.
5. What makes you a better candidate than the other applicant from your medical school?
6. What is greatest strength/weakness?
7. What motivates you?
8. What is your essence?
9. What was your biggest failure?
10. What was your greatest success or accomplishment? How did you accomplish it?
11. What is the greatest challenge you've ever faced? How did you overcome it?
12. Why was your Step 1/2/3 scores low compared to other applicants?
13. How do you deal with stressful situations as a medical student?
14. Tell me about a memorable patient experience.
15. What was your most/least favorite rotation?
16. How would your attendings describe you?
17. What is the most difficult thing you experienced in medical school?
18. What inspired you to pursue ____ specialty?
19. How would your friends describe you?
20. Tell me about a memorable patient experience during so and so rotation.
21. Why did you, or didn't, do any research in medical school?
22. What is the last book you read? Tell me about it.
23. Who influenced you the most in your life?
24. Who do you look up to?
25. What do you read for fun?

26. What are your hobbies?
27. Do you play sports?
28. How do you feel about a current news event?
29. Have you ever worked outside of medicine?
30. Tell me about your favorite movie.
31. If you were stranded on an island, what 3 items would you bring with you.
32. Tell me about your hometown and where you grew up.
33. What do you think will be the greatest challenge for you in residency?
34. How will you adapt to handle the challenges residents face?
35. What are your plans after residency?
36. Do you plan on doing a fellowship?
37. What did you think was the most difficult part about medical school?
38. If you hadn't chosen to pursue this specialty, what else would you have chosen?
39. What personal characteristics make you a good fit for this program and specialty?
40. Where do you hope to practice medicine? What kind of setting do you see yourself in the future?

Medical School Slang/Superstition and Rules

Here is a small collection of terms and slang you're bound to encounter in med school. I did not make these up, and they are not meant to be derogatory or anything, but they can be pretty funny.

"Gunner" – A term I had never heard until I was a few days into medical school. Gunner is a term used to describe the somewhat annoying and over-achieving students you're going to meet. These students go well above and beyond the expectations in class and make a concerted effort to make themselves look better than you, score higher than you, and make sure everyone in the class knows it.

"Punting" – This is a term used to describe the process of figuring out a way to transfer primary care of a patient to another service.

"Bounce Back" – Lets say you discharge a patient from the ER or from you medicine service and they end up coming back to your service almost right away, this is a bounce back.

"Golden Weekend" – You won't really appreciate having full 2-day weekends until you start med school rotations. Its ridiculous, but full weekends are not normal and very rare, like a unicorn. You usually only get like 4 days off a month and having two days off in a row can't be taken for granted. So when you get a full weekend off you get a *"Golden Weekend."*

Discharge – This is the term used when you decide to send the patient out of the hospital to a nursing facility or home. Usually, the ultimate goal of an intern.

SNF (Pronounced Sniff) – The term used to describe a Skilled Nursing Facility. This is where a lot of patients from the surgical and internal medicine services get discharged to and you'll often hear *"We are gonna discharge him/her to SNF."*

"The List" – As an intern and resident you'll have all the names of the patients you and your team are following on a *"list."* This is where you keep track of all the patients, things you have to do, labs/results to follow-up on.

"Winning the Game" – The ultimate goal of an intern is to *"win the game."* The so-called *"game"* is attempting to reach a census of zero on the "list," by either discharging or punting all the patients off their service. The reason for this is that when all the patients have been cleared from the list that intern therefore has nothing to do and can reach a state of peace. Winning the game lives on in legend most of the time and only a select few of interns can reach this state of bliss, which at times is only a fleeting moment.

"Pimping" – Definitely not what you think it means. I didn't hear this expression until my clinical rotations and it's a strange term to use but you'll hear it everywhere nonetheless. It's a code word for getting quizzed and potentially shamed during rounds about various medical topics and obscure trivia. You can use it in a sentence like *"Man, did you see how bad Johnny got pimped by Dr. Smith during rounds, it was brutal. I don't know how anyone could answer those ridiculous questions.*

"White Cloud" – Usually an intern or resident who has unbelievably good luck when working and rarely gets new patients or work.

"Black Cloud" – An intern with horribly bad luck and is known to get the most patients and the most difficult cases.

"Sundowning" – This is a term that refers to the delirium that older patients experience when they stay in the hospital a long time and start to lose their sense of day and night.

Superstitions/Rules:

- A full moon is thought to be the worst night to work, legends says that it's associated with lots of traumas, admissions, births, etc.

- If things are going well, don't talk about it. If it's a quiet day at work, don't mention it and act like nothing is happening. The second you mention something about it being an easy day it will immediately turn into a horribly difficult day and you have successfully jinxed it. Everyone will blame you.

- It's poor form to correct an attending or resident during rounds.

- Always be nice to the nursing staff and other ancillary medical staff.

- Never touch anything blue in the OR (operating room), it usually means it's a sterile field and you don't want to contaminate it.

- Respect the surgical tech in the OR. They are in charge of the surgical instruments, so don't mess with them.

178

Common Abbreviations

Many hospitals moving away from using these, but you're still bound to see them all the time.

BIBA - Brought in by ambulance
BID - Twice daily
CAD – Coronary artery disease
CTAB - Clear to auscultation bilaterally.
DDx - Differential diagnosis
DM – Diabetes Mellitus
D/W - Discussed with
EOMI - Extra-ocular muscles intact.
G/R/M - Gallops, rubs or murmurs.
HTN – Hypertension
LR - Lactated Ringers
NAD – No acute distress
NPO - Nothing by mouth
NS - Normal saline
NT- Non-tender
N/V/D - Nausea, vomiting, diarrhea.
OSH - Outside hospital
PERRLA – Pupils equal round and react to light, accommodation
POD - Post op day # (0 is day of surgery, day after is POD #1)
PRN - Give as needed
Q - Means how often something is given, like medication given q daily (once a day).
RRR - Regular rate and rhythm
RVR - Rapid ventricular rate.
S/P - Status post
TID - Three times daily
TTP - Tender to palpation
WWP - Warm and well perfused.

Conclusion

I hope that you found the material of this book helpful and interesting. These are some of the things my fellow residents and I learned on our journey through undergrad, medical school, and now residency. If you have more questions, suggestions for the next edition of this book, or would like us to expand on different topics, visit the website, or email us at premedadvisor.net@gmail.com.

I'll be attempting to update this book every so often as I compile more and more useful information. Wishing you the best in your journey ahead. It's worth the hard work.

AJ, M.D.

Notes

Made in the USA
Middletown, DE
09 November 2020